SILENT
BONES

VAL McDERMID

SILENT BONES

A KAREN PIRIE NOVEL

Atlantic Crime
New York

First published in 2025 in Great Britain by Sphere
an imprint of Hachette UK

First Grove Atlantic US hardcover editon: December 2025

Typeset in Meridien by M Rules

Printed in the United States of America

Library of Congress Cataloging-in-Publication data is available for this title.

ISBN 978-0-8021-6439-1
eISBN 978-0-8021-6440-7

Atlantic Crime
an imprint of Grove Atlantic
154 West 14th Street
New York, NY 10011

Distributed by Publishers Group West

groveatlantic.com

25 26 27 28   10 9 8 7 6 5 4 3 2 1

For Jo.
Who makes all things possible.

If we say that we have no sin
We deceive ourselves, and there's no
truth in us.

CHRISTOPHER MARLOWE
Dr Faustus

SILENT BONES

Prologue

New Year's Eve 2013

She'd never imagined a Hogmanay thrash like this, never mind that she'd be invited to it. Growing up in a lochside hamlet on the edge of the Trossachs, of course the year end had always been celebrated, though on a scale that reflected village life. But this? The midnight fireworks alone were legendary. She couldn't conjure up a notion of what the everyday life of these people must be like, given this was what they considered a party should be.

For a start, there had been a queue of taxis and honestly, *limos* waiting at the gates to be admitted. There was actually a stretch Hummer. Even as she marvelled at it, the sensible part of her thought it was the most ridiculous thing she'd ever seen on wheels. To get through the gates, she had to produce her invitation as well as the photo ID she'd been told to bring. She'd thought that was a joke. Fancy having to bring your passport to a party.

She'd leaned back in the taxi as it drove sedately down a wide gravel drive that swept between perfectly groomed waist-high hedges, with flaming torches set at regular intervals. The house itself was spotlit, its perfect symmetry making it look like a cut gemstone against the night. She was glad for their host that it wasn't raining. To go to all this trouble and have that perfect vision smudged and blunted by a typical Glasgow drizzle would have gutted her, if it had been her party. *As if.* She stifled a snort of derision.

She smoothed her sheer scarlet dress over her thighs. She'd gone way over budget in that new Italian designer boutique in the Merchant City, but it would be worth it if she made the right impression on the right people to-night. If she could market *herself* so well, then surely they'd have to realise she should be given a role where she could market their business with the same flair? The year they were about to enter was being boosted as the Homecoming, heralding the upcoming referendum that would sweep Scotland out from under Westminster's boot and usher in a new independent Scotland. A land of opportunity, equality and social justice for all, or so they promised. But Fraoch House wasn't her home, not by any stretch of the imagi-nation. Now she was on the threshold she was definitely feeling stage fright. What if she looked tarty? Or lumpy? Or just plain?

So many ways she could blow it . . .

The taxi drew to a halt and she fumbled with the catch on her new evening bag. She handed the driver a twenty, waited for the change then realised he was going to make her ask for it. She'd planned to give him a two quid tip; him expecting a fiver was taking the piss. But tonight, she'd left meek in the bathroom mirror. 'I'll take my change,' she said briskly.

He turned to face her, a sneer on his thin lips. 'What's a few quid tip to the likes of you?'

'My bus fare to my work next week,' she snapped, holding

out her hand. 'C'mon, you're not the only working stiff here tonight.'

He grumbled something under his breath then counted out ten fifty-pence pieces. She had to cup both hands beneath the cut-out in the partition to prevent them falling to the floor. She absolutely wasn't going to give him the satisfaction of seeing her scrabbling on her knees for her money. She shovelled the coins into her bag and said, 'You have a good new year when it comes.'

Before he could find a withering response, she was out of the cab and walking with every appearance of confidence up the wide stone steps. They led towards imposing glossy black doors, thrown wide for the evening. Two beautiful youths in glittering silver body suits held trays of champagne cocktails to greet the new arrivals and she swept in alongside a trio of perfectly groomed young women on impossibly high heels. She recognised one of them, an actress one step up from a non-speaking part in half a dozen minor Scottish TV dramas. It looked like she'd had a nose job since she'd last been a murder victim on *River City*.

She turned away and let herself be drawn into this exotic world. Marble floor, domed ceiling that could have given Govan Town Hall a run for its money, scantily clad statues in alcoves, a sweeping staircase with broad shallow steps, a Christmas tree covered in baubles and lights that wouldn't have been out of place in George Square – it was like stepping on to a film set. Or it would have been if it hadn't been crammed with people in their finery clutching champagne flutes and whisky tumblers and talking at a volume designed to disguise the fact that they had nothing to say worth listening to.

She moved through the throng, slipping easily between

groups of strangers, trying not to make it obvious that she only knew the other guests from screens, sports pages and TV debates. The politicians were there to give *faux* gravitas, she thought. They looked too eager, unlike the beautiful people who knew they deserved to be there.

At last, she spotted a familiar face. The man responsible for her invitation. Billy the Kidd, a star of the comedy circuit on both sides of the border, was holding forth, showering those around him with observations and quips, taking no prisoners in his usual style. The admirers around him seemed not to understand they were the butts of his often cruel humour; she knew from her own experience of William Kidd that his victims seldom recognised themselves in his slights. They told themselves his jibes were aimed at some other rich entitled tossers.

She knew better. She liked William in spite of his cruelties, not because of them. But then, he'd never used her for target practice. She wasn't important enough. Yet.

Absently, she checked out his audience. The usual hoorays and yaahs, she thought. Then one of them snagged her attention and her eyes stuttered back to him. He was watching her, a knowing smile twitching one corner of his mouth. She knew who he was. Everyone who was here tonight would know who he was. This was home turf for him, king of the high-end parties – Lord Haig Striven-Douglass, younger son of the Marquess of Friockheim, record producer and chairman of one of Scotland's leading conservation charities. She could never quite square those different elements of his profile, but he seemed to steer a passage through the gap without turbulence.

William came to the end of his excoriation of the Scottish Labour Party, his current bête noire, and gave a mocking bow to his audience before swinging round to face his host. 'Haig, my man, take me to the powder room.' Haig slung an arm round his shoulders and steered him towards a side corridor. But before they reached the corner of the passageway, he turned and caught her eye. 'Chloe?'

Until her invitation had arrived, she'd had no idea Kidd had even noticed she existed, never mind that he knew her name. She'd just been an insignificant intern on a BBC radio comedy programme when she'd started out. But somehow she'd made an impression and he'd remembered her.

William slid out from under Haig's arm and his face lit up, like he was genuinely pleased to see her. She'd seen that look too often to take it seriously. 'Chlo, the finest marketing assistant in the biz. Come away with me and His Lordship and we'll show you how the stars party!'

His Lordship grabbed him in a headlock. She'd seen plenty of that kind of horseplay before, so it didn't bother her. 'Ignore him, he's a pleb,' Haig said. 'Come and join us, escape the hoi polloi and have a drink somewhere you don't have to shout to be heard.'

William fought his way out of Haig's grip. 'Though you can scream if you like. Walls this thick, it's like *Alien*. Nobody can hear you.'

'We are the boys to be with,' Haig said, eyebrows raised, mischief in his expression. William was a known quantity. She knew he could help her build her career; he had a genuine streak of kindness. Haig Striven-Douglass she knew less about. Except that he had some of the keys to the kingdom she was ambitious to enter.

Why not? she thought.

It was a question that would be answered soon enough.

1

Spring 2025

Detective Chief Inspector Karen Pirie hated doing her expenses. Crafting a narrative that would justify the bundle of receipts she'd forgotten she'd even incurred was the worst aspect of running Police Scotland's Historic Cases Unit. When she'd first recruited Detective Sergeant Daisy Mortimer, she'd tried to convince her that doing the DCI's expenses was now her responsibility. Daisy had grinned and said, 'Good try, boss.' So the ringing of her phone was a welcome relief. But only for as long as it took her to read the screen.

In Karen's experience, a call from the Assistant Chief Constable (Crime) never brought tidings of comfort and joy. Nevertheless ... 'Sir,' she answered brightly. 'How can I help you?'

'I wanted to talk to you about a bit of reorganisation.'

Karen's heart sank. ACC Rowntree – aka the Fruit Gum – had announced himself as the new broom when he'd arrived at Police Scotland a couple of years before. If his predecessor had heard that line, she'd have gutted him at his first morning briefing. Ann Markie had been convinced *she* was the face of the future when it came to policing; the reality was that her brand of coppering was rooted in a historic world view that Karen thought had gone out with the abolition of slavery. If Markie had had a whip, she wouldn't have let a day go by without cracking it. Rowntree, on the other hand, liked to claim he was frank and open with the lower ranks. Karen had soon realised that only applied to the trivial stuff.

Trying to keep her tone upbeat, Karen said, 'What did you have in mind, sir?'

'I think I've made it clear what an asset I believe your team is to Police Scotland, Karen.' He paused for praise.

'You have, sir.' *Because we get the kind of results that produce great media reactions and you like getting your name in lights.*

'So I hope you won't take what I have to say as a criticism.' Another pause.

That was a question that demanded only one answer. She was damned if she was going to play his game. 'I have no problem with constructive criticism,' she said. That was mostly true. Most days.

And enough to tip him slightly off his stride. He gave a fake laugh. 'I'm under pressure to make sure Police Scotland gives great value for money. Which of course, the Historic Cases Unit continues to do.'

Karen could hear the 'but' all the way across the city. 'It's always a consideration, sir.'

'So in the interests of economy of scale, it's my intention to move your unit from the furthest recesses of Gayfield Square to an office space more commensurate with your prestige. How would you like to be based at Gartcosh?' Another question that demanded a single answer.

She knew he wouldn't appreciate her knee-jerk response

that she'd rather slam the car door on her fingers. 'I'd welcome the chance to give the suggestion careful consideration. Why don't I call your secretary and make an appointment to see you later in the week? Then we can discuss it fully.'

'I don't know that there's—'

She bulldozed straight over him. 'I'm sorry, sir, I've got to go now, I'm due at a meeting. Thanks for the suggestion, and we'll talk soon.' And she ended the call. Karen squeezed her eyes shut momentarily. The Fruit Gum might like to appear a different species from Ann Markie, but some days she thought you couldn't get a cigarette paper between them. Nobody wanted to work out of Gartcosh, the Bermuda Triangle of Central Scotland. Bounded by motorways on all sides, convenient for absolutely nothing and nowhere except itself, a desert with insufficient parking. She'd fight this one and she'd win.

Probably.

2

'I swear to God we never had tropical downpours like this when I was wee,' Detective Chief Inspector Pete Niven complained, pulling the hood of his raincoat closer to his narrow face. 'Can we get a fucking tent up here?' he shouted at the crime scene technicians battling the howling wind and the sheeting rain to erect a shelter over the collapsed section of the M73. A massive mudslide had careened down the hillside when the heavens had opened during the night, shifting enough mud and previously unseen rocks to bite a chunk out of the motorway. Bad enough that it had completely blocked one lane, destroyed the hard shoulder and caused mayhem on the morning commute, but when the road crew had finally turned up, the traffic problem swiftly morphed into a very different one.

The torrential rain had dislodged more than the steep bank beside the road; the layers of roadway had shifted downwards and sideways to reveal unmistakably human remains. DCI Niven had been dragged away from his warm office at the nearby Police Scotland Crime Campus to contemplate the grim sight of a skull grinning up at him out of the mud. Recovering the body would be a logistical nightmare in this weather, never mind figuring out how to secure the most chaotic crime scene he'd ever seen.

Niven glared at the body as if it was a personal insult directed at him. His dark thoughts were disturbed by his bagman, DS Richie Scott, who announced his arrival with a typically tasteless comment. 'Found Jimmy Hoffa, then, boss?' He leaned over the crime scene tape. 'Makes a change from all the stories about Glasgow gangsters bricked up in the Kingston Bridge.'

'Give it a rest, Scott. We don't even know if it's a man or a woman.'

'So you've not PLE'd it?'

Scott was, as usual, grating on Niven's nerves. 'I have done this before, you know. I have not only pronounced life extinct, I've spoken to the Fiscal's office. They think there's someone over at Gartcosh who can come across and formally confirm it so we can get the body removal under way.'

Niven turned away and headed for the shelter of the police Land Rover. Scott climbed in alongside him and the two men waited for the crime scene techs to secure the scene. A few minutes of silence passed, then Niven said, 'When was this bit of motorway built?'

'Not a scooby, boss. I don't remember it not being here.'

Niven rolled his eyes. 'Of course you don't remember it. You're just a bairn, Scott. Which means you're supposed to be a fucking genius with the technology. Get your phone out and do some research.'

Scott sighed, his cheerful expression swept away like rain under the windscreen wiper. 'Aye, right.' His chubby fingers stabbed his phone as if he was trying to injure it. At least, thought Niven, it shut him up.

Time trickled past and the crime scene tent slowly took

shape through the downpour. Then two things happened at once. The rain stopped as abruptly as if someone had turned off a tap. And their Land Rover door opened to reveal a diminutive woman who had materialised outside. She was sensibly clad in waterproofs, fisherman's waders and a bucket hat. A thick comma of dark auburn hair had worked its way loose in front, a single drip worming its way downwards towards an eyebrow. 'Hi, guys,' she said. 'I'm looking for DCI Niven.'

'That would be him,' Scott blurted out before Niven could speak. His smile was back at full wattage.

The woman ignored him and nodded to Niven. 'I'm Dr Wilde. River Wilde. I know, I know. Hippy parents.' Clearly it wasn't the first time she'd introduced herself thus. 'Forensic anthro. Lucky for you, this is the day I work out of Gartcosh. I understand you've got human remains?'

Niven straightened up. 'I've not got up close and personal, Doc. It's not what you'd call easy terrain. But there's a human skull that looks like it's emerged from the broken lip of the motorway, so I'd say yes, that's what we've got.'

'Unless it's a shop window dummy,' Scott said brightly.

Niven scowled. 'The only dummy round here is you, Scott.' He gave River a tight smile. 'Can't get the staff, Doc. What's the plan, do you think?'

'Let's go and take a look.' She turned away and set off towards the tent.

Niven followed her, Scott in his wake, sighing. 'There go my best loafers.'

As they approached, Niven thought it resembled a scene from *1917*, the last film he'd seen in a cinema before Covid hit. Which made it maybe the last film he'd ever see in a cinema. These days, he'd lost the desire to sit in a confined space with a lot of strangers at close quarters. Why bother when you could wait for it to show up on Netflix, in the comfort of your own living room with a beer and the chance to pause for a pee whenever you felt the need without missing a crucial plot point? Still, this reminded him of that last visit. A sea of mud, torn clumps of grass, random bits of rock, aggregate and tarmac, all mashed up around the forensic tent. The men picked their way across the morass, taking exaggerated care not to trip. River, in sharp contrast, moved with swift assurance and disappeared inside. 'Bloody mountain goat,' Niven muttered.

By the time the two police officers made it into the tent, River was already crouched by the body. It was more like a golem than a human form, with its thick coat of dark brown mud streaked with yellow and black like an abstract painting.

She looked up. 'It's hard to be absolutely certain till we get the remains cleaned up and examined properly but given the height and the relative breadth of shoulders and hips, I'd say it's a man.' She delicately moved the head. Flecks of white appeared through muck as thick as flesh and they could make out the catastrophic damage to the side of the skull that had been lying in the mud. 'And I'm in no doubt that he didn't die a natural death.'

'Murder?' Niven asked.

'It's the obvious conclusion. A remote possibility that it could have been an accident or suicide that someone was determined to cover up. But either way, you're looking at a crime.' She straightened up. 'These are skeletal remains. Far be it from me to tell you your job, but I'm thinking this is one for the Historic Cases Unit.'

Niven felt a burden shifting from his shoulders. Everybody

knew that the ACC (Crime) loved the publicity the HCU garnered. The Fruit Gum never put DCI Pirie in front of the cameras to deliver the soundbites. He always seized the limelight for himself. If he could sideline Niven and give the case to KP Nuts, he'd do it in a heartbeat.

With a bit of luck, Niven might get home in time to catch the second half of the European Cup game. 'Good thinking, Dr Wilde,' he said. 'I'll speak to Mr Rowntree right away.'

3

Detective Sergeant Daisy Mortimer rummaged in her desk drawer and came up with half a bag of dark chocolate Brazil nuts. She'd bought them the previous week, mistaking them for chocolate gingers, which was the only reason they'd lasted this long. She'd only just crunched her way through the first nut when the phone rang. Since the boss was working from home on her exes, Daisy reached for the handset. It was the front desk. 'Got a walk-in for you,' the civilian aide reported.

'We don't do walk-ins,' Daisy said patiently. 'Walk-ins are live cases, for CID.'

'No, Daisy, this is a death going back before the Covid. The guy, he says it was his brother. It was written up as an accident, but he never believed it. Now he says he's got new evidence and it should be reopened.'

Daisy rolled her eyes. One of few downsides of the Historic Cases Unit was relatives with bees in their bonnets. Nobody liked the idea of their loved ones committing suicide or dying after an apparently dodgy accident so they brought their unhappiness to the HCU. It seemed to be a growing problem. Even Karen, usually so compassionate, sometimes reached the end of her rope, blaming the rise of the citizen journalist industry. 'Everybody wants to be the star of their own bloody true crime podcast,' she'd muttered just the other week over a Friday-night negroni in their local.

Usually, Daisy managed to palm the dissatisfied off on Jason, but that afternoon he was in Dundee learning about new protocols in fire investigation. Karen liked her team to keep their forensic awareness current. With a sigh, she said, 'OK, I'll talk to him.'

'Interview room two.'

Daisy paused to sharpen a couple of pencils then headed down the hall. She found a lanky man leaning against the wall of the spartan room, ankles crossed and arms folded across his chest. He wore a navy canvas jacket in the style of a French labourer, a plaid shirt and a rather stylish pair of selvage denim jeans over black Docs. His head was cocked to one side, revealing a neat tattoo of a swallow flying up from his collar into his hairline. His face and neck were tanned and his light brown hair had sun-bleached highlights to match. He seemed clean, healthy and handsome. He didn't look at all Scottish. She introduced herself and gestured to one of the upright chairs at the table. 'How can I help you, Mr . . .?'

He pushed off from the wall and pulled out a chair. 'Jamieson. Drew Jamieson. Thanks for seeing me.' His accent was an odd mix she couldn't place. He sat down and folded his arms again.

'Pleased to meet you, Mr Jamieson. You wanted to talk to an officer about the death of your brother?'

'The murder of my brother,' he corrected her. 'You lot were in such a rush to get it off the books that you wrote it up as an accident. But it was no accident. My brother Tom was murdered.'

Daisy made a note of the name. 'And when did your brother die?'

'Five years ago. March seventeenth. Just before youse all went into lockdown. Covid hadn't really hit us in New Zealand at that point but we were already pretty wary of the rest of the world.'

'You live in New Zealand?'

'I do. I'm part owner of a brewery in Nelson. Top of the South Island. So many flights were getting cancelled, plus I was worried I might not get back into NZ, so I couldn't come running back here when Tommo died. But I didn't believe it even then. I called a couple of times, spoke to a Detective Inspector Caldwell. I'm told he's retired now. Frankly, he might as well have been retired then for all the use he was. As far as he was concerned, it was an accident. End of.'

'Forgive me, Mr Jamieson. I'm not familiar with your brother's case. Can you tell me how he died?'

He ran a hand along his jaw. 'He took a header down the Scotsman Steps. You know the Scotsman Steps?'

Daisy nodded. A wide spiral staircase that led from North Bridge to Market Street. More than a hundred shallow steps from top to bottom, it was technically classified as a road, though nobody in their right mind would consider driving a car, or even a bike its length. Now it was officially also an artwork, the original sandstone steps having been replaced with slabs from all the great marble quarries of the world. The artist, Martin Creed, said it was 'like walking through the world'. As far as Daisy was concerned, it was nothing more exotic than a shortcut from the Royal Mile to Waverley Station, usually adorned with empty beer cans and fast-food wrappers. Edinburgh, UNESCO City of Culture, right enough. 'I know the Scotsman Steps. They can get quite slippy when it's wet.'

'It wasn't wet, the night in question. My brother was the general manager of the Scott Monument Hotel, and he had a flat round the corner on Jeffrey Street. The steps were his daily route to and from work. He used to say he could run up and down them in his sleep.'

'But not that night?'

Jamieson gave her a level stare. 'Not that night, no. That night, he was found towards the bottom of the steps with a broken ankle and a broken neck.'

'What time of night was this?'

'He left work at 1.53 a.m., according to the hotel CCTV. He was found dead at 2.17 by a railway worker coming up from Waverley after the end of his shift.'

'What about CCTV? Were there any images?'

'The coverage back then wasn't comprehensive. Someone did enter the steps behind Tommo, but he was wearing a hoodie. He could've been anybody. He was moving quickly and he was out of the staircase a few minutes before Tommo was found. You'd have to think he had something to do with it, right?'

'I couldn't say, not without reviewing the file.'

He snorted. Not unreasonably, Daisy thought. 'It's the broken ankle that gets me. How do you break your ankle falling downstairs? Even if you trip?'

'I don't know,' Daisy said. 'But I'm not a medical expert, Mr Jamieson.'

'Well, I've spoken to a couple of orthopods back in Aotearoa and they don't think it's very likely.' He spoke with the air of a man quoting scripture. 'I've seen the footage, and he goes off down the street with his right arm stiff as a stookie. As if he has a metal bar or something up his sleeve.'

She took a deep breath. Now for the question that would

likely set him off. 'Don't take this the wrong way, Mr Jamieson, but had your brother been drinking?'

He threw his hands up in the air. 'I knew you'd go straight there. He was a hotel manager. Of course he'd been drinking. It's part of the job. Have a glass of wine with the punters, keep them happy. According to his blood alcohol, which your people tested, he'd had about a bottle and a half of wine. Now, that might make a slip of a girl like you trip over your feet, but my brother had a hard head for booze. I've seen him put away a couple of bottles of full-on Kiwi wine without any sign of being pissed. He drank regularly and he ran up and down those stairs every day without a single misstep.'

Until he didn't, Daisy thought. Sounded like the guy was an accident waiting to happen. 'I understand your unhappiness about your brother's death. But I'm not clear why you're so convinced he was murdered.'

He pulled a folded wad of papers from his jacket pocket and unfolded it dramatically before slapping it down on the table in front of Daisy. 'Because I've got bloody photographs of the bloke who did it. Same photographs youse have had all along. First you said there was no reason to believe he had anything to do with Tommo's death. Then you said nobody knew who he was. You even sent me the pix so I could confirm it was nobody I recognised. Well, Sergeant Mortimer, I've been doing Police Scotland's job for them. And now I know who killed my big brother.' He stabbed the blurred images with his finger. 'So what are you going to do about it?'

4

Even though Karen arrived at the office next morning in good time as usual, for once Daisy was there ahead of her. 'You're in early,' Karen said. 'Did you set your alarm for the wrong time?'

'I wanted to start the day on a cheerful note. Before we get overtaken by events.'

Karen frowned. 'Are you expecting events? We're pretty quiet just now.'

'I had to deal with a walk-in yesterday that's going to get right up some people's noses.'

Karen groaned. 'Tempting though that sounds, I need to sort something before we get into it.' She took out her phone and keyed in ACC Rowntree's number. His PA answered instantaneously. Her promptness always unnerved Karen. 'Hey, Susie,' she said. 'Karen Pirie here. How are you doing? How're the kids?'

'Och, Helena's driving me nuts, she's got Princess Fiona – you know, the female lead – in the school production of *Shrek*, and she keeps worrying it's because she's fat. And Kieran just keeps winding her up about it.'

'Threaten him with me if he doesn't leave her alone. Listen, Susie, I've to make an appointment with ACC

Rowntree for later in the week. What day's he going to be in a good mood?'

'Now, now, DCI Pirie, don't be like that. He's always in a good mood with you. So, he's got a wee lunch tomorrow with a couple of the Westminster Tories and they don't usually get into his ribs too much, so maybe if I was to slot you in around three? How would that be?'

'Magic, Susie, I'll be there.' Karen ended the call and turned her attention back to Daisy. 'So what's this about a walk-in? You know we don't do walk-ins.'

'That's what I told the numpty on the front counter, but it turns out the guy had a point.' Daisy started on a succinct report of her conversation with Drew Jamieson. She paused for breath when she reached the bit about the printout from the CCTV and Karen dived straight in. 'So where did these CCTV pictures come from?'

'I was getting to that.' Daisy knew by now that patience was not one of Karen's virtues, unless it was necessary for one of her own inquiries. 'Apparently we sent them over to him. If it was supposed to shut him up, it was an epic fail. The stills came from the CCTV inside the hotel, by the entrance.' She opened the images on her laptop and turned the screen to face Karen. 'The guy in the front of the first shot is Tom Jamieson.'

'You can only see a quarter of his head, and that's blurred.'

'I know, but his brother swears it's him. Then there's this figure in the background, coming up behind him.'

Karen frowned at the picture. 'It doesn't prove a thing. It's one man leaving a hotel a bit behind another man.'

'He's wearing a hoodie, though. And the CCTV from the Scotsman Steps, that shows a man with a hoodie pulled up hiding his face.'

Karen shook her head and sighed. 'And Drew Jamieson thinks there's only one man wandering round Edinburgh city centre late at night with a hoodie? He's not in small-town New Zealand now.'

'Well, no. But I checked back in the case files, and the team didn't manage to ID the man in the photo. He'd been drinking in the bar. Paid in cash, so no credit card to trace. He wasn't a regular, none of the bar staff on duty that night recognised him.'

'Did they make a media appeal?'

'No. I'm guessing they decided there weren't enough grounds for suspicion.'

Karen grimaced. 'Can't say I blame them. Looks like a duck, et cetera. I'd likely have taken the same decision. Maybe thought twice about the punter in the hoodie, but I'm assuming the investigating officers didn't find any obvious motive in the victim's life. No criminal connections, no affair with somebody else's partner, no dubious accounting?'

Daisy nodded. 'None of the above. So it was written up as an accident and laid to rest.'

'But not by brother Drew?'

'He's a bit like a dog with a bone. He admits he didn't know what to do with the images at first but he's got some pal in New Zealand who works in computer security who showed him how to do a reverse image search. You know what that is, right? You feed the image into a search program and it hunts for a match on the internet.'

'All the courses I send you on, nothing's ever wasted. So what happened?'

Daisy flicked on to the next screen. It showed the same man from the Scott Monument Hotel lobby, only now he was wearing a sharp business suit with a cutaway collar and a dark red tie. Superimposed on it was a graphic that read, 'Location match: Image 99.3% MATCH'. 'I'd say that's him.'

'I wouldn't argue. So who is he?'

'Marcus Nicol. He's not some shady hitman, boss. He owns a company called Surinco. They started out making surgical instruments, then when Covid struck they pivoted—'

'I bloody hate that word, "pivoted",' Karen interrupted. 'It usually signals the worst kind of opportunism. Sorry, Daisy, on you go. Mr Surinco "pivoted" to, don't tell me, let me guess. Crap PPE.'

'Not quite that scummy. He started off converting anaesthetic machines into ventilators, but there wasn't enough money in that. Then he moved on to producing' – she referred to her notes – 'CPAP machines. Not entirely reliable ones, according to some reports. But now there's a world shortage of them and he's still raking it in.'

'Just because he's morally bankrupt doesn't mean he murdered Tom Jamieson,' Karen said mildly.

'Drew Jamieson is adamant that it's new evidence. He says if we don't follow it up, he'll go to the media.'

'And that's so not the kind of coverage the Fruit Gum wants to see.' Karen pondered for a moment. 'We could go and have a chat with Mr Surinco. Take a witness statement and get the measure of him. Chances are it's not going to take us anywhere, but it'll maybe give Drew Jamieson some closure. At least he'll know he's gone down every avenue. Where's Surinco based?'

'Edinburgh Park.'

The industrial estate near the airport still looked somehow provisional to her, though Karen knew it was home to several thriving businesses now. She'd never noticed Marcus Nicol's company name on tram rides to and from flights, but that meant nothing. Not every firm shouted its name from the rooftops, especially if people associated it with making money out of the pandemic. Conspiracy theories had turned all sorts of businesses and individuals into targets. With some, like Michelle Mone, that response felt legitimate. Others, not so much. 'We'll take a wee run out there later.'

Before Daisy could respond, the Mint opened the door, juggling a cardboard tray of coffees and his shoulder bag. He looked shocked. 'Am I late?' he demanded, putting the coffees down on the nearest surface.

'No, we're early,' Karen reassured him.

'Scary, isn't it?' Daisy said. 'Pass me my mocha.'

Karen reached for her flat white. Right on cue, her phone rang. She glanced at the screen and answered it. 'River, what's up?'

A warm chuckle in her ear. 'And I'm very well too, Karen. Listen, I'm giving you a heads-up here. I was at Gartcosh yesterday, just my usual lab day, and I got called out to a landslip down the road from the Crime Campus. The monsoon weather took a chunk out of the side of the motorway and exposed skeletal remains. I'm pretty sure they went into the mix when the motorway was extended back around 2014, but one of the soil scientists from the Hutton is coming down today to confirm that.'

'And you reckon it's one for us, then? Who's the SIO?'

'A DCI Pete Niven. He's very keen to get it off his books and on to yours.'

'You'll get no complaints from me on that score. The fewer feet stomping all over the evidence, the better. Have you already managed to remove the remains?'

'I wanted to, but Niven wanted to wait for the pathologist. Who was busy in Bathgate. Not to mention the soil scientist.'

'Sounds like he's being thorough, at least.'

'Yeah. I'm going back over now, if you want to join me?'

'Now there's an offer I can't refuse. I'll have to stop off at Edinburgh Park to front up a witness, but I could be with you in a couple of hours. I'll send the Mint on ahead to hold the fort.'

Jason's ears pricked up and he gave Karen a thumbs up.

'Better warn him, it's like the Creature from the Black Lagoon. Well, the brown lagoon, to be strictly accurate. Tell him to bring his wellies.'

'Glaury, glaury Hallelujah.'

'What?'

Sometimes Karen forgot River hadn't had the benefit of a Scottish upbringing. 'Glaur. It means clarts.'

'Stop it. You know that's just as obscure. What's "glaur"?'

'Mud, glorious mud.' Karen ended the call and briefed Jason.

'I don't suppose there's any chance of an innocent explanation?' he asked, ever hopeful.

'You've got all the way to Gartcosh to think of one.'

Daisy gave him a look of commiseration. 'Better drive slowly, Mint.'

5

Surinco wasn't easy to find. It occupied a squat two-storey building in the furthest reaches of the industrial zone near the airport, but the signage was so discreet Karen had driven past it twice before Daisy spotted it. She struggled to find a parking space, giving up eventually and parking outside the main entrance. 'Not exactly the red carpet for visitors,' she commented.

'I don't think anybody who made a killing out of Covid wants to shout their name to the heavens.' Daisy followed Karen to the glass portico.

'Maybe not talk about "making a killing out of Covid"? The grasping shysters might be a wee bit sensitive about that.' Karen pushed the door, which turned out to be locked. She could see a woman sitting behind a tall curved desk at an angle to them, ostentatiously avoiding looking at them.

Daisy pointed to a keypad where the glass met the wall. 'I think that might be the entryphone?'

Karen crossed to it and pressed a button on the bottom of the brushed chrome pad. At first, nothing happened. Then the woman inside leaned forward and out of the box came a voice. 'Can I help you?'

'We're here to see Marcus Nicol.'

'Do you have an appointment?'

'No, but I am Detective Inspector Karen Pirie from Police Scotland.'

'You still need an appointment.'

Karen felt the slow burn of irritation building in her head. 'I don't believe you're thinking this through. It's an offence to obstruct a police officer in the commission of her duty.'

There was no reply, other than a buzz from the door. Daisy, who was closest, lunged forward and pushed it open. They made an undignified entrance under the disapproving glare of the receptionist. Judging by the lines on her face, she'd been practising that look of disdain for most of her adult life. 'We are a secure medical facility,' she said, stopping short of a snarl. 'We can't have any Tom, Dick or Harry breengeing in.'

'Mr Nicol,' Karen said. 'You might want to let him know there are two police officers here to see him.'

She sighed as she picked up a phone, tapped a key and said, 'Kayesha, there's two polis here to see Marcus. They're not saying why.'

'You never asked us,' Daisy muttered. The receptionist paid no attention, simply ending the call and glaring at them.

Karen exchanged quizzical looks with Daisy. She thought she'd experienced all the variations of reactions to her arrival, but this was new to her. Moments later, a door in the back wall swung open and a young woman in pressed navy overalls emerged, a broad grin on her face. 'Wow, police. This is a novelty.' Her accent was broad Ayrshire, her voice deep and warm. 'Come away through. I'll get Marcus to come and join us.' She waved them through and closed the door firmly behind them. 'Sorry about Claire, she acts like Marcus is the new Oppenheimer and we're building the next nuclear bomb. The rest of us are quite user-friendly.' She showed them into a small conference room with a round table, half a dozen chairs and a coffee machine. 'Help yourselves to a wee brew, I'll not be a minute.' And she was gone.

'This place is weird,' Daisy said.

Karen inspected the coffee machine. 'Looks like a decent cup of coffee though. At least it's not Nespresso.' She looked around and frowned. 'Shame there's no cups.'

He kept them waiting for exactly ten minutes. In Karen's book, the precision made it performance. He was recognisable from the images Drew Jamieson had passed over to Daisy, though she thought if push came to shove, a good defence advocate could cast a decent shroud of doubt over the ID. Medium height, carefully barbered hair, the skin of a man who knew what a facial spa was for. What hadn't been obvious from the photographs was the air of self-satisfaction he wore like Superman's cape. 'Good morning, ladies. Sorry to keep you waiting. I'm Marcus Nicol, CEO of Surinco.' He extended a hand to Karen, who was unsurprised by the strength of the grip.

'DCI Karen Pirie, Historic Cases Unit,' she said. 'And this is DS Daisy Mortimer.'

He nodded at Daisy, clearly deciding a handshake was above her pay grade. He pulled out a chair opposite Karen and sat down, hitching up his trousers to preserve their excellent cut. 'I'm at a loss to know why you're here. Is this something to do with the pandemic? There seems to be a vendetta running these days against anybody who rode to the rescue during Covid.'

Karen couldn't help admiring his chutzpah. 'No, sir. But if there's anything you'd like to confess ...?' She tailed off with a wry smile.

He guffawed. 'Good try, but you don't look like a priest to me. So why are you here?'

'Do you know a man called Tom Jamieson?'

He made a show of frowning, his eyes travelling to the corner of the ceiling. Then he pulled a grimace of failure. 'Sorry. Not even the faint tinkle of a distant bell.'

'He was the general manager of the Scott Monument Hotel.'

Nicol shook his head. 'Not one of my usual drinking dens, I'm afraid.'

'But you were there on the night of March seventeenth 2020.' Karen's voice was quiet.

He seemed taken aback. 'Was I?' He spread his hands. 'I don't think so.'

Karen produced the photograph from the hotel CCTV. She laid it in front of Nicol. That amused look was back. 'Looks like me, but it's not exactly in focus. And I don't think I've ever owned a hoodie that naff.'

'So you didn't walk out of the hotel and make your way down the Scotsman Steps?'

'Not me, officer. Why would I do that?'

'There's a taxi rank at the bottom of the steps. If you were heading home, it would be the best bet for picking up a cab.'

'If you say so. We have a contract with a taxi firm, though, so I tend not to hang around ranks waiting for a cab. But even if it was me, which it wasn't, that's not a crime. So why are you here?'

Karen stabbed her finger on the fraction of Tom Jamieson that was visible in the foreground of the CCTV image. 'The

29

man who walked out just ahead of you? He died on the Scotsman Steps a few minutes later.'

Nicol raised his well-shaped eyebrows. 'That's tragic. What happened? Heart attack? Jakie attack?'

'If you'd been right behind him, you might know the answer to that.'

'What are you implying?' Now the bonhomie was slipping a little.

'I'm investigating an unexplained death, sir. Trying to give some answers to Tom Jamieson's family.'

'You've taken your time about it,' he said, aiming for levity and almost making it. 'Five years is a long time to get nowhere.'

'Some evidence takes a while to reach us. But we never give up seeking explanations. I'm sure you get that, in your line of work. So, just to be absolutely sure. You categorically deny that you are the man who was in the Scott Monument Hotel and on the Scotsman Steps on seventeenth March 2020?'

'I've told you. It's not me in that pic. For all I know, it could be a deepfake. That'd be why it's taken so long to surface.'

It was, Karen thought, a line too far. 'Why would anyone deepfake you, Mr Nicol?'

'I was just . . . trying to make sense of the situation. Our line of business is very sensitive, we have competitors who might think this would be a way to throw shade on me.'

Karen just stared at him. Daisy knew her cue and picked up the baton. 'Do you have an electronic diary, sir? Or do you prefer old-school paper?'

'My diary contains commercially sensitive material. Unless you've got a warrant, which I very much doubt, you don't get to see it.' He pushed back from the table. 'You just ran out of goodwill, ladies. This has been an epic waste of all of our time.' He stood up and opened the door, gesturing that they should depart.

Back at the car, Karen stood for a moment looking back at Surinco. 'Did you believe him?'

Daisy shook her head. 'Not for a nanosecond.'

'The only reason he'd lie is that there's connective tissue between Marcus Nicol and Tom Jamieson. Now we just have to figure out what it is and join the dots.' She gave a savage grin. 'Gotta love the easy ones.'

6

Karen dropped Daisy off at Edinburgh Park Station. 'Time for a deep dive into Surinco and Marcus Nicol. Away you go and cultivate his nearest and dearest,' she said. When it came to digging through the internet for possible lines of approach, Daisy was in her element. Considering she had no interest in men, she had a rare knack of convincing them to open their hearts.

'It's *because* I have no interest,' she had explained to Karen one lockdown night after a few glasses of wine. 'It's a challenge to their ego. They want to show off the secrets they're supposed to be keeping. They can't help themselves. They think that's how they impress us.'

It had impressed Karen that Daisy had come up with a strategy that worked for her. 'Do you play the same game with women?'

'What, when I'm interviewing them?' Daisy had chuckled. 'No. I flirt. Not in a sexy way,' she added hastily, seeing Karen's eyebrows climb. 'I make them feel like I want to be their new best friend. Like I totally respect them.'

'Ah. So you don't really respect me? It was all a game to get into the HCU?'

'That's for me to know and you to find out, boss.'

There was a moment when it could have gone either way. But Karen didn't actually mind if she'd been played. Daisy was a valuable addition to the team and that was what mattered most. They had each other's back when it counted; Daisy was smart enough to understand that trying to get one up on her boss would not end well. As Karen drove down the motorway towards Gartcosh, she considered the awkward truth that she'd benefited from the Covid lockdown, both professionally and personally. The knowledge brought with it a burden of guilt; it was something she could never admit to, even to the people she loved most.

But there was no doubt of the benefits she'd accrued. She'd finagled Daisy into a permanent slot in the HCU, a slot that hadn't really existed but which had proved its value since. Jason had gone to hell and back in his private life, but he'd come out of it stronger and more mature. He'd lost his beloved mother, split up with his fiancée Eilidh (*praise the lord*, she thought) and forged a new relationship. Meera was an archivist at the National Library of Scotland; their paths had crossed when Karen had got into the habit of sending him off to the NLS to use their newspaper archives for research. It was, on the face of it, an unlikely pairing, but Meera challenged him in a good way, just as Karen thought she pushed him to become a better polis. And her?

She'd extracted herself from one relationship that had started to make her feel lesser, and now she seemed to be inching her way towards another that showed every sign of the possibility of happiness. Rafiq's life could not have been more different from hers; a Syrian refugee with a price on his head, an orthopaedic surgeon who had struggled to regain his former calling, a widower whose only child had been torn from him by war, he had known even more grief than she had. And yet there was undeniably something that drew them together, improbable as it seemed. Now he was living under a new name in Canada, which made the prospect of a life together slender. But the Assad regime had finally fallen; it seemed the target on his back had been painted over. He was close to qualifying for a Canadian passport, which meant they could meet on her ground as well as his. They'd never have the easy connection her happily married parents had, yet perhaps they could find something equally solid, in spite of its very different foundations.

And in professional terms? Lockdown had taught the three of them a new way of working together. They'd had to rely on each other because there was no support coming from anywhere else. The HCU had always been a beast apart and she thought it had maybe made them a bit chippy, a bit eager to take offence whether any was intended or not. Now, they'd learned to treat their independence as an absolute positive; they didn't have to measure themselves against anyone else.

That had been much easier with the departure of ACC Markie. She'd had her reasons for her hostility to Karen, reasons the DCI had only uncovered relatively late in their working relationship. It was the kind of resentment that would only ever fester. Markie carried blame in her heart towards Karen and the only way to resolve the hostility was for one of them to depart the ambit of the other. Karen could be thrawn as a mule; she'd been adamant she wasn't going anywhere. But the pandemic had struck, all across the board senior posts had been shuffled and Markie had packed her bags for a top job elsewhere. She couldn't have moved further from Police Scotland's borders and stayed within the UK. Karen liked to think she'd driven her away, but in her more honest moments, she admitted to herself she was probably bigging up her importance to Markie. She knew River wouldn't agree with that. But River was the nearest thing she had to a best friend; Markie wasn't worth falling out over.

A sign warning that the road was narrowing to a single lane told her she was nearing the landslip and crime scene, and she lowered her speed accordingly. She rounded a bend and the sodden fields gave way to a raw scar in the hillside where the grass and topsoil appeared to have been spread as if by a giant palette knife, a deep valley scoured out in the middle. A blue forensic tent had been erected to prevent rubberneckers gaining the satisfaction of vicarious disaster; a police Land Rover was stationed at one end, the anonymous black van of body removal at the other.

Karen signalled to the constable in high-vis that she wanted to pull in. He clocked her ID, and moved a couple of cones to allow her access. He pointed further down the hard shoulder to where presumably it was safe to park. She got out and donned the wellies from her boot then took in the disaster that had overtaken the road. It looked like a giant with a snaggletooth bite had taken a chunk out of the side of the hard shoulder, leaving the edge of the roadway to crumble like a chocolate brownie. Several shades of mud clung to the sides, made viscous by the rain and the surface water.

Towards the bottom of the exposed substrate a smaller white tent had been erected. Karen groaned softly at the prospect then began to make her way gingerly down the slope. As she went, a white-suited forensic technician emerged from within, carrying a short stack of clear plastic boxes that seemed to contain slabs of mud that looked disturbingly like fudge. The woman looked up, alerted by her peripheral vision to the presence of a newcomer. She nodded in recognition. 'River's still inside,' she said.

Karen negotiated the last part of the slippery descent without incident and stepped inside the tent flap. The light filtering through turned the scene unreal, bleaching colour and flattening shapes. She picked up a white suit from the trestle table by the entrance and wrestled herself inside. Even though she'd lost weight, more to do with anxiety than dieting, she still struggled with the suits that seemed not only to have a life of their own but to bear her personal malice. River looked up and chuckled. 'Swearing won't make them more obedient,' she said.

'A bit like forensic scientists, then,' Karen grumbled, slipping plastic bootees over her wellies and snapping gloves on her hands. 'Don't know why we're even bothering. It's hard to think of any locus more contaminated than this.'

'You missed the soil specialist.' River straightened up and stretched her back. 'Oof.'

'That was quick.'

'She was here and gone. Took some pics, a few samples, said it was pretty clear the body had been inserted when the road layers were being laid down. She's forwarding her report to you.'

'Fine.' Karen moved forward and took her first look at what had brought her here. It was still almost completely encased in its overcoat of thick mud, a bizarre clay maquette of a human sculpture. 'Looks like something out of a horror film. "They came from the primordial slime." What's the game plan for it?'

'I'm just waiting for the heavy-duty tarp then we're going to roll it. There's a small hoist on its way from Bathgate.

We'll raise it to the level of the road then put it on the trolley, load it into the mortuary van and take it back to Dundee.'

'You're taking it back to your mortuary? Not dealing with it at Gartcosh?'

River shrugged. 'I've got better kit back there. Not to mention it's a potential teaching opportunity for my students. I cleared it with the Fruit Gum. He's a lot easier to work with than Markie.'

Karen made a non-committal noise in the back of her throat. 'Has anything turned up that might help us with ID?'

'Not yet. The sooner I can get the remains out of here, the sooner the scene techs can start looking for any trace evidence. I don't envy them, it's going to be a thankless task.'

'But one we can't ignore.' Karen sighed. 'By the way, where is the Mint? I sent him over first thing.'

'Well, there was nothing for him to do here, so I suggested he went off to Gartcosh to plug in his laptop and see what he could find out about when this bit of road was built and who the contractors were.'

Karen nodded. 'Right up his street. Nothing he likes more than the kind of trawl through the records that makes my brain bleed.'

Before River could say more, the sound of a heavy vehicle slowly grinding above them alerted them to the arrival of the low loader. The two women left the scene techs trying to make sense of the mudscape around the body. They all knew the investigations were probably fruitless but they had to be done.

Karen stepped outside the tent and stared up at what remained of the embankment. The low-loader lorry was perched across the carriageway, blocking all oncoming traffic. Its onboard crane was lifting a bright scarlet hoist on to

37

the lip of the collapsed road. It swung gently to and fro, a giant metal insect whose outline made no sense to Karen. The finer points of engineering were beyond her; she could manage a hammer drill and an electric screwdriver, but that was her limit. Though once the hoist was in place, its configuration began to make sense.

She clambered out of the way as a trio of police officers in hi-vis jackets struggled down the slope with a tarp. They passed it into the tent and a surprisingly short time later, a neatly wrapped bundle emerged. Meanwhile, a cradle of chains and slings had descended from the hoist. With infinite care, the crime scene techs and the police officers placed the increasingly muddy bundle securely in the cradle. Then, inch by inch, it rose upwards, swaying gently from side to side. Karen watched, gripped by the apparently precarious process. Just one uncontrolled jerk or twist and they'd have a nightmare scatter of mud-covered bones cascading around them.

River joined her as the hoist operator manoeuvred the arm round so the body was suspended above solid ground. The trolley from the mortuary van was already in place to receive it.

In moments, it was all over. The trolley had disappeared from sight, and the hoist was back in the air, swinging on to the low loader. 'Impressive,' Karen said. 'Now what? You're off back to Dundee to work your magic?'

River grinned. 'That's right. We should be able to extract DNA, and we'll process the bones for location info. I'll keep you posted.'

'Thanks. Once Jason's figured out when the road was laid down, we'll check the timeline against mispers and see if there are any obvious matches.' She turned her gaze momentarily towards the mortuary van. 'This is definitely one for the HCU.'

'Good luck,' River said. 'Whoever did this, they didn't plan on their victim being discovered.'

'On the other hand, there's nothing subtle about it. I've got a feeling once we have the victim ID'd, we'll have a very good idea who put them here.'

7

Daisy started in the obvious place. She googled Marcus Nicol and found a Wikipedia page. He was older than he looked – she'd have put him in his early forties, but it turned out he'd been born forty-eight years before in Crieff. All Daisy knew about Crieff was that their former distillery cat was in the *Guinness Book of Records* for killing an insane number of mice in her twenty-four-year reign. And she only knew that because it had come up one night in the regular pub quiz Steph insisted on dragging her along to. Since the other two members of the team were, like Steph, teachers, Daisy always felt like the class dunce. Every day a school day . . .

Nicol had gone to school at Morrison's Academy, a private school in the town, which explained his posh accent. Then on to Heriot-Watt University to do a degree in Chemical Engineering. His early career was briefly described as 'several years working in the area of refining medical supplies' before he founded Surinco. The company was described as 'suppliers of market-leading surgical instruments and devices to the NHS and abroad'.

It stopped being quite so bland when it reached the Covid years:

At the start of the pandemic, Nicol was driven by the desire to help fight Covid. There was a fear that there would be a desperate shortage of ventilators as patients suffered respiratory distress, and Surinco quickly developed a method of repurposing anaesthetic machines to fill the gap. They were able to supply ample machines to the Scottish Government and beyond.

Surinco later switched their output to CPAP (continuous positive airway pressure) machines which use air pressure to keep breathing airways open.

Why the switch, Daisy wondered.

Back at the Google results, she found some media stories that gave her more colour. There was a photograph of Nicol next to a grinning Scottish cabinet minister at the opening of a new robotic production line just over a year ago. Probably where the Covid profits went, Daisy thought. Another photo from a charity dinner, this time in formal Highland dress with a stylish and rather beautiful blonde on his arm, captioned, 'Marcus Nicol with his wife Heidi at the Lord Provost's Burns Supper'. Not at the top table, though. Paying through the nose to dine out with the not-quite great and good, she decided.

There was more of the same. Rugby club dinners, glad-handing politicians, with and without Mrs Nicol. Daisy scrolled to the bottom of the page then turned to the next one. She knew the overwhelming majority of searchers never made it that far; it was often where the interesting stuff started. First up was a profile from the *Daily Clarion* Saturday supplement. *My favourite Saturday*, it was called. Daisy had yet to read one of those that sounded anything like the activities of anyone she knew. Marcus Nicol was no exception.

41

Up at seven, off for a run across the Braid Hills with his cockapoo, then home for a shower and breakfast of a green smoothie and a bowl of home-made Bircher muesli in the conservatory with the lovely Heidi. He'd read the papers for a couple of hours, then they'd play a round of golf on one of the East Lothian courses. His weekly treat was a fish supper at the Rocketeer in North Berwick. Daisy preferred the Lobster Shack, but she couldn't really fault his choice. Either way, the views of the Bass Rock and the Forth estuary were worth the trip, regardless of the weather. Then back to Edinburgh for a night out at one of the cinemas where you could sprawl on leather sofas and drink cocktails.

The golf she could believe, but she had a sneaking suspicion that the fish supper and the movie were a fabrication. She suspected Marcus Nicol was too invested in networking to give up the prime opportunities of Saturday nights to sit in the dark with his wife and a tub of popcorn. He'd be eating and drinking with the movers and shakers who could help his business. She'd have staked money on it. Though maybe not against Karen; her boss was too good at reading people to take that chance.

Digging down deeper, she found a profile of Nicol dating back to the early days of the pandemic, when he was being hailed as one of the heroes of the fight against the virus. It rehashed much of what Daisy already knew, but the journalist had also quoted the opinions of others. A Scottish government minister had praised Nicol's speedy stepping up to the plate; a consultant at Glasgow's Royal Infirmary commented that if every business took their responsibilities as seriously as Surinco, more lives could be saved. 'Aye, right,' she mumbled. An unnamed close friend talked about Nicol's ambition not just to be a success but also to support his community; another 'old school friend' spoke of his ambition not getting in the way of his integrity. She made a note of the byline on the feature. She had a feeling Karen might want to talk to her.

On the third page, she found the first dissenting voice. A social media thread from a community activist with the handle @DinnaeDrinkTheKoolAid complained at some length about the money Surinco had 'gouged' from the Scottish taxpayer for their 'often inadequate, sometimes useless equipment'. It was interesting, but it didn't take much investigation to establish that @DinnaeDrinkTheKoolAid was definitely not an alias for Tom Jamieson, since their most recent post had been only a couple of days previously. Unless Drew Jamieson had bizarrely decided to assume his brother's mantle, the rogue account had nothing to do with the death on the Scotsman Steps.

She decided there wasn't much more to be gleaned from the internet. But Daisy realised she knew another source who might have some inside skinny on Marcus Nicol. The pub quiz boasted half a dozen regular teams as well as Steph and her colleagues, and over the last couple of years, some of their rivals had become pals. One of the teams contained two spads – special advisers to government ministers – and a pair of junior civil servants. One of the spads had recently left his post with the health minister to join a think tank. Before she could get cold feet, Daisy grabbed her phone and called him. He answered on the second ring, which was a good sign.

'Hi, Paul, it's Daisy here. From the pub quiz?'

'Daisy, how are you doing? You looking to defect?'

'No chance, Steph would kill me. Besides, unless there's something you're not telling me, you've not got a vacancy.'

A pause. 'Actually ... there might be. I've been offered a promotion, but it's in London. I'm not sure I can afford to take it, though. With what I'd get for my flat, I'd be lucky to rent a cupboard down there.'

'But you'd be running with the big dogs, no?'

'It's a hard choice, though. Stay in Scotland and hope for another shot at independence and all the possibilities that brings, or go down south where so many of the major decisions are taken.'

Paul McCallum wasn't the first person Daisy had seen sitting uncomfortably on the horns of that particular dilemma. 'You could always raid their cupboard then come back?'

'I'd be accused of being a carpetbagger. With some justification.' He sighed. 'And I'd lose my place on the quiz team.'

Daisy chuckled. 'Right enough. Get your priorities in order, Paul.'

'So what are you after, Daisy? I know it's not my bonny blue eyes.'

'When you were at Health, did you come across an outfit called Surinco? And their boss?'

'Marcus Nicol?' A subtle change of tone.

'That's the one.'

A pause. 'It's nearly lunchtime. Are you in town?'

Clearly this was a conversation Paul didn't want to have over the phone, presumably where he might be overheard, 'I am.'

'I'll see if I can get us a table at Ka Pao. One o'clock, unless you hear back from me.'

The line went dead. That was the thing about spads, she thought. They loved being the ones in possession of the secrets. It was the nearest Paul was ever going to get to being a secret agent, but if it made him happy, that was half the battle. The Thai-based menu at Ka Pao was terrific, but most importantly, the acoustic was perfect. Even though it felt noisy, it was still possible to have a private conversation.

It was Daisy's idea of a perfect combination. The only real challenge was to order enough of the small plates for there to be leftovers she could take home for dinner.

8

Karen found Jason hot-desking in the corner of an office half-full of detectives staring into screens, hammering keyboards or conducting their end of conversations with their earphones plugged in. He was hunched over his own laptop, frowning, his fingers moving sporadically over the keys. Every now and again he'd make an entry in his notebook. He was the only person she knew under thirty who still preferred to write things down rather than make notes on their phones or take endless screenshots. She'd once asked him why.

He'd looked embarrassed, then said, 'It's not that I don't know how to do the techie stuff. But things stick better if I write them down.'

'It's always the right move to realise what works best for you,' she'd said. 'And you're bloody good at working your way through the routine research and pulling out the important bits.' Now she wove her way across the room to his side. 'How's it going?' She pulled up a chair.

'The carriageway in question was built in the spring of 2014. This particular stretch was mostly laid down in March and April. I got a contact number for the civil engineers who ran the contract, but they couldn't be certain exactly when this bit went in. They've got records but they're on paper and they're archived off site. The guy I spoke to reckoned they could get somebody out there later in the week.' He pulled a face. 'I couldn't get him to budge on that. He was, like, "it's more than ten years ago, how urgent can it be?"'

'Not everybody appreciates that to anybody who's missing a loved one, every day takes another wee bite out of you,' Karen said, weary that after all these years of fighting the cold case battle there were still people out there who didn't get it.

'But I did make a start on mispers,' Jason said, brightening. 'River said she was pretty sure it was a man so I thought I could pull the records on men that were reported missing in the first three months of 2014 where there was no resolution. See, boss, most of them turned up one way or another in a matter of days.' He gestured at the screen. 'I got it down to seventeen that were reported missing and never showed up.'

'That's good work. We'll be able to narrow it down even further when River's finished.'

He nodded. 'Thing is, though, if they're not on the DNA database, it'll not be easy to ID them. We'll have to rely on familial matches, and that's easier said than done. Meanwhile, I'm going to check them all against our databases, see whether any of them has a record or known connections to any organised crime groups.'

'We'll get there.' Karen checked the time on his laptop screen. 'I'm heading off to the Tulliallan. I've got a meeting with the Fruit Gum at three, and I don't want to keep him waiting.' Jason looked incredulous. 'I know that'll come as a shock to you, Jason, but sometimes I actively want to stay on the boss's good side.'

*

Daisy made a point of arriving ahead of Paul at the restaurant. If she was already seated when he reached their table, it avoided the awkward 'do we hug?' moment. 'Hey, Daisy,' he greeted her. For a moment she thought he was going for a high five, but then he thought better of it and settled on a sketchy wave. He was wearing a better suit than he had when he was a spad, and he had the air of a man who was sleeping well and occasionally experiencing fresh air. Life in the think tank clearly agreed with him.

They spent little time on the menu; both were sufficiently familiar with it to have their own preferences set in stone. Once they'd ordered half a dozen small plates, Paul sat back. 'So, Marcus Nicol. Or, as we used to call him, Marcus Nick-it.'

'"Nick-it"?'

'Let's just say he extracted more from the public purse than his products merited. What's your interest?'

'Good try. But you know I can't divulge details of an ongoing investigation.'

He made a circling gesture with his wrist that suggested she was delivering a hackneyed line. 'You've got to give a little to get a lot, Daisy.'

'All I can say is that he's a person of interest in a case we're investigating.'

'A suspect, then? I didn't think the HCU dealt with fraud. Or is it the Covid deaths of people who got his faulty equipment?'

'Stop fishing, Paul. I'm not going to fall for your nonsense. Tell me why you think he's dodgy.'

'This is between you and me, right? Even though I'm not working for the Scottish Government any longer, I'm still not supposed to give out privileged information. But the Covid inquiry's already opened this can of worms and I don't see why companies who screwed money out of the public purse should get away with it. Doesn't matter if it was incompetence or bad faith, the end result was the same. It magnified the damage of the pandemic.' His expression was pained. Some people became whistleblowers to big themselves up; others because they felt a genuine sense of outrage. Daisy was pretty sure which camp Paul sat in.

'I get that,' she said. 'I'm not going to drop you in it. But Marcus Nicol's public image is that he's one of the good guys. I'm trying to ascertain whether that's the truth or a well-constructed facade.'

The first couple of dishes arrived at the table and they both paused to attack the food. Eventually, Paul said, 'Surinco was one of the first companies to offer support to the health service. At that stage, none of us knew what we were facing. Every day, the news seemed to get worse and worse. We were desperate for anything that would help us fight Covid. And in fairness, we were maybe guilty of taking chancers like Nicol at their word. We didn't have enough bodies or expertise to scrutinise every offer as stringently as we would have done normally.'

'You were kind of on a war footing. Without much time to prep for it.'

More food arrived. Plates were rearranged. 'Don't get me wrong. We'd done contingency planning, but not for a contingency like this. So when Surinco came along with a plan, a successful company working in the medical sector, with a boss whose web of contacts made spiders look ham-fisted ...' He shrugged and helped himself to a wedge of hispi cabbage.

'Why would you doubt him?' Daisy sighed.

'He's a very smooth operator, is Nick-it. He does a lot of glad-handing, a lot of mixing and mingling. He doesn't come across as needy either, he's got genuine charisma.'

'And there's nothing politicians like more than a man with success *and* charisma. So when did the gloss start to wear thin?'

A pause for eating. And careful reflection. 'We believed we were going to need a shitload of ventilators. Nicol was proposing to repurpose anaesthetic equipment as ventilators. Seemed like a sound idea. Same principle, right?'

Daisy nodded obediently. But Paul shook his head and continued. 'Aye and no. The problem was consistency. Some of the adapted equipment worked not bad, up to a point. And some didn't. But the staff on the Covid wards couldn't tell for sure which was which until sometimes it was too late. What saved Surinco and a couple of other firms like it from a huge public outcry was that in the end we didn't need nearly as many ventilators as we'd feared. You might say we hit the panic button too early.' He pulled a face. 'But I don't think that's fair. We were facing something nobody working the wards had ever seen before, which meant we were whistling in the dark.'

'And there was no comeback?'

'At the time, we were focused on trying to keep people alive. When Surinco realised their ventilator conversions weren't really doing what it said on the tin, they very quietly swivelled away from that and started making CPAP machines. For a lot of patients, those were enough to meet their medical needs. Bloody uncomfortable, and scary to look at. But just as some of the PPE gear was pretty crap, so were some of Surinco's CPAP machines. They didn't fit properly, so not enough air was being pushed into the lungs. Around the office, I heard people calling them C-RAP.'

Daisy remembered how things had been at the height of the pandemic. She recalled the hell Jason had gone through when his mother had ended up on the Covid ward. That companies were cynically cashing in on suffering of that order was incomprehensible to her. 'How much did Surinco make?'

'I don't know the exact figure. It wasn't like your woman with the big yacht and the £200 million supply contracts but it wasn't nothing either. They got something around seven million. Obviously, that wasn't all profit. But it gave them liquidity as well as keeping their balance sheet healthy and paying dividends to Nicol and his investors. Seven mil was more than enough to keep Surinco on their feet when a lot of others were going to the wall.' He gave a deep, shuddering sigh.

Neither spoke for a couple of minutes. Then Daisy asked the question she knew her boss would want to know the answer to. 'Did we ask for our money back?'

Paul scoffed. 'What do you think?'

'I think we should have. And I suspect we didn't.'

'Yes, and yes. I saw a brief at one point where the writer argued that if we made a song and dance about getting our money back, it would open the door to NHS Scotland being sued for failing in their duty of care by allowing substandard equipment on the wards.'

They stared glumly at the wreckage of their meal, neither willing to meet the other's eyes. Daisy knew she had to be the one to break the silence; Paul didn't want to venture out on thinner ice. 'Have you actually met Nicol?'

He sighed. 'I met him a few years ago, at a reception

in Bute House, when we were trying to make nice with employers we were encouraging to expand their training schemes. He was very affable, very chatty, happy to discuss Surinco's aims of training school leavers. He wanted to see more focus on the sciences in secondary education, but I'd say he was wistful rather than pushy about it. "I appreciate it's a different minister I should be talking to," he said, kind of joking but not, if you know what I mean?'

Daisy nodded. 'Making sure you'd remember him for all the right reasons.'

'Exactly. But I was also in the meeting when he made his pitch for the Covid supplies.' He pursed his lips. 'No more Mr Nice Guy. He was very firm, very direct. Still charming, but making it absolutely clear that the country would not forgive us if we dropped the ball now. And not giving a contract to Surinco would be a cardinal example of dropping the ball. He produced one of his repurposed ventilators. It looked the business. He hit every hot button round the table.'

'So if you were going to sum him up in three words?'

Paul smiled. 'Charismatic, determined, ambitious.'

'Not crooked?'

He laughed. 'I know this is just between us, Daisy. But he's not a man I'd want to cross. Being sued is for the big boys. I can't afford the hit. You'll not get me to go any further than "necessarily ruthless".'

9

The rain had started again in earnest as Karen set off up the motorway towards Castle Grayskull, as Police Scotland's HQ was known among the lower ranks. She always marvelled that a modern police force would choose a 200-year-old castle for its HQ. She understood why the training college was based in a forbidding Gothic castle that wouldn't have looked out of place in a remake of *Frankenstein*, but to her, it didn't project an image of twenty-first-century policing. All those visuals were back at Gartcosh.

She crossed the Forth on the old Kincardine Bridge, her wheels reassuringly back on Fife tarmac. Karen knew it was sentimental tosh but she always felt on safe ground back where she'd cut her teeth as a cold case cop, on the territory of the former Fife Police force. She parked behind the main building and made her way to the admin wing where ACC (Crime) Graeme Rowntree had his office. The decor always set her teeth on edge. In a bid to replicate the style it had replaced, the wing sprouted Gothic doorways in flawless modern wood, stained in what she supposed was meant to give an authentic look. The wallpaper was so anodyne she could never remember its pattern from one visit to the next.

It looked and felt more like a discreet private medical facility than a cop shop.

She turned into the anteroom to the Fruit Gum's office, where Susie sat behind the desk, diligently typing away at her computer. 'DCI Pirie!' she exclaimed, looking up and smiling. 'He's just got back. You're a couple of minutes early, but I'll let him know you're here.' She picked up a phone and tapped a key. 'DCI Pirie's here, shall I send her in?' She waited for a response then thanked him. She made a rueful face at Karen. 'Give him five minutes.'

'Lets me know who's boss,' Karen said.

Susie shook a warning finger at her. 'Now, now, give the man a chance. He *likes* you, Karen. Not like her ladyship.'

'Right enough. How's *Shrek* coming along?'

Susie rolled her eyes. 'Don't ask. I'm dreading the first night.'

Karen strolled over to the window and looked out at the trees that were just coming into leaf around the manicured lawns. 'It's beautiful here. I'm not surprised he prefers this to Gartcosh.' She turned back. 'Has he said anything about moving us over there?'

Susie glanced at the door. 'It's on his radar. He wants all his key units under one roof.'

'Economies of scale?'

Susie's lips pursed. 'He doesn't like wasting time driving between locations,' she said, sotto voce.

Before Karen could reply, the door to Rowntree's office swung open and he greeted her with a warm smile. He was as memorable as the wallpaper, Karen thought. Forty-ish, mousy hair thinning at the temples, medium build, medium height, rimless glasses. She'd struggle to pick him out of a line-up but for the white scar that ran along the right side of his jawline. It was his badge of honour, the evidence that he'd once been a street cop who understood the front line of policing. 'Come away through, Karen,' he said now, gesturing for her to enter.

She followed him inside and sat down across the desk from his grand leather chair without waiting to be asked. There were no files or paperwork on his desk, just a clutch of photos. Him with the Princess Royal, with his wife and with the current First Minister. All the bases covered. 'Thanks for making the time to see me,' she said.

'It's me who should be thanking you for taking the time out from your investigations. How are we progressing with the body in the motorway?' He sat down and steepled the fingers of his hands. Not a good look when you had short fat fingers, Karen thought.

'Early days, sir. It's not so much a body as a skeleton, according to Dr Wilde. The crime scene techs are still trying to do a fingertip search around the immediate locus to see whether they can find anything useful. But having been to the scene – it'd be a bit like trying to find a pearl in a pile of gravel. Our best chance of ID is whatever Dr Wilde can give us.'

'We're lucky to have her. She's one of the best there is.'

'You'll get no argument from me on that score. We've resolved a fair few of our cases thanks to her information.'

'And of course, she's based at Gartcosh some of the time.'

There it was, out of the box and on the table. 'But her lab's still in Dundee,' Karen said mildly.

'I want to talk to you about Gartcosh.' He smiled at her again. 'It *is* our national Crime Campus, the beating heart of the leading-edge work we do.'

Karen doubted whether beating hearts had leading edges

55

but chose not to mention it. She was trying to be diplomatic and that took energy. 'It's where a lot of valuable work is done. But it's not the only place where that happens.'

'It's my view that the Historic Cases Unit should be one of the core units in that machine going forward. So many of the elements of your investigations are centred there. It would save time and money if your team was based there too.'

Karen gave him a long speculative look. 'I don't know who's put this idea into your head, sir, but I don't think they understand the bigger picture. Of course we utilise the facilities of the crime campus. They're without rivals, especially the forensics teams. But we don't need that daily. We can go for weeks without needing their expertise. In Edinburgh, we're a lot closer to Dr Wilde's Dundee lab, and to the fire and explosives experts there. Not to mention the soil scientists up in Aberdeen.'

'But these days you can have so many of those conversations remotely,' he countered smoothly. 'No need to drive anywhere.'

'All my team are based in Edinburgh, sir. We all live within easy access of the office. Bear with me a second.' She took out her phone. 'I'm quoting from the police strategic plan here, sir. "Police Scotland will make a significant contribution to the Scottish Government's 2040 carbon neutral and 2045 greenhouse gas emissions targets."' Karen gave him her most innocent face. 'How does having three officers driving a daily round trip of about ninety miles square with that strategy?'

The genial mask began to slip. The skin round his eyes tightened. 'There is such a thing as car sharing. Or public transport.'

'My team covers cases all over Scotland. Are you seriously suggesting we try to do our job at the mercy of trains, buses, and planes? Not to mention ferries. I don't see how that can work.'

'There's no need to be so melodramatic, DCI Pirie.' Gone was the 'Karen' now.

'I'm not being melodramatic, sir. Another important consideration is our access to research resources. For example, my officers and I regularly use the archives and reference sources at the National Library of Scotland. I don't think the North Lanarkshire Mobile Library's visits to Gartcosh on a Friday afternoon will meet that need. National records of births, marriages and deaths are held in Edinburgh. Some of them are digitised but by no means all of them. I've lost count of the number of times I've had to spend a morning poring over those lists.' He tried to interrupt but she kept on going, barely pausing for breath.

'The universities in Edinburgh are home to experts in all sorts of abstruse subjects, and they're right on our doorstep. And of course, the Parliament is in Edinburgh, and I've been known on occasion to have to deal with some of our politicians. And then there's Historic Environment Scotland, which I've also had dealings with in the past.'

His face had turned sour now. 'ACC Markie warned me of your lack of cooperation.'

Karen shook her head, more in sorrow than in anger. 'I'm not uncooperative, just practical. Judge me by my results, sir. We bring the dead home to the people who loved them. Our present location serves us very well. We perch at the back of Gayfield Square, getting in nobody's way, but still with our fingers on the pulse of the city. We aren't in some ivory tower, remote from the to and fro of everyday life and crime. Give me a year. If you still think we'd run a better operation out of Gartcosh, then you'll have my resignation on your desk.' She'd surprised herself with that last line. But it felt good to have uttered it.

'There's no need for that,' he spluttered. 'You know I rate you, DCI Pirie.'

'So give me and my team a year to prove that my way of doing things works.' She stood up. 'I've heard you're a fair man. So prove it. Put this date in your diary for next year and we'll discuss this again.' She turned on her heel and walked out, leaving him lost for words.

'How was it?' Susie asked as Karen walked past.

'Unexpected,' she said. 'But I'm still standing. Though I can't speak for your boss.'

Karen marched out of the building, head up, back straight. But she didn't return directly to her car. She rounded the front of the building and walked straight down the wide pathway towards three granite stones that stood erect, surrounded by landscaped shrubs and neatly trimmed hedges.

Whenever she came to Castle Grayskull, she always made time for the three stones of the Scottish Police Memorial. There, carved into the granite, were more than three hundred names, all of them police officers who had died on duty. She didn't have to search; she knew precisely where Phil Parhatka's name was carved into the blue pearl granite.

Phil had been the love of her life. They'd worked together and gradually realised there was more than friendship binding them. For the first time in her life, Karen felt seen, properly seen for who she truly was. And then he'd been killed on the job, trying to arrest a man who had brutalised and terrorised his wife.

The bottom had fallen out of her world. She literally felt

there was nothing under her feet, nothing holding her up-right. All she could manage was being a polis. And she had to hold that together for Jason, who adored Phil, who lived his life by the mantra, 'what would Phil do?'

Slowly, she'd started to heal. She'd fallen into a relation-ship with Hamish Mackenzie but it hadn't been built on solid ground. And then she'd met Rafiq. The attraction had been there from the start but his grief had also been too close to the surface. So they'd moved tentatively and slowly. Karen wanted to hope but was still held back by her fear of loss.

She put out a hand and traced the letters of Phil's name. 'I just delivered an ultimatum to the ACC Crime,' she said conversationally. 'Nice enough guy, but clueless. I can't be-lieve I said what I did. Now I've got a year to be spectacular.' She leaned forward and kissed the cold stone. Time enough to talk about Rafiq next visit.

10

The rain had given way to a pervasive dampness by the time Karen returned to the HCU, feeling cold to her bones. Daisy broke off from staring into her computer screen to bring Karen up to speed with the product of her lunch with Paul McCallum.

'That's a good start, Daisy. Remind me not to take the piss out of your quiz nights again. So what are you up to now?'

'I'm doing what you taught me. Victimology.'

Karen had worked out early in her HCU days that the answer to why someone ends up a murder victim often lies in their own hinterland. Which was the opposite of blaming the victim. It was about finding the point of intersection between the lives of victim and killer and working out why the killer wanted them out of the way. Sometimes it was a product of a drunken fight or a drug deal gone sour; those were the cases a probationer cop could resolve readily. But there were other motivations more deeply buried, where the *cui bono* shorthand of checking who benefited didn't provide an obvious answer. Those were the cases that stretched Karen's intelligence and diligence in equal measure. Those were the cases where the only place to find the loose thread that would allow her to unravel the stitch-up was deep in the life of the victim. 'Have you made much progress?' she asked.

'Not a huge amount,' Daisy admitted. 'I've got an address for his parents, thanks to his brother. He shared his flat with his partner, Jayden Shaw, who's the bar manager in Compadres, a Mexican-themed restaurant in the West Port. His brother said they'd been together for three years at the time of Jamieson's death. They'd met when they were both working at the Angus Arms.

'According to LinkedIn, Tom Jamieson had been general manager at the Scott Monument Hotel for two years and seven months. Before that, he held the same post in the Angus Arms in Carnoustie. It's a five-star hotel specialising in golfing holidays. Judging by the website, it caters to a lot of overseas visitors. Our man was there for three years. Before that, he did two years as night manager of the Glen Troon Hotel. Four stars, again aimed at golfers, mostly from overseas. Before that, he had a series of jobs, working his way up after he graduated from Queen Margaret University with a degree in Hospitality Management. No indication of any problems. Plus he was shortlisted for Scottish Hotel Manager of the Year in his last year at the Angus Arms.'

'And you think we should start with . . .?'

'His number two at the Scott Monument Hotel; the owner of the Angus Arms and maybe the Glen Troon? Find out who was close to him and move on to them.'

'Not the boyfriend and the parents?' Karen's voice was mild but her expression was not.

Daisy shifted in her chair. 'I figure it'd be good to get a more dispassionate take on Tom Jamieson before we talk to his parents and his boyfriend. Get a sense of what other people thought of him?'

It was a reasonable decision. Not the order she'd have chosen, but Karen reckoned she wasn't infallible. Daisy had to work out her own angle of approach. 'OK. Do you want to make a start on that now? The good thing about hotel workers is that they don't knock off at five. There'll be staff there who knew Tom Jamieson well. And don't forget to show them Marcus Nicol's pic.' Daisy nodded. 'Tomorrow morning, we'll take a look at the boyfriend, OK? You and me.' There was only so much freedom of action she was prepared to give her sergeant.

Daisy approached the concierge at the Scott Monument Hotel with more surface confidence than she actually felt. She couldn't help feeling a little daunted by the foyer. Unlike so many of Edinburgh's tourist hotels, it had avoided the faux Victorian decor of dark wood, tartan and tweed in favour of discreet lighting that emphasised a bright and airy atmosphere. The paintings on the walls were not brooding mountains, Highland cattle or bearded men in plaids and kilts giving the landscape a hundred-yard stare. Instead, they were splashy modern takes on the city itself. But in spite of that apparent rejection of tradition, it still maintained the insouciant air of superiority that had characterised the city since the Enlightenment back in the eighteenth century.

The concierge himself wore a dark navy suit that looked tailored to fit him. His gleaming white shirt was open at the neck, revealing a tiny triangle of hairless skin. Cleanshaven and pink-cheeked, somewhere south of forty but wearing it well, he seemed to carry the waft of fresh air with him. He gave Daisy a head-to-toe glance that clearly read her as a non-resident, but he smiled nevertheless.

'I'm DS Mortimer from Police Scotland,' she said, her voice discreetly lowered. 'Is Tom Jamieson's deputy still on the staff here?'

Disconcerted, he hesitated. Then when she produced her photo ID, he said, 'Yes, she is.'

'Perhaps you could tell her I'm here?'

He swallowed hard, struggling for the composure that is the hallmark of a good concierge. 'I can do that. Can I ask what it's in connection with?'

Daisy smiled. 'We're taking another look at Tom's death and I'd like to speak to any of his close colleagues that are still working here.'

Still with an air of uncertainty, he picked up a phone and tapped in a number. He forced a smile at Daisy as he waited for a response. Then he all but stood to attention. 'Good afternoon, Jakki. I have a detective here from Police Scotland who'd like to speak to you about Tom Jamieson.' He listened, then thanked her and replaced the receiver. 'She'll be right down,' he said.

'Thanks. What's her name?'

'Jakki. Jakki Livesey-van Dorst.' He looked towards the lifts. 'I thought ... we all thought that business with Tom was, what do you say? Case closed?'

'Loose ends,' she said vaguely. 'Often happens. How long have you worked here?' she added casually.

'Just over nine years.' He stood straighter. 'Since the current owners took over.'

'You must have seen it all.'

A knowing look. 'Same as you, I reckon.'

'Did you know Tom well?' It was, she thought, worth a try.

'I had a lot of time for Mr Jamieson. He was clear what

he wanted and how he wanted it done, but he was always fair. Friendly but fair. And he knew everybody's name, right down to the kitchen porters.'

'A good boss, then?'

He shrugged. 'In this business, people move around all the time. If you don't think you're getting a fair crack of the whip, or if you don't get along with your boss, or if you make a mess on your own doorstep, you don't have to stick around. There wasn't a lot of staff turnover when Mr Jamieson was here. Not at the senior levels.'

'Did he mix with the staff socially? Have a drink at the end of the shift? That sort of thing?'

He raised his eyebrows. 'No. He didn't need us to be his friends. He had other fish to fry.' Before she could ask what he meant, he straightened up. 'And this is Jakki Livesey-van Dorst. Jakki, this is Detective Mortimer.'

Petite, slim, hair a wavy chestnut cascade, subtle make-up, a dark navy skirt suit and low heels that flattered shapely legs. When she smiled, her greenish eyes sparkled and fine lines appeared at their corners. Daisy took it all in with an eye practised in noticing how women presented themselves. Jakki reminded her of a past mistake; Daisy would try not to let that prejudice her. Hopefully the days of bad choices were behind her now she'd settled with Steph.

Jakki held out a hand and Daisy shook it. Firm, cool, dry. A quick mutual introduction, then Jakki offered her office for privacy and a cup of tea for refreshment. Daisy said yes to both, hoping there would be scones, or at the very least, biscuits.

Jakki's office was on the third floor, a side window providing a view of the eponymous monument and Princes Street Gardens beyond. 'Some view,' she said.

'I've had worse,' Jakki said with a chuckle. She pressed a button on her desk and spoke into a microphone. 'Soraya? Tea for two in my office, please.' She looked up at Daisy. 'Earl Grey or English Breakfast?'

Daisy grinned. 'Builder's?'

Jakki nodded with a grin and said, 'Good strong English breakfast, please.' She gestured towards a pair of armchairs on the visitor side of the desk. They sat facing each other, Jakki with her back to the light. *She knows what she's doing,* Daisy thought.

'I thought we'd covered poor Tom's tragic death with your people already?' Jakki crossed her legs, apparently relaxed. 'There was a Fatal Accident Inquiry and the sheriff ruled that Tom had fallen and told the Scotsman Steps people they should consider better lighting and the provision of CCTV cameras. Isn't that the end of the matter?'

It was interesting that she had all the details at her fingertips. Or perhaps not; Daisy didn't imagine there were many violent staff deaths in a hotel like the Scott Monument. 'Not always, no. Sometimes fresh information emerges that requires us to look again at a case.'

'Even after all this time?'

Daisy nodded. 'There are all sorts of reasons for delays in information emerging. That's where we come in. I'm with the Historic Cases Unit.'

Jakki frowned. 'What's this new information?'

'I'm sorry, I can't go into details.'

'Well, there's no point in asking me, I wasn't on that night.' As she spoke there was a tap on the door and a young woman came in pushing a trolley. All the accoutrements of having a cup of tea, as well as a three-tier cake stand with scones, shortbread and two kinds of cake. For a fleeting moment, Daisy wondered whether she was in the wrong career. Did hotels still have house detectives? 'Thanks, Soraya,' Jakki said, dismissing the waitress. 'I'll let the tea brew a bit longer.'

'At this point, what we're interested in is finding out more about Tom Jamieson. His friends and associates, how he spent his spare time, what his interests were. That kind of thing. I believe you were his deputy manager?'

'Latterly, yes. I was promoted about five months before he died. I'd been Events Manager first.'

'You knew him well?'

She poured the tea in a dark brown stream. She pushed a cup towards Daisy. 'I don't know that I'd say "well". There were no issues between us, don't get me wrong. But Tom wasn't an easy man to get to know. He was a bit of a worka-holic. He didn't do small talk.' She picked up a slice of lemon with a toothpick and carefully added it to her cup. 'Help yourself, lemon or milk?'

Daisy poured milk into her tea. She'd been neatly di-verted, she thought. 'Why was that? I thought hotels were hotbeds of gossip.'

'They are. And we're no exception. But Tom didn't join in. I used to wonder whether he'd developed the habit of discretion because he was ambitious and he didn't want that to stand in the way of his climb up the greasy pole.' She shrugged. 'Either way, I really couldn't tell you anything about his private passions. I met his partner Jayden at a staff Christmas party once and I know they lived round the corner, but that's the extent of my knowledge.' She sipped her tea.

Disappointed, Daisy asked, 'Is there anyone else on the team who might have known him better?'

Jakki helped herself to a piece of shortbread. 'God, the shortbread here is killer. You must have a piece.' She pushed the cake stand closer to Daisy, who gave in and took a piece. It was so good she almost missed Jakki musing. 'Except, maybe ...'

'Maybe who?'

'Bob Watson,' she said slowly. 'He's the sommelier.'

'Were they friends?'

Jakki sucked her breath in over her teeth. 'I don't know that for sure. But I know they fell out quite badly before Tom died. Just after the New Year. Bob was distraught afterwards, he was genuinely upset that they were not talking to each other when it happened.'

Karen would love this, Daisy thought. Come to that, she loved it. 'Do you know what it was about?'

Jakki seemed embarrassed. 'It's really silly. It definitely wasn't a motive for murder.'

'You'd be surprised. When tempers flare—'

Jakki shook her head and laughed. 'I don't think anybody's ever committed murder over this, Sergeant.'

'Try me.'

11

The HCU started the next morning in what had become since lockdown their preferred way; Jason arriving with a tray of three coffees from Valvona & Crolla on Elm Row and, if they were lucky, a bag of bomboloni. No way would there be anything comparable within miles of Gartcosh, Karen thought bitterly. A debrief and a discussion of 'what's next?' would follow before they all set about their different tasks, fuelled by sugar and caffeine. 'Any joy at the hotel last night, Daisy?'

'He seems to have been well liked among his staff. But he did have a falling out with a guy called Bob Watson. He's the sommelier at the hotel.'

'What did they fall out about?'

'It sounds really stupid but it was the only thing Jamieson's deputy could think of.'

Karen made a circling gesture with her hand. 'Go on? Was Watson up to something dodgy with the wine suppliers?'

'Nothing that tasty. Five-a-side football.'

'How come?' Jason demanded. 'I mean, that's supposed to be fun, right?'

Daisy sighed. 'They've got a team at the hotel. They play every Thursday night in a hotel league.'

'Who knew?' Karen muttered.

Ignoring the interruption, Daisy continued. 'The Scott Monument guys were top of the league, not least because Tom Jamieson was their goalie. He had a great record of stopping balls. Anyway, a few months before he died, he pulled out of the team. He said he'd joined a book club that met on Thursdays and it wasn't fair on the team for him to miss one game a month. Bob Watson had a stand-up row with him in the staffroom when Jamieson insisted the book club was more important to him. Bitter words, apparently, on both sides. The pair didn't exchange another word for the rest of Jamieson's life.'

'Did they come to blows?' Karen asked.

'Only a war of words, but it got heated. Watson accused him of thinking he was better than the rest of them. Too big for his boots. That sort of thing.'

Karen shrugged, dubious. 'I can't believe a row over a football team could end up in murder. But maybe a ruck on the stairs that got out of hand . . . We should talk to Bob Watson, see what he's got to say for himself.' She turned towards the Mint. 'Jason, how did you get on with the mispers?'

'Not a single one of them had any recorded connections to organised crime. Four of the younger ones had drug problems, family issues. They probably hightailed it to London, disappeared into the homeless and hopeless. Never got back in touch with their families, which, reading between the lines, isn't that surprising. There's another group of older men, alcoholics, scraping by at the bottom of the pile, homeless or sofa surfing, they just disappear off the radar.'

'That's the thing with Scotland. Miles of empty space to disappear into. Plenty of deep lochs. And a lot of sea.' Karen shook her head. 'It's surprising there's not more of it.'

'There's three separate climbers missing in the Highlands,' Jason continued. 'The bodies tend to turn up eventually, but there's a lot of bits of the Highlands that don't see much action from the climbing community. The rest fall into the "fuck it, I've had enough" category of men who've just walked away from their families because they can't cope or they're up to the eyeballs in debt. I really can't see anybody in this list ending up buried in a motorway.'

'I tend to agree,' Karen said, wiping the bomboloni sugar off her lips. 'And if that's the case, for whatever reason, nobody reported our guy missing.'

'Organised crime is my bet,' Daisy said. 'Somebody got too big for his Docs and everybody will have gone, "aye, he's done one," and promptly erased him from their memory banks.'

'Let's keep an open mind for now,' Karen said mildly. 'He might not even be from our jurisdiction.' Catching Daisy's raised eyebrow, she shrugged. 'I don't think everybody's a refugee or an asylum seeker just because of Rafiq. But they might be. OK, Jason, you stick with this for now. Talk to Gartcosh, see whether forensics have anything for us, and stay across whatever River's up to. I'd like this man ID'd as soon as possible.'

Daisy helped herself to a second little doughnut. 'Once you've finished that,' Karen continued, 'you're with me, Daisy. We'll go and talk to the boyfriend. He's a bar manager, he'll be at home this time in the morning. I want to get as complete a picture of Tom Jamieson's daily life as possible. We need to find out whether anyone wanted him dead. Apart from his five-a-side team.'

'I could talk to Bob Watson?' Jason said. 'If he was het up enough with Jamieson, mibbes he'd know other guys who felt the same?'

70

Karen thought for a moment. Scots law required corroboration for interviews whose results ended up as court evidence. But if interviews were merely to further the investigation, they could be done single-handed. She really didn't think a row about football was going to end up in the witness box; time to let Jason fly solo. 'OK. But if it takes a turn into shark-infested waters, back off until you can return with Daisy or me. And don't take your eye off the ball on the skeleton ID.' She turned to Daisy. 'Let's away and see what Jayden Shaw has to say to us.'

Jayden Shaw was still living in the flat he'd shared with Tom Jamieson. According to the brother, they'd bought the flat jointly so the sole ownership had passed to Jayden with Tom's death. The street door was easily missed, sandwiched between a restaurant and a small ceramics gallery. Karen pressed the intercom bell marked 'SHAW' and waited for a response. A long pause, then a crackly, 'Hello? Who is it?'

'Detective Chief Inspector Karen Pirie,' she said.

'What's this about?'

'Your late partner, Tom Jamieson.'

Another pause. 'This is his brother stirring it all up again, right?' The buzz of the door opening cut across whatever else he might have wanted to say and Karen took her chance while it lasted. Faced with a typically narrow Old Town stone staircase, she sighed and started the climb.

They were both feeling it in their lungs and legs by the time they reached the fourth floor. Jayden Shaw leaned in the far doorway, wearing a plaid dressing gown over a pair of leisure pants. His tousled bed hair and the scribble of stubble revealed they'd woken him. He still looked better than most of the men Karen knew even after they'd showered and shaved. 'Takes it out of you till you get used to it,' he said, an annoying note of smugness in his voice. 'Now you're here, you'd better come in.'

He led the way through a small vestibule to the living room. The view from high above the railway lines was impressive; a slice of the imposing Balmoral Hotel, the old Royal High School and above, on Calton Hill, the National Monument commemorating the fallen of the Napoleonic Wars in classical Greek columns, and the Nelson Monument with its time ball that synched every day with the One O'Clock Gun fired from the castle ramparts. In a city with no shortage of breathtaking vistas, this was special. 'That's worth the climb,' Karen said.

'It still knocks me out every morning. It's like Tom bought us a slice of Scottish history.' He yawned and threw himself down on one of a pair of tweed sofas angled towards the wide screen TV on one wall. Beneath it sat a couple of games consoles, an untidy pile of games boxes and a wicker basket of controllers. 'I'm Jayden Shaw, as you'll have worked out, being detectives. And you are?'

'We're from the Historic Cases Unit,' Karen said. 'I'm DCI Karen Pirie and this is DS Mortimer.'

'And am I right about Drew kicking off?' He scoffed. 'He can't get over me ending up with this place. I've tried explaining how joint ownership works, and how either one of us dying would have meant the mortgage got paid off, but he still thinks I've done him out of something.' His Irish accent became stronger as the heat in his voice rose.

'I know this must be painful for you, but when someone comes to us with fresh information, even after all this time, we're obliged to take a look at it,' Karen said, her voice cool.

'So what's this fresh information? Has he persuaded

someone that I was there that night and not tucked up in bed after an infernally long shift?'

'No, not at all, Mr Shaw. There's no suggestion that you had anything to do with your partner's death.'

Something shifted in his face. 'He was my fiancé,' he said softly. 'We were planning our wedding. And he goes and slips on the stairs because he's hurrying home to me.' He studied his hands, fingers interlocked between his knees.

'Is that what you think happened?' Daisy asked gently.

'What else? There was no evidence of anything else. And who would want to kill my lovely man? I know people say things like, "he didn't have an enemy in the world" when people die. But genuinely, my Tommo – even the eejits he had to fire, they didn't go out the door hating him.'

Karen reached into her satchel and took out the pictures. 'Drew Jamieson persuaded my colleagues to hand over CCTV images from the hotel and the Scotsman Steps.' She handed him the first one, from the hotel. 'This was taken as Tom was leaving – it's hard to tell it's him, you can only see his shoulder, but we know from the previous shots—'

'Of course it's him, I'd know the cut of him anywhere. So who's this behind him? What's to say he's not just any old punter?'

Karen explained about the reverse image search and showed him the shot of Marcus Nicol. 'This is who the search engine identifies as the man in the CCTV. Do you recognise him?'

Shaw frowned, studying the image carefully. He covered the eyes then the mouth separately and shook his head. 'Never clapped eyes on him in my life. Who is he?'

'His name is Marcus Nicol and he runs a company called Surinco. They're in the medical instrument business.'

Shaw shook his head again. 'Means nothing to me. Tommo never mentioned him, or his company. Why does Sherlock Drew think he's anything to do with Tommo's death?'

Karen handed over the final shot. 'We think that's the same man, but we can't be sure because the hoodie slightly obscures his face. There's no reason to think he had anything to do with Tom's death, but because his brother has raised it with us, we have to pursue it.'

'I get that. It hurts, though, dragging it all up again.' He turned his head to take in the view, his jaw clenched.

'One of his colleagues suggested he'd had a falling out at work,' Daisy said. They'd agreed on this approach as they'd walked over from their convenient office on Gayfield Square. 'Something about Tom quitting the five-a-side football team?'

Shaw sighed. 'Honest to God, you'd think they were in the finals of the European Championship, the way Bob Watson was carrying on. He called it a betrayal of Tommo's colleagues. He came out with a load of nonsense about my lad getting ideas above his station and all that class warrior shit. This from a man who looks down on anyone who can't tell the Margaux 2020 from the 2013. Look, Tommo had been trying to get a foot in the door with this book club for ages. He loved reading, he always had a book on the go on his phone as well as a book by the bed. Me, I read nothing more serious than the sports pages. So he wanted to hang out with some proper readers and he heard about this club. It's a very select little band, no more than a dozen at a time. He heard about it from one of his regulars, and he was desperate to get invited. So when they asked him, he wasn't going to say, "No, I'd rather play footie with the same guys I see every day at work." Now, was he?'

'I can see how that would be a no-brainer,' Daisy said. 'And did it live up to his expectations?'

Shaw ran his hands through his hair. 'He only got to three meetings before . . . But he loved it. He came home the first time saying it was the best night out he'd had since the night we met. "These guys really know what they're talking about," he said. Who knew a bunch of middle-aged men talking about your woman King-something-or-other could be such a big deal?' He gave a grim little chuckle. 'But you're barking up the wrong tree if you think Tommo deserting the footie was reason to push him down the steps.'

'Can you think of any other reason why someone might have meant your fiancé harm?' Karen came back with the pointed question.

'Officer, it's been hard enough to recover from Tommo's death knowing it was an accident. I can't stand that Drew has shown up and tried to turn it into a drama. Does he not see how insulting that is to the memory of a good man? To presume that Tommo could have provoked someone to murder.' Shaw's lip curled in disgust. 'I loved Tommo. I've not looked at another man since the night I lost him. He was a good man, a kind man. He was as honest as anybody in the hospitality business is, which is to say he'd sometimes sneak a drink from the bar or bring home some leftover pastries.' Another deep sigh. 'He just slipped on the steps. Yes, he might have had a wee drink. Yes, he might have been running, because he liked to shake the hotel from his heels and get back to his own life. But was he murdered? You'd have to say there are far more likely candidates for homicide in the hotel trade than my Tommo. You're wasting your time.'

It was hard to disagree, Karen thought, getting to her feet.

'And we won't waste any more of yours, Mr Shaw. I'm sorry for what you've been through. And sorry we've brought it all back.'

He walked them to the door. 'It never goes away, Detective. You're only doing your job. Imagine if Tommo had been murdered and nobody was paying attention? How much worse would that be?'

12

They were walking through Waverley Station en route to the office when Karen's phone rang. Seeing it was Jason, she stepped to one side allowing the stream of passengers on the walkway to pass. 'We've got an ID on the motorway skeleton, boss,' he said, diving straight in. 'I was just on my way out the door to go and talk to Bob Watson when River rang.'

'That was quick. How come?'

'River says they did the DNA extraction as a priority soon as they got the remains back, so they were able to run it against the database first thing. And it turns out we have the victim's DNA on record. And here's the thing, boss. It's because he's the number one suspect in a murder case.' He sounded like a small child at a birthday party.

It wasn't what Karen had expected, but given they'd thought it might be a gangland killing, it wasn't exactly shocking. Punishments weren't always advertised to the wider community. 'That's wild. I can't really talk right now. Daisy and I are in the middle of Waverley, but we're on our way back. You can tell me all about it then.'

She shared Jason's news with Daisy, who was even more excited than Jason had sounded. 'That would explain why nobody reported him missing, no?'

'Possibly. Let's not leap to conclusions, though.' But they picked up their pace and made it back to Gayfield Square in record time, narrowly escaping being mown down by the Newhaven tram.

Jason hadn't wasted any time. He'd already put together the beginnings of a dossier on the skeleton from assorted online sources. 'Wait'll you see this, guys,' he greeted them. 'It'll blow your socks off. I've sent you links to the basics but there's a lot out there.'

'Give me the ten-second version,' Karen demanded, hanging her coat up.

'It's definitely a cold case. The victim is Sam Nimmo. Mean anything to you?'

'I'm coming up blank,' Daisy said.

'Before your time,' Karen said. 'You were still living off Pot Noodles and Jägerbombs in Aberdeen.'

Daisy scoffed. 'Hardly! I was still at school, doing my Highers. I know you think my parents are ridiculously liberal, but even they drew the line at Pot Noodles. So who's this Sam Nimmo?'

'Sam Nimmo was a freelance investigative journalist. A pretty good one too. The minute the Queen gave the referendum Royal Assent back in June 2013, it was the only thing Scottish journos were interested in. Sam Nimmo was one of the pack and I remember he broke some big stories at the start of the campaign. And then his pregnant girlfriend was beaten to death in their flat. He had no alibi and what forensics there were pointed to Sam. The murder team were about to lift him when he went AWOL.' Karen shook her head, incredulous. 'Everybody thought he'd done one. He sent a bunch of texts – to his parents, his closest pals, the news editors he mostly worked for.'

'Even the publisher he'd just signed a book deal with, it says here,' Jason chipped in. 'He said he was devastated by what he'd done but he couldn't face a life behind bars so he was leaving.' He pointed at his screen. 'That's the text of one of them.'

Daisy and Karen leaned over his shoulder and read:

Dear mum,

You'll know by now I've done a terrible thing. I've got no excuses. I just lost control and I'm devastated. You know I couldn't do a life sentence. So I'm leaving. As of today, Sam Nimmo no longer exists. I have contacts who can help me disappear with a new identity. I'm so sorry for all the grief I have caused you. Please try to forgive me. Or forget you ever had a son called Sam. I love you both.

'I seem to remember nobody came up with a reason why he'd murdered his girlfriend. Rebecca, was it?' Karen said.

'Rachel,' Jason corrected her. 'She was five months pregnant and they were planning to get married after the bairn was born. Everybody said Sam was thrilled about the baby, that he adored Rachel.'

'Did they do a DNA test on the foetus?'

Jason flushed. 'I've not got that deep into the investigation notes yet.'

'Make a note to follow it up, please.' Karen frowned as she dredged her memory for details. It hadn't been her case so she didn't know more than any random member of the public with an eye for headline murder cases. And this had made the headlines because the people who wrote the news knew who Sam Nimmo was. 'Were there not alleged sightings of him until the Ref itself knocked everything else out of the headlines?'

Jason nodded. 'Mostly in Spain. Which would have been a pretty stupid place for him to try to hide out, with his face being all over the papers, given how many Scottish folk go there on their holidays.'

'Where would you have gone?' Daisy asked.

'America,' Jason said. 'It's a big country with big cities you could easy get lost in. How about you?'

'I'd go to New Zealand,' Daisy said. 'You'd stand out a lot less there than in America. And so many of the population have Scottish roots, they'd welcome you without thinking about it. Plus, you being a ginger, you'd stand out less.'

'But it turns out, he didn't go any further than the substrate of the M73. Who knew the Gartcosh Triangle could give Bermuda a run for its money?' Karen's smile was wry. 'Does this change our view about Rachel's murder? Everybody was so sure it was Nimmo, but it doesn't look quite so open-and-shut now.'

'From what I've seen so far, they jumped on Sam as the obvious suspect because everybody loved Rachel,' Jason said. 'She was a lawyer, but one of the ones that doesn't make enemies. Conveyancing, apparently.'

'Aye, but nobody likes to speak ill of the dead, especially the pregnant dead. Let's see how it plays out now. In other business – Jason, you didn't get the chance to talk to Bob Watson, did you?'

He looked guilty, 'No, I didn't get out the door because River—'

'Chill, I'm not having a go. Daisy, you should go and talk to Bob Watson now we know a bit more about the row between him and Tom Jamieson. Before you do that, can you organise a Family Liaison Officer to track down Rachel Morrison's parents and inform them, out of courtesy? Jason, with me. We need to go and do a very overdue death knock. Can you rustle up an address for his parents from the original files?'

She settled in front of her own computer and skimmed the file Jason had already started. Sam Nimmo, thirty-three. An older sister. Parents Janet (primary school teacher) and Dermot (dentist). Born and raised in Knockentiber, a dot on the map near Kilmarnock. Left school at sixteen to start work on the local paper. A couple of years later, he stumbled over a story of corruption on the local council that involved blackmail and the sexual abuse of children in care. Instead of saving it for his own paper, he'd walked into the newsroom of the *Scottish Daily Clarion* in Glasgow and sold them the story. It had grown wings and legs and made Sam a big enough wedge to take a chance on going freelance. He'd pulled together a collective with three other journalists – two reporters and a photographer – specialising in investigative journalism. They'd stuck their fingers into all sorts of pies. They'd exposed corruption in government, in the arts establishment, in banking. They'd caught all sorts of public figures with their trousers down in the wrong bedrooms. They'd turned over scammers and idiots, bent bobbies and arrogant athletes who thought they were above the law. Stings were their speciality. Whistleblowers turned to Sam with confidence because they could see his only loyalty was to the truth. Not to media moguls or political parties. Not to business bosses or bankers.

It was a reputation for integrity that died the night Rachel Morrison was found in a pool of blood in the living room of their penthouse flat by the Clyde. Nimmo himself had raised the alarm. He'd been out to dinner with a Scottish

Government minister and a couple of party officials who wanted to brief him about the dirty tricks campaign being waged by their opponents in the forthcoming Independence Referendum. According to Nimmo, he'd come home to find his fiancée lying on the floor with catastrophic head injuries. There was no sign of a break-in. Rachel Morrison had died from a compound skull fracture, seemingly from a collision with the corner of a marble fire surround. The pathologist had been sceptical about the possibility of an accident. 'In my opinion, her head was forcibly smashed against the stone,' his post-mortem report read. The only fingermarks on the mantel were two partial prints that matched Nimmo himself.

Officers who'd attended the scene reported he seemed shocked and distraught. He appeared catatonic with grief and could not respond to initial interrogation. But there was no forensic evidence to contradict the theory that Nimmo had killed his partner. The couple's cleaner had been in that day; apart from her prints, the only fingermarks in the living room were from Nimmo and Rachel. There was a single print on the underside of the rim of the bathroom sink, but it didn't match Nimmo or the cleaner and there was no way of knowing how long it had been there. There was no bloodstained clothing in the flat. The forensics team examined the bathroom plumbing; they found traces of Rachel's blood, but no signs of anyone else's presence.

Time of death, that measure notoriously inaccurate outwith the pages of detective fiction, gave a big enough window for Nimmo to have killed her and still made it to dinner on time. Or near enough. Nobody would have gone into the witness box to argue otherwise.

None of their friends wanted to believe it was possible

for Nimmo to be guilty of so brutal a crime. But there were still serving police officers whose careers had felt the sting of his investigations. Karen could imagine only too well the conflict between the ones who wanted to see him serving life in Barlinnie and the others whose careers had benefited from putting some of the criminals he'd exposed behind bars. But the bottom line was that there was nobody else in the picture for the murder of Rachel Morrison. And nobody with any motive other than to devastate Sam Nimmo.

A week after Rachel's death, the Procurator Fiscal caved in to pressure. A warrant was issued for Sam Nimmo's arrest. But Nimmo had friends in the Crown Office and one of them had warned him. When the officers rocked up to the service apartment Nimmo had rented after the murder, the bird had flown. Once they'd tracked down the building management employee with the master key, they'd found Nimmo's apartment keys in a glass bowl on the table with a battered second-hand copy of Frank Abagnale's supposed autobiography, *Catch Me If You Can*. Jason had found a quote from Nimmo's colleague, photographer Linda Lawrence, who said, 'He always had a tendency towards bad taste. Most journalists do.'

That was as far as Jason's researches had taken him. Karen stared out of the window at the blank wall of the building across the vennel. All the background they had was meaningless, she thought. All the assumptions that underpinned it were mistaken. Sam Nimmo hadn't smashed his own skull in and placed himself at the bottom of a motorway. But the person who had done it had been very clever.

Clever, or panicked and lucky? For Karen couldn't help wondering whether Rachel Morrison's death had happened purely because the intended victim was out for the evening.

13

Knockentiber stood a couple of miles to the west of Kilmarnock, a village that seemed to consist almost entirely of housing estates that had been built in the previous twenty years. It looked smart and bright, the harling showing little sign of the attrition of weather. Jason drove slowly down the main road, allowing Karen to check out the house numbers as they passed.

'Pull over,' she instructed him as they passed a detached sandstone villa with a sharply peaked single gable. 'That's it.' The house stood incongruous among its modern neighbours with its red sandstone and black slates.

'I suppose if you're the local dentist, you'd want to live a wee bit out of the town,' Jason said. 'You don't want people huckling you in the street or the Tesco Express going, "my gums are nipping".'

'Right enough,' Karen said absently, noting that the Vauxhall Corsa in the drive had a seven-year-old registration. Either the Nimmos were too thrifty to change up their cars regularly or they were too skint, which seemed unlikely. They walked up an asphalt drive pocked with weeds and potholes, and Jason rang the bell by the front door. The black paint was starting to chip and fade. Karen thought the place felt unloved, uncared for.

The woman who answered the door was definitely not Sam Nimmo's mother. She was at least twenty-five years too young. Karen tried not to show she was wrong-footed. 'Hi,' she said. 'I'm looking for Mr and Mrs Nimmo. I'm not sure I've got the right house?'

'You're half-right,' came the curt reply. 'Who's asking? Are you journalists?'

'No.' Karen produced her ID. 'I'm DCI Karen Pirie from Police Scotland. Historic Cases Unit. And this is DC Jason Murray.'

Her eyes widened. 'Has Sam turned up? Has he been spotted?'

'We need to talk to Mr or Mrs Nimmo,' Karen said, firm but friendly. 'Are they at home?'

The woman's mouth tightened. 'Your information's out of date. My dad doesn't live here any more. But my mum's in. I'll go and get her—'

'It might be better if we came in?'

The woman paused, her face crumpling. 'This isn't good news, is it? I'm a doctor, I know all about delivering the hammer blow.' Her voice was bitter, a prophylactic against tears. She pulled the door wide open. 'Come on in, then, do your worst.'

They dutifully followed her down the hall. It was spotlessly clean but leaning towards shabbiness round the edges of the carpet and the wallpaper. There were no pictures on the wall, just a mirror with a heavily gilded frame and a barometer that looked old-fashioned rather than antique. The woman showed them into a living room that faced on to the main road. 'Take a seat, I'll get my mum.' Halfway to the door, she turned back. 'I'm Jess, by the way. Dr Nimmo. Sam's sister.' And she was gone.

'Probably should have checked the electoral roll,' Jason muttered sheepishly.

'Might have helped.' Karen looked around, taking in a room where comfort clearly ran ahead of style. A large black-and-white cat was curled in an armchair under the window. It had raised its head when they entered, then stood up, stretched and returned to its original position, clearly uninterested in the new arrivals. Karen had once mistakenly picked up a novel where the detective had been a cat; she was reminded once again of how preposterous a premise it had been. But she also remembered how the position of a cat was an indicator of the ambient temperature. She decided to follow the cat's tip and keep her coat on in this chilly room.

The door opened to admit Jess Nimmo, followed by a woman who looked like a shrunken monochrome version of her. Where Jess was tall and straight, her mother was narrow and slightly stooped. Instead of a thick dark head of hair held back loosely in a clasp, Janet Nimmo had iron grey hair cropped in a ragged bob. Her face was lined and weary; Karen thought she looked as if she lived with chronic pain.

Jess stepped aside as her mother made her way to an armchair next to the elaborate wooden fire surround.

Karen went through the introductions again. Janet Nimmo nodded and sighed. 'You'll have worked out that I'm Janet Nimmo, Sam's mother. And we've worked out that your arrival on our doorstep is not good news.'

'I'm afraid not. I'm sorry to have to tell you that human remains found earlier this week have been identified by DNA analysis as being your son, Sam.'

Janet bowed her head and squeezed her eyes tight shut. Then she looked up, her eyes bright with unshed tears. 'I've had eleven years of living with the knowledge that my son was either a murderer or dead. I could never decide which was worse. Now at least I know.'

Karen didn't want to point out that the two were not mutually exclusive. Not yet, anyway. It was still remotely possible that Sam Nimmo had killed Rachel Morrison then almost immediately killed himself in remorse. 'I'm sorry,' she said.

'Where was he found?' Jess demanded.

'The recent heavy rains caused a landslip on the M73, and his remains were uncovered. They were carefully removed. Subsequent tests revealed that it was your son.'

'Under the motorway?' Janet sounded bemused. 'How can that be?'

'Somebody must have put him there, Mum. Do you have a cause of death?' Jess again.

'There is evidence of a blow to the head which broke his skull. It's impossible to say how it was caused but we are treating it as a suspicious death.' Karen hated these encounters; it felt as if every sentence she uttered was a devastating blow of its own.

'Of course it's suspicious.' Janet Nimmo's voice was strengthened by grievous anger. 'He didn't hit himself on the head and bury his body under a motorway, did he? And he obviously didn't send all those messages saying he'd killed Rachel and run away because he couldn't face the consequences. I knew that text didn't sound like Sam. It wasn't his style. We said at the time that he could never have behaved like that. He adored Rachel. He was thrilled that he was going to be a dad. But you lot? You wouldn't listen. You didn't look beyond the obvious. It was easier to write my son off as a violent heartless killer.' She turned away and covered her face with her hands.

'I wasn't part of that investigation. I'm not making excuses but sometimes it's hard to escape the obvious narrative that the evidence indicates. I'm sorry it has turned out to be the wrong narrative.'

Janet struggled to her feet and stumbled out of the room. Jess looked after her, fists clenched. 'It's a "narrative" that destroyed this family. My father doesn't live here now because he believed it and he couldn't cope with the shame. You know what he is now, my handsome father who ran the busiest dental practice in East Ayrshire? He's an alcoholic who lives in a hostel in Glasgow and has a part-time job as a cleaner in a shopping centre. That's what your "wrong narrative" did to him. I had a brilliant job in a New York hospital when the wheels came off our family. I had a fiancé of my own over there. But I had to give it all up because my family needed me.' Her face softened. 'Don't get me wrong. I love my mum. But we've all lost so much because of your "wrong narrative".'

Karen reached for a response that didn't feel dishonest. 'This is my case now, Dr Nimmo. I can't bring your brother back but what I can promise is that I will do everything in my power to uncover the truth of what happened eleven years ago. I'm not going to talk about "closure" or "healing" but I will do all I can to help you understand what happened and how it happened.'

Jess raked her from head to foot with a scornful look. 'Oh well, that's all right, then. Next you'll be telling me that whoever did this will pay the price. Let me tell you, Chief Inspector, whatever price they pay, it won't come near to covering the cost of losing a brother, a future sister-in-law and nephew. Not to mention a father who might as well be dead for all the use he is to my mother and me.'

'I do understand that. I know it's not relevant to you, but I lost my man to an act of senseless violence. I appreciate that nothing feels like justice after that.' Karen surprised herself by her response. Normally, she barely shared her feelings about what had happened to Phil Parhatka with her friends, never mind complete strangers. But something about Jess Nimmo had penetrated her armour. 'All I can say is that there is something to be said for silencing the questions.'

'And you think you can find some answers after eleven years? You think you can find credible witnesses?'

Karen shrugged. 'I've gone further back in time than that. Can I ask you some questions about Sam?'

Jess lowered herself into the armchair her mother had vacated. 'I probably don't know the answers,' she said wearily. 'I'd been in New York for three years before ... before Rachel was murdered.'

'Do you know why anyone might want to kill Sam?'

She shook her head. 'People liked Sam. I'm not going to be stupid enough to say he didn't have an enemy in the world. Of course he'd pissed people off over the years – he was an investigative journalist and his work had consequences. Politicians had lost office. Businessmen had been exposed as frauds. Cops had been driven out of the force for corruption.'

'But the damage had already been done,' Karen countered. 'People talk about revenge being a dish best eaten cold, but in my experience, for most people, once the immediate sting is past, common sense kicks in and they settle for nothing more violent than hatred. They wouldn't turn the hose on you if you were on fire, but equally, they wouldn't start the fire either. They've learned enough about consequences.'

There was a pause while Jess considered Karen's words. 'I guess that makes a kind of sense,' she said, grudging.

'So, do you know what he was working on when he died? Who he might have offered a threat to?'

Another shake of the head. 'When we talked on the phone, we talked personal stuff. He didn't talk about his work, I didn't talk about life on the wards. You'd have to speak to the other people in his team. Well, I say team. It was more of a loose affiliation. They all worked their own stories, but they'd chip in if one of the others needed a hand. The only person who covered all the bases was Linda Lawrence, the photographer. Photojournalist, I suppose would be more accurate. But I've no idea where she is these days.'

'Who else was in the collective with Sam and Linda?'

Jess didn't have to think twice. 'Keir Stevens and Alan McParland. But you'll not find Alan. He was killed in a Russian mortar attack in the Donbas in 2022. I don't know anything about where Keir is or what he's doing. I don't even know whether he's still a journalist. He wasn't at Alan's memorial service.'

'Was Linda at the memorial?'

Jess nodded. 'We said hello, but that was about it. To tell you the truth, I was only there out of a sense of duty, I didn't want to have to deal with people asking if I'd heard from Sam. The innuendo lurking underneath the surface, that we knew where he was hiding, after what people believed he'd done to Rachel.' Her lip curled. 'That's journalists for you, the story trumps every human emotion.'

90

Karen let that hang in the air for a moment. Of course even people who had known Sam believed her brother had done a runner to escape the consequences of what he appeared to have done. She also understood Jess's need to believe that Sam wasn't a man who would have murdered his pregnant girlfriend. Whenever there was a domestic murder, there was always a mother or a sister or an auntie adamant that their lovely boy couldn't have done it. Time to move on. 'What about friends? Who did Sam hang about with when he wasn't working? Other couples he and Rachel mixed with socially?'

Again, Jess seemed to have nothing. Then she sat up abruptly. 'He used to go to the football when he could. He had a couple of pals from schooldays he'd hook up with and go to the match with. Eamonn Sharkey and John Baxter. The three of them had season tickets, even though Sam only got to about one game in three.'

Jason was industriously making a note of the names. 'Do you know where we'd find them, doc?'

'John's still in Kilmarnock, he's got an electrical supplies business. Eamonn's up in Glasgow. He used to work for a venture capital outfit, I don't know the name.'

He shouldn't be too hard to find, Karen thought. 'And there's nobody else you can think of who was close to your brother?'

'He was careful with his confidences. He protected his stories and his sources. The one person he confided in was Rachel.'

Jess's face told the whole story. Karen understood she'd hit a literal dead end.

14

Daisy found Bob Watson in a brick-lined room deep below the public areas of the Scott Monument Hotel. Racks of bottles stretched the length of the cellar; the opposite wall held a series of fridges containing the golden crowns of champagne and the plain foils of white wine. Daisy couldn't help imagining the parties it could fuel. She'd be set for life.

The sommelier was filling a column of pigeonholes from a stack of wine boxes three deep, ignoring her arrival as he worked. He wore a brown apron over his white shirt, sleeves rolled up and top button undone. His movements were effortless, his arms and legs powerful. Daisy couldn't escape the fleeting thought that he'd have had no difficulty in kicking the feet from Tom Jamieson and pitching him down the Scotsman Steps if he'd been so inclined. She cleared her throat and he paused mid-action, turning to face her. 'Mr Watson? I'm DS Daisy Mortimer from the Historic Cases Unit of Police Scotland.' Her smile matched the warmth in her voice.

He raised well-groomed eyebrows and scoffed. 'Historic Cases? The only historic cases I know anything about are the 1992 Screaming Eagle California Cabernet. If you could lay your hands on one of them, I'd be your pal for life.' He grinned, pleased with himself. He was, Daisy thought, a man whose regular features, gleaming white teeth and neatly barbered hair gave him plenty of opportunities to be pleased with himself in the bathroom mirror.

'I'm guessing I wouldn't be able to afford one of those on a police officer's wages.'

'I doubt it. Not unless Elon Musk needed a speeding ticket cleared. What can I do for you, Sergeant?'

'I'd like to talk to you about Tom Jamieson.'

The smile vanished as he drew his eyebrows down in a frown. 'Tommo? Was that not all done and dusted ages ago? He slipped on the Scotsman Steps, broke his ankle, took a header down the stairs, end of. I've nearly done it myself before now on a wet night.' He pointed at his shoes, turning one foot up to show the thin leather soles. 'No grip on dress shoes, Sergeant. We don't get to wear Docs to work here. That's why it was ruled an accident.'

'We have some new evidence that may suggest otherwise,' Daisy said mildly.

'What kind of evidence?'

'The kind we're duty-bound to follow up.' A rueful wince. 'It's routine, and I'm sorry to bother you. I assume you worked closely with Mr Jamieson?'

'Of course. He knew every aspect of his business, did Tommo. We keep an excellent cellar here, we've got a great range and a good balance of prices. That was partly down to Tommo. He went to bat for me with the board a few times.' He gave a wry smile. 'Sometimes they're more interested in boosting the profit margins than keeping the customers on side.' He paused, waiting for her to agree.

Daisy shrugged. 'I suppose they're looking to protect their investment.'

'Sure, but the kind of customers we get here, they've got a lot of decent wine at home. They notice when you're offering a wine at sixty quid a bottle when they paid twenty for it at their online wine merchant. And they don't like being gouged. So they stick at one bottle instead of making a night of it.' He pulled a wry smile.

'Were you close socially, you and Mr Jamieson?'

He drew in a breath. 'Ah, Sergeant. You've been listening to gossip. Look, Tommo and I were pals, not best buddies. And yes, we had a falling out, like.' His accent slipped down the social scale a fraction. He spread his hands and smiled again. 'And that's all it was. A falling out.'

Daisy gave him a level stare, letting him know she wasn't going to be palmed off by his charm. 'Take me through it.'

He rolled his eyes and folded his arms across his chest, the muscles tensing. 'Here's how it went. We've got a five-a-side football team. We play in a Thursday night league against other hotel and pub teams. Tommo joined when he started here and he was a bit of a star. Best keeper in the league, like. We were in line to win the league for the third time in a row when he announced he was quitting.' He looked down, shaking his head. 'It was a blow.'

'I imagine so.' Daisy tried to sound sympathetic.

He flashed a quick glance up at her. 'Look, I'd have understood if he was carrying an injury, like. You're on your feet a lot in this trade. But it wasn't that. He was leaving to join some bloody book club. A book club?' His expression revealed disgust. 'They only met once a month but he was adamant that he didn't want some other poor sod feeling like they were second fiddle, standing in for him every fourth week. A flaming book club. He was letting his mates down to sit around in some poncey New Town private library to blether about books. Talk about social climbing. It's like we weren't good enough for him any more.' It spilled out in a rush, then stopped abruptly.

'Sounds like you were pretty angry with him.'

'You could say that. We had a bit of a bust-up about it in the staffroom.' He shook his head. 'No shortage of witnesses, if that's what you're after. It got bitter. But it never came to blows or anything like. I won't lie to you, I was pissed off. Especially after we lost the first game after he jumped ship to go and hang out with his fancy new pals.' He sighed. 'You might think it's a stupid thing to get so heated about, I know it sounds that way. But the five-a-side, it's a real bonding thing. It makes us a team at our work as well as on the pitch. We've got the sous chef, the deputy chief concierge, the head waiter in charge of the lunch service and me, plus the replacement goalie – the head of maintenance. So between us, we know what's what around the place. I'm telling you, it felt like a betrayal when Tommo walked away.'

It sounded like a bunch of wee boys complaining that the big guy had found a new pal, Daisy thought. 'Did he fall out with anybody else over this? Or anything else?'

One corner of his mouth rose in a sneer. 'Nobody else wanted to go head to head with the boss. And to be fair, people liked Tommo. He was a decent boss. He was always open to ideas about how we could do things better. But I thought this nonsense was going to make that harder down the line because he wouldn't discuss it. It wasn't like him to be so set in stone, like. His mind was made up and the matter was closed.'

'So you stopped communicating with Mr Jamieson off the pitch?'

'I couldn't *not* speak to him, obviously. But I kept it

95

formal, did a lot more WhatsApp-ing and texting. And it's not like he came crawling to me, asking to be pals again. I'm sorry we didn't make it up before he died, like. I mean that, honest. But it's something I can live with.' His jaw jutted, making a defiant point she didn't entirely buy into.

Daisy waited; she knew the value of silence. 'I went to his funeral, like,' Watson blurted out. 'We all did. And I miss him, you know? Till we fell out, we had a good relationship. Banter, and that. Look, I'm sorry Tommo's dead. I get that he was trying to better himself, I just thought he was going about it all the wrong way.'

'What was so special about this book club that he was willing to risk his friendships and his working relationships for it?'

He turned his head, staring at the massed ranks of the red wine. 'He said it was a once-in-a-lifetime opportunity to make important connections.' He looked back at her. 'He was ambitious. He wanted to break into the front rank. The kind of place where people know the name all over the world. The Ritz, Raffles in Singapore, the Plaza in New York, the Georges Cinq in Paris, Atlantis the Royal in Dubai. We were just a stepping stone for Tommo. Well, he thought so anyway. I don't know who these guys were that he was hanging with, but he was convinced they'd give him a boost up the ladder.' For a moment, genuine sorrow seemed to cross his face. 'Instead, the poor bastard only got to three meetings before he ended up taking a tumble down the stairs.'

15

Karen told Jason to pull over before they rejoined the main road. 'We need to find out what Sam Nimmo was working on before he died.'

'Or who had it in for him, boss. Sounds like he stood on a lot of people's toes.'

She nodded. 'True. Jason, can you hold your own on the subject of Kilmarnock FC?'

Jason looked affronted. 'Course I can. You don't just follow your own team if you're into fitba. You have to keep your finger on the pulse across the divisions.'

'That's good. All I know about Killie is they're supposed to have the best pies. I want you to track down his football mates. They're more likely to talk to you than to me or Daisy. Get alongside them, see what they remember about the period before Sam disappeared. Double-check how he talked about Rachel and the baby. Do your best to find out what he was working on, who he'd pissed off in the recent past.'

He nodded vigorously. 'I can get with that, boss. It sounds like they'll not be too hard to find.'

'I can't help thinking that for the likes of Sam Nimmo who liked a bit of stirring, there was a lot going on at the time, with the build-up to the Indy Referendum. Arguments about the currency, the economy. Winners and losers. Who would get what if the Indy movement won.' She paused for a moment. 'And big picture stuff. What would happen to the Trident nuclear submarine base at Faslane? Or the Yanks at Holy Loch?'

'Not to mention all the controversy about the Edinburgh trams,' Jason said. 'If we're talking corruption. The tram cost more than a billion quid. Remember the joke? They nearly bankrupted the city for a line that only ran from the airport to the comedy clubs on York Place. Built by comedians for comedians.'

Karen managed a wry smile. 'Right enough. It's got a bit better since then, for folk like you living down the bottom of Leith Walk at least. So you've got plenty to get your teeth into. Drop me off at the station in Kilmarnock and I'll head back on the train. See if you can get hold of Baxter for a chat and then move on to Sharkey up in Glasgow. Try to find out whether Sam Nimmo gossiped or boasted about the stories he was interested in. Meanwhile I'll try and track down Linda Lawrence and Keir Stevens.' Karen knew a couple of journalists who weren't exactly hostile; perhaps one of them would be able to help her out. In the meantime, she could use the train journey for a bit of blunt googling.

To her satisfaction the search engine gave her a few threads to tug on. She hit pay dirt early on with Keir Stevens. He'd given up on the hard graft of investigative journalism and moved into PR, working as a comms officer for a digital accounts software company based in Livingston. She found a recent photo of him showing the local MP round their new production line, which would make it easier to recognise him and approach him after work. If he still had the journalists' habit of going for a pint after a hard day at the office. She could check whether he was in work and, if her luck held, get off the train at Livi and Uber it round to his office.

Linda Lawrence was harder to nail down. Her most recent photo credits were from Gaza, but she'd also been in Ukraine. Her pics from the devastated buildings and their inhabitants had stopped abruptly after Alan McParland's death in the Donbas, and shortly after that, she'd moved on to the destruction of Gaza and the dire straits of its population. Her most recent photo essay had appeared in a Sunday supplement; a series of heart-rending images of refugees, their lives stripped back to what most people would not regard as even the bare necessities.

Karen knew from Rafiq's reluctantly shared stories of his own life in Syria and beyond that those lives could never be the same again. He had been forced to flee Syria after the security forces discovered his part in the revelation of appalling torture inside President Assad's jails. A refugee charity had supported his whistle-blowing and had helped him escape. She read the short text that accompanied Linda Lawrence's self-explanatory photographs, and noted the name of the charity working with the Gazan refugees that she had spotlit. Perhaps they might have pursued the same route with her? It wouldn't hurt to ask.

Karen found the charity online and explored their website. She took advantage of an email link to their press contact. 'Hi,' her message began. 'I'm a detective with Police Scotland's Historic Cases Unit and I need to get in touch with Linda Lawrence. I have some information to pass on to her and I'd welcome the chance to discuss it with her.' She read it back, hoping she'd hit the right note. She sighed then listed the various ways to contact her and pressed *send*. If that didn't work, she'd figure something else out.

By the time she'd put a call in to DigiLivi and confirmed Keir Stevens was in the office, the train was pulling into Livingston North, so Karen hastily closed her laptop and shoved it in her backpack. She checked her phone and worked out the quickest way to DigiLivi. It was a fifteen-minute walk, but she reckoned there was still time to make it before the end of the business day.

The software company occupied a squat red-brick building surrounded by car parking areas on all four sides. It looked prosperous; no weeds sprouted in tarmac cracks, the window frames were in good order and the foyer was brightly lit, the walls decorated with photographs of motherboards, their colours enhanced to eye-popping levels. Karen pressed a buzzer to alert the receptionist. What was it with companies these days? They all seemed to have more ID-based security than the average police station. As if they were expecting Jason Statham to launch an attack at any moment.

But once she identified herself and made it inside, the reception was warm enough to satisfy Karen. She was shown into a side room and supplied with iced coffee and a plate of biscuits while she waited for Keir Stevens to arrive from his domain.

She barely had time for a single Biscoff before her target arrived. He was dressed in a pair of skinny jeans and a sweatshirt with the company logo across the chest, an outfit that would have looked more suitable on a man fifteen years younger and without a beer gut. If Karen had been an accounts manager looking for software, she wouldn't have been impressed. When she introduced herself, he seemed bemused. 'The front counter said you were Police Scotland,

I assumed it was something to do with the outfit that tried to scam our customers out of their personal data last month. Surely that's not a historic case already?'

'Nothing to do with us, I'm afraid. I'm here to tell you we've reopened the investigation into Rachel Morrison's death in the light of new information.'

He sat down heavily in a chair across the table from Karen. 'But that was eleven years ago. And it was an open-and-shut case.'

'That's what it appeared to be, yes. I don't know whether you saw the reports yesterday about the recent torrential rain leading to a landslip on the M73?'

He frowned. 'Vaguely. Wasn't there something about a skeleton? What's that got to do ... Oh my God, you're not telling me you've found Sam?'

It was a surprising conclusion to leap to, Karen thought. 'What makes you say that?'

He clenched his fists. 'Why else would you have started this conversation by referencing Rachel? Is it Sam? Tell me, is it?'

Karen nodded. 'I'm sorry to have to tell you, the skeletal remains have been positively identified as those of your former colleague Sam Nimmo.'

Stevens flushed dark red and drove one fist into the palm of his other hand. 'Fuck. I knew he hadn't done it. I knew it.' His mild expression had transformed into a fierce glare. 'So all this time, you've been calling him a killer on the run, he's been lying dead, what ...? A stone's throw from the bloody Police Scotland Crime Campus?'

'The place wasn't actually officially opened till a few months after Rachel was murdered and Sam disappeared. There wouldn't have been many polis working there then.'

'All the same, he was right under your noses. You really are a bunch of incompetent cunts, aren't you?'

'You need to calm down, Mr Stevens.' A pointless line, she knew, but necessary none the less.

'Calm down? Calm the fuck down? Eleven years ago, you labelled my best pal a murderer and you tell me to calm down?'

Karen returned his rage with a measured stare. He slammed the flat of his hand on the table that separated them. Then the air seemed to leave him like a burst balloon. His eyes brimmed with tears and he wiped them away angrily.

'I'm sorry you had to learn about your friend's death like this,' she said gently. 'Some news, you can't sugar-coat it. Sam was murdered, just as Rachel was murdered. Right now, we don't know the whole story and we certainly don't know who committed these crimes. And that's why I'm here. Because you were Sam Nimmo's friend and colleague, and if anyone can point us in the right direction, it's probably you.'

His shoulders slumped and he clasped his hands between his knees. 'Poor Sam. All this time, everybody blackening his name, and he's lying dead under the fucking M73. It doesn't get much more ignominious than that. Fuck's sake.'

'I can only imagine how upset you are.'

His head jerked up. 'Can you, though? Can you? I doubt it.'

'There's nothing I can do to bring your friend back, but my team can change what the world thinks about Sam. We can investigate this with a scope that wasn't available to the original investigation. Rachel's death was set up to make it look as if Sam was the only possible suspect and that he'd fled to avoid prosecution.' *And maybe that's because he actually did kill her.* Karen didn't want to lose sight of that possibility. Nevertheless, she spoke with full-on sincerity. 'We need to find who was really behind those murders.'

'After all this time? You think you can manage what your useless colleagues couldn't achieve eleven years ago?'

'We've resolved cases going a lot further back than that. And I'm not afraid of nailing past failures. I am the woman who put an assistant chief constable behind bars.' She turned down the stern a notch or two. 'Look, you must be about finished for the day. Why don't we find a pub with a quiet corner and talk this through over a pint?'

He sighed. 'I put this to bed in my head a long time ago. If I take it out again, you're better make it worth my while. I swear if you lot fuck me over again, I'll shout it from the bloody rooftops.'

'Fair enough. I can live with that.'

Keir gave her a long hard look. He seemed satisfied with what he saw for he nodded sharply. 'I don't want to have this conversation here. Not in my place of work. You based in Edinburgh?'

'I am.'

'Do you know Portobello?'

'I do.'

'Meet me at Smith and Gertrude on the High Street in an hour.'

'I've not got my car with me. Make it an hour and a half.'

He scoffed. 'What? A bobby on the bus?'

Karen shrugged. 'Like I said, Historic Cases Unit.'

The smile he gave her felt like a truce. 'See you later.'

16

John Baxter's electrical supplies shop turned out to be more than Jason had bargained for. He'd envisaged a wee establishment in a side street with shelves of plastic bins containing fuse wire and assorted plugs, light bulbs and white plastic light switches, cables and cable clips with nails already inserted, ready to be hammered in to fix a new extension to the top of the skirting board.

The reality was JB's Illumination Emporium. It sat at the heart of Kilmarnock High Street, its windows gleaming with light and glittering with crystals, gilt and chrome. Chandeliers, wall sconces, bedside lights in the shape of ceramic crows with spotlights in their beaks, ceiling spots, doorbell cams and giant globes for mounting on gateposts. Just for starters. Jason, who had never given much thought to the lighting design of his tenement flat, felt momentarily ashamed, as if he were letting the side down with his IKEA concertina paper shades.

He entered with some trepidation, wishing Meera was with him. At least she'd know the names of things. The middle-aged woman behind the counter smiled pityingly, as if she was used to men who didn't know what they wanted. 'What can I do for you, son?' she said.

'I'm looking for John Baxter,' he said, gathering what shreds of authority he possessed around him. He produced his ID. 'DC Jason Murray, Police Scotland.'

She didn't seem startled. 'This'll be about the break-in,' she said. 'You've taken your time. Anyway, you don't need to see the boss, I can fill you in on all the details.'

Jason flushed. 'No, it's nothing to do with that. I'm from the Historic Cases Unit, I need to speak to Mr Baxter about . . . a historic case.'

She tutted. 'Why didn't you say so? Hang on, I'll get him for you.' She bustled off towards the rear of the shop, disappearing amid a copse of free-standing floor lamps. She returned soon after with a man who was much closer to Jason's expectations than his shop had turned out to be. John Baxter's hair was a tousled dark mop threaded with silver and his brown eyes were alert, sizing Jason up as if measuring what his bank balance would stand. He wore tan overalls, the breast pocket bulging with a folded wooden rule and pencils of varying thicknesses. 'Detective Murray? You're not here about the break-in? We phoned you first thing, man. What's going on at Police Scotland?' He sounded exasperated rather than angry.

Jason took a deep breath. 'I don't know anything about the break-in, I'm from the Historic Cases Unit in Edinburgh and I need to speak to you about a case we've got some new evidence on.'

Baxter's eyebrows rose into his jagged fringe. 'Cold cases? You hear that, Auntie Ellie? Cold cases, like that show with Nicola Walker and yon Sanjeev guy that's married to Meera Syal?'

'Aye,' Jason said. It felt like the easiest option.

Baxter frowned. 'Wait a minute . . . Don't tell me Sam

Nimmo's finally broken cover?' He turned to the woman. 'You remember my pal Sam? Went mental and murdered his wife then went on the run? Nobody's seen hide nor hair of him for . . . what, must be ten years, getting on for. Is that it? They've run Sam to ground?'

'I'm sorry to tell you Sam Nimmo's body has been found.' It seemed the only option to slow Baxter's flow.

And it did. His mouth fell open and he grabbed the nearest lamp for support. 'No. What? He died abroad?'

'His body was found buried in the substrate of the M73 near Gartcosh. He appears to have been murdered at around the same time as his fiancée.'

Baxter disagreed 'There's got to be a mistake.'

'I'm afraid there's no room for error, the DNA from the skeleton matches DNA on the record from Sam Nimmo.'

'That doesn't make any sense. So, what? He murdered Rachel then somebody murdered him? Out of revenge? Or what?'

'Or someone murdered them both,' Ellie remarked casually. 'And made it look like Sam killed Rachel then did a runner. That's the kind of thing you'd get on the telly.'

Jason felt this interview was running away from him. 'I understand you and Sam were pals?'

Baxter nodded. 'You'd better come through the back. Auntie, be a doll and make us a pot of tea.' Ellie looked disappointed but went off to do as she was bid. Baxter led Jason through the shop and into a neat office at the back. 'Hell of a business,' he said. 'How did he turn up?' He waved Jason to a plastic bucket chair and settled himself behind his desk.

'The rain,' Jason said. 'The embankment collapsed and took a slice out the motorway with it.'

'That's some story.' He blew out a stream of air. 'Growing up with somebody, you never imagine they're going to end up like that. So, what do you want to know?'

'Anything you can tell us about Sam that you think might be relevant.'

John scratched his cheek, fingernails rasping on stubble. 'We'd been pals since primary three, when my family moved to Killie. Sam and me, we played football together right up through high school, and we were Killie daft. Even after we left the school, we met up for the match, along with our pal Eamonn. Every game at Rugby Park, and whatever away games we could get to. Man, we went on a bender for three days after we won the League Cup in 2012. Sam couldn't always get to the game, if he was out of town on a story. But he kept the flame burning. He was Killie to the bone. He even brought Rachel along once they started going out serious-like.' He shook his head, sadness breaking through. 'She was a lovely lassie, Rachel. I could never make sense of Sam being supposed to have killed her. He worshipped the ground she walked on. You know that old story about Sir Walter Raleigh putting his coat over the puddle so the Queen's feet wouldn't get wet? Sam would have gone one better, he'd have laid down in the puddle and let her walk on top of him.'

'That's saying something. So you never believed Sam had killed her?'

He sighed. 'All the evidence pointed to Sam, and when he did a runner . . . I couldn't square it with what I knew of him, but there didn't seem to be any other explanation.'

Ellie pushed the door open with her hip and put a tray with two mugs of tea, a carton of milk and a bowl of sugar lumps on Baxter's desk. 'He was always getting up people's noses, though, John. All those stories he did, embarrassing folk and even getting them sent to the jail.'

'Did he talk about his work much?' Jason was grateful for the steer in the direction he wanted to go.

'Only after he'd nailed his target to the wall. When he was working the story, he never spoke to us about the details. I asked him one time, and he said it was better we didn't know. That way we couldn't let something slip. And if he fucked up further down the line, we couldn't be caught up as co-conspirators.' An ironic grimace. 'I always thought he was mibbes bigging himself up a bit, putting on the swagger to impress us.'

'But he did break some big stories, John,' Ellie pointed out. 'That shocking one about the disinfectant company getting a contract with the Lothian Health Board then sup-plying stuff that was no more than perfumed water. That could have cost lives.'

'I know, Auntie. But this is Scotland, not Turkey or Russia. Journalists don't get bumped off because of a few inconvenient stories. And anyway, once the cat's out of the bag, what's to be gained from knocking off the journalist who broke the story?'

It was a good point, Jason thought. 'Unless you were hiding an even bigger story, I suppose,' he said.

'But you've no way of knowing which particular crook that might be, have you?' Ellie said. 'What about Sam's notes? Or his laptop? He must have had something written down somewhere.'

'Gone,' Baxter said. 'That was one of the reasons they thought Sam had done a runner. All his notebooks, van-ished like snaw aff a dyke. The only people who might know are the other members of the collective. And there's only two of them left – Keir and Linda.'

'We're tracking them down,' Jason said.

'Good, because I can't remember their second names.' He stood up. 'Look, I'm sorry I can't be more help. Give me your card, and if I come up with anything, I'll bell you. But don't hold your breath. When it came to his work, Sam trusted nobody. Not even Rachel.'

17

Daisy peered into the fridge and snagged a couple of Heidi-Weisse. She loved the clean taste of the wheat beers, made in Glasgow according to German purity laws. Steph had been momentarily taken aback when Daisy had announced this the first time she'd brought some home. 'These are the *good* German purity laws,' Daisy had promised her. 'Beer, not eugenics.'

She popped the caps and carefully poured them into the glasses designed to best promote the beer's virtues, then carried them through to the tiny conservatory Steph had built out from the front window of her basement flat. She passed the glasses over the sill, then followed, stepping up on the milk crate that provided access. Daisy squeezed next to Steph on the narrow bench and they clinked glasses. 'How was your day?' Daisy asked.

'We had a visit from an author,' Steph said. She taught thirty-five seven-year-olds in a local primary. 'The kids loved it. Well, the kids love anything that doesn't involve them doing any proper work, to be fair. But he was good with them. He got them using their imagination, which does make them more unruly, but in a good way. How about you?'

Daisy filled her in on Drew Jamieson's hand grenade. 'I don't think we're going to be able to take it anywhere, though,' she said. 'Just because his brother has unearthed a photo of a man who walked out of the hotel behind Tom Jamieson and emerged from the Scotsman Steps ahead of him is no kind of evidence of foul play. There's nothing to say the guy in the hoodie didn't run down the stairs and pass Jamieson well before he got to the bottom.'

'And there's no apparent connection between Jamieson and the man identified in the photo?'

'Not an obvious one that we've found so far.'

'You said Jamieson was gay. Is Hoodie Man gay too? Maybe that's the connection?'

Daisy was embarrassed to realise neither she nor Karen had considered that. It might even have explained the sudden shift in Marcus Nicol's attitude during their interview. 'He's got a very glamorous wife. I know that means nothing, but I didn't get any twitches on my gaydar. Maybe I'm going to have to do some more digging,' she mused. 'And I maybe need to talk to a couple of other guys from the football team. I can't just take Bob Watson's word for it that Jamieson walking away wasn't more of a big deal than he made out to me.'

'I'm with your guv'nor on this one, my love. People don't commit murder over a non-league five-a-side footie team.'

Daisy took a long pull from her beer. 'I know. But there's something feels off about the whole set-up. Here's a guy, well thought of by his colleagues, puts heavy emphasis on team spirit at his work. Then he just walks away from that whole camaraderie thing, and for what? What makes someone turn their back on their crew like that?'

Steph shrugged. 'Love would be the obvious first choice.

But you said he's loved up at home? No sign of him slipping over the side?'

'What kind of love affair takes place only on the second Thursday of the month? And requires having read a particular book in advance?'

They both pondered the question. At length, Steph said, 'Maybe it's somebody he met through work? A supplier who comes up to town once a month, stays at the hotel?'

'But Tom didn't stop out all night. He went to the book club for seven, they all had dinner together somewhere in the New Town and he was home by midnight. You'd have to be totally besotted by somebody to think that spending five hours together once a month was worth breaking long-standing friendships for, never mind cheating on the man you were planning to marry. I know I wouldn't.'

Steph chuckled. 'That's because you've got me. Wouldn't you think five hours a month with me was worth it if that was all you could have?'

'I'd find a way to plant you front and centre in my life.' Daisy was firm; she landed a kiss on the corner of Steph's mouth to emphasise the point.

'But this Thursday-night thing had only been going a wee while, you said. Maybe he'd just started seeing someone but then they got cold feet. Or they had a partner who found out and decided to do away with the competition.' She grinned. 'If you hadn't been single when we met, I'd have been tempted to do just that.'

'Nice of you to say so, but I don't believe you'd have done it.'

Steph leaned back and contemplated the legs walking past at street level. 'If not love, then what?'

'Money's the other big motivator. Gain, specifically, but

money generally. But I don't see how that comes into play. He lived in a lovely flat, but there doesn't seem to be any significant debt. The life insurance paid off the mortgage, which wouldn't have happened so readily if they'd remortgaged.'

'There's a motive right there, for the partner. Lovely flats sell like hot cakes in Edinburgh these days.'

'If that's what Jayden was thinking about, he's had years to capitalise on it. He seems to love the flat, for itself and also because it reminds him of the man he was planning to marry.'

'Talking of money . . . you said Tom Jamieson was ambitious. Maybe he wanted to get enough of a pile together to buy a hotel of his own? Maybe he was thinking of selling the flat as a down-payment on building a deal with someone who could make that happen?'

'He'd have had the expertise to run it, for sure. I suppose it's possible he had a regular meeting with his potential investors one Thursday a month. But surely he wouldn't have kept it a secret from his fiancé? And surely he could have arranged it for a time that wouldn't clash with such an important regular feature in his life? Especially if he was looking towards branching out – presumably these would be some of the guys he'd be wanting to take with him?'

Steph stared up at the street, frowning. 'What if it looks like a duck, walks like a duck and quacks like a duck?'

'What?' Daisy had a momentary sense of dislocation. It was one of the boss's favourite lines, not what she expected to hear at home.

Steph turned to her and grinned. 'Just for a moment, consider the improbable. What if he really was going to a book club?'

*

Karen arrived at the Portobello wine bar ten minutes early. She'd passed it often enough, glancing in at the simple decor, the clean lines, the sudden blurt of colour from a turquoise sofa, the comfortably chattering wine drinkers. She'd been tempted by the prospect of charcuterie and cheese boards, but she'd always been in too much of a hurry to be somewhere else. Now she was actually here, she was giving the wine list her full attention, trying to decide what to go for when she could avoid the strictures of not drinking on duty. There were plenty to choose from but although she recognised some of the styles, there were a lot of unfamiliar names. She'd have to drag one of her pals down here for a night of experimentation. River or Giorsal would appreciate it, that was for sure.

It wasn't somewhere she could bring Rafiq if he ever managed to get over to Scotland again. When she'd first visited him in Montreal, she'd been well aware of how little they knew about one another. Their paths had crossed when he'd been tracked down by a hitman from the vicious Syrian regime he'd fled from. As an orthopaedic surgeon, Rafiq had been well placed to see the handiwork of Assad's torturers; his conscience had turned him into a whistleblower, a decision that had cost the lives of his wife and son.

Karen's connections to the Syrian community she'd helped with setting up their social enterprise café had brought them together when the regime picked up Rafiq's trail. They'd spent precious few hours in Edinburgh before he'd been smuggled out aboard a container ship bound for Antwerp. And although they'd spent hours talking online, there was still so much to learn. It was only after they'd gone out for dinner on the night she'd arrived for the first time in Montreal that it occurred to her that she didn't even know whether he was the kind of Muslim who really didn't drink at all, or the kind who liked a glass of wine with dinner.

So she'd asked. He'd given a sad smile. 'After I lost my wife and my son, I also lost my religion. I couldn't hold fast to the idea of a god who could care so little for us. So I stopped observing most of the rituals of my former faith. I don't go to the mosque, I don't observe Ramadan. I have an occasional glass or two of wine.' He gave a mischievous grin. 'But I still don't eat bacon sandwiches. So let's have a bottle of good Frontenac Noir to celebrate your arrival.'

And so to her relief, they had. She'd have felt awkward opening a bottle of wine just for herself. And she certainly didn't want to give up the metaphorical journey round the gin distilleries of Scotland that she'd embarked on with Phil's former boss as a kind of tribute to the person they'd lost. Gin Mondays still happened at least once a month when Karen and Jimmy Hutton met up in her flat to share gin and gossip, ice and lemon and advice. The realisation that this wasn't something Rafiq would judge her for had cheered her up.

Before she'd made her choice, Keir Stevens shouldered his way into the bar. He'd added to his work wardrobe a tweed flat cap and a battered waxed jacket with enough pockets to carry a weekend's shopping. She really wasn't sure what look he was going for but she hoped the barista didn't judge her by it. Stevens sketched a wave in her direction, stopped to lean on the bar, pointed to the blackboard and ordered a bottle of something Karen had never heard of. He marched over to the table and plonked himself down opposite her, hands on manspread knees. 'I hope you like muscular red wine,' he said. 'Because you're paying for it.'

'I expect you think that's the least Police Scotland can do for your pal Sam. Thanks for meeting me.'

'So how come you guys never entertained the possibility that Sam was dead?'

'First, I wasn't one of "you guys" back then. I wasn't on the case. I was working a different beat. I'm sorry to say Rachel's murder barely tweaked my antennae. So I'm coming at this with a completely open mind.'

He raised his eyebrows. 'I'll take you at your word, then. Since you're the only show in town. I'll tell you for nothing, I never believed Sam had killed Rachel.' As he spoke, he poured two generous glasses and swallowed a substantial gulp of his. 'From the first time they went out, he knew she was the one for him. We were all a bit wild in our younger days, you know? Work hard, play harder. But for Sam, all that stopped as soon as he started going out with Rachel. And when she told him she was expecting? He was like a dog with two dicks. I couldn't imagine then, and I can't imagine now any set of circumstances that would have driven him to kill her.' Another gulp of wine. 'Turns out I was right all along.'

Karen sipped hers, enjoying the blackberry fruit on the nose. When he showed no sign of continuing, she said conversationally, 'Everybody has a trigger. Most of us never squeeze it, but it's there.'

Stevens shook his head decisively. 'I'll never believe Sam did away with Rachel. He was devastated when she was killed. It totally knocked the feet from under him. My ex-wife said at the time, he was like a boat unmoored, drifting without an anchor.' His mouth twisted. 'She's a poet, my ex-wife. Just one of the reasons she's my ex. If it had been her that had ended up dead, there would have been a fair few folk completely unsurprised. But Sam and Rachel? Never in a million years.'

'So what did you think when he disappeared?'

Stevens drained his glass and poured another. 'He was nobody's fool, Sam. He saw the way the wind was blowing. He could see your lot measuring him up and deciding he fitted the killer-shaped hole in their heads. So he fucked off before they could put the cuffs on him. He had all sorts of contacts, he had the resources to disappear. He probably thought youse might turn your attention elsewhere if he took himself off the board, but he got that one wrong.'

'But he didn't take himself off the board. Somebody else did that for him.'

'So you're telling me. And it makes a kind of sense since he never killed Rachel.'

'If he didn't, who did?'

'Obviously somebody who had it in for Sam. They framed him and did a bloody good job of it.'

He was seeing the same light that had dawned in Karen's head. 'Who hated him enough to break his heart before they killed him? Because according to you, that's what they did. If they wanted rid of him, why not just jump him in a dark close in the Old Town and gut him there? Or arrange to meet him some place out of the way with the promise of a story then run him down? Why go to all the trouble of an unnecessary murder before killing your real target?'

Stevens sighed. 'You're supposed to be the bloody detective, you tell me.'

'You can't think of anyone who'd fit the bill?'

He looked around at the other patrons in the bar, as if one of them might put their hand up with the answer. 'Some twisted psychopath, I suppose.'

117

Karen thought she understood now why Keir Stevens wasn't freelance any longer, why he'd turned his back on a world where he had to dig and dig and make a leakproof jar out of the shards of pottery he'd found. He was, she suspected, the dogsbody, the one who was enlisted to do the scut work in their loose grouping. Every organisation had to have its useful idiot. 'I think there was something else altogether going on here. I agree with you that whoever murdered Rachel also murdered Sam. But they didn't just want to take him off the board. I think they wanted to discredit him.'

18

'He was researching the people behind the Indy Referendum campaign. Both sides. Looking for the dirt that had been swept under the carpet,' Karen said without preamble when Jason arrived at the office first thing Monday morning bearing his tray of coffees, a brown paper bag balanced on top of them.

'We talking Sam Nimmo?' Jason said, passing Karen her cup as Daisy burst in.

'Sorry I'm late, bloody number five bus, never runs on time,' she gasped. She reached for a coffee and smiled. 'What's that in the bag, Jase?'

He looked pained. 'Not sure, sounds a bit like tagliatelle but it's a pastry with lemon cream in it.'

Daisy tore the bag open. 'Oh, Jase, you're a hero. Sfogliatelle, that's what they are. I could kiss you.'

Jason's head retreated like a startled turtle. Daisy grabbed one of the pastries and plonked herself down on her chair.

'Could we maybe all focus on what we're supposed to be here for?' Karen's tone was enough to make Daisy straighten up, put down her pastry and wipe the crumbs from her jacket.

'Sorry, boss.' Daisy looked the opposite of penitent as she eyed her sfogliatella.

Still sounding frosty, Karen continued. 'I tracked down Keir Stevens last night. We had an interesting chat about what Sam was working on around the time he died. According to Keir, he was up to his oxters in Indy Ref backgrounders, trying to get the story behind the stories.'

'Which side?' Daisy asked.

'Either. Both. According to Stevens, Sam didn't have strong convictions on either side. He knew enough about the dirty side of politics to think they were all as bad as each other. But he was hoping for a "yes" vote because there would have been an absolute tsunami of stories afterwards. Stevens said they were the kind of journalists who fed off chaos.' She shook her head in wonder. 'He sounded proud of it.'

'There would have been plenty of chaos for them to get their teeth into if the country had voted "yes",' Daisy said. 'So was he any more specific about what Sam was sticking his nose into?'

Jason raised a finger, 'I might have something. It's not much but it's maybe a start?'

'Let's hear it,' Karen said. 'At this point, I'm open to anything.'

'I tracked down Sam Nimmo's other football pal, Eamonn Sharkey. Our info was wrong – he works in Edinburgh, not Glasgow. He's a partner in an investment brokerage. He manages folks' money.' Jason shrugged. 'Whatever that means. I spoke to him last night.'

'What's he like, this Eamonn Sharkey?'

'He's come a long way from Killie,' Jason said. 'You'd never guess. He's turned into a total Edinburgh posh boy, right down to the accent and the floppy haircut.'

Daisy spluttered her coffee. 'Nailed it there, Jase. Sharkey by name, sharky by nature.'

'I thought he was on the level, all the same. He took the news about Nimmo on the nose – he said he wasn't surprised the man was dead, but him being buried in the motorway was pretty shocking.'

'Why was Nimmo being dead no surprise?' Karen was intrigued. 'His family, other people, they seem to have thought he was capable of disappearing. Reinventing himself some other place. Why was Sharkey so sure he must be dead?'

'He didn't believe Sam would be able to cut himself off from his family,' Jason said simply.

'That's more than his family thought,' Daisy said.

'We never know people as well as we think,' Karen said. 'Everybody has the capacity to surprise us. My dad was always a "charity begins at home" kind of guy until the pandemic. Now he volunteers at the food bank three days a week and he's got half his bowling club buddies doing the same. That's why we try to get multiple takes on victims and mispers, to see if we can find where the surprises are. So, did Mr Sharkey have any surprises for us?'

Jason looked pained. 'It's not exactly a surprise as such. I mean, knowing what we know now about what goes on, right?' Karen nodded, waiting patiently. 'He went on about how loved up Sam and Rachel were, then I asked if Sam ever talked about his work. He said, Sam never usually got into the details, but he'd been all fired up about the Indy Ref, and he was doing some deep diving into the backgrounds of some of the campaign activists on both sides. And he thought he might have struck gold.' He paused. With anyone else, Karen thought, it would have been for dramatic effect. With Jason, she knew he was gathering his thoughts into the right order.

121

'Wow,' Daisy chipped in. 'So what's the roadmap to El Dorado, Jason?'

A quick flash of puzzlement crossed his face, but he stuck doggedly to his story. 'According to Sharkey, the last time they were at a game together, Sam was excited about a lead he'd picked up about a couple of major players in the campaign, and sexual harassment. Serious stuff. Like, maybe rape. There had been some high-end fundraising party in Glasgow, at a big house, and the story was some lassie had been assaulted by these two men and everybody had kept stumm because of who they were. Sharkey didn't mention this conversation to the detectives at the time because that was the night Rachel died. When they got round to questioning him, all the polis asked about was whether Sam had been angry or upset about Rachel. Nobody asked him what Sam had been talking about.'

Karen's interest quickened. Eleven years ago, there had been no 'Me Too' hashtag; 2014 was well before women felt emboldened to speak out against powerful entitled men. In the run-up to the Indy Ref an accusation like that would have exploded on the Scottish political scene like a starburst firework. Depending on who was caught up in it, if Sam Nimmo had broken that story it could have changed the future of Scotland.

'Do we have any idea who the victim was? Or the perpetrators?'

Jason shook his head, sorrowful. 'Sharkey says he's got no idea. Nimmo was full of it, though. He said he'd found a source and was close to firming it up. They were playing Hearts and they came back for a 4-2 win after being all square at half time.'

'How do you know that?' Daisy exclaimed.

122

'I didn't, Sharkey did. When you're a diehard, you remember stuff like that. It was their first season in the Premiership and they got caned a lot. But that day they turned the tables and it was a big result for Killie, and Nimmo was in an especially good mood because he'd just got the tip on a big story.' It wasn't often Jason got the chance to school Daisy and he was making the most of it.

Karen broke off a piece of her pastry and contemplated it. 'OK. It's thin. But it's maybe a thread we can pull on. We need to get a lead on this fundraiser. There can't have been that many big money fundraisers, surely? There were plenty of celebrities involved, but not the kind who have big fuck-off houses in Glasgow.' She paused for thought. 'We need to do some digging. Who do we know who was involved in the Indy campaign?'

'I got a selfie with Nicola Sturgeon,' Daisy said with a smirk.

Karen rolled her eyes. 'Away you go and interview her then, she's used to Police Scotland officers rocking up to ask her stupid questions.' Sometimes Karen wondered if Daisy's occasional lapse into childishness was what attracted her primary school teacher girlfriend.

'There's must be a record somewhere,' Jason said. 'It's politics. They're bound to have some kind of register of donors.'

'The Electoral Commission, are they the ones?' Karen weighed in.

He pulled a face. 'I guess. And if this was a really fancy do, there'll be stuff online. And newspaper cuttings. I bet Meera will have some ideas too.' He was off. Thanks to Karen honing his skills and boosting his confidence, he'd developed a knack with the kind of records that gave her a headache just thinking about them.

That was Jason sorted. 'Daisy, this book club thing with Jamieson. It's niggling at me. See if you can find out from the boyfriend or the brother who runs it, what it's called, where they meet, who else is in it. And I will be talking to someone who's forgotten more than I ever knew about the viper's nest that is Scottish politics.' Karen picked up her sfogliatella. 'Just as soon as I've demolished this.'

19

Karen waited to make her call till she had the office to herself. It wasn't that she distrusted her colleagues but some sources were too valuable to risk burning. Cath Gray definitely fell into that category. It ran against Karen's instincts to get close to politicians; she thought the benefits of cosying up to each other didn't merit the risks to either person's integrity. She valued friendship and knew that she went the extra mile for friends without thinking twice. But politics was often a dirty game and she didn't want to find herself on the wrong end of an obligation. Even though the cold case world seldom intersected with contemporary politics, there were always ancient skeletons lying around in cupboards whose seals could be broken all too easily, especially when journalists like the late Sam Nimmo were on the prowl.

But Cath Gray had been tucked away in Karen's back pocket since she'd been a probationer back in her late teens. She was the mother of her first boyfriend. To her surprise, Douglas 'don't call me Doug – or Dougie' Gray had homed in on Karen at the Senior Christmas Dance when they'd both been fifteen. It had taken her aback because lads like Douglas – rugby player, drummer in an enthusiastic but tuneless post-punk band, earmarked for Edinburgh University down the line – went for lassies with long hair, eyelashes like road sweeper's brushes and very short skirts.

The first dance had been a Military Two-Step, calculated to set the pulses racing and the temperature rising. Every PE lesson for the term had involved Scottish Country Dancing. There was no excuse for not knowing the steps, and sadistic teachers chivvied everyone on to the dance floor, no matter whether they preferred to lean against the wall. Douglas had sauntered along the line of lassies, pretending not to notice the disappointed looks as he passed, and stopped opposite a bemused Karen. 'You dancing?' came the time-honoured call-and-response starter.

'You asking?'

'Ah'm asking.'

Karen nodded, still not sure if she was somehow being mocked. 'Ah'm dancing.' They whirled and jumped and staggered and bumped their way round the dance floor, laughing when they lost the plot. When the trio of accordion, fiddle and drums struck the final chord, they edged their way to the side.

'That was a laugh,' Douglas said.

'I enjoyed it.' Her smile was tentative.

'I thought you would. I've listened to you at the Debating Soc, you've got a sense of humour as well as a sharp tongue on you.'

The compère, Miss Peterson from the History Department, announced the next dance. A ladies' choice. Before Karen could open her mouth, one of the identikit lassies from her year breenged in and demanded Douglas dance the Gay Gordons with her. He shrugged and allowed himself to be dragged off. Karen had thought it would be the last she'd see of him that night.

She'd been wrong. They'd had three more turns round the floor together, including the St Bernard's Waltz, which almost counted as a slow dance. As he swung her inelegantly around in the waltz section, he asked her whether she fancied coming to see a film at the weekend.

It had been the start of a few months of awkward teenage jockeying for position, neither of them entirely sure how they were supposed to behave. She liked being with him, liked that he made her feel more confident in herself, but she didn't get any rushes of emotion when he walked into the room or obsessive anxieties about what he was doing when he wasn't with her. Snogging was all right, but it didn't send her heart racing. None of it was how she expected it to be. Eventually they drifted apart with no hard feelings.

But in the process, Karen had got to know Douglas's parents. Cath and Keith Gray welcomed Douglas's friends into their home, encouraging them to play endless games of Monopoly and Risk, engaging them in conversation. What was unique in Karen's experience was that they were actually interested in the opinions of their teenage visitors. They'd listen to their complaints and push them to come up with solutions. It took Karen a few weeks to realise this was because Cath was one of the town's representatives on Fife council, always on the lookout for vote-winning ideas.

Even after Karen and Douglas had ceased to be an item, Cath had made it clear Karen wasn't banished from the board games or the conversation. When she'd left school to join the police, Cath had taken her out for a pizza to celebrate. 'You're exactly the kind of young person who should be a polis,' she'd said. 'You've got a good heart and a good brain. I know you might not feel as comfortable coming about the house once you're a member of the force, but I'll always think of you as a pal. I've got a lot of contacts, not only in the world of politics. My reach extends well beyond the narrow world of the Scottish National Party. So if you're ever up against a brick wall that you think I might help you to climb over – or, knowing you – to bulldoze through, don't be shy about picking up the phone.' She gave a knowing smile. 'Maybe more discreet to do that than chap the door.'

Karen had stayed in loose touch with Cath over the years but had never needed to call in the proffered favour. And when Douglas had confided in her a few years ago that he was gay, she'd helped him smooth the way with his parents. Now she felt pretty sure that Cath could provide what she needed. She was a Member of the Scottish Parliament, a former whip, so she'd know where the bodies were buried among her own party, as well as having her ear to the ground when it came to their rivals. And she'd been around for long enough to remember what sharks had been swimming around under the surface in the run-up to the Indy Ref in 2014. The question was whether she'd still be willing to be Karen's Deep Throat.

There was only one way to find out.

Daisy made it to Compadres ahead of the lunchtime rush. She'd phoned ahead to check that Jayden Shaw was on the premises, though she hadn't identified herself on the call. She liked to catch people on the back foot. It did backfire sometimes, but on balance, she thought it worked in her favour.

The bar occupied two floors in an old building on the West Bow, right in the heart of tourist Edinburgh. It was nobody's local; not even the people who lived and worked in the West Bow were regulars here. But its range of craft beers and cheap tapas appealed to the passing trade. They also had a side gig in catering for off-site events, she'd noted from the website. Compadres seemed to have adjusted well to the post-Covid exigencies that had decimated the city's hospitality business.

A young woman in a peasant blouse and a cowboy-style neckerchief was mixing jugs of sangria behind the bar. She glanced up at Daisy and said, 'What can I get you?' without pausing.

'I'm looking for Jayden.' A smile intended to reassure.

'We're not taking anybody on right now.' The barmaid tipped some diced and sliced fruit into the jugs.

'I've already got a job, thanks.' Daisy flashed her ID. 'Jayden?'

An eye-roll. 'You probably get better perks. He's in the office.' She gestured over her shoulder towards the hacienda-style staircase. 'Up the stairs, door in the far wall, says "El Jefe". Spanish for wanker, I believe.'

Daisy was still grinning when she knocked on the door. Without waiting for a reply, she wiped her face clean and walked in. There was nothing showy about the dingy office. A cheap desk and office chair, a run of open shelves that held box files and promo gifts from brewers and distilleries, a couple of folding chairs set against the wall by the door. The only personal touch was a framed photo of Shaw and Tom Jamieson in shirt sleeves in a bar, glasses of fizz raised in a toast.

Jayden Shaw was working at his computer, apparently checking delivery notes against orders. 'Sergeant, right?' he said, walking his chair along the desk so they could have an unobstructed view of each other. It was, she thought, the action of a man who wanted to demonstrate frankness.

'That's right, Mr Shaw. I hope you don't mind me turning up like this, but I wanted to follow up a couple of things from our previous conversation. I appreciate we came at you out of the blue after all this time, and I know how easy it is not to remember everything in the moment.'

He sighed. 'I don't know about that. I often think my life would be easier if my memory was kind of crap. There's so many little things that bubble up every day to remind me what I've lost.'

'I get that. Did you ever think about moving away?' Daisy reached for one of the chairs, unfolded it and sat down.

'Why would I? I like my job, Edinburgh's a great city. I love our flat and in spite of the pain the memories bring, I don't want to wipe the slate clean of Tommo.' He ran his fingers through his hair. 'So what brings you to my door? I can't think of anything I know that I didn't talk about at the time. It was like I had verbal diarrhoea, I couldn't stop telling you guys everything about our life together. As if talking about it would bring it back to life.' He tutted at himself. 'If only it was that easy.'

'To be honest, the one thing my boss and I keep coming back to is the book club.'

'Why're you so interested in that?'

'We're interested in anything out of the ordinary in his life. Clearly your Tommo loved his job and he built a loyal team around himself. To put those relationships at risk, that must have taken some weight on the other side of the scales.' Daisy let that hang for a moment. When Jayden said nothing, she went for the direct line. 'What did he think was in it for him?'

130

He gave her a level stare. 'Now why would you think there had to be something in it for him other than spending time with a bunch of guys who shared his love of books?'

'This is a UNESCO City of Literature. There's no shortage of book clubs. It couldn't have been too hard to find one that didn't meet on a Thursday. Just off the top of my head, I know one of the indie bookshops has an LGBTQ group.'

His lips twitched in a wry smile. 'No offence, but I can't see Tommo in a room with a gaggle of lasses talking about what's-her-name Winterson's oranges.'

But Daisy was not to be diverted. 'You said before, he'd been trying to hook up with them for ages. What was so special about this particular bunch of guys? Why them, why then?'

He sighed. 'It's really not that big of a deal. A couple of years back, Denise Mina was dining in the restaurant with a couple of pals. She's very distinctive-looking, apparently. One of Tommo's regulars asked him if that really was the lassie Mina, and they got talking about books. Next time this customer came in, he told Tommo about the book club and said how he'd fit right in. Tommo came home full of it. He said it sounded right up his street. To be honest with you, I'd rather stick needles in my eyes, but I could see how keen he was on the idea so I told him to go for it.'

'How come it took ages, then? Did he not see his customer again for a while?'

'No, nothing like that. This guy was a regular, like I said. He'd be in every couple of weeks. Business entertaining. They get a lot of that at the Monument. The problem was, there wasn't a vacancy. This reading crew like to keep it exclusive. Just a dozen members. So he had to wait till somebody left.'

Daisy winced. 'Dead man's shoes? I'm not sure I'd have been comfortable with that.'

Jayden scoffed. 'Jesus, Sergeant, you've got a dark mind. Not everybody dies. People move away, or their circumstances change.'

'Was that what eventually happened for Tommo? Someone left town?'

Jayden shifted in his seat. 'As it happens, somebody did die. You maybe remember it making the headlines? Bryce Gordon, the architect? Went off the road in a forest in the Highlands, they didn't find him for a couple of days. Dead on arrival. Tommo said, "Thank God for the Jaguar F-Type."' Seeing her look of confusion, he added, 'Sorry, that was a bit dark. Only, if he'd had a big fuck-off SUV, he'd probably still be alive today. Soft-top convertible, no chance.' He had the grace to look embarrassed.

'And that opened up a spot for Tommo.'

'Aye, it did. And he was over the moon. He was doubly chuffed because he'd already read the first book they were going to discuss and he really had something to say about it. Won the Booker Prize, apparently. Set in South Africa. *The Promise*, I think it was called. Have you read it?'

Daisy shook her head. She went for the little white lie. 'Like you, I'm not much of a reader. But Tommo? He was happy with his introduction to the group?'

'He said he thought it was just what he'd been looking for.' He chuckled, smiling at the recollection. 'He was buzzing when he got back. I thought it would just be a couple of hours, but he didn't get home till nearly midnight. I said, "I know it wasn't exactly a short book but that's one helluva book craic." Tommo said no, the book conversation only lasted about an hour, but they had drinks beforehand then more talk afterwards. He liked the company. He said the other members, they were all top people in their line. He thought they might come in handy. He wanted to run a world-class hotel, you know? Something people like us can only dream about.'

Daisy felt the faint tug in her gut that she liked to think was intuition. 'What did you make of that?'

'Ach, I thought he was just being Tommo. Getting carried away with his first encounter with one or two big players. In a different environment from where he usually met the likes of them. I thought, a few more meetings and your feet'll be back on the ground where they belong, my lad.' Something in his expression shifted and the shadow of grief crossed his face. 'He never got long enough in their company for that to happen. Two more meetings and he was in his grave.'

'I'm sorry.'

'Not as sorry as I am.'

'Did they have a name, this book group? Where did they meet?'

'They called themselves Justified Sinners. I thought it was a bloody strange name for a book club, but Tommo said it was a tip of the hat to a Scottish classic. Some shepherd guy back in the day.'

It rang a vague bell somewhere in the back of Daisy's head but she couldn't nail it down. Never mind, that was what Google was for. 'And where they met?'

'It was somewhere in the New Town. I don't think Tommo ever said exactly where.'

'How did he get there? Did he drive? Take the bus?'

He scoffed. 'What? Rock up to his fancy book club on the bus? Not on your nelly. He got a contract cab, there and back.'

Daisy tried not to show she was rejoicing at that nugget of news. 'I don't suppose you have the details of which company he had a contract with?' She tried to sound casual.

'It was the hotel's contract, I'm sure the concierge can give you the details. I doubt their records will go that far back though.'

'We can try.' Karen Pirie had built up a relationship with Gartcosh's digital data expert Tamsin Martineau over the years. In exchange for premium chocolate biscuits, Tamsin would manage to organise the digging up of data its creators thought had been dead and buried long ago. Daisy reckoned that uncovering a relatively recent contract cab record would almost be an insult to her skills. 'One more thing before I leave you in peace, Mr Shaw.'

'Ask away, Sergeant. You're only keeping me from making sense of my bloody invoices.'

'Did Tommo mention any names? Who hosted the meetings? Who else was there?'

He shook his head. She'd run out of road.

Daisy got to her feet. 'Thanks for your time, Mr Shaw.'

An anxious frown furrowed his brow. 'Do you think there's anything to this mad notion of Drew's? It really upsets me, to think there's even a chance that someone killed Tommo and got away with it. That they could be walking around without a fucking care in the world and he's in the ground? If that's what happened, I feel like I let him down.'

'You didn't let him down, Jayden.' Daisy put a hand on his arm. 'If there's any substance in what Drew is alleging, it's not on you. It's on us. And our team will make sure you get the answers Tommo deserved.' She saw the sparkle of tears in his eyes and patted his shoulder. She didn't want to imagine how he felt. Nothing could make that better.

But if Karen Pirie had taught her anything, it was that unanswered questions deserved to be resolved. As she headed down the Cowgate towards the office, she thought she knew at least one place to start looking.

20

That Cath Gray picked up on the second ring was reassuring. 'Hello, Karen,' she said, hearty as ever. 'Long time no speak.'

'I'm sorry, Cath. I've not really got back to staying in touch with folk since Covid.'

'Don't feel bad about it. You're not the only one. We all crawled into our wee shells like hermit crabs and I think we've kind of lost the knack of being easy with each other. I can't remember the last time I just dropped a text to someone at half past six, going, "Fancy a wee swallie on the way home?" Now, I just head back to the ranch, ready for another night with Holyrood paperwork and Netflix. Keith's the same. So what brings you out of your buckie?'

'I'm ashamed to say it's work. Not that I don't love you for your company, but I need to pick your brains.'

Cath snorted with laughter. 'Good luck with that. Ever since I had the Covid, finding my brain's been like wading through a plate of mince. Is this the kind of brain-picking that requires a secure location? Like, lunch?'

'You beat me to the draw. Where would you like to eat?'

Cath paused but not for long. 'What about the bistro in the Scott Monument? The tables are far enough apart.'

'Can't do that, Cath. Conflict of interest with another investigation, sorry.' They settled on the café at Holyrood Palace. In spite of it being across the street from the Parliament, it was generally sniffed at as a tourist mecca, which meant neither was likely to be spotted by anyone who knew them.

Karen arrived first and ordered a plate of scones with jam and cream, a pot of tea for Cath and a flat white for herself. Cath arrived swathed in an elegant navy wool coat that had more swagger than a catwalk model. A few heads turned, but there was no recognition in their stares. She shrugged her coat off, revealing a stylish asymmetric sweater. Cath was on the downward slope of her sixties, a decade described by the late comedian Janey Godley as 'sniper's alley', but Cath showed little sign of succumbing to vulnerability. Her hairstylist was doing a fine job of making her hair look as if the shades of mid-brown were as nature had intended and her skin glowed. Karen wondered if she'd have managed to look that soignée if she and Douglas had stuck together. Somehow she doubted it.

Cath leaned in for a perfunctory hug then settled down opposite. They performed a quick catch-up, both knowing that wasn't why they were there. 'So, Karen, I'm guessing the cloak-and-dagger means this isn't just the usual gossip?'

'Years ago, you said if I was ever up against a brick wall that you might help me get over, I should ask.'

Cath's eyebrows rose. 'I thought you'd forgotten about that, since you never asked.'

'Well, you have shared quite a bit over the years.'

'Nothing that you couldn't have found out elsewhere. You never pressed me to break a confidence. You never even asked me to intervene when you were helping your Syrians get their café going.'

For a moment, Karen wondered if that omission had caused offence. 'It wasn't your constituency,' she said. 'And I had an in with the local MP.' She gave a wry smile. 'I didn't want to use up your goodwill unnecessarily.'

'Good for you. But now it's time?' Cath poured a cup of tea, adding milk and one sugar.

'I don't know anybody else who has the kind of knowledge I need. And a memory like a steel filing cabinet.'

Cath grinned and reached for a scone. 'It's true, I could go on *Mastermind* with "what's lurking under stones in Scottish politics" as my specialist subject. And since it's you I'm talking to, I'm assuming it's something that's stayed in the dark for a long time.'

'Cast your mind back to 2014.' Karen followed Cath's example, splitting a scone and slathering it with jam.

'The year of living dangerously. When we thought we could take our future into our own hands. And we've had to live with the failure ever since.' She sighed. 'When I can't get to sleep at night, I like to imagine that we won the referendum. That I'm sleepless in an independent republic run by a government dedicated to a socially responsible agenda, committed to ending child poverty and homelessness.' She put down her scone, her eyes suddenly tired.

'I'm sorry to drag it all up again.'

Cath shook her head. 'It's never far from the surface, love.' She pulled herself together, physically squaring her shoulders and straightening her spine. 'So. The great Independence Referendum. What's caught your attention after all this time?'

'It's not the ref itself that concerns me. It's the campaign.'

Cath groaned. 'You're not digging up the old stories about dodgy under-the-table funding from foreign sources, are you? That's all been well and truly knocked on the head.'

'No, no, nothing like that,' Karen said hastily. Though she wasn't sure she wouldn't end up going down that road eventually. 'Did you see the reports in the media about the skeleton that emerged from the landslip on the M73? Near Gartcosh?'

Raised eyebrows. 'I wasn't expecting *that*. What's that got to do with the Ref?'

'We've identified the body. Sam Nimmo. You probably remember him?'

'Nosy wee hack? I remember him. He had a habit of making a Munro out of a molehill. I've not heard that name for years.' She frowned then her face cleared as memory kicked in. 'He murdered his girlfriend then did a runner, wasn't that the story?'

Karen nodded. 'That was the story at the time. It was a neat fit, given there were no forensics to put anybody else in the picture. He knew the kind of dodgy guys who could have fixed him up with fake ID and he likely had the money to pay for it. The only problem was that there was no credible motive. And by all accounts, he was shattered by her death.'

'Aye, but he might have been shattered when he realised what he'd done. And you never know what goes on inside a relationship behind closed doors, Karen. Maybe he found out she was cheating on him?'

'She was pregnant. With *his* baby, Cath. And he was over the moon about it. Nobody could come up with a satisfactory reason why he might've killed her. Except all the evidence pointed that way.'

'So what's changed?' Cath returned to her scone, her moment of angst past.

'Well, he didn't hit himself over the head and bury himself in the substrate of the M73, that's for sure. So we started digging, metaphorically as well as literally. And we got a wee bit of a lead.' She gave Cath a hard stare. 'This has to stay between us.'

'I think you know you can trust me, Karen. I'm not going to interfere in your case, I care too much about justice to risk it.'

'Sam had a couple of pals he'd been tight with since school. Nothing to do with the media. They went to the football together. Not long before he died, they were at Rugby Park and Sam told his pal he'd got hold of a major story. Sam was excited because he'd heard a rumour about a couple of major players in the Yes campaign. Serious sexual harassment, maybe even rape. It happened at a big house in the Glasgow area, some big-ticket fundraiser. The whisper was that two men had sexually assaulted some lassie but it got swept under the rug because of whose house it was, or who the two guys were.'

Cath's face gave nothing away.

'All I'm looking for is a steer on big fundraisers in the run-up to the Indy Ref that might fit the bill.'

'It was the No campaign that had the big money,' Cath said carefully. 'We were always scrabbling for what we could get our hands on. You know that.'

'I assumed it, I didn't know it for sure.'

Cath cleared her throat. 'I'll need to check my diaries. I kept a note of stuff like that, just in case there were ever any question marks about where the cash was coming from. When I could, I tapped up people I knew who were there. People on the fringes, you understand?'

'Obviously. Not spies as such.'

Cath's face relaxed and she chuckled. 'More like double agents. The ones with their eyes on the main chance, keeping a foot in both camps to make sure they were still chief with whichever side won.'

'You had one or two big cheeses on your side as well, though?'

A hollow laugh. 'The upper crust keep their hand on their ha'penny, Karen. That's how they keep their castles and their shooting estates. Even the ones who were most vocal in their support stopped short of putting their hands in their pockets.'

'You must have had some big nights, all the same. You had so many showbiz types on the Yes side. Musicians, actors, comedians, writers, artists. Surely somebody had a jamboree or two for the big names?'

Cath shook her head. 'It wasn't really our style. We tended to use our big names to make an impact on actual voters. Meetings in community centres, church halls, social clubs, comedy nights. Better to roll out Elaine C. Smith to talk to five hundred folk on a council estate than to spend ten times that pouring prosecco down the necks of yummy mummies and rugger buggers. If they were for us, they'd be voting anyway. If they were agin us, to quote Boris, we'd just be spaffing it up the wall.'

Karen wondered if Cath was maybe laying it on too thickly. But she could circle round that way again when the MP passed on the fruits of her research. And in the meantime, Jason could be relied on to attack the newspaper files. The Scottish media had been so avidly against independence, they could be guaranteed to fall on a big pro-Indy hoolie like a pack of starving wolves. 'I don't suppose you ever heard of anybody who had the knives out for Sam Nimmo?'

'No more than any other journalist. One thing I will say for the Nimmo lad – he was even-handed when it came to dishing out the pelters. An equal opportunities bastard, you might say.'

'Did you ever cross paths directly with him?'

Cath's smile was broad and genuine. 'You know me, Karen. I might push at the borders, but I never cross the line. I love my life too much to take risks with it.' She raised her scone to her lips. 'And that's why you came to me.' The smile disappeared behind a mask of jam and cream.

Karen hoped she was right. But she'd been doing this job for too long not to have a niggle of doubt in the corner of her mind.

21

Karen had barely hung up her coat when Daisy bounced into the HCU office. 'You look like you've had a result,' she said.

'I might have a loose thread to pull on.' Daisy sat down, shrugging out of her puffa jacket and letting it settle over her chair.

'Sounds intriguing.'

'Jayden was a bit more forthcoming. I think we just didn't know the right questions to ask before.' As she spoke, Daisy opened her laptop and began typing. 'Justified Sinners, that's what Tom Jamieson's book group was called. I thought it rang a bell . . .'

'It's a book,' Karen said. 'I've not read it, way too highbrow for me. But it's one of the books Scottish crime writers talk about when they're trying to sound literary.'

'Found it! They did a walking tour of it at the book festival last year.' Her voice slowed as she read the content. 'Published two hundred years ago. Some guy called James Hogg wrote it. The central character is a fanatical Calvinist who thinks he's preordained to be one of the saved, so it doesn't matter what crimes he commits, up to and including murder. Whatever he does, he's on the fast track to heaven when he dies.' Daisy frowned at her boss. 'It's an odd choice to name your book group after.'

Karen scoffed. 'I've arrested a fair few guys – and they've all been guys – who think they've got a God-given right to destroy other people's lives. But you're right, it's not exactly sending a positive message.'

'Maybe that's why they're so secretive? They don't want people to know what they believe in?'

'If they do actually believe in it and it's not some clever-dick joke we're not getting,' Karen said gloomily. There were times when she almost regretted having passed on going to university in favour of joining the police straight from school, but this wasn't one of them. She had no time for people who used their learning as a fence to keep others from understanding. 'Did Jayden have anything else to say about the book group? Like who else belongs to their happy wee band of sinners? And where they meet?'

Daisy smiled, her satisfaction showing. 'I don't have a location yet, but I'm checking out the cab firm the hotel has a contract with. I rang the concierge and he told me. Jayden said Jamieson went to the meetings in one of their cars.'

'Good thinking.'

'There's more, boss. I don't have names of the membership yet, but we may have a way into that. This limited membership routine, a dozen places? The slot that Tom Jamieson filled was literally dead man's shoes. Do you remember Bryce Gordon, the architect whose car went off the road in the Highlands? Took them three days to notice his car down a gully.'

Karen frowned, pulling the information from storage to the front of her mind. 'There was a stooshie about that, wasn't there? He disappeared on his way home from ...'

She paused. 'Spean Bridge, was it? It's all coming back to me now. His wife reported him missing, the local tackety boot boys didn't take it seriously. They assumed he was off shagging someone else. A gamekeeper came across the car when he was out checking his crow traps.'

'Wow, your memory for detail never ceases to amaze me.'

Karen shrugged. 'It only stuck because it was the first time I'd come across a mention of a crow trap. Usually it's dog walkers that stumble across bodies, not gamies. Another reason why I don't have a dog.' A wry smile.

'Another?'

'Warm poo on cold mornings, Daisy. So tell me more about Bryce Gordon. Do we know why his car ended up in a gully off a Highland road?'

Daisy's fingers flew over her keyboard as she sourced the reports in the local press. 'He was driving a Jaguar F-Type. It's a soft-top convertible. It flipped over a couple of times on the way down. He broke his neck.'

'That's not really why, it's how. What caused him to go off the road, do we know?'

Daisy speed-read to the end of the newspaper story. 'He'd been working on a project near Letterfinlay, he set off for home just before nine p.m. He was over the limit. Not much, but enough. It happened on a bad bend, they think he lost control then over-steered.'

Karen gave it some thought. 'Are there any quotes from the local polis?'

'An Inspector Garvey. "We wish to express our condolences to Mr Gordon's wife and family. This was a tragic accident. Unfortunately, due to the steep side of the gully, it was impossible to see Mr Gordon's car from the road."'

'Did nobody think to track his phone?'

145

Daisy spread her hands. 'No idea.'

Karen rolled her eyes. 'What a fuck-up all round. I think I might have a wee word with Inspector Garvey. I need to talk to the widow and I can use getting her address as a pretext to ask one or two questions.'

Her sergeant seemed perplexed. 'What? You think there was something dodgy about the accident? Why?'

'I don't need a reason, Daisy. I have a naturally suspicious mind.'

Inspector Garvey had immediately taken the huff as soon as Karen uttered Bryce Gordon's name. 'Not this again,' he complained. 'Look, I told the widow *and* her lawyers till I was blue in the face that there was nothing suspicious about her husband's death. Just a bit of careless driving after an ill-advised drink or two before he got on the road.'

'I'm not suggesting—'

'And now she sets the cold case team on me.' He steam-rollered on. 'She probably saw your face all over the papers with that Edinburgh student lassie that disappeared.' He let out a mighty sigh. 'Well, you're wasting your time if you're on a headline hunt here. There. Is. No. Story.'

'I'm not investigating Bryce Gordon's death,' she said, raising her voice just enough to cut him off. 'All I'm after is contacting his next of kin to make some inquiries about a club he belonged to.'

'You should have said,' he grumbled.

'You should have let me.'

'Aye, well, you'd be the same if you'd had your head dirled by the Widow Gordon like I did. Give me a minute.'

Karen waited, accompanied by the percussive sound of a heavy hand on a keyboard. Then he read out Victoria

Gordon's address slowly enough for her to scribble it down. 'Thanks for your help,' she said. 'One thing though – I get that the car couldn't be seen from the road, but when he was reported missing, how come you didn't manage to trace his phone?'

A pause. 'Are you sure you've not been on to the widow already? She had a bee in her bonnet about that very thing.'

Hardly surprising these days. 'I thought that one up all by myself, Inspector.'

'The answer's simple. The roof of the car was ripped clean off in the crash and the phone flew out of the car and smacked into a bloody great boulder three metres from the car. Smashed to buggery fuck. That's how come, DCI Pirie.'

Bryce Gordon had nailed his architectural colours firmly to the mast with his own home. It sat in its own substantial grounds on the edge of Barnton, probably the only part of Edinburgh where it didn't look like it had been dropped from outer space. Glass and steel were his preferred materials, with a base layer of rich red sandstone. The colour was picked up in stained glass panels in the top sections of each giant pane, splashes of shades of red from geranium to deepest crimson arranged seemingly at random. It must be like living in a vast aquarium whose inmates had been slain, their bloody corpses floating on the surface. 'Wow,' Daisy said.

'Rather them than me,' Karen said. 'I like a wee bit of privacy from the neighbours.'

Daisy looked around theatrically. 'The only neighbours they've got are sheep.'

'Exactly. Who wants a flock of spectators for those wee moments of intimacy? Or just when you're watching something embarrassing on the TV. Like an old black-and-white movie on a Sunday afternoon instead of some highbrow four-hour Swedish exploration of tortured human relationships.'

Daisy giggled. Karen was good at sounding grumpy when she was cracking a joke. The only problem was that she also sounded very similar when she was actually grumpy. Daisy had learned that the telltale was her mouth; an upward twitch at one corner granted permission to smile. 'I kind of like it. I bet you can press a button and it goes dark.'

The front door was a tall oblong of densely grained oak, the door furniture brushed steel. Karen pressed the doorbell; they waited and a disembodied voice issued from it, asking who they were. Karen explained. 'I'll come down,' the metal box squawked.

The woman who opened the door was dressed for yoga. Karen couldn't decide whether it was an affectation or purposeful. She certainly looked sleek and fit enough for their arrival to have been an interruption to Downward Facing Dog. Only the faintest crepe around her neck placed her in her fifties rather than her thirties. She cocked her head to one side, brown eyes considering them.

'Mrs Gordon?' Karen asked. 'Mrs Victoria Gordon?'

'Yes, that's me. Why are you here?' she asked, curious rather than concerned. 'What has Police Scotland to do with me?'

'It's complicated. In our corner of the building, it usually is.' A deprecating smile. 'DS Mortimer and I are with the Historic Cases Unit. Can we come in?'

'Is this to do with Bryce?' Now she sounded anxious.

'Indirectly, yes.'

Mrs Gordon sighed. 'You'd better come in, then. I'll put the kettle on.'

They followed her inside and into a space so light it felt as if the sky had been imported. Daisy and Karen exchanged looks as they took in the extravagantly beautiful ceramics that topped waist-high steel plinths and free-standing panels that held immaculately detailed drawings of modern buildings. A scatter of leather chairs and small sofas stood around the space, carefully arranged to look random. Karen couldn't imagine living like this. It felt contrived for display rather than life. *You might as well take up residence in the city's Modern Art Gallery,* she thought.

They followed her through a door at the rear of the room and found themselves in a room recognisable as a kitchen. This time, it was clear that function was as important as form. It was equipped with modern kit, from matching dark red Kitchen Aid appliances to an air fryer that looked like something Darth Vader could have worn. A young man with a man-bun and a bushy beard was sitting at a polished limestone breakfast bar. He looked up from his laptop as they entered. 'My son, Gavin,' Mrs Gordon said. 'Gav, these women are from Police Scotland.'

His eyebrows quirked. 'I told you not to run that red light.'

'Very funny.' She turned back to Karen and Daisy, inviting them to sit at a circular steel-topped table with a view of long landscaped lawns. 'Tea? Coffee?'

'Or don't you drink on duty?' Gavin offered.

'Ignore him,' his mother said. 'I try to.'

'We're fine.' Karen sat with her back to the view. 'I'm sorry to impose on you but we believe you might have some information that could be helpful to us in one of our investigations.'

Mrs Gordon sat down heavily. 'You're Historic Cases, yes? Does that mean you're finally going to investigate my husband's death properly?'

149

Wrong-footed, Karen managed to keep her face straight with an effort. 'Are you unhappy with the outcome of the Fatal Accident Inquiry?'

'Of course we are. Bryce wasn't a drunk driver. He loved to drive fast but he wasn't irresponsible. His client swore on oath that Bryce had only a single glass of wine before he set off. There's no way of verifying that because it took your officers so long to find his body.'

Gavin chipped in. 'I did some research into the subject. It's really not possible to establish someone's blood alcohol level with any precision three days after their death. There's microbes and fermentation inside the body that can produce alcohol.'

Karen was nonplussed. But Daisy had skimmed the post-mortem report while Karen had been tracking down the Gordons' address, and she cut in. 'It's my understanding that Mr Gordon didn't die instantly. He had head injuries that meant he could have been unconscious for hours before he died. But his liver would have carried on processing any alcohol in his system. So it's impossible to be definitive either way.'

'But that's not why we're here,' Karen said firmly. 'I understand that you're still grieving. It's natural that you want to get to the bottom of what happened to your husband. But sometimes an accident is just that, and nothing more.'

Gavin again. 'My dad was a good driver, he'd passed the Advanced Driver test. No way was he going to lose control on a simple bend in the road. I mean, there wasn't even a crash barrier there, that's how, like, not-dangerous it was.'

'I'm sorry, but there's nothing I can say. Not because we're keeping anything from you but because I'm not familiar with the details. We're here on another matter entirely.' Karen spread her hands in a gesture of openness.

Mrs Gordon sighed. 'I should have known it was too good to be true. Expecting Police Scotland to own up to a mistake.' Her mouth had turned into a bitter line.

'So why are you here?' Gavin stood up and crossed to the table, noisily pulling out a chair and throwing himself into it.

'We're investigating the death of a man called Tom Jamieson. You may remember it. He died in a fall on the Scotsman Steps by Waverley Station a few years ago. He was one of the managers of the Scott Monument Hotel?'

The Gordons both shook their heads.

'This is probably going to sound a bit bonkers, but bear with me,' Karen said. 'His brother, who lives in New Zealand, has come back to Scotland and alleges his brother was murdered. He claims he has some new evidence to back up his claim. So we scrolled back through the case notes. One of the things we always look for in a case like this is what changed in the victim's life ahead of the fatal incident. Because that can sometimes be the key to what happened.'

'Makes sense,' Gavin muttered. 'That is, if you've already ruled out everybody else who had it in for them.'

Karen thought Gavin Gordon was well on the way to proving the maxim that 'nobody loves a smartarse'. 'One thing in Tom Jamieson's life that had not just changed his diary but also affected things that had previously mattered a great deal to him is the reason we're here. The new thing was being elected to membership of a book club. Tom Jamieson was the man who replaced Bryce in the Justified Sinners book club.'

22

These days, Jason felt different about spending the day in the National Library of Scotland. Until he'd joined the HCU, he'd never been inside the imposing building that dominated the east side of George IV Bridge. Truth to tell, he'd felt intimidated by the very frontage, with its seven larger-than-life statues apparently floating in deep bays in the facade, below inscrutable carved insignias representing who knew what.

But Karen had noticed Jason had an eye for detail that trumped his lack of intellectual heft. It was, she believed, part of her job to identify the individual skills of her team and work with them to enhance their strengths. And then to exploit them to the greater success of the HCU. So she'd exposed Jason to the wonders of research in assorted databases and the National Library, particularly in the resource of its newspaper archive.

That morning, he'd summoned the bound volumes of a selection of Scottish newspapers for the year before the Independence Referendum of 2014. It didn't really matter which titles he selected; hardly any of the Scottish press was an advocate of independence, so they'd all have been more than happy to pick up on big-ticket fundraisers – on the Yes side, to have a go at the spendthrift nationalists who were demonstrating how they'd squander the country's cash if they won; on the No side, to praise the truly patriotic Scots who were willing to put their hands in their pockets to ensure they remained in the union with the rest of the UK.

Jason had still been a teenager – just – when the referendum had happened. He was more interested in football and girls and his new career as a probationary constable working the beat; politics had barely registered on his radar. But a dozen years on, and under the tutelage of Karen – and his girlfriend Meera – he'd grown to take more of an interest. Now, he was actually looking forward to getting stuck into this task.

But inevitably, there was a delay while the library staff located his requested items and ferried them to him from the stacks in the floors below. Jason hoped that was where they were; he knew from his own experience, as well as what Meera had told him, how much material was stored off site. It was, she'd explained, the peril of being a Legal Deposit Library, charged with holding a copy of everything published in the UK and the Republic of Ireland. Every day, there were deliveries of books, magazines, newspapers, pamphlets, maps and other assorted printed material. In spite of the advent of the digital world, a daily deluge of paper still flowed into the library. More than two thousand items a week, Meera had said. He couldn't even imagine what that looked like. Even if they shelved every wall of their flat, there would still be overspill, he reckoned. So it wasn't surprising he had to wait.

The weather was dismal, which discouraged a sortie into

the city. He'd already had enough coffee, which ruled out the café. Jason mentally reran the morning briefing and realised the boss had more to do this morning than to chase up Linda Lawrence, the photographer who had been the fourth member of Sam Nimmo's agency team. Maybe he could help out there?

He started with Google, soon discovering what Karen had already learned – Ukraine and more recently, Gaza had been her beats. She'd been working with a refugee charity in Khan Younis. It was, he thought, a good route into finding stories that would touch a nerve beyond the Middle East. But there was no sign of her having published anything in the past five weeks. When the tenuous ceasefire had been in place, had Linda Lawrence moved on? Was she in another hellish war zone? Or had she stepped sideways from death and destruction to recover? He didn't think anyone could blame her if she had.

He started to check out which titles had most recently published her work. He soon noticed she'd worked with the same journalist a few times over recent months; their joint features had appeared in three different news magazines that still ran photo essays. Two were in France, one in Germany. As far as he could work out, with the help of Google Translate, all three pieces were about the spread of extreme right-wing politics seeping into the mainstream.

It looked as if Linda Lawrence was covering a different kind of war now.

Jason made a note of the name on the byline and turned to the socials on his phone. He struck gold on Instagram. There was a story posted by the journalist about an AfD rally the previous evening in Rostock; it was clear that the writer and photographer had been undercover, but Linda was tagged at the bottom of the story. @FindingLinda.

It looked like he'd done just that.

The Gordons' reactions to Karen's words were wildly different. Mrs Gordon flushed and said, 'That's ridiculous!'

Her son shrugged. 'Nothing about that lot would surprise me.' Karen wasn't certain whether his comment was based on anything significant or if it was simply attention-seeking behaviour. He could wait, she thought.

'Don't get me wrong, Mrs Gordon. I'm not suggesting anyone in the book group was responsible for Tom Jamieson's death. Or your husband's, come to that. It's simply that we need to form as full a picture as we can of Tom Jamieson's contacts and the Justified Sinners seems to have been important to him. I'll be honest, we're clutching at straws here.' Karen produced her most apologetic smile.

Mrs Gordon remained unmollified. 'I no more knew the details of the Justified Sinners than Bryce knew the names of the women in my Pilates group. We did many things together, Chief Inspector, but we also had our own interests.'

'He didn't have any paperwork relating to his membership?'

'It wasn't that sort of club. It was a group of like-minded men who came together to share what they were reading and enjoyed each other's company. It was about friendship, and helping each other out when they could.'

'How do you mean, "helping each other out"?'

'Nothing sinister, I can assure you.' There was an faint note of exasperation in Mrs Gordon's voice. 'Bryce said that friends in the group had put a couple of projects his way, that's all.'

'Saved him having to tender for them, he said,' Gavin chipped in.

His mother cut across him. 'Don't presume to talk about things you know nothing about, Gavin. Inspector, I really can't help you any further.'

'Mrs Gordon, all we know is that the club meets on the second Thursday of the month. We don't know who belonged to it. We don't even know where it meets, except that it's somewhere in the New Town. Any information at all would be helpful at this stage.'

The woman shook her head. 'I'm not being difficult. I just don't know.'

Daisy leaned in. 'Cast your mind back, if you will. He never mentioned any wee details about the venue? Or the other members?'

'I said, didn't I?' Her tone was becoming hostile again.

Gavin leaned back in his chair and exhaled noisily. 'I might just be able to help,' he said loftily, as if this was almost beneath his dignity.

The three women's heads turned to face him. 'How do you know anything about this?' his mother demanded.

'I scrounged a lift from him one night. He said he was going into town and I asked if he could drop me off. He said he was going to Stockbridge, if that was any good to me. As it happened, I was meeting friends up the hill, in Thistle Street, so he extended the cab journey after it dropped him off.'

'He was always generous about things like that,' his mother said.

'Where did he get out?' Karen asked.

'That short street that runs from Ann Street to Danube Street. At the Water of Leith end. I don't know what it's called. I watched him head up the path to the topmost house. Number eight.'

'Well remembered,' Daisy said.

Gavin gave her a superior smile. 'I knew it was his fancy book club night. I expected them to hang out in some arsey New Town club, not a private house.' He shrugged. 'Though I suppose that might not have been his final destination. Maybe he was just hooking up with another one of the bookworms for a quick dram before they hit the books.'

It was a start, thought Karen. 'And you're sure that was his book club night? Not just a casual get-together for a drink with a friend? Or a business colleague?'

Gavin rolled his eyes. 'Well, duh. Of course I'm sure. It was like a religious observance, the book club. Second Thursday of the month. He never missed it. We even had to schedule our holidays around it. You remember, Mum? That time in Tuscany, back when I was still at the school? He flew back two days before us so he wouldn't miss it. You were really pissed off.'

Mrs Gordon pursed her lips. 'You do exaggerate, Gavin. I was just sad because we'd been having such a lovely time, and it was always a struggle to get your father to take a proper holiday.'

His grin was wolfish and irritating. 'Like I said, really pissed off.' He pushed his chair back. 'If that's all, I've got things to do.'

Karen stood up, neatly moving between him and the door. 'Did you see anyone else at the house? Walking up behind your father, or opening the door?'

He sighed. 'It's a pretty short path, there was nobody on my dad's heels. And I didn't see the door open. We'd pulled away by that time. Sorry, Detective, you're going to have to do some detecting.' He stood up and sidestepped round her on his way out of the room.

Mrs Gibson sighed. 'I apologise for my son's rudeness. I know it sounds silly, but it's as if he hasn't forgiven his father for dying on us.'

Karen understood exactly what she meant. Mostly what she felt about Phil was a deep sadness at what she'd lost, but sometimes the burn of anger caught her unawares. Since she'd grown close to Rafiq, that had happened less. But still there were moments when she was engulfed by the rage that Phil wasn't there to share some moment of joy or sorrow or frustration. 'It's hard to lose a parent at any age. But when you're young enough to still need them as a parent, it's worse,' she said. 'I'm sorry we were the cause of him being upset.'

Mrs Gordon looked startled, as if the last thing she'd expected from a polis was empathy. 'Yes, well,' she said.

'Does your son's description of your husband's destination mean anything to you? Do you recognise the house? Or know anyone he'd be visiting in that part of Stockbridge?'

She shook her head. 'We used to have some friends in Ann Street, but they moved across the park to Inverleith.'

The well had definitely run dry, Karen thought. 'If you think of anything that might be relevant, even if it seems trivial, let us know.'

Daisy stood up and together they followed Victoria Gordon to the front door, Karen marvelling again at the space and the decor. By the time they got into the car, Daisy was already checking Google Maps for the location Gavin Gordon had described. 'Upper Dean Terrace,' she announced.

'I'll message Jason and get him on to it. Finding out who

lives there is right up his street.' But as she took out her phone to send the text, she saw he had beaten her to the draw on coming up with fresh information. Linda Lawrence is working undercover in Germany she read. Trying to track down where exactly. She grinned. Jason was showing he really did deserve his sergeant's stripes.

23

Karen arranged to regroup with Daisy and Jason back in the HCU office in the morning. After they'd left the Gordons' house, she'd put a call in to the only architect she knew well enough to ask a favour. She'd met Tavish Adam when he'd worked pro bono on Aleppo, the Syrian café Karen had helped get off the ground down in Leith. When Covid came along and scuppered so many small businesses, Tavish had clung on by his fingernails, due in no small part to the goodwill his efforts at Aleppo had garnered. He was a man to whom a problem was only ever a challenge; Karen had recognised in that a kindred spirit and they'd taken to meeting up in a variety of bars in Leith where the cocktails suited their taste. It was a constant source of amusement to Karen that mixologists had come to resemble chefs. As soon as their reputation spread and customers began to flock to sample their concoctions, another venue would poach them and the merry-go-round would begin again.

When he answered his phone, Karen was confused by strange background noises before he spoke. A couple of clacks, a thud, then a metallic shiver followed by a clink. 'Hi, Karen,' he said softly. 'Gimme a minute.' And muted her.

When he spoke again, he was his usual ebullient self. 'Sorry about that.'

'Where are you?'

He chuckled. 'Snooker club. More than my life's worth to disturb a client when they've got a difficult shot on. Talk quickly, I'll be due back on the table before you can say, "pot black".'

'OK. Can we meet up? I'd like to buy you a coffee.'

'I'll be done here in half an hour. I'm nowhere near Aleppo though. Meet me in FIKA. You know it?'

'Dundas Street?'

'That's right, corner of Great King Street. Should satisfy your soul's coffee craving.'

Tavish was already in possession of a table and a cup of what looked like a decent double espresso. He was absorbed in the *Edinburgh Reporter*, a free sheet whose coverage of the city gave *The Scotsman* a run for its money. Karen ordered herself a flat white then took a moment to check him out. Since she'd seen him last, he'd acquired a pair of oversized round glasses with cloudy white frames. He'd always borne a faint resemblance to an owl, with his small pointed nose and cupid's bow mouth; now the comparison was irresistible. His brown tweed jacket and chocolate-coloured polo neck sweater only enhanced the similarity.

He folded the paper up as she sat down and grinned at her, destroying the illusion. 'Hey, girl, how're you doing?' he asked, cheery as always. He'd grown up in a cottage in the Borders, the only son of a painter and a potter, both moderately successful. As far as Karen could make out, his childhood had been a ridiculous idyll. Because his parents hadn't fallen into the middle-class Edinburgh habit of sending their offspring to private schools, he'd developed the survival skills of the state sector and avoided the attitudes that often set Karen's teeth on edge. He'd been nudged into the Aleppo project because his work on the transformation of a Victorian workhouse into social housing was coming to an end and he was up for working with the Syrian refugees.

'My great-grandmother was a refugee,' he'd told her. 'She escaped the Turkish genocide in Armenia and arrived here at the end of the First World War with the clothes she stood up in and a gold bracelet sewn into the hem of her coat. I wonder whether that's where Coco Chanel got the idea of stitching a gold chain into her jacket hems to make them hang properly.'

'I doubt the hang of her coat was on your great-granny's mind,' Karen had said. They'd laughed, and that had been the start of a friendship.

'No' bad,' she said, with the traditional Fife grudging understatement. 'Been worse. You?'

He grinned. 'I've just landed a lovely job out Haddington way. A wee Georgian gem that's been thoroughly neglected. Happily it's been bought by a lassie who wants to restore it, not rip it back to the bare walls and start again.'

'Right up your street.'

'It was her I was just playing snooker with. She's a demon with the cue. Luckily there's room enough for a full-sized table in her new house.' He gave a mischievous wink. 'She'll have to lose the dining room, though. Unless I can work out some kind of up-and-over cover . . .' His voice drifted off and his eyes lost focus momentarily. 'But that's not why we're here. What gives?'

'I'm looking for a bit of background. It's a tangent to a case

I'm working. What do you know about an architect called Bryce Gordon?'

His eyebrows rose. 'I know he's dead. Which I suspect is not news to you?'

'I'm interested in the period when he was alive.'

'I thought you might be. I never knew the guy, we moved in different periods. He was very much a Modernist but he wasn't really part of any one school. Do you know the Maggie's Cancer Centre in Kirkcaldy?'

'Of course, that's where I grew up.'

Tavish nodded. 'I'd forgotten that. Well, he took inspiration from that for some of his domestic architecture. Lucky Zaha Hadid's dead or she'd have come after him for copying her.' That grin again.

'So apart from nicking other people's ideas, what do you know about him?'

'We all do that in this game. Only, we call it standing on the shoulders of giants. But seriously. He had a rep for doing good work. His buildings didn't leak or develop cracks or have creaky floors. Or gimmicky plumbing. You wouldn't believe the number of designers who try to reinvent the wheel. Or in this case, the flush. Bryce Gordon, though, he did a good job.'

'Successful, then?'

'Very.' He gave her a slightly cagey look. 'Before he died, he was a bit of a golden boy.'

Karen sipped her coffee, waiting for him to continue. But he said nothing, leaving it to her to probe. 'How do you mean, Tavish? You just said, he was known for doing good work.'

He sighed. 'That's not enough though, is it? You've got to have the right contacts in the right places. There are hoops to jump through, mountains to climb, nimbys to massage. You don't just get to breeze in and say, "You want a new headquarters building just off the Newbridge Roundabout? I'm your man. Izzy wizzy, let's get busy."'

'I get that. So you're saying Bryce Gordon had a magic wand?'

A one-shouldered shrug. 'Most of us spend a ridiculous amount of time trying to get projects through boardrooms, council planning committees. Sometimes even public inquiries. Gordon was more successful than most.'

The implication was there. Karen picked it up and ran with it. 'You saying there was dirty work at the crossroads?'

Tavish stood up. 'I need more coffee.'

She watched him as he crossed to the counter and ordered his brew. He moved confidently, as he always had, sure of his place in the world. It was unlike Tavish Adam to step sideways to avoid the direction of travel in a conversation. When he'd been working with the Syrians on the Aleppo project, he'd never been shy to take up the cudgels on their behalf to make the café the kind of space they wanted it to be. But Bryce Gordon was making him uncomfortable and she wanted to know why.

He returned to the table and placed his cup down carefully, back to his usual composed cheerful self. 'That's better,' he said. 'Never have serious conversations when under-caffeinated. So, Gordon's magic wand. I'm not accusing anyone of corruption here, let's be clear. I have no knowledge that money or lavish foreign holidays changed hands. And sometimes in our game, success begets success. Like, after Zaha Hadid designed the Maggie Centre in Kirkcaldy, it dawned on lots of organisations that a world-class architect might not be out of their reach after all.

Everybody wanted her – or at least her studio – to give them a beautiful building that came ready-festooned with reputation. So a good name will get you a long way. But I will say that Gordon managed to get the go-ahead for surprising buildings in places most of us wouldn't even attempt.'

'Like?'

He pulled his phone out of his jacket pocket and raised one finger to pause her while he interrogated its screen. Then he turned it on its side and passed it across. Karen saw a wide pavilion with a central tower of curved glass panels in an astonishing abstract pattern of blues, greens and aqua, shot through with comet trails of scarlet and purple. It was spectacular. 'That's beautiful,' she said.

'You should see it at night. It blazes across the Assynt sky like a weird version of the Northern Lights.' He reached for the phone and expanded the area the screen covered. In one corner, a rocky cove was exposed with a narrow sandy beach.

'What's not to love?' Karen said. 'I'd go there for my holidays.'

'But it's right in the heart of a key geoheritage area. You could maybe justify it if it was some sort of field-trip centre, or a base for studying the environment. But it's not. It's a private house. It's owned by some impenetrable trust. The clever money says there's some American tech bro behind it. One of their bunkers for when the end of the world comes around, if they've not made it to Mars in time.'

'And it just sits there, empty?' Incredulous, Karen stared at Tavish.

'Mostly. Five years since it was built, it gets used a couple of times a year. Every now and again, a bunch of American yahoos rock up in a fleet of massive SUVs and spend a few days drinking and feasting on venison and salmon and going for wee walks. Or so I'm told. Your ex, Hamish Mackenzie? His hobby gin distillery supplies them with spirits. He could tell you better than me what the story is.'

Karen scoffed. She'd have to speak to him first and she didn't think that would be happening any time soon. 'I always thought he'd eventually get round to capitalising on his years in the States. I'm surprised they used a Scottish architect, not some Californian wunderkind.'

Tavish pushed his glasses up his nose and frowned. 'I doubt a foreigner could have got the planning permission through. It would have needed a particular kind of pull. Being able to trumpet it as "Scottish talent in a unique synergy with the landscape"?' He enclosed his sentence in finger-quotes. 'That'd stand a better chance. I know I'd never have got a project like that off the ground.' He grinned. 'But that's not my kind of schtick anyway.'

'Do you think Bryce Gordon was dodgy, then?'

He sighed. 'I don't think he was one of the bad guys, I never heard that about him. But he certainly knew people who could put him in the right place at the right time. We all need a helping hand and he must have had one or two in high places.'

'How high? Are we talking local government? Or higher?'

He drained his cup. 'Not for me to say, Karen. Maybe just big money. You know how that talks. Starts in a whisper but if it faces opposition, it shouts loudest. I don't know who Bryce Gordon hung out with, but whoever they were, they had access to the right ears.'

'Had he always been the golden boy, Tavish?'

He paused, cocking his head as he thought. Slowly, he said, 'He used to be in partnership with a couple of other guys. But he split off on his own about eight years ago and that's when he really started to make a name for himself.'

'How do you think that happened?'

He puffed his lips out in a long breath. 'Karen, I never gave Bryce Gordon that much thought. Like I said, we moved in different worlds. If you pressed me, I'd guess his partners weren't in tune with the direction he wanted to go in.'

'Or maybe they didn't like his route map?'

His eyes met hers in a level stare. 'It's possible. Karen, why are you so interested in this? Are you thinking maybe his fatal accident wasn't an accident after all?' He scoffed. 'Come on, girl. This is architecture we're talking about, not drug running or people smuggling. I know folk in the New Town sometimes feel murderous about their neighbours' renovations, but they don't actually act on it.'

Karen forced a smile. 'Don't be daft. Like I said, it was a tangent in another investigation. You know me, Tavish. Give me a loose end and I've got to unravel the whole jumper. I don't think you've got anything to worry about. Nobody's running about Edinburgh bumping off architects because they don't like their work. If they cared that much, there are a few buildings in the city centre that would have been blown up by now.'

He laughed. 'I can think of one or two right off the top of my head. You're right, of course. Sometimes an accident is just an accident.'

As she set off for home, Karen reflected on their conversation. At the start of the day, it hadn't crossed her mind that Bryce Gordon was anything other than a victim of an RTA. Now she wasn't so sure.

24

Warriston Path, Victoria Path, Newhaven Road; Karen was oblivious to her surroundings as she walked home from her meeting with Tavish. Past cemeteries, through parks, alongside busy roads, her mind was turning over what they'd learned that day, looking at it from every angle. That morning, both cases had resembled a jigsaw puzzle with pieces missing. But now the circumstances surrounding Tom Jamieson's death seemed more like a kaleidoscope. Each time she gave it a shake, the pattern took on a different shape. Was his death really an accident? Was Marcus Nicol the mysterious man in the hoodie? And if so, was he intentionally following Jamieson? And why? Or was it the kind of coincidence Karen instinctively distrusted? Were the Justified Sinners nothing more than a book club playing at bigging themselves up? Or were they a cover story for something more sinister? Or both?

Too many questions, and no answers by the time she reached home, hungry and cold. She took a pizza – fennel salami and mozzarella – from the freezer and turned on the oven. She had just enough time to cook and eat it before she was due to FaceTime Rafiq. He'd have finished his surgical list for the day so he could take a break to talk to her before writing up his notes. Inevitably, that would make her feel better.

He was, as ever, punctual. On the stroke of eight, there he was, still in scrubs, minus hat and mask, his brown eyes crinkling in a smile, a lock of dark hair falling across his forehead. No matter how often he pushed it back into place, it fell like a comma above his left eyebrow. Karen's spirits lifted at the sight of him. He raised a hand in greeting, wiggling his fingers at her. She couldn't help the grin that spread across her face. 'It's good to see you.'

'You too, always. How was your day?'

'Busy, trying to unravel two cases at once. I'm so glad we've got Daisy on the team now, it takes a lot of the pressure off. The Scottish rules about corroboration in interviews meant we used to waste a lot of time when it was just me and Jason. An extra body means one of us can get on with research while the other two are out and about talking to people, taking witness statements and the like.'

He nodded. 'But of course the work expands to occupy the extra capacity.'

'Always. And you? What kind of day have you had?'

He grimaced. 'Also busy. Two patients, three knee re-placements. It felt a bit like a conveyor belt.'

'But at least you get to ply your trade.' There was a pause while they both drank each other in. 'I swear, you look better every time I see you.'

He pulled a face and turned his head so she could see his temples. 'Not true, there is more silver among the dark hair with every week that passes. And I feel it in my hips when I spend seven hours straight in the operating theatre.'

Karen ran a hand through her own thick mop of brown

hair. 'And me still in my prime. You're getting the best end of the bargain.'

He laughed. 'I can't deny that. Having you in my life, that feels like a bargain I never expected.'

'Somewhere in your youth or childhood . . .' she teased.

He frowned. 'I don't understand?'

Another one of those cultural references that tripped them up from time to time, in both directions. Somehow, it never felt like an unbridgeable distance. 'It's from a classic film, *The Sound of Music*. Two people from very different backgrounds whose paths cross and they fall in love. It's a musical, so they have to have a duet where they sing about how extraordinary it is that they found each other.'

'You should sing it to me.' His smile was wry; he'd heard Karen's attempt at singing when he'd shown her around Montreal and she'd been moved to launch into Leonard Cohen's paean to Our Lady of the Harbour.

'Maybe not, I don't want to send you running for the hills. So, tell me, what excitements have you got planned for us for next month? I can get away from Thursday to Tuesday in the last week.'

'I thought we could go to Quebec City? You liked it so much there when we went last year.'

And they were off, making the kind of plans that kept Karen's spirits up in the grimmest days of a murder inquiry. Hamish had been fun to be with, but with Rafiq, their pleasure felt as if it had a solid foundation. She couldn't wait for the day when he'd get his Canadian passport and he could apply for a work permit. She'd walked along the front at Portobello after her drink with Keir Stevens the previous evening, imagining the two of them living in one of the houses that faced the Firth of Forth, watching sunrises over Fife. It felt like a dream that could come true.

In a job like Karen's, there had to be some light at the end of the tunnel.

25

When Karen arrived in the office next morning, Daisy and the Mint were both wiping sugar and crumbs from their faces. Karen dived straight into business. 'I know we felt Drew Jamieson came to us with a bee in his bonnet about his brother's death. Probably watched too many Scandi crime dramas—'

'Do they get Scandi crime dramas in New Zealand?' Daisy interrupted. 'Is it not all *Lord of the Rings*?'

'Or Aussie ones, like where they found all those bodies in barrels?' This from Jason.

'For pity's sake,' Karen exploded. 'Have you two had too much sugar this morning?' She gestured at the empty paper bags strewn on their desks. 'I'm trying to make a point here. At the beginning of this, I thought we'd be going through the motions, taking a look at the file, maybe chatting to the boyfriend and the boss and putting it back to bed where it belonged. But the more we dig into this Justified Sinners business, it feels like there's a lot more going on.'

'What makes you think that, boss?' Jason asked, nervous.

'We keep hitting brick walls. And that always makes me suspicious. We only found out what they call themselves because Daisy thought to ask Jayden if they had a name. Turns out it comes from a book written two hundred years ago by a guy called James Hogg. *The Private Memoirs and Confessions of a Justified Sinner*, it's called. Not a very catchy title, but it caught on all the same. The basic idea is that if you were one of God's chosen ones, the elect, you could do what the hell you liked on earth because your place in heaven was guaranteed. Right up to and including murder.'

Jason gawped. 'And folk believed that?'

Daisy scoffed. 'Sure they did. Same as they believe Donald Trump is the finest president America ever had.'

'Not that I'm suggesting they're naturally a bunch of crooks. On its own, it's mibbes no big deal, just a private joke among a bunch of guys who think they're a bit special. But if that's all it is, why all the secrecy? The only reason we know where they have their monthly meetings is that Bryce Gordon's son Gavin happened to be in the room when we were talking to his mother. And he couldn't resist the chance to show off that he knew more than she did about where his dad disappeared off to on the second Thursday of the month.'

'So now we've got an address,' Daisy said. 'I made a detour on my way home last night and swung by the street Gavin described to us. Upper Dean Terrace. Number eight is a three-storey Georgian townhouse with a basement. Classic Stockbridge. If you wanted to buy one like it, you'd need to win *Who Wants to Be a Millionaire*, and then some. The shutters were closed, so I couldn't catch a glimpse of the inhabitants.'

'You weren't the only one doing a bit of digging,' Karen said, 'I checked the electoral roll. No surprise, but they've withheld their name from the public register. So I looked up the Land Registry Service and coughed up three quid to find out who owns the property.' She paused, keeping them dangling.

'Who is it, then?' Daisy demanded.

'Somebody I'd never heard of. Hugh Grieve. Ring any bells?'

Daisy looked at Jason, who seemed to have as much of a clue as she did. 'Never heard of him,' she said. Followed immediately by an anxious, 'Should I have?'

Jason was already busy on the keyboard. 'There's a Hugh Grieve who's a director of Brochan Enterprises. Registered offices in Braemar. Do you think that's him?'

'I wouldn't be surprised.' Karen gave a snort of incredulity. 'You know what brochan is?' Again, she was met with two shaken heads. 'It's a word for oatmeal porridge but it's more like thin gruel than the creamy stuff you get for brunch around the city.' With a pang, she remembered the steaming bowls Hamish used to concoct, laden with fruit and spices and nut butters. 'Think peasant food.'

'That doesn't sound like a get-rich-quick scheme,' Daisy said. 'I mean, I know we're all supposed to be getting back to simplicity in our diets, but I'm not even remotely tempted by a plate of gruel.'

Jason, king of the bacon roll, chipped in, not to be outdone by Daisy. 'Me and Meera went to see *Oliver!* down in Leith a while back and they were singing about gruel. It sounded like something you'd have to be starving to fancy.'

Karen rolled her eyes. 'What does the web say about Brochan Enterprises?'

Jason wasted no time. 'Brochan Enterprises ... There's an address ...' He fiddled with the trackpad and the keys.

'OK. It's on a road heading out of the village. Not far from the Highland Gathering site, according to this. But it turns into a private road so that's where Google Street View runs out.' He turned the screen round to show Karen and Daisy. 'It's hard to tell but the only building in sight looks like one of those timber-clad kits you get from Norway or Sweden. It's not like an office or a factory, more like a house. Or a holiday place.'

'Right in the middle of Royal Deeside,' Karen mused. 'Plenty of money around there. Castles and big houses galore. Not to mention the visitors. Government ministers and foreign dignitaries.'

'And not to mention the scumbags Prince Andrew invites to Balmoral,' Daisy muttered.

'What does Brochan Enterprises actually do?' Karen said. 'Any clues?'

Now Daisy was at her keyboard, determined not to be outdone by Jason. She knew she was supposed to be the smart one, after all, Karen thought, amused at the rivalry that kept them both on their toes. 'According to their website, they work with innovators to bring emerging technologies to the marketplace.' She scoffed. 'Which tells us the square root of bugger all. Let's see what "About us" has to say . . . OK. No names, it just says "their experienced financial team invests in creative thinkers who are willing to go the extra mile".'

'Interesting,' Karen said. 'It could be anything from anonymous tech bros to international drug runners.'

'In Stockbridge?' Daisy sounded incredulous.

Jason weighed in. 'Well, when you think about it, Stockbridge has one thing in common with drug dealers.' Both women raised their eyebrows. 'Loads of big

SUVs that never get a speck of mud on them,' he said triumphantly.

Karen laughed. 'Good point, well made. Either way, we need to find out more about Mr Gruel. Any pix of him online? Anything on the socials? Daisy, see what you can dig up on Brochan or Grieve himself.' She turned to Jason. From the minute she'd walked in, she'd seen he was in a state of poorly suppressed excitement. It had been cruel not to unwrap the reason for that, but she'd wanted to push on with what was in the front of her mind before it slipped away. 'How did you get on with the papers?'

'I've found three big-ticket "No" campaign fundraisers – Edinburgh, a castle in Perthshire and another one in Aberdeenshire. And there was one really sniffy story in *The Scotsman* about a "Yes" ball. They clearly didn't get across the door, so there's only a couple of snatched pix of people getting out of their motors.'

'Where was this?'

'Glasgow.' He checked his notebook. 'Fraoch House. Over on the Southside, near the Royal Infirmary. Hosted by Lord Haig Striven-Douglass, younger son of the Marquess of Fr ... Fry ...'

'Friockheim,' Karen finished. 'I know it looks weird but it's pronounced Freak-'em.' She frowned, searching her memory. 'Back then, Striven-Douglass owned a record label. Ran a few indie bands, I seem to recall.' Slowly, the wheels kept turning. 'He was a big noise in the Greens. Had something to do with Save Scotland's Shores.'

'So were they big independence supporters back then, the Greens?' This from Daisy.

Karen had to remind herself that the Indy Ref had been more than a decade ago. Jason would have had no interest in it, and Daisy would have been too busy studying for her Highers. She couldn't realistically expect them to be familiar with the personalities or the loyalties at the heart of the campaign. 'The Greens were part of the loose coalition that was pro-Indy, yes.'

'I thought all the landed gentry supported staying in the union?' He could still surprise her, Karen thought.

'Mostly they did. I think Lord Friockheim was a unionist.'

'But somehow Striven-Douglass talked the old man into letting him have the use of Fraoch House for a fundraiser.'

Karen nodded. 'And a year later, Friockheim and his elder son were dead and Haig had inherited the lot.'

'Sheesh,' said Daisy. 'What happened?'

'Johnny Striven-Douglass OD'd on heroin at a party in London, and his father collapsed with a massive stroke when he heard the news. He never recovered. So Haig inherited the title and the stuff that goes with it.'

Light dawned on Jason's face. 'I remember that, it was all over the papers. I just forgot the name, it's like my brain just beeped over it.'

'Like the Russian names in Dostoyevsky,' Daisy said.

Karen rolled her eyes, wondering whether they'd ever grow out of their attempts at one-upmanship. 'OK, well done, Jason. What I want you to do—'

'There's something else, boss. While I was waiting for the newspapers to come up from the stacks, I did a wee bit of digging to see if I could get a fix on what Linda Lawrence is covering in Germany. It turns out she's undercover with the AfD. That's the German far right party, pretty much neo-Nazi.'

'They came second in the latest elections,' Daisy said.

'Everybody says they're a real threat to democracy in Germany.'

'I got hold of the journalist who wrote the story with Linda,' Jason continued doggedly. 'He was pretty cagey about her. He wouldn't tell me where she was based, just that she's deep undercover. He didn't even want to pass on a message to her.'

'How did you leave it?' Karen asked.

'I said I thought she'd want to know we'd found Sam Nimmo. I didn't want to say any more than that – I thought that might be enough to push her into making contact. I left your number.'

'Good thinking. I guess all we can do is hope that the message gets through and she cares enough to break cover. If she contacts Keir Stevens rather than me, I'm pretty sure he'll tell me, but I'll mark his card just in case. In the meantime, I want to know who these Justified Sinners are. If they stick to their usual pattern, they should be meeting this Thursday. We need to be prepped for that. Jason, I want you staking out the house, snapping anybody who goes in or out. Daisy, you're with me. We'll let them settle in then we'll chap the door and ask to talk to them. Either they'll let us in and we can take names, or they'll give us the polite Stockbridge version of "get tae fuck".'

'Or Hugh Grieve might invite us in and keep us at arm's length from his guests. A house like that, there'll be more than one reception room,' Daisy said, an atypical note of gloom in her voice.

'One way or another, we'll have made some progress. And Jason, check out the Friockheim party. See if you can find out the names of any of the guests. If something bad did happen, there's bound to be gossip. Nothing in this country is safe from social media, there'll be—' Karen's phone abruptly cut across her words. Seeing Keir Stevens' name on the screen, she said, 'Talk of the devil. I have to take this.'

As soon as she accepted the call, Keir Stevens spoke. 'I went back through my old notebooks. I think I've got something that might interest you.'

26

Karen drove to Livingston, Jason in the passenger seat. She wanted to pick his brains en route and she didn't entirely trust him to focus on two things simultaneously. Keir Stevens hadn't wanted to go into detail on the phone, but he'd said enough to make Karen realise she didn't know enough about gambling scams to ask the right questions.

'I understand the point of trying to fix sporting events,' she said. 'You bet on the unlikely outcome and you bribe one side to lose. I see how it works in something like golf or tennis or snooker where you can throw a match without it looking too dodgy. But I just don't get how you make it work in football. Or rugby.'

Jason sighed. 'You really don't know much about betting, do you?'

'I'm like a lot of folk – I bet once a year on the Grand National. I put a fiver on a horse that I like the name of. Maybe it reminds me of a place I went on my holidays or a film I loved. Nine times out of ten, I lose my money but every now and again, I win a few quid.'

Jason chuckled. 'It's not folk like you that have the bookies worried. It's the ones that work out how to beat the system. Betting's got so complicated now that there are more ways to beat the odds. Your serious gamblers, they don't just bet on which team's going to win a match. They bet on who's going to score a goal, whether a goalie can keep a clean sheet, when a goal's going to be scored.'

'How can they know when a goal's going to be scored?' Karen was bemused.

'Say you've got a goalie in your pocket. You'll lay a bet that he's going to concede a goal in the first fifteen minutes of the second half. And lo and behold, he lets one in. We've all seen those goals when everybody goes, "What the actual? How did he not stop that, my granny could have stopped that without her glasses on." That's just one example. Here's another one. The gambler bets that a particular player's going to be sent off in the last quarter of the game. And suddenly the guy gets into a ruck for no reason, the red mist supposedly descends and bingo! Off he goes, knowing that he'll be trousering a pay-off that'll more than cover the fine he gets from his club. We're talking big money here, boss.'

Karen was becoming uncomfortable about the extent of Jason's knowledge. 'How come you know so much about this, Jason?'

He gave her a sideways look. 'My dad likes a flutter. It's the main reason my mum kicked him out. She couldn't stand the uncertainty of not knowing whether we'd be flush or skint every week. I've seen her literally going through all our pockets looking for enough to put some tea on the table.' His voice grew subdued, as it always did when he spoke of his beloved mother, snatched from them by the Covid pandemic.

'Sandra was some woman. It takes nerve to end a marriage.' Karen had often thought of the Murray family as a living exemplar of the Jekyll and Hyde story. Sandra and Jason, trying to do the right thing, constantly thwarted by his big brother Ronan and their dad, always looking for the easy way out, regardless of the finer points of the law. She'd never met his father, but she'd gathered enough over the years to know he was less than a model husband.

'Aye, well.' He sighed. 'I picked up a lot about betting, just being around my dad.'

'It's a mug's game, though, right?'

'Not if you're a bookie.' A long silence. Then he said, 'And then there's spread betting. That works best with a high-scoring sport like rugby or basketball. Especially if one team's the hot favourite. So you bet on the gap between the winner and the loser. Say it's the rugby, and you think Scotland will beat England by ten points. So you might bet a spread between seven and thirteen points. If you're right, you win. If you're way off beam, you lose. Honest, boss, you can bet on anything. There was a guy at the end of the eighties who bet an accumulator—'

'What's that?'

'You bet on several different things, and the odds multiply the more there are. So he bet on things that he believed were going to happen before the millennium. I can't remember them all, but there were half a dozen different things – Cliff Richard getting a knighthood, *EastEnders* still being a BBC soap, U2 still being a band, that kind of thing. Anyway, they all happened and he got nearly two hundred grand for a £30 stake.'

'But you only know about that result because it's so gobsmacking,' Karen objected. 'Surely there must be dozens, if not hundreds, of folk who do bets like these and never win a penny?'

Jason grinned. 'You can see them every afternoon in the bookies. They've bet on an accumulator, the first three horses have come up and they're watching the fourth race and their horse is going gangbusters, but it runs out of gas on the last furlong and the punters just about burst into tears as they see their payday go up in smoke.'

Karen sighed. 'I just don't understand it. Everybody knows the house always wins. How can you not know that?'

Jason shrugged. 'I don't get it either but I grew up in a house where my dad was always convinced the next bet would be the one that would lift us out of the back streets of Kirkcaldy into . . .' He spread his hands. 'I don't know. The sunshine, mibbes. Every now and again he'd try to knock it on the head, then he'd hear something like that couple down in Ayrshire that won more than a hundred and fifty million on the Eurolottery and he'd go, "That could be us, Sandra," and off he'd go to the supermarket and blow a week's wages on lottery tickets. I tell you, after she got him to move out, our life ran a lot more level.'

'I had no idea. You never said.'

'My mum was ashamed, I think. That's why she got so upset when Ronan got into bother with the law. She was scared he was going down the same road as my dad.'

Jason's brother had ended up spending the best part of two years behind bars for assaulting a nurse and a doctor while impersonating a police officer. It would have been a lot longer if the sheriff hadn't taken pity on him for the death of his mother in the Covid ward he'd been trying to burst into. 'What's he doing now – Ronan?'

'He's driving a lorry. Long distance. He does a lot of trips to the continent.' His mouth closed in a tight line. Karen didn't want to think too closely about what Ronan was up to. With luck, nothing more serious than smuggling a few boxes of cheap fags.

'Back to the gambling. Presumably, the crooks are all about fixing the odds?'

'I would think so.'

'So, what? They'd bribe somebody to let a goal in at a pre-set time? Or a set number of times in the second half?'

'That kind of thing, yeah. It's cheaper if you go for lower league sides, obviously, because their players are not on the big money so they're easier to tempt into cheating. But there are still plenty of punters who'll bet on those games even if they're on the other side of the world.'

'Do you think these are the kind of people who'd murder a pregnant woman and an investigative journalist, Jason?'

He exhaled noisily. 'Honestly? I wouldn't have thought so. But people do end up going to jail. Conspiracy, you see? Like you're always telling me, conspiring to commit a crime often ends up landing folk with a longer sentence than actually committing the crime itself. So maybe if they'd got a big coup planned and Sam Nimmo got wind of it, there might have been a lot at stake.'

Karen nodded. Now at least she felt she had a tenuous grasp on what Keir Stevens had to offer. She followed the satnav directions to a chain Italian restaurant. When she walked in with Jason, Stevens was already set up in a booth, a substantial selection of food already arranged in front of him. Three different flavours of chicken wings, two kinds of arancini and a stack of bruschette with assorted toppings. 'I thought it would save time if I ordered some nibbles,' he said, reaching for a wing as they sat down and Karen introduced Jason.

'I'm guessing you think I'm paying,' she said, as the waitress arrived with a pint of lager.

'I am helping you with your inquiries. Seems the least you can do,' he said through a mouthful of chicken.

Jason went to reach for the arancini but the look Karen gave him made him hastily reach for a napkin instead. 'You said you thought Sam had a lead on something to do with match-fixing,' she said.

'Like I said, I went through my old notebooks. Something was niggling at the back of my mind after we spoke yesterday. And I found a shorthand note of a conversation I'd totally forgotten about. Rachel being murdered, that put everything else out of my mind.' He bit down on a bruschetta and crunched vigorously, sticking his tongue out of the corner of his mouth to capture a daud of tomato sauce that had escaped into his beard.

'And what did this note say?'

Stevens washed the bruschetta down with a swallow of lager then pulled a wing apart, expertly stripping flesh from slender bones. 'That's the problem, you see. We use a form of shorthand called Teeline. The outlines are notoriously difficult to interpret after the passage of time if you don't already know what they're about.'

'What's the point of that?' Jason beat Karen to the punch, for once.

'It's really fast and if you transcribe your quotes without too much delay, it's accurate.' Stevens reached for a couple of arancini and popped one in his mouth whole. Karen looked away, trying to hide her revulsion at the sight of the half-chewed rice ball. He swallowed and continued. 'I spent ages last night trying to make sense of it.' He sounded injured. 'I knew it was important.'

'And how did you get on?'

'Sam had stumbled across a bit of dressing-room gossip

from a couple of the lads in the Kilmarnock team, drinking mates of his. He couldn't follow it up directly himself because they'd told him when they were all a bit pissed and they panicked afterwards because they realised not many people knew about it and the guys behind it all were real heavies. They were scared if Sam followed it up, somebody would join the dots and they'd get a doing.' More lager, more chicken wings. 'These are bloody lovely, guys, you need to get stuck in.'

'What did they tell Sam, these mates of his?'

'Piecing it together from the notes I made and the distant stirring of memory, the whole thing was orchestrated by a couple of guys from Singapore and a likely lad from, I think, Irvine. Though it could maybe be Erskine.' He spread his hands in a gesture of uncertainty.

'What thing?'

'It was a betting scam. They had a couple of referees in their pocket in the Scottish lower divisions. They were waiting for the cup ties, when the wee teams face the big boys and folk get tempted by the "giant-killer" narrative. I'm not sure of the details of how it was going to work but it was basically down to the referees making some questionable decisions.'

'Nothing new there, then,' Jason said gloomily.

'There speaks a Scottish football fan,' Stevens said. 'Sam said he had enough to start us off on setting up some kind of sting. He had the names of the refs involved, but he didn't tell me. All I know is that one of them was based in the North-East, up Elgin way, and the other one in Fife.'

'No way of narrowing it down?' Karen asked.

Stevens shook his head. 'I don't see how.'

Jason chipped in. 'No idea what cup ties we're talking about?'

'No. But for it to be worthwhile, it would have had to involve one of the top teams.' He helped himself to more wings, sucking the bones clean.

'But Sam was definite about organising a sting? How would that have worked?' Karen asked.

'Pretty straightforward. He knew who the bent referees were, so we'd have set up meetings with them and pretended we were part of a betting syndicate in the Gulf or the Far East. We'd have pitched them a deal to fix a game, have it all recorded on audio and video then we'd have sat back and watched it play out before selling the story. Bob's your uncle and Fanny's your aunt.'

'But Rachel died and it never happened?'

Stevens nodded. 'That's about the size of it.'

'How much money are we talking about, Keir?' Karen leaned in.

'Organise it right, six figures, easy.'

That seemed extraordinary to Karen. 'On a match involving a lower league team that punters in East Asia would know nothing about? Really?'

'You have no idea, Detective. Have you never been in the casino late at night when the restaurants close? These guys – Chinese, Filipino, Malay – they come in and punt a hundred quid on a single number on a roulette wheel. Thirty-seven to one, that's the odds. And when they lose, they do the exact same thing again till they run out of chips. So yeah, betting on an obscure Scottish football game, that's right up their street.'

27

Karen drummed her fingers on the steering wheel. 'Well, that was frustrating,' she complained.

'And we didn't even get anything to eat,' Jason sighed.

'What kind of journalist can't even read their own notes?'

He perked up. 'I know. I don't expect anybody but me to read my scribble, but at least I can make sense of it. Still, I reckon we can find out who was on the take, boss.'

'How do you work that out, Jason?'

'So, we know what season we're looking at, right? So I can look up the cup ties, starting with Celtic and Rangers and working my way down. The local paper match reports always give the names of the match officials. A wee bit of googling and I should be able to narrow down any refs from Fife or from the Elgin area. I should be able to identify other games they've officiated at and see if there's any pattern. Are they prone to sending folk off? Controversial penalty decisions? Contested goals?'

'You think?' Karen tried not to sound incredulous. Whether it was the influence of Meera or his determination not to be outdone by Daisy, Jason was definitely turning into a serious asset to the HCU. Nobody could write him off as a dogsbody any longer. Though thankfully, he still had his moments as a comedy copper . . . 'That sounds tedious.'

He nodded, his enthusiasm obvious. 'I don't mind, it'll be worth it. And it might even lead us to Sam and Rachel's killers?'

Karen wasn't convinced, but she had to concede it was a possibility. 'One step at a time, Jason. Let's get back to the city so you can get stuck into your research.'

'What about the party inquiries I was on?'

'Leave that with me for now. I need to speak to a contact about Haig Striven-Douglass and the company he keeps. Plus we need to work out what we're going to do about interviewing Linda Lawrence.'

'Aye, and then there's the Justified Sinners to cover on Thursday. We've got a lot on our plates right now. I don't know how you keep it all straight in your head, boss.'

Karen started the engine and headed for the motorway. 'What makes you think I do?'

Daisy had to admit she was struggling with Brochan Enterprises and Hugh Grieve. The accounts filed at Companies House led her into a maze of shell companies and distant jurisdictions. Their declared turnover for consultancy work was just over £100,000, which seemed suspiciously small to her. She reckoned the plumber they'd employed to put in a new bathroom in Steph's flat had a bigger turnover, and he wasn't living in a seven-figure townhouse in Stockbridge with a lodge in Braemar on the side.

Online searches came back with next to nothing. Brochan sponsored a minor award for schoolkids who'd come up with innovative ideas in the sciences, but that was it. She even called in a favour from a university pal who'd gone into financial services; he'd never heard of Brochan or Grieve. She felt it as a personal insult that when Karen and Jason walked back into the office she had nothing to offer, especially when Jason said, 'I'll get straight on to that lead, boss,' shrugging off his jacket and attacking his keyboard.

'Sounds like you had a more productive morning than me,' Daisy grumbled, filling Karen in on her lack of progress.

'Sometimes getting nowhere is as instructive as finding the next obvious step. At least we know now what Brochan isn't. Which makes my antennae twitch. We'll maybe know more after we've staked out the book club and got across the threshold.' Unlike Jason, Karen hadn't removed her coat. 'I'm going out now to talk to someone about Haig Striven-Douglass, as was. I'll be back later. In the meantime, Daisy, see if we can get to see Linda Lawrence. We'll go over to Germany if need be, because I really want to talk to her face to face.' She put a hand on the door handle then turned back. 'And Jason – good luck with your searching.'

Daisy watched the door close behind her boss then said, 'She's in a funny mood. She'd usually so focused, but she's bouncing around like pinball today.'

He looked up. 'She gets that way sometimes when she can't see a straight line. Right now, we're not really getting anywhere. Soon as we get a sense of direction, she'll get her mojo back.'

'You know best,' Daisy said, her tone tart. 'I'm still the new kid on the block. Even after four years.'

Cath Gray agreed, reluctantly, to meet Karen in her office in the Parliament. 'I can't leave the building, I've got to vote on an important bill,' she'd explained. 'And I can't sit in a café with my phone broadcasting government business to the world. Just try to be a wee bit discreet.'

Karen looked around Cath's office in admiration. Its clean modern lines contrasted with her team's cramped quarters, and the view of Arthur's Seat and a corner of Salisbury Crags beat their one of a brick wall across the alley hands down. But even if moving to Gartcosh meant she'd get a space like this for her team, it still wouldn't make her happy. 'Nice gaff,' she said.

'Long service reward. Cheaper than a gold clock.'

'I promise I won't keep you long,' Karen said, settling into one of the visitor chairs. 'Lord Friockheim, or Haig Striven-Douglass as he was back then. He hosted a big Hogmanay jamboree at Fraoch House in 2013, a pro-Indy fundraiser. Quite the hoolie by all accounts?'

'I wasn't there. Karen. It wasn't aimed at the likes of me. It was targeted at the under-thirty-fives, the ones we knew wanted independence but needed a bit of a cattle prod to get them into the polling booths.'

'How did that happen? I thought the old marquess was a bred-in-the-bone unionist? Didn't he fund the Scottish Tories?'

Cath gave a dry bark of laughter. 'It's complicated. He'd always been a big donor to the Tories, but he put his wallet away when they elected Ruth Davidson as their leader. Bad enough that she's a woman, but a lesbian too? It shrivelled his wee misogynistic heart to a dried prune.'

'And of course, it was still Alex Salmond running the SNP. Much more his kind of guy?'

'It wasn't exactly a road to Damascus conversion. The old man didn't do a complete U-turn. But he wasn't in great shape back then. He'd retreated to their Highland house, a pocket-sized castle near Strontian, well out of the whisky-and-gossip circuit. He didn't even have the strength for stalking the stags, so I heard. Which tells you all you need to know about the state of his health. So Handsy Haig had the run of Fraoch House without Daddy looking over his shoulder.'

'"Handsy Haig"?'

Cath shrugged. 'He had a reputation for being a bit of a ladies' man. This was well before MeToo, remember. For a lot of guys it was a badge of honour.'

'Still is.'

'And Haig's a good-looking guy. A real charmer when he wants to be. Not so much his sidekick from those days.'

Karen frowned. 'Who was that? I don't recall.'

'William Kidd. AKA Billy the Kidd.'

'The comedian?'

'Depends on your definition of comedian. He never made me laugh. There was a cruel streak to his schtick. And our Douglas was really offended by the homophobia in his material. "Only joking, only joking." Remember, that was his catchphrase.'

'I never heard him live and when he was on TV, he was heavily censored, I think. He never did it for me. So Billy the Kidd used to hang out with His Lordship? Talk about the odd couple.'

'For a while, they were like a dodgy Batman and Robin. You never saw one without the other lurking nearby. Usually surrounded by lassies.'

Karen knew she had to pick her words carefully. 'But Handsy Haig's rehabilitated himself, right? He's a government adviser these days, isn't he? On the Land Reform Commission?' Cath nodded, her mouth a thin line. 'So our present Lord Friockheim is at the heart of the independence movement and he's managed to shake off his past reputation?'

'He cleaned up his act around the time of the Indy Ref. And even before we lost the ref, Billy the Kidd shook off the dust of these shores for Australia. I hear he's big with the ex-pat community in Dubai now. Though the way things are going across the Atlantic these days, he could end up as Trumpty Dumpy's court jester. But Karen – I have to ask you. Why are you so interested in this pair?'

'I wasn't interested in them specifically, Cath. It was the hoolie I wanted to find out about. I told you Sam Nimmo was working on a story about a sexual assault at a big fundraiser. And you told me, quite correctly, that it was the No campaign that had the big-ticket events. But we made some inquiries and came up with Haig Striven-Douglass's big night out. And all I was going to ask you was whether you'd heard any rumours about that night.'

Cath's expression was tight and unforgiving. 'And I shot my mouth off and gave you the bullets to fire.'

'That's not like you, Cath. It makes me wonder.'

A long pause. Karen was determined not to break it. At last, Cath said, 'Wonder what, Karen?'

'I think you know what was raised that night is dirty money.' More silence. This time, Karen spoke first. She knew she'd have to tread carefully. Just as Cath must have done since they'd last spoken. 'I don't mean that there was something crooked about the donations or the funds themselves. I mean that things happened that night that tainted the event. I think you asked some questions and you didn't like the answers. And you guessed I'd be coming back for more so you confected a version of events that you hoped would head me off at the pass.'

Cath stood up abruptly and crossed to the window. Her back to Karen, she said, 'Some things are consigned to the dustbin of history for good reason. Who benefits from digging this particular dirt now? Even the Tories wouldn't be interested these days. They've got their own mountain of dirt to dig through. And it's not like there's going to be another Indy Ref any time soon. Alex Salmond went to his grave a disgraced man. Nicola Sturgeon's had her legacy trashed by a bunch of pygmies.' She turned back to face Karen, her eyes sparkling with unshed tears. 'I'm as passionate about Scottish independence as I ever was, but I feel like our enemies were better organised than us and we've been driven backwards. So what's the point of dragging up a slice of ancient history nobody gives a damn about?'

'I give a damn,' Karen said. 'And Sam Nimmo gave a damn. And that might be what got him killed. You might be able to brush a sexual assault, or even a rape under the carpet, but a murder? What happened that night, Cath? What got out of hand? And what did Handsy Haig do to make it go away?'

'Leave it, Karen. I don't believe you want to damage the cause of independence any further.'

'This isn't about Indy, Cath. This is about whatever it was that happened to a young woman – I'm presuming it was a young woman, because the likes of Haig Striven-Douglass with his privilege and Billy the Kidd with his fame aren't interested in anything else – whatever happened to her was covered up. I'm guessing she was either paid off or threatened. We know how that one goes, don't we?' Exasperated, Karen struggled to make sense of the turn the conversation had taken. 'I always thought you were a good feminist, there to support other women. Not the rich and famous.'

194

'I have it on good authority that she was taken care of. Materially and emotionally. I know the lassie, our paths cross from time to time. She's over it. Which, in fairness, she likely wouldn't be if Sam Nimmo had got his hands on her and turned her into tabloid fodder.' Cath was breathing heavily now; Karen didn't think she believed the words that were coming out of her mouth and it was taking a toll on her.

'Well, we'll never know, will we? Because somebody shut Sam Nimmo up for good before she got the chance to tell her story. Who was she, Cath?'

Cath's mask of bonhomie slipped, betraying her age. 'You're way over the boundaries, Karen. You know full well I'm not going to tell you that. Not only because I want to see an independent Scotland in my lifetime but because yes, I am a good feminist and I'm not willing to throw another woman under the bus. I know you'll say you'd protect her, but she'd be crushed under the steamroller of the media. They might not identify her but you know as well as I do that her name would be all over the socials.'

Karen knew when she'd hit the buffers. She stood up. 'I'm not walking away from this, Cath. And you can tell whoever it is you've been speaking to about that night in Glasgow that I'm not going the same way as Sam and Rachel.' She turned on her heel and walked out, slamming the door on years of friendship.

28

After Karen had gone, Daisy asked Jason for the details of the journalist Linda Lawrence was working alongside in Germany. He was already staring into his screen, searching for whatever it was that Karen had set him on to. He looked up, an uncharacteristic scowl on his face. 'How come I do all the digging and you'll get all the credit when you get her to talk?'

Daisy felt cross, justifiably so in her view. She knew she was the better performer in interviews, unless a detailed knowledge of Scottish football was the key to building rapport. Somehow she didn't think that would cut any ice with Linda Lawrence. 'Jase, you know as well as me that the secret of success on this team is to do what the boss decides we do best. You're right, it's not fair that you did all the spadework and you don't get to follow through. But look at it this way – you've got strengths I don't have and this investigation would plough straight into the sand if I had to wade through all those bloody lists that you crunch your way through like they were a bowl of granola.'

'All the same,' he grumbled, flicking back a couple of pages in his notebook. He reached for his pad of Post-it notes and jotted down a name and number. He peeled it off and handed it to Daisy. 'Klaus Beck. That's his mobile.'

'Thanks. It's a joint effort, Jase, the boss recognises that.'

He said nothing, settling for giving her the side-eye and turning back to his screen, fingers busy on the keys and the trackpad. What was it with men and their hurt feelings, Daisy wondered. She never had to put up with this nonsense with Steph; they knew each other's strengths and weaknesses and ran their life accordingly. Steph would no more expect Daisy to empty the bins than Daisy would expect Steph to accurately load the dishwasher, and neither thought any the less of the other for it. Allocating tasks to fit people's strengths was the best way to get things done, and Daisy thought the boss mostly got it right. Honestly, Jason needed to grow up.

She plugged in her earphones and dialled the number Jason had given her. Klaus Beck answered on the fourth ring. 'Beck, hello?' He sounded abrupt but Daisy knew this was simply the regular German phone response. When she'd first come to know German speakers, she'd made the common mistake of assuming they were bossy and abrupt until it dawned on her that when they said, 'You will meet me at seven,' it wasn't a command. Rather it was nothing more domineering than a direct translation of the German. Thus were national stereotypes created.

'Klaus Beck? Can I ask, do you speak English?'

A deep chuckle. 'Well enough to recognise you are from Scotland. I went to university in Bristol.' He spoke as clearly as if he'd been educated in an English public school.

'That's a relief, because I'm ashamed to say my German is almost non-existent. Herr Beck, I'm Detective Sergeant Daisy Mortimer of Police Scotland's Historic Cases Unit. I wonder if I could ask for your help on a case we're working?'

'That sounds intriguing. Tell me more.'

'I saw your pieces about the rise of the AfD and I was very impressed. I realise that as a journalist, you're always look- ing for the story. But this matter is at a very delicate stage and I'd like to talk to you off the record. Is that something you'd be willing to do?'

A pause. 'Will there come a point where I can write about it?'

'I hope so. You'll have a front-row seat if it does.'

'And is this something happening in my backyard or yours?' His tone was amused and knowing.

Daisy struggled for the response that would win the desired effect. She could feel her skin warming, and knew she'd be literally sweating it any time now, Fuck it, she thought. This isn't the time for game-playing. 'I need to make contact with Linda Lawrence. I realise she's working undercover and the last thing I want to do is to blow her cover, but this is a murder case involving one of her oldest friends and colleagues.'

'With the greatest respect, Daisy Mortimer, I don't have any evidence that you are who you say you are. I would not put any journalist at risk on the basis of a phone call from a stranger.' His voice was chillier now.

'I can give you the number of Police Scotland and you can ask them to put you through to me?'

'Ah, Daisy, I've been burned before by clever people on the wrong side of a story. I know how possible it is to set up all kinds of fake trails. If you are serious about this task, you will come to Rostock and bring evidence that you are who you say you are. And evidence of the murder case and how it connects to the journalist you say you need to speak to. I'm sorry if this seems ridiculous to you. But we are work- ing to expose some dangerous people and if, for the sake of argument, we had someone working under cover, we could not take any risks with their life. So, you will come here and we will talk further. Is that acceptable?' His tone brooked no argument.

'I suppose it will have to be.' She hated to give ground like this, but she couldn't see a way round it. And Daisy was honest enough to admit to herself that in his shoes, she'd feel the same. She wasn't sure Karen would see it the same way but she'd do her best to convince her. 'I do understand your position. I'll call you back later, when I've had a chance to speak to my chief.'

'Thank you. I look forward to hearing from you.'

And that was that. Daisy took a deep breath and opened her browser. 'Travel Edinburgh to Rostock,' she typed and hit return.

Jason was having a more productive time with the Scottish football statistics for the 2013–14 season, which went some way towards soothing his wounded pride. From the sounds of it, Daisy had swiftly hit the buffers with the contact he'd given her. Meanwhile, he'd set up a spreadsheet of cup tie matches and was now populating it with the names of the referees and linesmen who had officiated at them.

It was slow, tedious work, but it was, he thought, pretty mechanical. The next part was more demanding, He worked his way down the Premiership, putting them in order from Celtic and Motherwell at the top down to Hibs and Hearts at the bottom. No Rangers, still languishing two tiers below after the scandal that had seen them demoted from the Premiership to the bottom league. Jason continued to the championship teams and the two lower divisions. The outcomes of league games were more broadly predictable, since opponents were of broadly similar standard so he decided to concentrate initially on cup ties, where teams were drawn randomly. There were invariably shock results, particularly in the early rounds. Every season, there were giant killers who played out of their skin and knocked out a side that were odds-on favourites.

He studied the result of his painstaking collation with a degree of satisfaction. So far, it had been relatively straight-forward. But now he'd have to trawl through newspaper reports and catalogue surprise results, controversial decisions and unexpected penalties to see whether there were officials in common. There was only one place to do that. Jason checked the time and realised with satisfaction he still had three hours before the National Library reading room closed. He could make a start on his research and still be home in time for dinner.

With luck, he'd unearth a seam of information that would point straight at the match officials who'd been the focus of Sam Nimmo's investigations. And then it was only a matter of finding one who was susceptible to the persuasions of the boss. Jason had no doubt that KP Nuts was more than capable of breaking open the defences of a football referee. He was a football fan; he knew that although most referees were honest and incorruptible, the only explanation for some of the decisions he'd seen on the field of play was that they'd been well and truly induced either by cash or by threats.

If their inquiries exposed men at the heart of the beautiful game who were greedy lying bastards, that was a heroic endeavour in Jason's eyes. Probably even more significant than anything Daisy would come up with.

*

Karen stalked out of the Parliament building, her pace driven at first by anger. But halfway up the Canongate, her fury abruptly leached away, replaced by a swift surge of sorrow. Although she'd been a background rather than a pivotal figure, Cath Gray had been part of her life since her teens. She'd been one of the few women Karen had seen as a role model, carving out space for a woman in what had been the man's world of local then national politics. Cath had encouraged her when nobody else seemed to think she was fitted for a career in the police. She'd epitomised the notion that you had to see it to be it and although Karen had never entertained the notion of a life in politics, she'd clung to Cath's successes as evidence that she could not only survive but succeed in a male-dominated career.

And now she'd crashed through the limits of their friendship, broken a boundary she hadn't even realised was there. Though if she'd ever stopped to think about it, she'd have understood that Cath was bound to have divided loyalties. You didn't have to be a politician to experience that. It was a bind everybody was liable to.

But this encounter had left her feeling shoogly; as if she'd stepped on what she thought was solid ground only to find it a floating pontoon. And before she got her sea legs, she'd gone overboard. She was almost afraid to reach out to anyone else that she was close to. That was the trouble with a small country; cross-currents happened more often than was comfortable.

Karen turned into the Scottish Storytelling Centre. Their coffee was decent and they got a better class of tourist, the general appetite for tartan tat being well catered for elsewhere on the Royal Mile. She'd barely settled down in a quiet corner with her restorative flat white when her phone pinged with a message from Daisy. How do you feel about a trip to Germany?

Wrong time of year for Christmas markets, she responded. Will Linda not come to the phone?

They want to see the whites of our eyes.

It was the logical next step. But it was Tuesday already. There was no way they could get to Germany and back before Thursday evening and Karen wasn't about to wait another month to find out what was happening inside the house on Upper Dean Terrace. They'll have to take a number. We need to check out the book club. See if we can get there on Saturday.

A minute passed. Then, Maybe better to leave it till Monday? We might have things to follow up after Thursday?

Karen knew her sergeant well enough to realise Daisy had plans for the weekend that likely included Steph. Sorry if that screws with your weekend but sooner the— She stopped herself. Really, did she want to alienate yet another person in her life? Just because she had nothing to fill her weekend but a Zoom call with a man an ocean away?

She erased the text and tapped instead, Good call. Monday it is. Figure out the best way to get there. See you in the morning.

👍 🎉 came the reply. Karen tried not to envy Daisy her easy happiness. She finished her coffee and set off on the long walk home.

29

There would be no coffee waiting in the office next morning; Jason had sent a message saying he was going back to the library to finish off his research. Going well, just need a bit more time, his message said. So Karen had stopped en route and picked up a couple of brews. If Daisy wasn't prompt, it would be on her own head if her coffee was cold.

Karen had sat up late, staring out at the sea from her living room window, interrogating herself over the conversation with Cath. How could she have managed it better? Surely she could have dug deeper for a note of conciliation? A step back from the brink? Somewhere between two and three in the morning, she realised the gulf probably wasn't unbridgeable. She suspected that Cath was equally unhappy at the idea of their friendship ending. And Karen knew Cath was fair, as well as being a woman of principle; all she had to do was to craft an argument that put her on the side of right and Cath would fall in behind it. It was a resolution that gave her enough of a measure of peace to make sleep possible.

In the office, she printed out a series of images of Upper Dean Terrace: a map, a couple of Google Street Views and a satellite shot. There were cars parked on either side of the street, some spots only available to residents.

Ideally, they'd set up later that day or overnight into Thursday so they could be sure of a line of sight to whoever arrived at the house. Karen had called in a favour from a colleague at Divisional HQ and managed to requisition a surveillance van for the evening. She reckoned they'd need two vehicles so they could cover arrivals coming from either direction. Daisy and her in one car, Jason in the van should do it. One major advantage of this location was that the houses had no rear entrance that gave on to the street; the back garden was entirely enclosed by the gardens of other houses. No inconvenient vennels or back passages here. Another advantage was that it would be dark; the street was in a conservation area and the Georgian-style street lights were far from brilliant. Even better, there were no houses on the other side of the street to cast light or eyes on the narrow pavement. That footpath was flanked by shrubs and trees on the bank of the Water of Leith, so the chances of the stake-outs being obvious to passing pedestrians were low. And if the book club members were being dropped off by car, the detectives would have an opportunity to snap them full on rather than in profile walking from car to pavement.

Daisy arrived in a flurry of umbrella and raincoat. 'Bloody rain came down the minute I got off the bus,' she said, shaking them out and hanging them up to dry.

'I managed to avoid it,' Karen said. 'Pity you didn't, your coffee would still be hot if you'd caught the earlier bus.' She grinned to take the sting out.

'I do try. But somehow, every day morning takes me by surprise. Where's Jason?'

'Up to his oxters in reports of football matches. I suspect he might be secretly enjoying himself. Me, I'm planning tomorrow's stake-out. It's going to be demanding but I want pics of everybody who goes into that house.'

'What if we don't recognise them? I mean, Tom Jamieson and Bryce Gordon weren't exactly public figures, there's no reason to expect that the other members will necessarily be guys we know by sight.'

'No, but Gordon and Jamieson were both men who moved in the kind of world where they were photographed in the course of their working lives. I reckon if we drop the images across to Tamsin at Gartcosh, chances are they'll find them in a reverse image search if Grieve won't cooperate.'

Daisy looked doubtful. 'So, shall I just get on with sorting out the travel arrangements for Rostock on Monday?'

'Leave that to me, I've got the patience for it.' That was such a blatant lie, even Karen recognised it and couldn't hide a smirk. 'What I want you to do is head over to the traffic wardens' HQ and make sure we don't get any tickets for being illegally parked in residents' parking spaces. I've got the details of the surveillance van that Jason's going to be driving.'

'What? Persuade them to give us a free pass?'

Karen laughed. 'They'll be able to see that incredulity from space. Look, tell them it's legitimate police business. Write a letter in my name, I'll sign it. We're all supposed to be on the same side. Use your natural charms. The ones I don't have.'

Daisy groaned. 'Why am I being punished?'

'Could be worse, I could have sent you to help Jason with the football reports. Don't forget, we're away to Germany on Monday. Just think of the duty-free . . .'

*

205

Jason retuned to the office just after noon, a definite spring in his step. 'You look like the man who landed a cup final ticket,' Karen said.

'Better than that, boss. It's amazing what you find when you start looking. I can't believe nobody picked up on this kind of thing before. No wonder Sam Nimmo thought he was on to something.' He pulled his laptop out of his backpack and opened it with a flourish, not even pausing to take his coat off. 'Wait'll you see this.' He reached across his desk and turned the printer on. 'It's easier to show you if I print it out.'

Jason grabbed the pages as the printer spewed them out and laid them side by side in front of Karen. 'I went through every match report I could lay hands on, and I highlighted all the controversies I found. For most officials, there were one or two bad decisions or questionable cards. But for these three' – he pointed them out – 'there were significantly more. Either they're really crap, or there's something dirty going on.

'I focused on the first three rounds of the cup, where there's more likely to be an ability gap between teams. And look – Number one: five instances of penalties, six offside decisions where the linesman was overruled, one disallowed goal, two red cards and fourteen yellows. All of them provoked howls of outrage from the fans, and some definite question marks from the match reporters. Number two: four penalties, five offside, three disallowed goals, four red cards, eight yellows. And number three: four penalties, three offside, two disallowed goals and five red cards. I couldn't get a proper tally of his yellow cards. These three are way out of line with the rest of the match officials.' He grinned triumphantly. 'Honest, boss, this is bang out of order.'

'It certainly looks like it,' Karen said slowly, studying the evidence he'd spread out in front of her.

'And it tallies with what we were told about where the bent boys are from. Number one, Don Rougvie, he's based in Fife, in Cardenden. His day job's a plumber. And number two, Robert Lumsden. He lives in Buckie. He's a transport coordinator for an oil company. The other guy, Jordan Macaleese, is from Gourock and believe it or not, he's a Church of Scotland minister, so he's maybe not inclined to organised dishonesty.'

'More vulnerable to blackmail, mibbes,' Karen scoffed.

Jason rolled his eyes. 'I never thought about that, boss. Plus they're not very well paid, are they?'

'Well done, Jason. You've done an amazing job. I'd have been tearing my hair out. Did you check to see if they're still in charge of matches?'

'Lumsden and the minister, they're still refereeing. Rougvie's retired from frontline stuff but he's on the board that governs match officials. What do you think? Have we got enough to front them up?'

Karen sighed. 'I'd like nothing better, but I don't know, Jason. On the face of it, they look dodgy. But we've not got any connectivity. We don't know for sure that Sam Nimmo was on to them. And we don't know who their presumed paymaster was or still is. All we've got is Keir Stevens' illegible shorthand notes about a couple of guys from Singapore and one from Irvine or Erskine. Without more details, the crooked refs could slide out from under with, "Everybody has a bad day, I'm just a crap referee, ask the paying customers in the stands."'

His disappointment was obvious. 'I see what you mean.'

Karen stared at the evidence in front of her. 'Mibbes there is one possibility . . .'

'What's that?' He perked up immediately.

'Daisy and I are off to Germany on Monday. We've

tracked down Linda Lawrence. She's undercover in Rostock with the AfD. I want to talk to her about the allegations of sexual assault in the run-up to the Indy Ref that Sam Nimmo was chasing up. But the guy she's working with will only connect us if we go there in person. She worked closely with Sam. I think she was more in the loop than Stevens. He seems to me to have been more of a follower, less of a go-getter. But Linda took the pix for Sam's stories, so if he was setting up a sting with these guys, she might have known more about it than Stevens.'

He looked crestfallen again. 'That's a pretty long shot,' he sighed.

'It's all we've got.'

He returned to his seat and slumped into it. 'Sometimes I wish we were like private eyes in the movies. Or like the FBI or something where we get to go undercover and catch these buggers out.'

'*Agents provocateurs.*'

'Aye. That. It's so frustrating when you know somebody's at it, and we don't have enough evidence to nail them.'

'I know. We just have to console ourselves with being the good guys, Jason. Even when that means the bad guys sometimes walk.'

He pulled a face. 'Then what's the point of us, boss?'

'The things we get right. That's the point of us. When we find out who killed Sam Nimmo and Rachel Morrison.'

30

Sometimes the gods smiled on Karen. Not often enough, she considered, but every now and again, something good landed in her lap. She'd no sooner started to check out flights to Berlin than her phone rang. The number was unfamiliar, but anything was better than wrangling the Ryanair website so she accepted the call. 'Historic Cases Unit, DCI Pirie,' she announced.

'It's Jess Nimmo.'

Karen wouldn't have put money on that. 'Hello, Dr Nimmo. How can I help you?'

'I think it might be me that can help you,' she said. 'Your visit the other day, it stirred things up for my mother. Some part of her's been clinging on to the notion that Sam was still alive. That one day he'd walk through the door and go, "Hi, Mum, what's for the tea?"'

'That's a natural reaction. None of us wants to consign the people we love to the grave unless we're sure.'

'I gave up on ever seeing Sam again pretty soon after he disappeared. I knew he was dead. Because I did not ever believe he could've killed Rachel and their baby. And if he'd still been alive, he'd have walked through fire to find out who did. He'd have been following every lead,

209

however slender, and he'd have been shoving it down Police Scotland's throat.' Jess was emphatic.

'I understand that.'

'But that's not how it was for my mum. To let you understand, she was the kind of parent who didn't want to let us go. Even when we went off to university, when we got jobs, when we started living with other people, she still held fast to the idea that we'd be coming back home one day. She expected us home for dinner at least once a week and our favourite teas were on rotation. Macaroni cheese with ham, roast chicken with mash and gravy and cabbage, meat loaf with potato fritters and pickled beetroot. I had to move to New York to get out from under, but I still had to come back. When Sam disappeared, she made it clear she couldn't cope without either one of us under her wing.' The words tumbled over each other in a rush.

Karen couldn't imagine living with that kind of pressure. She loved her parents, and couldn't help believing that persisted because neither half of the relationship made demands like those on each other. 'That can't have been easy for you or Sam.'

'I'm not looking for sympathy, DCI Pirie. I'm trying to explain the dynamic in our family, so you'll not think we've been holding important information back. So, one of her ways of hanging on to us has been to keep our rooms as we left them. Not pickled in aspic like a shrine. Over the years, Sam and I, we both chucked things out and added other stuff. But where some parents would box up their kids' stuff and stick it in the attic or the basement, the only people who got to mess with our stuff was us. Back when I was at uni, I binned a lot of stuff by stealth that I'd outgrown, but after that, I never really lived at home, so there's still all sorts of dumb crap tucked in the back of drawers and in holdalls under the bed. Anyway, all these years, Sam's bedroom has stayed the way it was. She dusted and hoovered it, that was all. But you came along and threw a rock in the stagnant pond.' Jess drew in a sharp breath. 'And now she's taken it into her head to do a room clearance.'

Karen didn't want to allow hope in. But she couldn't help herself. 'You found something?'

'The last time Sam was at the house was the night Rachel died. He'd been at the football in Kilmarnock with his mates and he dropped round to see Mum for a quick cup of tea and to get changed. He was meeting some political contacts for dinner, and he still kept a smart suit at Mum's for convenience sake. We were going through his clothes this morning, sorting them out for the charity shop and Mum got all tearful over the Killie replica shirt he'd been wearing that afternoon. It was bundled up in the bottom of his wardrobe with a pair of jeans and his parka—'

'Did the investigating officers not take those away for forensic examination?'

'Why would they? He wasn't wearing them that evening, he got changed into his suit right after the football. Anyway, I went through the pockets, and found his notebook. He always used those wee black notebooks, the ones like cops use. Small enough to tuck into a jeans' pocket.' She sighed. 'There were a couple of pages written under that day's date. I can't read it because it's in that daft shorthand he used, but he always wrote names out in full because he was afraid he'd get them wrong if he just used the phonetic form.'

'And were there names?'

'Kind of. Not in full.'

'Can you tell me what there is?'

211

'Do you think this could have any bearing on his death?'

Karen clenched her free hand. 'I really have no idea. Howsabout I come over to Knockentiber and collect it? I can consult someone who reads shorthand, then we'll know for sure.'

A pause. 'I'm not at home. I brought it into work with me. I didn't want to leave it lying around for my mother to stumble across. It'd only upset her even more than going through his stuff has. I'm on shift till ten tonight so if you can come over . . .'

'Where are you working?'

'Crosshouse, just outside Kilmarnock.'

'I know where it is. Cops always know where the hospitals are. Which ward are you on?'

'4C – surgical high-dependency unit. I'll tell the nurses' station to let you in.'

'I'll be with you in a couple of hours.'

Karen struggled to keep the car within touching distance of the speed limit as she hammered down the motorways. Was this the break she'd been hoping for? She tried to tamp down her excitement, reminding herself that Keir Stevens had warned how problematic old Teeline notes could be.

Meanwhile, Daisy had returned from the traffic wardens' office with assurances that their cars would be free from interference. Karen hoped they'd be as good as their word; she didn't relish having to unravel the red tape that would otherwise ensue. Sometimes it actually was easier to seek permission than forgiveness.

She'd instructed Jason and Daisy to swing by Upper Dean Terrace at the end of the day. If there were vacant parking spots available, they were under orders to park their vehicles and leave them there. Failing that, they should both share the van and hang around till there was a slot. Then Jason could remain with the van while Daisy returned to her car and waited for the word that another space with a different sight line had come vacant.

'How late do we have to stay?' Daisy had demanded. 'I don't see much point in staying too late, everybody will be parked up for the night.'

'Give it till nine,' Karen had decided. 'If it's not worked out for you both by then, you can pick it up tomorrow morning at seven.'

Daisy groaned. 'This'd better be worth it,' she muttered.

'Nothing's ever wasted,' Karen reminded her. 'You can work on your expenses once you get parked up, they're already a month overdue.'

Karen turned into the hospital and cruised round the car park, looking for a space. An SUV pulled out across her bows without looking and she slammed the brakes on, swearing loudly. But at least it gave her access to a space that was more than adequate for her Juke. She turned off the ignition and sat for a moment, enjoying the ticking of the engine as it cooled down.

She made her way into the maze that was Crosshouse and followed the signs down corridors, up stairs, round corners, into a lift and eventually ended up outside the surgical high-dependency ward. A porter was leaving as she arrived and Karen dodged inside, avoiding the pressing of buzzers and complicated explanations. She produced her warrant card at the nurses' station, where a handsome nurse who reminded her irresistibly of Rafiq immediately greeted her with, 'You're the polis here for Dr Nimmo, right? I always said Jess would come to a bad end.' He grinned. 'She's on

213

the ward, I'll get her for you. Take a seat,' he added, pointing to a couple of basic orange polypropylene chairs.

Her discomfort didn't last long. Jess Nimmo came striding down the corridor after a few minutes, taking a black notebook from the pocket of her white coat as she approached. 'Thanks for coming,' she said. 'Good luck deciphering my brother's scribbles. I'm sorry, I can't hang around, I've got a patient just back from surgery.' She handed over the notebook and turned back in the direction she'd come from.

'I'll keep you posted,' Karen said. Jess didn't break stride. Karen sat down again and opened the notebook. It contained page after page of small tight outlines that made no sense to her. There were recognisable dates at the top of some pages, occasional names printed in full and sometimes initials. The last couple of pages were dated the day of Rachel's murder; all that was decipherable were CHLOE, HSD and BtheK. 'Haig Striven-Douglass,' she said under her breath. 'The party boy.'

It was a moment of discovery that provoked a new sense of urgency for Karen. She racked her brains, trying to come up with a journalist she could trust with so potentially incendiary information. But nobody came to mind.

Was there another way of coming at this? Didn't journalists have to take exams in the skills of their trade? Did they still have to learn shorthand or did they rely on their phones? Surely there must still be people who taught them?

And then light dawned. She jumped to her feet and made for the car park, calling her mother's mobile as she walked. 'Hi, Mum. This is going to sound mad, but bear with me. Have you got Ella Gorrie's number?' she began.

31

Ella Gorrie had been what they called a commercial teacher at Fife College. She'd been teaching shorthand, typing and bookkeeping since it had been Kirkcaldy Tech, probably before Karen had even been born. In spite of being in her eighties, Ella was still a stalwart of the bowling club her parents belonged to, although arthritis had crippled her hands, hips and knees. But like Karen's mother, she was a regular at the card games that occupied a tranche of the women members on Tuesday and Thursday afternoons. They played a fiendishly complicated version of canasta called Bolivia involving three decks of cards. It confounded Karen in spite of her mother's attempts to initiate her into the mysteries of melds and escaleras. If Ella Gorrie could still manage Bolivia, Karen reckoned a stranger's Teeline would be a walk in the park.

Her mother had smoothed the way for her, once Karen had reassured her that there was nothing illegal or even illicit about what she'd be asking Ella about. 'It's a dead man's shorthand note, so there's no issue of confidentiality,' she'd said with more confidence than she felt.

Ella had a flat in a sheltered housing complex at the top of Bennochy Brae. Her apartment was on the second

215

floor, accessible via a lift for those who couldn't manage the stairs. 'Did you get the lift up? I don't use it,' Ella said dismissively as she showed Karen in. 'Use it or lose it, that's what I say about mobility. It takes me a wee while to get up and down, but determination goes a long way.' It was clear from the stiffness of her movements that flexibility was a distant memory. But other than that, she looked more like mid-sixties than her true age. Her hair was a silver bob, her glasses had fashionable oblong black frames and her cotton floral blouse was crisp and spotless.

Karen followed her into a small living room with space enough for a two-seater sofa and a pair of high-backed arm-chairs. 'It's gey wee, but we've got a couple of communal lounges on the ground floor if we want to have a gang of pals round. Sit yourself down, Karen. My, it's been a few years since I saw you last. Your mum keeps us up to date, though. She probably doesn't tell you, but she's very proud of you.'

'She's a proper Fifer, she wouldn't dream of telling me. I might get too full of myself.' Karen sat down on the sofa, taking in the family photographs arrayed along the windowsill and hiding the contents of the bookcase. She recognised a couple of faces from her own youth but didn't say so, for fear of Ella launching into the entire backstory of their lives since schooldays.

Ella hovered in the doorway that led to her tiny galley kitchen. 'Tea or coffee? Your mum says you're a coffee girl, but I only have instant so that might not be the ticket.'

'I'm fine, Mrs Gorrie. I've not long had one.'

Ella gave her a look that mixed humour and disbelief and settled herself on the chair that was angled towards the TV. 'Fine, but if you change your mind . . .' She straightened her shoulders. 'Now, your mum tells me you've got a bit of a puzzle on your hands that I might be able to help you with?'

Karen took out Sam Nimmo's notebook. 'You taught Teeline, I believe?'

Ella tutted. 'It's an abomination of a system. Pitman, Gregg even, they're standardised. But Teeline? It's based on handwriting, and I don't have to tell you how much handwriting can vary from person to person. I was an examiner for the National Council for Training Journalists for a time back in the 1980s, and we regularly had to return scripts to the tutor to ask if these were really the examinee's actual outlines.' She shook her head, her mouth a prim line.

'But you can read it?'

'Although I say it myself, if anyone can read a stranger's Teeline, it's probably me.'

'That's a relief. I don't know if my mum explained what I do in the polis?'

'Och, we all know you're like Trevor Eve in *Waking the Dead.* "Only less shouty," your mum says.'

Karen grinned. 'That depends. So, what it is ... This notebook recently came into our hands. It belonged to a journalist called Sam Nimmo who disappeared back in 2014. His body only turned up the other day—'

'He's the one that was entombed in the M73! Well, that's how Fiona Stalker put it on Radio Scotland. You don't get a story like that every day.'

'No, thankfully. We're trying to figure out what he was working on when he died. He was freelance, and he did a lot of investigative journalism, so he often didn't share what he was looking into till he'd got it nailed down. At first we didn't have a clue what he was working on, but now this notebook has come into our possession and frankly, it might as well be in Ancient Greek for all the sense we can make of it.'

Ella pulled out the drawer in the end table by her chair and took out a large square magnifying glass. She pressed a switch in the handle and a bright light shone out of the frame. 'I'll need this. My eyes are pretty good since I had my cataracts done, but it never hurts to get a good look at somebody else's outlines. Do you have any idea what this might be about? That's always a good place to start with Teeline.'

'There are some names and initials in ordinary writing, but the rest of it's in shorthand. I'm not sure exactly what it's about but I believe it may concern an alleged sexual assault at a fundraising gala. If that's something that would be a problem for you, I'll find someone else.' Heaven forfend she should appal an old woman.

But Ella chuckled. 'I've not lived under a stone all my days, Karen. I'm not afraid to confront the evil in the world. If you need this looked at, I'll do my best.' She held out a hand for the notebook and Karen passed it across.

'It's the last couple of pages,' she said. 'The date's at the start of it.'

Ella flicked forward to the notes in question. 'The outlines are pretty small, that makes it a wee bit harder to tell what's supposed to be above the line and what's below it. That makes a big difference in meaning ...' She held the magnifying glass up to the page and frowned at Sam Nimmo's last notes. 'Where did this event take place, do we know?' she asked. 'If I can make sense of that, it's a good starting point.'

'Fraoch House. In Glasgow.'

Ella shrugged. 'Never heard of it. But there—' She pointed to a couple of outlines. 'That could translate to Fraoch House. So I should be able to get a feel for this person's hand.' She looked up. 'I'll work better on my own. Why don't you away to your mum's and I'll phone her when I've got something? It should only take a couple of hours.'

Karen stood up. 'Thanks, Mrs Gorrie. I'm in your debt.'

'Don't be daft. Your mum's a good pal. She'd do the same for any of mine. From what I hear, you're your mother's daughter.'

Karen walked back to her car, not at all convinced that Ella Gorrie was right.

32

Karen arrived at the office next morning with a couple of neatly typed pages, courtesy of Ella Gorrie. Daisy had left a message to say she was back in Stockbridge, still trying to get a spot with a better line of sight than she'd managed the previous evening. Jason tried not to look smug about his parking success. 'I got lucky, boss.'

He'd managed to find a parking space for the surveillance van on Upper Dean Terrace with a perfect view from the one-way rear window. He'd already set up the camera with its long lens on a tripod. He'd see anyone walking up the hill to number eight. Daisy would be aiming for the opposite side of the street, facing downhill. Come evening, he'd be squatting uncomfortably on a wee stool in the back of the van, but she'd be sitting in a comfortable passenger seat; a driver sitting in a car looked dodgy but anyone sitting waiting for the driver to return aroused no suspicions.

'I also definitely got lucky.' She waved the papers at him. 'My mum's pal Ella Gorrie is an old-school retired shorthand teacher and she took a pass at Sam Nimmo's notes.'

'Amazing. Can I see?'

She handed the top sheet over and Jason frowned in concentration as he read:

Fond/fund raising ball/bell at Fraoch House. HSD & BtK hosted. Packed/picked/poked with money and beautiful people. Plenty pretty girls. Live/love bands/bonds/bends & DJ. +card/cord room for poker & blackjack. Live/love auction/action for special days & events. HSD & BtK reputation for exploiting wealth & fame/foam to pick/pack/peck up women for sex. Drink/drank/drunk. Drugs – coke/cake. CHLOE ??? taken/token from party. Clams/claims assault? Rape/rope? Scared/scarred/scored to go to police or yes team/tame/time. Job on line/loan marketing. Not first/forced/frost time I heard/hard/hoard stories/stars like this. Source DD from yes. CHLOE's name???

'Bloody hell,' he said.

'And this is Ella's note,' Karen said. '"Thanks for the challenge, Karen. I've done my best, but Teeline has a tendency to miss out vowels. It's not a problem if it's your own note and you remember what it's about, but it can be hard to be certain when it's come from a stranger. I've put in the options as I see them, but it's pretty clear that the HSD and BtK are being accused of taking advantage of a lassie called Chloe, probably drunk and drugged. It's hard to see another interpretation. The information came from someone with the initials DD, but they didn't know Chloe's surname. I don't know how you'd find that unless you had a guest list for the party. Good luck with bringing these rats to justice!"'

'She's some woman, this Ella. So what do we do now?'

Karen sighed. 'This is a serious allegation. The big question is what Haig Striven-Douglass or Billy the Kidd – or even the Yes campaign bosses – would do to stop that coming out.'

'You think they'd go so far as a double murder?' Jason was clearly dubious.

'I'd struggle to say so. But let's not forget the stakes couldn't have been higher. The future of Scotland was on the line. At this distance, it's easy to forget how high passions were running in 2014. On both sides. The No campaign's Project Fear would have fallen on this kind of story like a pack of hyenas.' Karen stared out of the window at the brick wall opposite. 'We need to find out more about Chloe. It sounds like she was something to do with marketing? Maybe working for the events team? Do we know who organised the Fraoch House hoolie? They'd have a guest list, presumably?'

Jason shook his head. 'I don't know.'

Karen wished she could rerun and reframe her conversation with Cath Gray. She was the only person she trusted enough to ask, and that was probably out of the question now. She'd have to rebuild bridges before she could burn them again.

Was there a remote possibility that Chloe was still involved on the Scottish political scene? It was hard to believe she'd have stayed inside the fold after such an experience at the hands of so prominent a pair. But sometimes a political ideal could survive even worse excesses.

Linda was the only possible line of approach. But until Daisy returned from Upper Dean Terrace, it would have to sit on the back burner.

Daisy finally secured the perfect spot just before noon. It complemented Jason's viewpoint; it was hard to picture how anyone would manage to get into number eight without being captured by either one of them.

All that hanging around had given her an appetite. So she walked down the street to the Swedish bakery and bought a savoury scone the size of a baby's head, a cardamom bun and a coffee. Sufficiently replenished, she set off up the hill towards the office, glad that the rain was still holding off.

She found Karen at her desk, wrangling plane and train travel to Rostock. 'Sorted,' she announced, shedding her coat and settling into her chair. 'Perfect view of anyone coming round the corner and down the hill.'

'Well done. We'll set ourselves up at half past six.'

'Where are you going to be? With me or Jason?'

'I'll be in my own car wherever I can get parked. There to pick up any slack. You and me, Daisy, we're going to chap the door once they're all inside. Twelve members. Right? We don't know whether that includes Grieve, but we'll busk it.' She turned back to her screen. 'You did right, by the way. Changing the travel day from Saturday to Monday. The Saturday flights to Berlin Brandenburg are at the crack of sparrow fart but the Monday ones are midday. And then there's a direct train every hour to Rostock. So we'll be there in time for dinner. I know that's what you're interested in.' Karen grinned, Daisy's legendary appetite provided all-you-can-eat fodder for humour in the HCU.

Daisy curled her lip in scorn. 'When do we get to see Linda?'

'You can set it up with Klaus Beck soon as I've got the tickets booked. Meanwhile, take a look at this.' She passed over Ella Gorrie's transcript.

Daisy took her time to digest it then waited for Karen to finish the travel bookings. 'Nice work. Just as well we've got somebody plugged into the Fife mafia.'

'The old dears love to be useful. But this only goes so far. Until we get a full ID for Chloe or we manage to identify who DD, the source, was, we can't get any momentum.

223

There's something in there about marketing and Jason and I were wondering whether she might have had something to do with the marketing team for the fundraiser? Or even for the Yes campaign generally. Which didn't help much because, oddly enough, there isn't a Wikipedia page for the people who did the marketing for Yes campaign fundraisers.' Karen scoffed. 'It's really not true you can find anything on the internet.'

'So we're hoping Linda can fill in the gaps?'

Karen nodded. 'She should be able to tell us whether Sam's investigation had gone further than this notebook tells us. Had he actually confronted Haig Striven-Douglass or William Kidd? Had he spoken to anyone connected to the Yes campaign who might have revealed his interest to someone who was prepared to do whatever it took to protect the fight for independence?'

'You really think there were people who would have killed for it?'

'You don't remember what it was like,' Karen said. 'There were some complete bams on the fringes of both sides of the campaign. There were death threats on the socials, and people got into fist fights in pubs. Even normally placid guys like my dad got their dander up. He still won't play bowls with one of the men from the club who chucked an egg at the First Minister on the campaign trail. And he didn't even hit him!'

'OK, I get it. We need Linda.'

'We really do. With a bit of luck, she'll be able to tell us where Chloe is now. With so much water under the bridge, she might finally be willing to talk about her ordeal. There's a lot less tolerance of the "boys will be boys" bollocks these days.' Even as she spoke, Karen wondered whether she was whistling in the dark. Her determination to find justice for the dead seldom wavered, but sometimes it felt as if the biggest obstacles were the living.

At half past six all three were in position. Karen had decided to join Jason in the van. It was more secure from prying eyes than sitting in the car with Daisy. He was routinely snapping everyone who walked up the hill towards number eight, deleting the shots once they'd passed the target house. Many were dog walking, at the end of the working day, letting themselves into the private Dean Gardens through the locked gate at the end of the street. When she'd first moved to Edinburgh, Karen had railed against the many private gardens in the New Town, until someone had explained to her that most of the flats in that part of town had no outside space. It still felt like privilege to her, but she conceded the point; after all, her own wee balcony with its pots of herbs gave her access to fresh air that she enjoyed.

Just after quarter past seven, a man came down the hill and turned in at the gate. 'Hope Daisy got him,' Jason muttered. Karen's view had been partial – short, ginger going grey, fussy walk, tweed overcoat. He didn't seem at all familiar.

She recognised the next arrival though she couldn't put a name to him. He was something to do with financial services, she thought. He'd been interviewed on the news when there had been all the fuss about boycotting festival sponsors that the righteous thought were inappropriate. Lovely suit, she thought.

In ones and twos, the rest arrived. She spotted an academic who'd famously made a killing setting up a company to exploit a gadget that made heart surgery less risky, and a

former Member of Parliament who she knew ran a successful consultancy that provided speakers to businesses and
organisations who needed ideas and sought prestige. But the
majority, they were strangers to her, distinguished only by
the quality of their tailoring and shoes. Some carried books,
a couple had designer backpacks and one even had a tote
bag from one of the city's indie bookshops. They all looked
prosperous; none seemed at all anxious.

By half past seven, nine men had entered the house. The
opening door obscured who was welcoming them, but they
were all whisked inside without ceremony. Nobody here
was unexpected. 'Is that it, boss?' Jason asked, shifting his
position and trying to straighten one leg.

'There's supposed to be twelve. There should be three
more.' Karen stirred and moved towards the front of the
van's compartment. 'Two, if Grieve's one of them.' She slid
a partition open, cautiously making sure no one was visible. 'I'm going to join Daisy. We'll give it five minutes and
if nobody else turns up, we'll go for it.' She slipped through
and emerged between the front seats. She waited till someone passed her with two cocker spaniels frisking on their
leads then eased out of the van.

Moments later, she was walking briskly downhill in the
dogs' wake. She drew level with Daisy's car but instead of
getting in, she kept going until she passed a black Tesla
whose driver she recognised. He had no eyes for her, so focused was he on his phone. Karen reached the corner and
turned into Danube Street, almost colliding with a man
who was ambling past and heading up the hill, a book bag
over his shoulder.

Karen almost lost her footing, so stunned was she by
the moment of recognition. The man reached out to steady

her, a solicitous look on his face. 'Sorry, are you OK?' She nodded, momentarily lost for words. 'Take it easy,' he said, releasing her elbow and stepping around her with an apologetic smile.

Lord Friockheim had lost none of the charm that had made him one of Scotland's most eligible bachelors.

She sneaked a look round the hedge and saw him turn into the house of the Justified Sinners. If ever a man needed that absolution, it was probably him. A moment later, the Tesla driver stepped out of his car, a hardback in his hand. He caught up with the first man and joined him on the doorstep where they waited briefly to be admitted.

Which raised an interesting question. Why had Marcus Nicol acted as if he'd never heard of Tom Jamieson? And what was Handsy Haig Striven-Douglass doing with the Justified Sinners?

33

Karen hustled back up the hill and climbed into the driving seat of Daisy's car. 'Why did you walk past me before?' her sergeant asked. 'Did somebody spot you?'

'Quite the opposite. There was somebody in the car behind you that I recognised.'

Daisy looked thunderstruck. 'You're kidding? Somebody we both know?'

'You could say that.' Karen's mouth twitched in a wry smile.

'Who was it? How come I didn't notice?'

'I presume because you were so focused on anyone coming down the hill. Plus it's dark now and probably not too easy to see the details in your rearview mirror.'

Daisy swivelled in her seat. 'Come on, boss. Who?'

'Marcus Nicol.'

Daisy looked as baffled as Karen felt. 'What the actual? What's he got to do with this?'

'I've got no idea. But this gives us the ammo to go back and push him harder. He must have known Tom Jamieson. Or if he joined after Jamieson died, I can't believe nobody's mentioned his name since, especially in light of Bryce Gordon's death. Even if it was just a throwaway line – "to lose one member is unfortunate; to lose two seems like carelessness". We definitely need to front him up again.

'But he's not the only surprise of the evening. Didn't you recognise the man who went in with him? Bloody Lord Friockheim.'

Daisy's eyes widened. 'Handsy Haig?'

'The same.'

'I can't believe it. Edinburgh is a village, right enough.'

'We'll unwrap that later. But in the meantime, we've got our dozen members inside number eight. It's time to shake up their evening.'

The doorbell was a gleaming brass knob; when Karen pulled it, an old-fashioned bell sounded distantly. Footsteps followed soon after and the door swung open to reveal a slender middle-aged man in herringbone tweed trousers and waistcoat over a startlingly white shirt and a pearl-grey tie in what Karen suspected was a Windsor knot. The hand that held the door sported a gold signet ring, the shirt cuff was held closed with a pair of discreet gold knots. 'Mr Grieve?' Karen chanced.

'Yes? And you are?' His voice was calm and soft, his accent hard to place.

Karen produced her ID and introduced them then waited for his response.

'I'm sorry, but I have no idea why you are here.'

'We'd like to talk to the Justified Sinners. The book club meeting here tonight? It's our job to investigate cases whose historic outcome has raised fresh questions.'

He frowned. 'I don't think that will be possible.'

'You're not quite getting it, sir. As I said, we're responsible for investigating new evidence in old cases and this book club has come up in our inquiries.'

'But this is a private residence, not somewhere you can just walk off the street into. This book group is not a public event. Members attend by invitation only and their privacy is paramount to them. So I'm afraid you can't just walk in here and demand to question the members.' His indignation was obvious. Karen didn't think he was planning to dismount his high horse any time soon.

'That is your prerogative, of course. Though most people do consider it their public duty to help the police with our inquiries.'

He scoffed. 'What? That old chestnut about having nothing to fear if you have nothing to hide? Nobody who's witnessed the activities of Police Scotland over the past couple of years and seen the wreckage they've made of people's lives and reputations would give that a moment's credit.'

Privately, Karen couldn't disagree with Grieve, but like the Justified Sinners, she didn't want to give up the privilege of privacy right then. She loved her job too much. She stepped into her most charming mode. 'I can't force you to let us speak to the book group. But they've got to go home at some point. At least, I assume you don't put them up for the night for some kind of literary sleepover. But when they leave the confines of your beautiful home, my officers and I will be waiting outside to ascertain their names and contact details. Uncomfortable for them but very entertaining for your Stockbridge neighbours and the Dean Gardens dog walkers. I imagine it'll make a nice wee reel on Insta.'

'You have no right. There are laws about obstructing the pavement.'

Karen smiled and turned to Daisy. 'DS Mortimer, have you ever heard of Police Scotland enforcing laws about pedestrians blocking the pavement?'

Daisy thought for a moment. 'Not unless you're running an abortion clinic?'

He glared at her. 'There's no need for facetiousness.'

'Nor for threats, Mr Grieve. Why don't you go and put the proposition to your members and see whether they'd prefer a public interrogation or a simple private conversation?'

He flung open the first door on the left, 'Wait in here.'

Karen demurred. 'Out here will do fine. We don't want anybody getting embarrassing ideas about trying to sneak out into the night. Apart from anything else, they'd run straight into the long arms of the law.'

'DS Murray's arms are not that long, boss.'

'They're long enough, Sergeant. They're long enough.'

Grieve rolled his eyes. 'You sure your names are not Laurel and Hardy?' He turned on his heel and marched down the hall. When he opened the door at the end, a brief gust of conversation leaked out before it was silenced again by the closure.

'You rattled his cage,' Daisy said.

Karen shook her head, her expression rueful. 'Not nearly enough. He's a classic Edinburgh Number Two. I don't mean a shit, though they often are. I mean the second in command, the one who's got the boss's back. You remember the late Queen? Whenever she went walkabout, there was always a big polis at her shoulder. Often with a raincoat over his arm?'

Daisy nodded, 'Close protection.'

'That too. But he was an Edinburgh Number Two. See when the Queen farted? Don't look at me like that, the

231

Queen was human, of course she farted. Well, the close protection guy, one of his jobs was to look pained and apologise. Hugh Grieve looks to me like a man who takes the blame for the boss's farts.' Before she could say more, her mobile blurted out the opening bars of Taylor Swift's 'Look What You Made Me Do'. 'Oh, fuck,' she said.

Daisy knew why. It was the ringtone Karen had chosen for the Fruit Gum. 'Somebody in there's got some serious pull,' she said as Karen answered.

'Good evening, sir,' she said, her voice neutral. She summoned Daisy close enough to hear once she'd slanted the phone away from her face.

'What on earth are you up to, DCI Pirie?'

'What I'm supposed to be, sir. Following where the evidence takes me.'

'I've just had my dinner interrupted by a very senior city councillor wondering why his book group meeting is being disrupted by one of my officers.'

'To be fair, sir, we've not actually managed to do any disrupting yet. We're still in the lobby.'

'Spare me the comedy routine, Pirie, it doesn't work with me. What are you doing, bursting into a private gathering of friends?'

'Like I said, sir, I'm not doing any bursting in. One of the cases I'm investigating touches on this book club. One of its members died in an unexplained incident not long after he joined. His brother lives overseas and came home recently, determined his brother's death was murder. When we started investigating, we discovered another questionable death of a member.'

'And you think there's what? Some kind of Agatha Christie plot going on in the New Town?' His contempt was obvious.

'I don't know what I think, sir, on account of having no statements to look at.' As she spoke, Grieve appeared at the end of the hall, moving towards them, a slow smirk on his face. Bastard thought he'd won. She turned her back on him and tucked her phone into her neck. 'All I want is names and contact details. I can follow it up discreetly. Can you make that happen for me?'

A pause so long Karen thought he'd hung up on her. Then he said, 'Promise me you'll walk out of there without another word?'

She couldn't help herself. 'Maybe just, goodbye?'

'Christ, Pirie.' He sighed in exasperation. 'I'll get you the names.'

'Thanks, sir.' She ended the call and turned back to face Grieve. 'You shouldn't creep up on folks, Mr Grieve. Especially not police officers trained in martial arts. My boss tells me you've agreed to cooperate and provide us with the names of your members. I'll look forward to seeing those on my desk in the morning. And meanwhile, we'll let you all get back to *A Big Boy Did It and Ran Away*.'

Grieve pursed his lips and stepped around her to the door. 'I can't say it's been a pleasure to meet you, DCI Pirie. But it's a pleasure to see you depart.'

'You've been saving that line up, I can tell,' Karen said on her way out. 'I'm happy to have given you the chance to use it out loud instead of just thinking it.'

And they were on the path, the door closing firmly behind them. Jason was hovering by the gate, anxiety and eagerness mingling on his face. 'How'd it go?' he demanded.

'Could have been worse. We should have the names tomorrow morning.'

'I've got a couple already,' he said. 'I thought I recognised their faces on the way in so I checked once you'd gone inside. Dermott Kennedy, the housing developer. And Frankie Khan, used to be a boxer, won gold at the Commie Games, runs that fast-food chain, Frankie Says Eat Snax.'

'Interesting career path,' Karen said.

Daisy groaned. 'I could murder a serving of their crispy chilli roast potatoes with parmesan mayo.' Then she looked a question at Jason. '"Commie Games"? Is that some kind of Cold War shit?'

They both looked at her as if she'd dropped in from outer space. 'Commonwealth Games,' Karen explained.

Her face cleared. 'Like Glasgow's having next year? I bet Frankie Khan'll have his food trucks front and centre at all the venues.'

It was, Karen thought as she tucked it away for future exploration, an interesting point. 'There's one down the bottom of Leith Walk, near you, isn't there?' Jason nodded. 'Then let's take advantage of the early cut and go down the Walk and get stuck in. My treat.'

34

Karen took a slightly circuitous route back home to give her stomach a chance to digest the delights of Frankie Says Eat Snax. They'd made the fatal mistake of letting Daisy do the ordering, which meant that they'd ended up with approximately double what three normal adults would consume. They'd each eaten their fill of a succession of small plates, which still left enough for Jason to take home a couple of containers for Meera and for Daisy to pack up enough 'for breakfast'. Even Jason confessed himself stumped at the amount Daisy could pack away without apparently gaining weight.

'You sure you've no' got a tapeworm?' he'd once said.

'Don't care if I do,' she'd replied cheerfully. 'It doesn't hurt and it means I can really enjoy my food without turning into one of those calorie-counting bores with their finicky diets.'

'Just wait,' Karen said. 'It'll catch up with you. The menopause will hit you like a runaway train.'

Jason had flushed at the introduction of women's business but Daisy just shrugged. 'Sufficient unto the day, boss.'

'First thing, we'll get stuck into the Justified Sinners,' Karen said. 'We've got four names to start with, until Grieve comes across with the rest.'

'I can't get over Lord Friockheim being one of them,' Jason muttered.

'I'm not surprised,' Daisy said. 'Birds of a feather.'

'Careful where you say that, Daisy. At least, until we have a shade more evidence. Jason, you take Frankie. Daisy, you see what you can dig on Kennedy. I want everything – school, uni or college, partners, kids, career path, recreation, how many houses they've got. Mistresses, divorces, tabloid scandals. I'll take Friockheim and I'll screw the nut on Grieve if he doesn't come across with the goods. We've got the weekend to put together back stories on all of them before Daisy and I go off to Germany. I'd like to be in a position of strength by the time we come back, and I don't expect you to do all the heavy lifting, Jason.'

She waved at the waiter for the bill and pushed back her chair. The others took the hint and reached for their leftovers and coats. 'I'll see you both in the morning. Thanks for your work tonight.'

Karen slept better than she felt she deserved, waking with a clear head and the beginnings of a plan. But first, she needed that list of names. She checked her messages and her email, but there was nothing from Grieve. Before she called the Fruit Gum, she needed a coffee. For his safety, if not her own.

He answered on the sixth ring. She took that to mean he wasn't eager to talk to her. 'Good morning, sir,' she said, injecting full-on bounce into her tone. 'I don't seem to have the promised information from Hugh Grieve. I wondered whether he'd sent it to you and you'd just not had time to forward it on to me?'

'Yours is not the only item on my agenda, DCI Pirie.'

'No, sir, I get that. But here in the HCU, we think every day counts just as much as in live cases. I don't like my team to be twiddling their thumbs waiting for the next lead to land. And you did say . . .'

'I know what I said. Leave it with me, I'll follow up with Hugh Grieve if it's not in my in-tray.' And he hung up on her. She never thought she'd entertain the possibility, but she almost missed his predecessor. For all her many faults, Ann Markie would never have let Hugh Grieve give them the runaround.

But by the time she'd showered and dressed, there was a message from Grieve in her inbox. No contact details or background; just a list of twelve names. She vaguely recognised a couple of them, from dimly remembered news stories about some sort of investment project. One was something to do with the film industry, another concerned a green energy start-up in Perthshire. It was a start, at least. She forwarded it to Daisy and the Mint, with the message that they should carry on with the backgrounders they were already covering then move on to the rest of the list once they'd got as far as they could.

And she would focus on Lord Friockheim. There was one person in her contacts book who moved in entrepreneurial circles. When Tavish had brought his name into the conversation, she'd ignored it. But she couldn't maintain that brick wall, not when demolishing it might open up the way forward. She'd even allowed herself to consider he might be a Justified Sinner himself. She thought she knew him better than that but deep down she'd recognised it was a possibility.

Thankfully, his name wasn't on the list, however. Karen couldn't put it off any longer. She was going to have to speak to Hamish Mackenzie. Coffee roaster, gin distiller, hobby crofter, mover and shaker. And ex.

When Karen's email landed in her inbox, Daisy had felt relieved. She'd woken early and slipped out of bed, leaving Steph to have a final hour of sleep before girding her loins for the stress of Friday in the classroom with thirty-five seven-year-olds convinced the weekend had already begun. She set herself up at the kitchen table with a pile of buttered toast and a mug of tea and started exploring the online life of Dermott Kennedy.

By her calculation, he was closing in on his forty-fifth birthday. According to a puff piece in a property magazine, he'd started with a holiday job, working for his carpenter father on new-build commuter homes down the coast in Dunbar. Then he'd inherited his grandparents' house, a ramshackle cottage on the unfashionable side of the blurred boundary between Portobello and Joppa. He'd held a finger up to the wind and realised the area was on the way up so instead of partying away his student years at Edinburgh Napier, he'd put his studies in construction management to practical use. He'd completely renovated the cottage and turned it into a showcase of what could be done to revivify properties that people had given up on. It had been the first step on a ladder that had taken him to his current position as one of the most effective developers of repurposed property in Scotland.

It wasn't all sunshine, though. She came across a couple of less complimentary pieces that questioned how he managed to gain permission for some of his projects, apparently sidestepping their listed building status. The laws of defamation clearly prevented out-and-out accusations, but the implications were there.

Kennedy married his wife Bridget on her twenty-first birthday, when he'd been twenty-seven. She was the daughter of the electrical contractor who had been closely involved in Kennedy's business and they had four children. They were still married, still seen out together at public functions. Now they lived in the Borders in a restored bastle house, one of the fortified dwellings built as defences against the reivers who plagued the so-called Debatable Lands between Scotland and England in earlier centuries. Daisy looked at the images in a swanky photographic essay and wondered what it would be like to live in a house that looked like *Game of Thrones* kitted out by John Lewis. She felt no envy. Apart from anything else, the Wi-Fi would be a nightmare in a building where the stone walls were two feet thick. And how far would you have to drive for a tub of ice cream on a Saturday night?

On the face of it, he was a poster boy for hard work and imagination. But something unsettled Daisy. She'd heard too many horror stories from friends of Steph about the struggle they'd had trying to get planning permission from the council for apparently straightforward things like putting a radiator in a basement or turning a boxroom into a toilet. How was it that Dermott Kennedy managed to sweep all that aside for the bijouterie that was required by his clients?

You have to wonder, she thought. And if she'd learned anything from working with KP Nuts, it was that, whenever you had to wonder, there was usually something dodgy going on.

35

The warmth in Hamish's voice when he'd answered Karen's call surprised her. When they'd split up, there had been acrimony enough in the moment, but they'd gradually realised they wanted to try to remain friends. It hadn't quite worked out that way; she thought now that he'd believed he'd charm her into getting back together, but the longer she'd kept flying across the Atlantic to Montreal, the more strained it had become until they'd largely drifted out of each other's orbit. Asking for his help now felt like taking advantage rather than the free exchange of favours that she enjoyed with other friends. But as usual, her commitment to the job trumped her finer feelings and she responded to his tone.

'So how are you doing?' she said.

'I'm pretty much wearing a groove in the A9. Between the croft and the distillery half the week, and the coffee shops the other half . . .'

'Nothing changes, huh?'

'Yes and no. Everything took a dent with Covid, but I guess people are more picky now about how they spend their money so if you give them quality products like ours, it's a pretty good survival tactic. And I'm working on a new project – we're setting up a series of residential events where people can come and learn foraging, fermenting and smoking over a weekend.'

Of course he was. 'You'll be on to a winner with that. Trump might be even worse for the economy than Liz Truss, but there are still plenty of folk with cash to splash,' she said, letting her amusement show. 'Listen, Hamish. Can we meet up? I'll be honest, I need to pick your brains, for work. But I'd like to see you regardless.'

A momentary pause. Then, 'You free for lunch?'

'Your lucky day.'

He gave a dry little laugh. 'It is, because you're buying. Meet me at Cardinal at twelve thirty?'

And so she found herself in one of the city's classiest restaurants. Which, these days, was really saying something. Hamish had better come across; it'd have to be good for her to get her money's worth. She thought the Fruit Gum would choke when he found this receipt on her expenses claim; she considered pushing back on the venue, but she was the supplicant here and she knew Hamish would relish demonstrating that she wasn't in his league.

Karen arrived first and decided she was going to break her own rule about not drinking cocktails before six. For a committed gin drinker, a gimlet with forced rhubarb instead of lime juice was irresistible. It arrived at the same time as Hamish. He raised his eyebrows, and bent to give her a soft kiss on the cheek. The feel of his beard on her skin reminded her irresistibly of Rafiq; it was good to have that recollection to replace her memories of Hamish's physicality.

'You're hitting the hard stuff early today,' he said, settling into the chair opposite her. He smiled up at the waitress and said, 'Any chance you can make me an espresso martini?'

'Not a problem, Mr Mackenzie. With your robusta beans?'

He nodded. As she left, Karen shook her head. 'You can't help yourself, can you?'

'No reason not to. They buy my beans, I eat their food. So tell me, how are you?'

The small talk took them through the ordering and the snacks, then Hamish ran a hand through his reddish gold hair and said, 'How's Rafiq's quest for a passport going?'

She'd been expecting it, thought she was braced for it, but still it cut through her defences. 'I didn't come here to talk about Rafiq,' she said. 'I don't ask you about your personal life.'

He drained his glass and crunched the coffee beans. 'I'd tell you, if you did. I'm not ashamed or embarrassed.'

'Neither am I. But I don't consider it any of my business. So now we've got the catch-up out of the way, let's just cut to the chase. Have you ever heard of a book group called Justified Sinners?'

Hamish frowned. 'Doesn't ring any bells with me. Should it?'

'It has an interesting and highly limited membership. I thought you might have heard about it on the grapevine.'

'I'm not known for the breadth of my reading. You should know, there were enough complaints from you and Sergeant Daisy when you were camping out in my flat during lock-down. I'm not the obvious recruit for a book group.'

'Which would be the case if it was just what it says on the tin. But I think it's a bit more than that. You get the reference in the title? Justified Sinners?'

'Vaguely. Some Calvinist crap about the elect having the freedom to do whatever they like and still make it into heaven?'

'I'm impressed.' It was more than she'd expected him to know. 'We don't know enough about the members, but I'm beginning to think there's a bit of back-door economic activity going on with them.'

'You scratch my back, I'll scratch yours?'

'Kind of. A bit like the Freemasons without the hand-shakes and the leather aprons.'

'How we all think the tech bros operate?' He was fully engaged now; she could almost hear his brain working. 'In a city like Edinburgh, in a small country like Scotland, that could be very profitable if you could keep the lid on firmly enough.' He cocked his head to one side, his eyes sparkling. 'What is it you're looking for from me?'

'All we've got is a list of names. We know a bit about two or three of them, but these are not the kind of guys who are household names so getting a fuller picture isn't straight-forward. I hoped you might be able to colour in some of the grey men for me?' Karen paused, meeting his direct stare.

His smile was rueful. 'You've always had the knack of get-ting your friends to go the extra mile for you. I've seen you do it with River, with Jimmy Hutton, with Giorsal. Not to mention the Mint. It's a pretty good team to be relegated to.'

'It's not a relegation. My friends have always been in the premier league, Hamish.' Her voice was gentle and she reached across to pat his hand.

He nodded and sighed. He reached out and rubbed thumb and finger together. 'Let's see it then, this list of yours.'

She opened her phone and passed it across to him. He took his time, scrolling through it and studying it carefully. 'Can you ping it across to me?' he asked. 'Then I can make notes.'

Karen shook her head. 'I can't do that, Hamish. This is

an active investigation and I can't risk this falling into the wrong hands. I'm already skating on thin ice, showing you.'

The waitress arrived with their starters and Hamish immediately turned her phone face down, all smiles for the staff. 'This looks great, I'm glad I brought my appetite along.'

When they were left alone with their food, Karen took out her notebook. 'One by one.' She'd deliberately put Lord Friockheim's name halfway down the list; Hamish was smart enough to pick up any biases in her interest. 'You tell me what you know, I'll write it down.'

'Always the careful one. Another cop would just record it on their phone. Not you.'

'I'm protecting you as much as me. I suspect it wouldn't do your business empire any good if certain people found out you've got a finger in this particular pie.'

He shrugged. 'I get that's what you're trying to do, but it's not exactly a state secret that you and I used to be an item. People will simply assume that I'm the person you've turned to for inside information. But if taking notes makes you feel happier, be my guest.'

Between eating, talking and Karen's scribbling, it turned into a long lunch. By the time she'd finished her second coffee, she had thumbnail sketches of eight of the members of the group, plus more details on the three they already knew about. When he'd reached the marquess, he'd given a knowing smile. 'His Lordship Haig. Now there's a man who likes to play his cards close to his chest.'

Karen didn't even look up from her plate. 'Meaning what?'

'I know him, but I don't *know* him, if you see what I mean? I'm not surprised to see him in this company, though. If they talk about books for more than five minutes, I'd be astonished. Haig's one of the quiet movers and shakers. He knows everybody but he never stands in the foreground. A bit like Macavity, in *Cats*. If you had a business problem you couldn't solve, Haig would be your go-to guy.'

'He'd make your troubles disappear?'

Hamish grinned. 'For sure he'd know who could. And he's not the only one on that list with that kind of pull.'

'Interesting. I heard on the grapevine he was a bit of a ladies' man,' she said casually.

Hamish chuckled. 'No argument that he's a babe magnet. Single, good-looking, loaded, castle in the Highlands. I imagine he's never short of female company. Why, are you interested?'

Wearily, she shook her head, reassured that she'd made the right decision when she'd walked away from Hamish. She still enjoyed his company, he was still easy on the eye and she had no doubt he'd still be fun in bed. This conversation had demonstrated he had his uses yet, but the reasons she'd given up on him remained. He'd been what she needed to distract her from the pain of losing Phil, but she was past that raw-edged necessity now. And he definitely wasn't Rafiq.

Back at the office, she found Daisy and Jason wrangling the internet. She pulled them into a huddle to examine what they'd discovered. The boss of a private equity company who owned two golf courses and the associated five-star hotels; a senior civil servant in Scottish Government circles; a director of a commercial bank; a senior member of the city council and a prominent member of the planning committee; a road-building contractor; a former MP with a successful consultancy and motivational speaking business; a top lawyer with a broad roster of clients. And of course, the Marquess of Friockheim. Still swimming with the kind of sharks who moved under the surface of Scottish life. Men – and it was still men – who could bend the world to suit their needs and those of their friends, sustained by a kind of invisible network of words in ears and unspoken understandings.

'A book club, my arse,' Karen snarled.

'Perfect cover, though. A bunch of guys walk up the street with a book under their arm, who's going to call them out on it?' Daisy scoffed.

'I bet none of them actually open the books,' Jason said.

'Tom Jamieson did, according to his fiancé. He was a proper reader. I don't think that actually disqualified him, though.' Karen leaned back in her chair. 'But where does it take us, in terms of putting a case together?'

Jason and Daisy exchanged looks. 'We don't know what order they all joined in,' Jason said. 'Like, was Marcus Nicol already a member when Tom Jamieson died?'

'How does that make a difference?' Daisy asked.

He looked at his notes. 'Well, it might help us to a motive? If he was a member and Tom Jamieson was some kind of obstruction to Nicol's plans? Or somebody else's?'

'What? We're talking Murder Incorporated now? You think the Justified Sinners are into removing roadblocks? And what could Tom Jamieson have stood in the road of?'

'For all we know, Jason could have a point, Daisy,' Karen weighed in. She couldn't be bothered with the children fighting. 'But let's think about it the other way round. What if Nicol wasn't in the club but he wanted to be? What if he saw Tom Jamieson as an easy target to create a vacancy?'

'How could he be sure he'd get the slot, though?' Daisy's scepticism was in full flow now.

'Hear me out ...' Karen paused, putting her thoughts in order. 'Let's say for the sake of argument that Marcus Nicol was desperate to get his feet under the Justified Sinners table. He wanted what he thought they could give him.'

'How did he even know about them, though?' Jason now, and he had a point.

'We don't know how they recruit,' Karen said. 'Mibbes his name had come up as a potential member, a nod from a pal? And they had a word with him, sounding him out. "If we had a vacancy, would you be interested?" kind of thing. And yes, our Marcus was interested enough to create a vacancy for himself.'

'It still doesn't take us any further forward,' Daisy complained. 'How would he even know Tom Jamieson was the last man in?'

Karen felt the synapses snap in a lightbulb moment. 'We're going in the wrong direction here. We shouldn't be looking further forward, we need to be looking further back.'

36

Saturday morning just after ten found Karen pulling off the road south of Pitlochry at a café recommended by Hamish. Nae Limits served an amazing eggs and avo benedict, but more importantly, their coffee was, according to Hamish, the best on the road north. He'd been trying unsuccessfully for years to persuade them to swap to his beans but they were loyal to their existing supplier. No skin off her nose, though, and it had become a regular stop for Karen to raise her caffeine levels to cope with the stress of the hated A9. Just as she was paying the bill her phone rang. She didn't recognise the number but that was hardly unusual. 'DCI Pirie,' she said.

'This is Drew Jamieson. Tom Jamieson's brother. I've not heard from you people since I gave you the evidence in my brother's murder.'

Just what she needed. 'Good morning, Mr Jamieson. The reason we've not been in touch is that we're following various lines of inquiry, none of which has come to fruition yet. I promise you, we're not ignoring the information you brought to us.'

'So what are you actually doing?'

Karen gentled her voice. 'I can't discuss operational

details, I'm sorry. That's not how it works. I understand
your pain and distress at not having satisfactory answers
but I can assure you that as soon as we know anything for
sure, we'll tell you.'

'That's all well and good but I'm going back to Aotearoa
next week. I wanted some answers before I leave.'

'We'll contact you when there is something concrete to
report. I'm not fobbing you off – we are working on the
case, but the time lag does make for additional difficulties.
We've got your details and we'll be in touch.' The line went
dead. She felt for him and wished she could say more but
in her experience, relatives pounced on the tiniest flicker of
possibility and fanned it into the flames of certainty. That
was a cruelty she tried not to generate. She paid the bill and
returned to her car.

Unusually, she was flying solo, chasing a hunch that had
taken shape during her conversation with Daisy and the
Mint the previous afternoon. It was such an off-the-wall
idea that she'd been reluctant to share it with them, settling
instead for telling them to carry on with their background
research. She'd gone home and left them to it, pursuing her
own wild goose.

She'd put a call in to Inspector Garvey, who was no more
pleased to hear from her than he had been the first time.
On this occasion, she dived straight in. 'Inspector Garvey,
right up front, this is not meant as a criticism of anybody in
your team. When I spoke to you before, I said I wasn't investigating Bryce Gordon's death. And that was the truth. But
the picture has changed since then and I've got good reason
to suspect it may not have been the accident it appeared.'

He sighed. 'So what's this new information? Have you
lifted a stone and found a witness? Or has the Widow

Gordon found a pipeline to somebody more senior than the sheriff who sat on the Fatal Accident Inquiry?'

'Honestly, it would take longer than either of us has got for me to explain and, even if I tried, you'd probably hang up on me long before I got to the end. I'm not asking you to reopen the case, not at this point certainly. I genuinely don't think your people missed anything. But I believe Bryce Gordon's death links to another one I'm dealing with that was also written up as an accident initially. There's a connection between the two men that sets all my polis' instincts jangling. I'm betting you know that feeling?'

'We're supposed to base our investigations on evidence, not feminine intuition.' His voice was flat and cold.

'I don't believe you've never followed up on a hunch. Because our hunches are based on observation and experience. And they pop up for guys like you as well as women like me.' She let out a long breath. 'I think we've got a killer out there and I hate the thought that he might get away with it. Especially since he's not motivated by anything except pure unfettered greed.'

The silence lasted so long she feared he'd put the phone down and walked away. At last, he spoke, grudging every word. 'Always supposing I was as bored as you seem to be on a Friday afternoon, what would you be wanting from me?'

'The traffic reports from the afternoon and evening of the day Bryce Gordon set off from Spean Bridge. Anywhere on the route. Anything and everything, because at this point, I'm not sure what I'm looking for. It might be a speeding ticket handed out to a name I recognise. It might be a drive-off from a service station. It might be somebody phoning up to complain that an eejit has parked across their driveway.'

His laugh was humourless. 'Is this how you normally go about solving cold cases? Because if it is, it's a blooming miracle you ever get a result.'

'I have been accused of being a law unto myself, it's true. But I've been doing this historic case schtick for long enough to know when something doesn't feel right. And then I have to find the right thread to pull on. I'll be honest, it doesn't always get a result. I used to drive Ann Markie absolutely tonto.'

By happy chance, she'd found Garvey's hot button. A bark of sardonic laughter. 'You were obviously doing something right.' Then another sigh. 'That woman pissed off more folk than Nigel Farage. Look, I'll tell you what I'll do. If you can get yourself up to Inverness tomorrow, I'll set you up with Donny Taylor. He's our traffic coordinator, he's got access to all the relevant data from cameras and patrol vehicles. I'll get him to pull up whatever he's got from that day. It might not be much, but you can knock yourself out going through it all. If that's not too far below your pay grade?'

'I don't mind getting my hands dirty. My team have got enough digging of their own to be getting on with. Thank you for this. And like I said, there's no criticism of how the original inquiry was handled.' *Apart from not noticing the wrecked car and the dead body at the bottom of the slope . . .* 'We just happened across a link that wasn't there to be stumbled over back then.'

'Good luck with it. Come in to Inverness HQ and ask for Donny. I won't be around myself but he'll sort you out.'

And so she'd set off that morning with absolutely no conviction that she was going to find a thread worth pulling on. It was the slimmest of chances, but it wouldn't be the first time she'd tiptoed out on a limb that hadn't snapped under her. And Sergeant Donny Taylor looked like a man who was more than strong enough to take the weight in his stride.

He was already waiting for her in the reception area when she arrived ten minutes ahead of schedule, a broad blond giant with pink skin and a ginger beard. She'd have bet he'd been called 'pig' often enough when he'd been on the streets instead of behind a desk. He enveloped her hand in a surprisingly gentle grip and ushered her up to his office on the first floor. Maps on the walls, three computer stations, comms terminals and the usual assorted piles of paper; every HQ in the country had interchangeable rooms like this.

'Good to meet you at last, DCI Pirie. I've been following your cases ever since Joey Sutherland's murder. He was practically a local,' he said, pulling up a second chair alongside his so she could see his screen. 'You guys make us all look good.'

Somebody has to ... 'Not everybody would agree with you. Some officers think we revel in showing up our fellow officers.'

He chuckled. 'Nobody's perfect. We all screw up sometimes, it's good there's somebody coming behind us with the brush and dustpan.'

It was an attitude Karen didn't come across often and she appreciated it, especially since she was afraid she was going to waste Donny Taylor's Saturday afternoon. 'Fingers crossed I find something of interest today.' She opened her backpack and took out her list of Justified Sinners names. 'These are the guys I'm interested in,' she said. 'We're in the very early stages of building a maybe-case, so I'm afraid I can't divulge details. But if any of them connect to any incidents on your patch that night, it could help us build a solid foundation.'

He ran his eyes over the list and shook his head. 'Nobody I recognise.' He tapped a key and his screen came to life. 'Let's look at hard stops first. Almost all of them are speeders, a couple of red-light jumpers and a bunch of minor bumps. One or two driving without a licence.' He turned his monitor so she could see more clearly. 'We breathalyse routinely, you'll see a few positives in there.'

Karen read her way down the list of names, addresses and car registration numbers. She was mildly disappointed but not really surprised that she recognised nobody. She pointed to a handful of Edinburgh addresses. 'Can you print them out for me? I'd like to check none of them link up with the names on my list – partners, colleagues, offspring.'

Tayor nodded and did as she asked. 'I also pulled any reports from members of the public calling us about traffic-related matters.' He brought up a different file. 'So, here's one from Dalwhinnie, complaining about three boy racers with noisy exhausts blasting their way round the local roads after ten o'clock. We didn't have a car in the area, they weren't actually endangering anybody's life and limb except their own, so, NFA. If it had carried on, we'd have taken a look. But mostly we know who these eejits are and we get one of the patrol cars to chap their doors and have a word.'

And so the list went on, half a dozen petty misdemeanours and mildly anti-social behaviour ranging from a nine-year-old on an ATV terrorising sheep to a teenager covering the car of a love rival in shaving foam. Nothing spoke to Karen till they reached the final page.

'And then we have Alexander Monckton.' Taylor sighed. 'He's one of our regulars. He lives outside Perth and he's a mad keen long-distance cyclist. He's up here most weekends on his fancy titanium bike. You know the ones, you can lift them with one finger, cost about the same as a second-hand family car. He's got all the kit, including a camera in his helmet and another one on his handlebars. Pretty much every other weekend, he comes in with footage of cars cutting him up on one of the main roads. He accuses them of dangerous driving, speeding, reckless driving, littering. The whole kit and kaboodle. He's a total waste of time. When you examine his files, either the number plates are unreadable because of rain or general shoogliness, or there's no way of proving how fast they're going. He's a bloody nuisance, gives cyclists a bad name. As far as I can see, this is a typical bit of nonsense.' He clicked on the arrow on the video window attached to Monckton's complaint.

Heavy breathing. The image of tarmac and roadside undergrowth shuddered as the bike moved forward. Then, apparently out of nowhere, a car appeared from behind his shoulder, cutting hard in front of the bike. 'Fuck!' the voice screamed as the bike wobbled and a clearly identifiable Jaguar F-Type convertible disappeared in the distance. Even as it vanished, its brake lights blazing as it approached a bend, an SUV sped past the bike, again the slipstream causing Monckton problems. The SUV fishtailed as it passed the bike, slamming on the brakes before accelerating into the curve. 'Now, you might say that was dangerous driving, if you were being picky,' Taylor said.

'You might also say that it's not very likely there were two red Jaguar F-Types on that stretch of road that night. The first one, that was Bryce Gordon's car, surely?'

Taylor flushed. 'Shit. That's the first time I've seen that particular footage. We concentrated on the accident scene once we found the car. I don't know how . . .'

'Run it again, please?'

He did as she asked. It was hard to make out any details of the SUV's number plate. But she knew Tamsin Martineau at Gartcosh would know someone who could manage it. 'I'd like to take a closer look at that footage. Can you ping it across to me?' She took out a card as she spoke. 'And pass on Alexander Monckton's contact details too, please? I'm thinking we might want to take a witness statement from him.'

'You think that's got something to do with Bryce Gordon's accident?' He sounded – and looked – stricken.

Karen gave him the hard stare that her team knew only too well. 'Only one way to find out.' She pushed her chair back and stood up. 'Thanks for your help,' she said on the way out. Somehow, she thought Donny Taylor would be less keen on the brush and dustpan in future.

37

Karen got off the tram at Picardy Place and walked round to the office. She wanted to see Jason face to face on her way to the airport to congratulate him on the job he'd done on the Justified Sinners. The memo that had landed in her inbox late on Sunday evening had both his name and Daisy's on it, but she could tell most of the groundwork had been his. Not least because she knew Daisy and Steph had been at a party on Saturday night.

'Nice work, Jason,' she said as she walked in.

Startled, he gave her a faintly worried look, as if he thought she might be winding him up. 'Thanks, boss,' he mumbled. 'Daisy weighed in too.'

'We're booked to come back from Germany on Wednesday. In the meantime, I'd like you to see what you can do with the footage I picked up from Traffic in Inverness. It's probably worth going over to Gartcosh yourself so you can talk to Tamsin about getting her help to get a licence plate from the mad cyclist's video. I'd also like you to go up to Perth and talk to Alexander Monckton about the incident. See if he can tell us anything at all about the SUV and its driver. As far as I can tell, this incident happened about ten miles north of where Bryce Gordon went off the road. There's probably a more accurate GPS reading on the original video.'

'No problem. Boss?'

'Yes?'

'If this Monckton guy is as much of a geek as you say, he'll have been posting his rides online. There'll be Facebook pages, or websites where guys who ride his particular kind of bike share their exploits. Fan boys and nerds, showing off to each other. "I did that route in four minutes thirty-one seconds faster than you, and I had a headwind." That sort of bollocks. Might be that somebody else was on that road that same day?'

'Really? It's not enough that they have competitive Lycra? Who knew. Good idea, Jason, see what you can dig up. I want to know who that SUV was registered to. And I want to know whether it had any bodywork repairs after Bryce Gordon went over the side. Do your best to make me smile when I walk back in this door.'

He grinned at her. 'Will do. Bring me back a bottle of *Schwarzbier*. We discovered it when we went over for the Euros, you can't get it over here.'

'Deal. Happy digging.'

'You too.' He took a deep breath. 'I hope one of us gets lucky.'

Karen couldn't believe how hassle-free the journey to Rostock had been. The flight was on time, they made the train connection and they'd found their accommodation without a single wrong turn. She had booked them into an anonymous-looking hotel in a residential street near the station in Rostock. Her poky room had been surprisingly well designed, with a single bed, a tiny shower room, a slender hanging space and a fold-down table top, an upright chair next to it. She tried the bed, with its square duvet and single pillow. It would do for a couple of nights. Now she was waiting for the other shoe to drop.

When she'd messaged Klaus Beck to tell him where they were staying, he'd responded by suggesting they meet in a brewpub on the promenade of the city harbour. 'It's a busy bar, popular with tourists so you won't stand out,' he'd said.

When she'd asked how they would recognise him, he'd replied, 'We have Google here in Germany! I checked you out online and I think I will recognise you from your media coverage.' Why, then, she wondered, all the palaver about ID and Linda's connection to their case?

'Paranoia,' Daisy had said. 'Journalists have never been more at risk from the nutters on every side of every argument. Just look at how many journos have died in Gaza. And if Beck and Linda Lawrence are running an undercover operation against the far right . . . well, I'd want to cover my back, and then some.'

They'd arrived in good time for the arranged appointment, but the bar was already busy. They had to wait for more than ten minutes to secure a table for four then fend off a pair of boozed-up middle-aged Americans who wanted to join them. Karen had been about to launch into the attack but Daisy pre-empted her with a tirade of cross-sounding French. The Americans had backed off, wrong-footed by the alien tongue. 'That was neat,' Karen said once they were out of earshot.

Daisy giggled. 'Just as well they weren't French-Canadians or we'd have friends for life.'

As she spoke, a short man with neatly barbered dark

hair and a tightly trimmed beard pulled out one of the two empty chairs facing the women. He placed a half-empty glass of dark beer in front of himself. 'DCI Pirie, I presume?' he said with a smile. 'I'm Klaus Beck. But before we go any further perhaps you could discreetly pass me your IDs?'

They'd prepared for this moment. Daisy took a leather folder from her bag and passed it across. Beck unzipped it and studied their police IDs, and their passports. He withdrew a couple of folded sheets of paper, one of which was the Companies House registration of the quartet of journalists that included Linda Lawrence and Sam Nimmo; the other was a printout of a news story trumpeting the identity of the body in the M73. He studied both, nodded in satisfaction, returned them to the folder and passed it back.

'I'm sorry to be so mistrustful. But the people we are working undercover to expose are not averse to violence. For example, one of their elected members distributed Kubotans at a campaign event. You know Kubotan? They're sometimes called Ninja keychains and they're actually illegal in the UK. And that's just the tip of the iceberg. There's a party-within-a-party that are avowedly neo-Nazi and espouse violence against people they don't want here in Germany. They want compulsory DNA samples to be taken to prove where migrants come from so they can deport them to their supposed home countries. Remigration, they call it. So the work Linda is doing to expose them is fraught with danger.'

'I understand that,' Karen said. 'But the work we do is important too. Somebody murdered her friend and colleague back in 2014. And they're still out there. We have no idea what level of threat they present but the very fact of our inquiries could well provoke more violence. If anybody knows the details of what Sam Nimmo was working on, it'd be Linda, and we do need to talk to her.'

He nodded. 'I've talked this over with her and she's willing to meet you. At the mouth of the river is the Warnemünde. It's part of Rostock but it likes to think of itself as separate. There's a big red-brick church in the centre of the town, you can't miss it. It's popular with tourists so you won't be obvious. Linda will be there tomorrow morning from eleven. If you sit down in the third row from the back, she'll join you when she's sure it's safe.'

Karen resisted the temptation to roll her eyes. She was all for being careful, but this was starting to feel like a bad parody of a Le Carré novel. 'We'll be there,' she said.

Beck drained his beer and stood up. 'It's been a pleasure. Can I suggest eating here? The food is good and the beer is better.' He nodded farewell and was gone.

Daisy reached for the menu. 'Always trust the locals when it comes to food.'

'Not a principle you can rely on,' Karen said. 'Have you seen the state of the locals who flock round the kebab shop near the office?'

'Good point. But let's chance it. Pretend we're on our holidays.'

She was, Karen thought, incorrigible. But in a good way. 'OK,' she sighed. 'If I'm up all night with indigestion, I'll be blaming you.'

Jason's travel had not been as free from stress as Karen and Daisy's. Heavy traffic on the motorway, an accident on the slip-road he'd wanted to take that added an extra ten miles to his journey and the usual headache of finding a parking place once he'd reached Gartcosh had taken the shine off his day. He wished he'd just messaged Tamsin Martineau for the info he wanted. But Karen always liked her team to maintain face-to-face relationships with their contacts whenever possible. At least he'd remembered the required bribe for Tamsin, whose preferred currency was good quality chocolate biscuits. He'd stopped off at an Italian deli near his flat and bought a packet of *baci di dama* which he hoped would fit the bill even though they weren't actually covered in chocolate.

Tamsin had eyed them with some suspicion. 'A bit out of the usual run, Jase,' she said. 'Whose idea were these?'

'Meera likes them,' he said, defensive.

'Are you confusing this' – pointing to her punked-up green and electric blue hair – 'with librarian hair?'

'They're nice. Don't knock them till you've—'

Too late. She'd already ripped open the packaging, sniffed one and bitten into it. She closed her eyes and chewed. Then her face lit up in a grin. 'OK, Meera has better taste in biscuits than in men. So why are you here, Jase? What is Karen after today?'

He explained, pinging the video clip across to her in the process. 'I'm going to try to get the original, but what I really need is the licence plate.'

She nodded. 'I'll take it over to my pal Devon in Digital Enhancement myself in a bit. Are you hanging around for an answer?'

He shook his head. 'The boss is away to Germany and I've got a to-do list. Can you get them to give me a bell if they get anywhere with it?'

'Sure thing. And if you get the original, just whizz it across to me and I'll see it gets into the right hands.'

Having left it in the lap of the goddesses, he found a quiet corner in the Gartcosh canteen to see where he might find Alexander Monckton. The cyclist was, according to Karen's notes, a green energy project manager, which as job descriptions went, was a word salad where Jason understood all the ingredients without being any further forward. Google delivered more detail which left him none the wiser except that his office address was the same as the home address that turned up on the electoral roll. It was late in the day to be trekking up to Perthshire; Jason decided to leave it till the morning. If he turned up early, chances were good he could arrive ahead of any departure Monckton might have planned.

Despite his early start, it took Jason longer to reach Alexander Monckton's home than the satnav had promised because it turned out its directions didn't quite correspond to the narrow lanes around Monckton's cottage. Worried that he was going to be too late, he finally got there on the third attempt, thanks to flagging down a passing shepherd on an ATV.

The cottage was almost hidden behind a thicket of hawthorn with honeysuckle threaded through it. Jason parked further up the lane where it widened slightly and walked back. The flagged path led round the gable end of a low-slung cottage and into a well-stocked kitchen garden. A black-and-white cat sat perched on the bottom half of an open Dutch door. As he approached it stood up, stretched, made a noise halfway between a yowl and a purr and disappeared inside. Moments later, a man appeared, frowning.

'Better than a doorbell, your cat,' Jason said.

'Who are you?' There was nothing welcoming in his tone or in his face.

'I'm Detective Sergeant Jason Murray, Police Scotland. Are you Mr Monckton? Mr Alexander Monckton?'

He inclined his head. 'I am he. What brings you to my door?'

'We're investigating an incident you brought to the attention of my colleagues just over five years ago.'

He snorted in derision. 'You've taken your time. But that doesn't narrow it down, Sergeant. I've made many reports about dangerous driving on these roads. Nothing ever happens. I supply your uniform colleagues with dates and times and video footage and still nothing happens. So what has it taken to finally provoke a visit from you?' His tone was peevish; it matched his expression.

'I work with the Historic Cases Unit and we have new evidence to suggest that a death that was recorded as an accident may not have been as straightforward as it appeared.'

His thin lips tightened in a self-satisfied smirk. 'I knew it,' he said. 'I knew it would take a death before you lot took the behaviour on these roads seriously. But *five years*? That's something of a record even for Police Scotland.'

'As I said, sir, new evidence has emerged. And we were hoping you might still have the original recording of the incident. And that you might recall more details than you reported at the time.'

Monckton rolled his eyes. 'Of course I still have the original recording. Not because of the so-called incident but because I keep a complete record of my journeys.'

'That must be quite inspiring to look back on.' Jason was deadpan and Monckton cast a suspicious glance at him.

'Are you taking the piss?' he demanded.

'No, really, I mean it. It's important to keep track. Memory's such a fragile thing. I lost my mother during Covid and not a week goes by that I don't wish I had more photos, more videos. So yeah, I see the point of what you're doing.'

Even Alexander Monckton couldn't find it in himself to doubt Jason's sincerity. 'You'd better come in if you want me to dig it out,' he said, opening the bottom half of the door to allow Jason to step inside.

Half of the room was a working kitchen, with an array of equipment that looked well used. The other half was an office dominated by a pair of monitors. One showed a large-scale map; the other a spreadsheet incomprehensible to Jason. 'What exactly is it you do?' he asked.

'I work with local communities to help them raise money by installing wind turbines that feed into the national grid. Up here in the Highlands, we've got all the wind and water we need to generate Scotland's power and more.' He caught himself and gave a whinny of laughter. 'Sorry, once I get started . . .' He opened a drawer and took out a laptop. 'Here's my records. Have you a precise date?' He booted up the machine and went online.

Jason gave up the relevant information and Monckton typed it into a search bar. Within seconds, up popped two results. 'I have two cameras. One on the bike, one built in to my helmet. Obviously you don't want to see the whole ride . . .' He spoke softly as he opened another window. 'I clipped the section out of the video that shows the reckless drivers that nearly had me off the road.' Again, a search, and again, two clips appeared. Mockton played one after the other; to Jason's untutored eyes, they looked the same as the ones he'd already seen.

'I hoped they'd be a bit clearer.'

'You can blow them up a bit further, they've got a higher PPI.' Seeing Jason's puzzlement he added, 'Pixels per inch.'

'Can you send me those files?'

'If I send them to your phone, it'll compress them and you'll be back to square one,' Monckton sighed. He opened another drawer and took out a memory stick. 'I'll put them on here, that's the best I can do.'

'Thanks. I wonder, did you post them to any websites, anywhere you share with other enthusiasts?'

He smiled at Jason, as if he was a particularly smart schoolboy. 'Oh yes. And sometimes my fellow cyclists share their experiences of similar bad driving on these roads.' More tapping on keys and opening of windows. Triumphantly, he pointed to his screen. 'What do you think of that?'

Jason gazed in awe at the screen. There in front of him it sat like an answer to a prayer he hadn't known to make.

38

Jason was back on the road within twenty minutes, the words he'd read on the screen whirling round his head. *Go, Alex! That shit in the SUV just about had me in the ditch fourteen minutes after he passed you.* Alexander Monckton had reluctantly passed on the details of his fellow cyclist, muttering under his breath about confidentiality and that he wouldn't mind a police state if it took less than five years to swing into action. Armed with a name – Dan Smart – an address – Culloden village near Inverness – and a place of work – FourCode in Inverness itself – Jason was a man on a mission.

He was tempted to slam the blue light on top of the car but he resisted. Karen had scolded more than once that it was for genuine emergencies only. 'Like when you think your wingman might be lying at the bottom of a flight of stairs with a broken leg,' she'd said, poking a finger into his bicep.

'Good point, well made,' he'd grumbled. And he'd recalibrated his own definition of 'emergency' to exclude, 'I really want the answer.' Then it dawned on him that this actually was one of those times when more haste meant less speed. If Dan Smart did still have his journey record, it would be stored at his home, not his work. So there was no point in fronting him up there. Cursing his own stupidity, he pulled off the A9 at Aviemore and found a decent-looking café.

He called the number Monckton had reluctantly handed over. It rang out half a dozen times before a man with an unmistakably English accent answered. 'Hello, Dan Smart here. Are you the dude Alexander said was going to call?'

'I'm DS Murray from Police Scotland, if that's who you mean?'

'Yeah, right. Wow, I've never been a witness in a crime case before. Do you want to come and interview me?' He was as eager as a nine-year-old.

'I'd like that to do that, yes. Do you keep your bike ride records at home or at work?'

'I can access them either place. We've got bigger screens here at FourCode, if you think that would make a difference?'

'It might. When do you close?'

A chuckle. 'When we're done for the day. We're a small operation, Sergeant. Just the four partners. So we're pretty flexible. Where are you now?'

'I'm in Aviemore. About forty minutes away, I think.'

'Excellent. That gives me time to look out the relevant footage and put the kettle on. You know where we are?'

This time, the satnav provided a perfect delivery. FourCode looked like a repurposed corner shop, only with sturdy metal grilles over door and windows. Given the speed with which he opened up, Dan Smart was clearly hovering. 'Come in, come in,' he greeted Jason. He looked like a man who spent his down time in the saddle. He was wearing electric blue Lycra tights that revealed powerful thighs and calves. A lightweight zipper jacket completed his business attire. His face was chiselled, his cheeks hollow but his skin glowed with health. Jason felt tired just looking at him.

They walked straight into an open-plan office that must have been the original shop floor. There were two work stations, both occupied by young men in cargo pants, T-shirts and headphones. Neither even glanced up from their screens. Dan led the way up a flight of narrow wooden stairs and into what had probably once been a bedroom. Now all it contained was an L-shaped desk, a trio of monitors, a clutter of peripherals, two chairs and a metal filing cupboard. There wasn't even a printer in sight. 'This is where the magic happens,' Dan said, dropping into a chair and waving Jason to the other. He turned to the screen and his fingers flew over keyboard and trackpad. 'Alexander's a bit of a freak,' he said. 'He gets a total bee in his bonnet about drivers being at war with cyclists. Me, I think you just have to be vigilant, you know? I don't think drivers hate us, they just don't realise how much space we need to be safe.'

'But you record your rides?'

'Sure, but that's mostly so I can look back on them and enjoy them all over again. And share them with other riders. A lot of cyclists come over here from abroad, they want to see Scotland at first hand and it helps them plan their routes if they can get a taste of them in advance. I do the same when I'm going to France or Germany or Italy. That's why I keep my vids and post them.'

'And you've still got the one from this particular date?'

'Yeah, I kept it mostly because there was a really spectacular sunset. Amazing colours, lighting up the mountains and the lochs.' The file had loaded now and Dan was fast-forwarding to the relevant section. 'So here I am, heading down the back road from Spean Bridge to the back of Ben Nevis, towards the resort down there.'

The screen filled with the image of a road unfurling through a dusky landscape of rough grassland and clumps of trees. The sky was greying out, but it was the time of day when everything seems surprisingly clear. All at once, the roar of an engine blots out the rider's breath and a boxy SUV cuts right across in front of the bike. The number plate was clearer than in Monckton's footage; Jason could almost make it out even in the fleeting moment. And then it was gone, swinging out to take a wide sweep at a bend.

'No sign of the penis extension Jag that Alexander was moaning about, though,' Dan said cheerily.

Jason didn't think he agreed with that opinion. 'Can you take me back through it, slo-mo?' Dan nodded and obliged. 'There. Pause it. Back a couple of frames. Now can you zoom in?'

'Zoom in where?'

'Nearside wing, above the wheel arch. Towards the door.'

'I'm not seeing—Oh.'

Jason could scarcely believe what his eyes were telling him. There on the dark paint there was a definite scrape. It might be wishful thinking, but he thought it might be scarlet.

The sun was shining in Warnemünde, making the red-brick church glow like a beacon at the centre of the port. The town's years as part of East Germany had left a legacy of drab buildings in the surrounding streets, though Karen had enjoyed their earlier walk along the Alte Strom, where yachts, day-tripper craft and fishing boats brightened the vista. Typically, Daisy had sniffed out a craft bakery which she'd raided for treats and they'd found a bench to watch the waterway as they ate and drank takeaway coffee.

She felt uncharacteristically nervous about the coming interview. Revisiting what they had so far, she realised Linda Lawrence could be the make or break witness. Not just for the Sam Nimmo case but also maybe for the football bribes too. If she'd worked as closely with Sam as everyone said, she might be the only surviving source for what Karen needed. Obviously Linda would be nervous about her cover being blown, which put even more pressure on them to get the interview right. Karen had laid out the plan over dinner the previous evening and had revisited it on the waterside bench. Daisy hadn't been overly thrilled at her proposed role, but she knew better than to argue with the boss once she'd made her mind up.

Karen was first in, fifteen minutes ahead of the arranged hour. Although it was as plain as she'd expected a Lutheran church to be, she recognised the same beauty she'd seen in the simple interiors of Scottish Presbyterian kirks. No statues, no icons, nothing elaborate to come between worshippers and their god. The only decorative feature was a perfect scale model of a sailing ship, flying above the pews on one side. But the wooden ribs of the ceiling, and the arches of the sanctuary led the eye inexorably forward, past the rows with their carved and painted ends. If, unlike her, you were a person of faith, Karen thought this building would speak to you.

A couple of elderly women were busy with polish and dusters in the sanctuary. She hoped they wouldn't be moving on to the pews any time soon. She made a slow tour of the nave, pausing to consider what the information plaque told her was a Votivschiff, donated to the congregation by local fishermen and boatbuilders. Finally she stepped into the third pew from the rear. She bowed her head slightly, slipping her hand into her pocket and turning her phone on to 'record'. Then she tried to empty her mind and prepare for what lay ahead. The door opened and closed and she heard footsteps. A pause. Silence. Then more footsteps and a woman slid into the pew next to her.

'DCI Pirie?' came a soft voice.

'Good to meet you, Linda.' Thankfully, the acoustics swallowed their low tones. 'I'm Karen Pirie. I don't want to alarm you or make you feel ambushed but my sergeant will be coming into the pew behind you in a moment. You'll remember Scots law's insistence on corroboration.' She sneaked a quick sideways look. Linda Lawrence was a slight woman, dressed in a nondescript pea jacket and jeans, hair covered with a beanie. Her profile was sharp, nose and chin pointed. A pair of round steel-rimmed glasses sat on the bridge of her nose and the beginnings of frown lines lurked across her forehead. You wouldn't remember her well enough to describe her clearly if you'd spent a train journey sitting opposite her.

'That's fine. You're covering my back as well as yours that way. I understand you've found Sam Nimmo?'

'I'm afraid so.'

'I read about it online. I always knew he was dead.' She lifted a hand from her knee to cut off whatever Karen had been about to say. 'Not because I had any pertinent information but because I knew Sam. I couldn't think of a reason why he'd kill Rachel. But equally, I couldn't think of a reason why anybody else would. But if Sam had been alive and innocent, he'd have found a way to let me know. And he'd have moved heaven and earth to uncover what had really happened to her. That would have been front and centre in everything he did, well ahead of doing a runner.'

Karen let that one go. 'I appreciate you agreeing to meet us. I do know you're taking a big risk. And I'll do everything I can not to blow your cover.'

Linda nodded. 'First sign of trouble, I'm off. I may have to punch you in the process.'

'Understood. I won't hold it against you. Linda, everybody tells me you were closer to Sam than anyone else, certainly in professional terms?'

'I'd say so. Alan McParland, our fourth member, my partner? He was in the loop too, to a lesser extent.' Her face tightened. 'But you'll know what happened there.'

'I'm sorry—'

'I know you get that. I remember Phil Parhatka too. So, what did you want the inside track on?'

'I heard Sam was working a tip about a sexual assault at a big gala evening during the Indy Ref campaign.'

'You're well informed.'

'Not well enough, Linda.'

'What do you know?'

'We think it happened at Fraoch House. Hosted by Haig Striven-Douglass before he inherited the title.'

'Go on. I'll stop you when you start to go wrong.'

Karen could feel a slow prickle of sweat on the back of her neck in spite of the cool of the church interior. 'Striven-Douglass was having fun with his pal Billy the Kidd. William Kidd, to give him his Sunday name. Drink and drugs were allegedly involved, some of them more narcotic than recreational.' She paused.

'Plenty of Colombian marching powder,' Linda confirmed. 'And a lot of champagne, which masks GHB perfectly. Because there's naturally occurring GHB in fermented wine. And of course it metabolises quickly.'

'And the upshot was that a young woman was sexually assaulted.'

Linda pushed up her glasses and rubbed the inner corners of her eyes. 'I think I'd say "brutalised" rather than assaulted. She was stripped naked and then brutally raped. Vaginally, anally, orally.' She cleared her throat. 'Haig liked to see how far he could exploit his position in those days. Showing off what he could get away with in front of Billy, who knew better than to try to stand in his road.'

The notion that Linda was better informed than the victim herself disturbed and disgusted Karen. 'So how did you come by the story?' Nothing. 'Linda, I know all that stuff about protecting your sources, but Sam Nimmo and Rachel Morrison and their unborn child died and I think it had to do with this. I didn't know any of them. I don't have skin in this game except that it genuinely grieves me to think people walk away from taking a life. I suspect you feel the same way, doing what you do.'

A deep sigh. 'Billy the Kidd and I go way back. We grew up on the same scabby street and we were the two who made it out relatively clean. We both understood how to protect ourselves. I let them copy my homework. Billy made them laugh – the crueller his jokes, the safer it kept him from the bullies. I always knew it was a performance, not the real lad.' *Why did we not know that*, Karen wondered. But she didn't want to break Linda's flow.

'One night, not long before all the wheels came off, Billy came round to mine and got very, very drunk. It came out in bits and pieces – how Haig had got this lassie out of her head on drugs and drink and he'd treated her like she was less than human. He didn't just dominate and degrade her, he had to do the same to Billy, trying to goad him into being part of it. Even though Haig didn't succeed in that, he managed to cow him into silence. Billy was genuinely traumatised about what he witnessed that night.'

Not enough to do anything about it. 'What happened with the young woman?'

Linda drew a breath in then bit her lip. 'Haig got Billy to put her in the shower and clean her up, then got his personal driver to take her home. With Billy to nursemaid her and make sure she didn't shoot her mouth off while she was still out of it. Next day, Haig sent a massive bouquet of flowers. The poor lassie didn't remember anything that had happened.' She pressed her eyes closed momentarily. 'All she knew was what was written on her body.'

'She didn't go to the police?'

'She knew there was no point. She couldn't point the finger because she didn't remember what had happened. Billy had showered her clean of any forensic traces. It would have barely been "he said, she said", and who were you lot going to believe? A working-class lassie off her face by her own admission, or a rich entitled bastard and one of the nation's favourite comedians?' Her bitterness was obvious. 'I hated what Haig Striven-Douglass had done, not just to the lassie but by making Billy complicit.'

Karen couldn't escape the conviction that William Kidd was a grown man who could make his own decisions. 'Surely Billy could have supported her if she'd reported it?'

'And you think Haig would have hesitated for a moment before he threw Billy under the bus? You're a polis, look at it like a polis. It was Billy who walked the lassie out to the car, Billy who took her home in Haig's motor. It would have been Billy carrying the can. He wouldn't just have lost his career, he'd have lost his freedom.' Linda bit her lip. 'Billy fought so hard to escape his background. But everybody's courage runs out of road at some point.'

'So what happened?'

'Haig finished cleaning the house. He gave his victim a job on his team. She was just starting out in PR, Billy said. Fraoch House is open to the public, they've got a shop and a cafeteria and they hire out space to conferences and weddings. For fuck's sake,' she added in an undertone. 'And Billy went off to Australia on a pre-booked tour and never came back. He knew only too well that if push came to shove, Haig would point the finger at him. Wild boy from a council house, you know that script.'

'Did you tell Sam? Is that how he started investigating?'

'No.' She shook her head. 'I was torn. I truly didn't want to destroy Billy. And the lassie seemed to be doing OK. And frankly, I thought taking on Haig Striven-Douglass would be disastrous for us, in business terms. He's got a lot of powerful connections and we were just a wee freelance agency dependent on the goodwill of editors who mostly didn't share our world view. So I took the coward's way out.'

'So who did talk?'

'Haig's driver. He'd given Sam stories before, but nothing on this scale. And Sam was fired up about it.'

'Do you remember the driver's name?'

'Derek ... Drummond, I think? But it'll not do you any good. I heard he didn't make it through Covid.'

This case had more bloody dead ends than a new town housing estate. 'Did you ever think Striven-Douglass might have been implicated in what happened to Rachel and Sam?'

'He'd never have got dirt under his fingernails. And it's not like this was the only story we had on our books.'

'So who would His Lordship have called on to do his dirty work?'

'That I don't know. People swallow their principles around men like Haig, men with money and position.'

'People like Billy?'

Linda gave her a quick glance laced with contempt. 'Don't be ridiculous. Billy's not got it in him. He could be easily led with a drink in him, but violent? I never saw him violent. And believe me, I couldn't put my hand on my heart about that when it comes to most of the men I grew up around.'

Time to move on before she lost Linda. 'I need to know more about the victim,' Karen said. 'All I know is that her name was Chloe.'

'I heard she changed her name. Apparently Haig told her Chloe was a bit too common and if she wanted to get to the top in her line of work, she needed an upgrade. She must have been in a fragile state, she'd have snatched at anything that felt like a lifeline.'

'What did she change it to?'

'I don't know what she's calling herself now. Her second name was Grange, or something, she might have kept that? All I know for sure is that Billy told me she's worked her way up to being Haig's marketing manager.'

And that, thought Karen, shouldn't be too much of a reach. The only question was whether they could persuade her to talk after all these years. But 'accessory to murder' was, in her experience, a very valuable tool for loosening tongues.

39

It seemed Linda had reached the end of what she was willing or able to offer. But everything Karen had heard clarified the story growing in her head, a story that made sense of the limited evidence they already had. 'I don't care what Linda says about William Kidd, everything points to him being Haig's scapegoat, the one to clean up the mess. Why bring someone else in? It's only one more mouth to keep shut,' she said as they walked away from the church.

'Plus Billy the Kidd was already in it up to his oxters. Even Linda admits that he was there. And we've only got Linda's word for it that Kidd wasn't party to the sexual assault. Linda's predisposed to believe him – not just because he's her old pal but because that plays into her narrative of class war.' Daisy shook her head. 'And Haig Striven-Douglass doesn't strike me as the kind of guy who'd take chances by bringing anybody else on to the team.'

'So, taking that as a working assumption, two things we need to do. We need to find out the name of Lord Friockheim's marketing manager and talk to her. And we need to find a way of getting William Kidd into our jurisdiction so we can interview him under caution. The first bit I can manage easily enough. But the second? Any ideas?'

'I need caffeine and sugar before I can think,' Daisy said.

Karen sighed, knowing she meant it. They walked back down to the waterside and sat outside at an ice cream parlour that boasted it served the best coffee on Alte Strom. Daisy ordered a mocha and a sundae that came with two spoons while Karen chose an affogato. While they waited for their order to arrive, Daisy said, 'What about finding a way to invite him to a surprise party? A private affair?'

'Why would he come?'

'Why wouldn't he?'

'He didn't even come back for Alex Salmond's memorial service. If you don't show up for the man who led the party into the 2014 referendum and nearly won, who would you show up for?'

Daisy greeted her sundae and coffee with a beaming smile. Two large spoonfuls into the boule of pistachio, she sighed in satisfaction and said, 'That's better. The trouble with a surprise party, I suppose, is that he'd be bound to call up whoever was supposedly organising it and they'd have to be in on the plot. Do we know anybody in the political sphere who we could trust not to blow it?'

Karen sipped her espresso. 'I just burned my bridges in that area.'

'How?'

'It's a long story.'

Daisy knew a slammed door when she heard it. She tucked into her ice cream, frowning in concentration. Karen was intent on her phone, working on the first piece of missing information. 'Claudia Grainger,' she said. 'Head of marketing at Fraoch House.' She turned her phone to face Daisy. 'She looks the right sort of age and the right sort of glamour to be the former Chloe, wouldn't you say?'

'From Chloe to Claudia, it's not such a big leap. His Lordship probably just calls her "Clo". Saves him some breath.' Daisy took the phone and zoomed in on the pic of a perfectly groomed Claudia Grainger. Her hair was an expertly maintained blend of shades of blonde and light brown, her make-up immaculate. It took a lot of time and money to look that understated, Daisy knew. And Claudia was by any standard good-looking enough to turn heads. 'Looking like that, it adds around ten per cent to what they can get away with charging when the clients are men.'

'Harsh. But probably true. What do you think?'

'Given what we know, she ticks the boxes.'

The only person Karen could think of who might be able to confirm that Chloe and Claudia were one and the same was Cath Gray. And that ship had sailed out to sea under the broken bridge. She stirred her affogato, slipping a tiny wedge of vanilla ice cream on to her spoon. 'Going back to Billy the Kidd – do you have a sense of how big a name he is on the comedy circuit?'

Daisy dug her spoon into her sundae and opened her phone. 'He's got 230k followers on YouTube, which is pretty good for somebody who's not been working his home crowd for years. He's just started doing some gigs in the US, which has boosted his numbers.' She resumed her dessert journey.

'Do you think he might be tempted back to the UK for a one-off massive arena event? Say, headlining something at the Hydro in Glasgow? I mean, it's huge, right? Twelve, thirteen thousand capacity.'

'The return of the prodigal! It would work because he's still got a big Scottish following, I reckon. I think that'd be a big draw for him. And a big payday too, presumably. But how on earth do we set it up?'

'Do you think there's any chance we could get the Glasgow International Comedy Festival on board? There must be some big star they're doing a tribute event for at the festival?'

'It's worth a try. People like to feel they're part of some big secret operation, don't they?'

'Mibbes if we ask them to bill a special surprise act as part of the tribute, then we can pitch it to William Kidd as his massive return to the Scottish scene. Or just a one-off, if he'd rather do it that way? And tell him he's got to keep it top secret, because we want it to be a genuine wow moment?'

'And we meet him off the plane and take him into custody?'

Karen gave a wry smile. 'Something like that, Daisy. Something like that. And in the meantime, get online and see if you can wrangle us a couple of flights home tonight.'

It was late when Jason arrived back in Edinburgh. Too late to bother Karen an hour ahead of him in Germany, but not too late to stop off at the office. He loaded up the footage of the SUV that Dan Smart had passed over to him and zoomed in on the number plate. He could make out the first four digits and make a decent guess at the last three. So he started working his way through the possibilities. He'd gone through fourteen before he got an SUV. He made a note of the full number plate and the details of the registered keeper, but kept on searching. By midnight, he had five other possibilities. None of the owners' names was familiar. And there was no way of checking who had owned the vehicles in question when Bryce Gordon had died without speaking to a human being. Jason sighed, turned off the computer and made his way down the hill and home.

To his surprise, Meera was still awake, sitting up in bed reading. 'I thought you'd be spark out by now,' he said, greeting her with a kiss before he changed into sleeping shorts and T-shirt.

'I'm enjoying this book. And besides, you'd only have woken me up when you got in.'

'I'd have been quiet,' he said, injured.

'Doesn't matter how quiet you are, I always sense your arrival.'

He slipped into bed beside her. 'Well, you can go to sleep now.'

'Only after you tell me about your day.'

So he did. Then drifted into the easy sleep that was the hallmark of his nights now. If for no other reason, he knew because of this that Meera was the one. Jason couldn't imagine existing as his boss did, chasing sleep like a fugitive half the time. When he woke, he felt ready for whatever the day might throw at him. Except for the mornings after a night out with the lads, obviously.

As soon as he was showered and dressed, Jason called Karen. But her phone went straight to voicemail. He assumed she and Daisy were still hot on the trail of Linda Lawrence, so there was no point in trying Daisy either. So he cleared his throat and spoke. 'Morning, boss. I've got some better footage from another cyclist further down the same road and here's the thing. No sign of the Jag. It's only the SUV and I think there's a paint scrape on the nearside wing. So I'm going to take it across to Gartcosh to see what they can make of it. Plus—' He swore under his breath as the beep cut him off.

He dialled Karen's number again. 'Sorry, got cut off. I've managed to read enough of the number plate to do a PNC search. I've got five possibles and I'm going to get on to my contact at DVLA to find out who the registered keepers were back when Bryce Gordon died. Hope that's all OK and that you're making progress. Talk later.'

It hardly seemed worth going into work when the boss wasn't due back for hours, but he didn't want to chance her calling him from the airport and finding him on the missing list. So he marched up the hill to the empty office and subsided into his chair, He scrolled through his contacts for 'Kayleigh at DVLA' and called her.

'DVLA,' came the answer.

'Kayleigh, is that you?'

'Is that Detective Constable Murray?'

'Not any more, it's Detective Sergeant now.'

'Congratulations! I thought I recognised your voice. Me, I'm still a lowly clerical officer. How can I help you today, Jason?'

He explained what he needed. 'Is that something you can help me with?'

'Shouldn't be a problem. I'll try to get back to you later today, but it depends what else lands in my lap.'

'Appreciate it, Kayleigh. How are you doing these days?'

'Pretty good. But you'd better make the most of me. I'm off on maternity leave in a fortnight.'

'Really? That's great news. I'll miss you, though.' And he meant it. Although they didn't talk often, he knew he could rely on Kayleigh to go the extra mile for him. Now he'd have to start from scratch with someone else.

'You'll be fine. Just charm whoever answers the phone with your Scottish accent and you'll be sorted.'

He ended the call, wondering whether his accent really made that much difference to some stranger in Swansea. He'd heard that some Scottish accents were the most trusted in the UK; others, like broad Glasgow, simply filled listeners with anxiety. He was glad he had one of the trustworthy ones. Anything that made him better at his job was something to be grateful for. He messaged Tamsin with the key clip of Dan Smart's footage and a note.

This is a different image of the Mercedes SUV I left you with yesterday. The licence plate's a bit clearer, but I'm more interested in what looks like a scrape on the nearside wing, just above the wheel arch. Anything your guys can get me on that – colour, relationship to the side of a Jaguar F-Type – and the boss will be even more in your debt. Thanks.

He'd barely sent the message when his phone buzzed and the screen told him 'Kayleigh DVLA' was on the line. 'That was quick,' he said. 'Thanks. Any joy?'

'It was really straightforward. I've traced the registered keepers for all five of those plates and I've pinged them across to you in an email. Hope it helps the case along.'

'That's brilliant. You're a star.' Jason couldn't get off the line quick enough. He logged on and scrolled down through Kayleigh's email. When he reached the fourth set of details, he drew his breath in sharply.

The boss was going to love this.

40

Staring at the information on his phone, Jason realised he wasn't done with Kayleigh. He called her back and told her what he needed to know. 'Can you access that?' he asked, anxious.

'It'll all be in the data,' she'd reassured him. 'I can pull up the entire history of the vehicle and give you all the information we have. Previous owners, current owner, when it changed hands, all that.'

'What about insurance claims? Do you keep records of those?' Not that he thought anybody would be making an insurance claim over this particular incident. But still . . .

'Not as such, no. You'd need to check that with the Motor Insurers' Bureau. They'll have the information but you'd maybe need a warrant, I don't know.'

'That's OK, I can cross that bridge if the boss thinks I need to. But the other stuff . . .'

'I know, you hate to ask, but asap, right?' There was laughter in her voice. 'It's fine, Jason, I like feeling part of what you do. Cold cases matter to people, thanks to you I get that. I'll ping you the info as soon as I can.'

She'd been as good as her word. Within the hour, he saw that the person he was interested in had been the first registered keeper of the car. It had been sold over the border in England to a dealership in Newcastle, two days after Bryce Gordon had died and before his body had been discovered. The condition of the car would have been recorded by them before they sold it on to its current owner. 'Ya dancer,' Jason murmured. This was getting better and better.

He debated whether to wait for Karen's return before he pursued that angle. But there were still hours to go before her flight landed. To cover his back against any complaints about taking too much of an initiative, he called her phone and left a voicemail saying he'd got a bit of a lead. Now he could start the ball rolling; maybe even get it in the back of the net ahead of her return. He found a number for the dealership and called it. He explained to the receptionist who he was and what he wanted to know. 'You'd be best talking to our sales manager,' she said, putting him on hold.

He listened for what felt like a very long time to an electronic version of some classical music he vaguely recognised from a TV advert before he heard, 'Hello, this is Seth Rothwell, sales manager at Berwick Motors. Jane our receptionist says you're a policeman, is that right?' His accent was unmistakably from the North-East, right down to the throaty rolling 'r' sound that was peculiar to the town itself.

'That's right. DS Murray from Police Scotland. I'm after some information about a vehicle that passed through your hands.' He gave the date and the details.

Rothwell repeated it, checking the registration number to make sure he'd written it down correctly. 'So what is it you want to know? I can't give you any information about the vendor or the buyer. GDPR regs, you know?'

Jason rolled his eyes. GDPR had become the catch-all bullshittery for anything people didn't want to reveal. 'That's fine, I've got all those details already from DVLA. What I'm interested in is the condition of the car when you bought it.'

'The condition? What, like, was it clean?' He chuckled. 'I think if there had been bloodstains we'd have noticed.'

'The bodywork. I want to know about the condition of the bodywork. Any scratches, scuffs, dents. Did it have to go through the bodyshop?'

A pause. 'Can I ask why you want to know?'

'You can ask, but I'm afraid I can't tell you anything material about an ongoing investigation.' Jason had the jargon off pat these days. It still felt awkward in his mouth though.

'Do you not need a warrant for information like that? Is it not confidential, like?'

'Why would it be confidential, Mr Rothwell? It's a simple question about the cosmetic condition of a car you sold years ago. I don't see how it can pose any issues for you.'

'I don't know … Look, I'm going to have to talk to my boss about this. Give me your number, I'll call you back.'

Jason could hardly bear the waiting. But Rothwell was as good as his word. Within half an hour, his phone rang. 'Sergeant Murray? It's Seth Rothwell from Berwick. Me and my manager, we've talked this up hill and down dale and we can't see any reason for not giving out the information you're after.' Jason held his breath, not daring to hope. 'The car in question did have to go through the body shop. There was a scrape on the nearside front wing, the actual wheel arch was dented out of shape. More than that, the rear nearside alloy was well battered.' He chuckled. 'That's a technical term the grease monkeys use.'

Jason punched the air with his free hand. 'I don't suppose there were any traces of what the Land Rover might have hit?'

'They'd obviously tried to clean it up. You couldn't tell from the wheel arch.' Jason's heart sank. But Rothwell continued. 'The wheel, now that was another story. It had really ground into something and there were definite streaks where it had scored into red paint.'

Jason closed his eyes and breathed freely again. 'You've been incredibly helpful, Mr Rothwell. Would it be OK if we got one of your local officers to come round and take a statement confirming what you've just told me?'

'I don't see why not, we'll give him a nice cup of tea and a choccy biscuit. We're nice like that. And happen next time he's changing his car, he'll think of us.'

I might just do the same, Jason thought.

It had been so late – no, early, since it had been well after midnight when they'd landed, that Karen had told Daisy they should take the morning off. When she'd woken to find a voicemail from Jason asking her to call, guilt had catapulted her out of bed, into the shower and up the road to the office, pausing only to alert Daisy and instruct her to join them there. As soon as she walked in the door, it was clear Jason had news; although he was undoubtedly maturing both as a polis and as a man, she was glad he still retained a childlike delight when he'd achieved something more than he'd expected.

'I can see you've got something to tell me,' she said. 'Daisy's gone to grab a sandwich, will it wait till she gets here?'

It was an obvious struggle, but Jason managed to contain himself. 'I did get some interesting stuff but it was a bit too complicated for voicemail. It can wait for Daisy. You're back early. How did you get on in Germany?' he gabbled.

'We rearranged our flights yesterday, but the last leg was delayed so I decided we deserved a long lie. Sorry about that. We made some real progress. Linda confirmed that Haig Striven-Douglass and William Kidd got a young woman off her face at a fundraiser at Fraoch House and raped her. She was too scared to go to the police, and Striven-Douglass bought her off with a job on his staff. Where, bizarrely, we think she's still working.'

Jason gaped in disbelief. 'You're kidding? Why would she do that?'

Karen sighed. 'It's hard to credit, but I think I can see why she might have made that choice. For one thing, she apparently has no memory of what happened to her.'

'What? No flashbacks, no weird reactions for no apparent reason? No triggering she can't account for?'

'So Linda implied. Which made it even more difficult to go to the police. Her befuddled word against theirs. And zero forensics. Striven-Douglass was taking no chances – he got William Kidd to scrub her clean in the shower. So that's point one. Point two is that Striven-Douglass gave her a good job. A real leg-up in her career. She's ended up head of marketing at Fraoch House. Which must be a pretty cool job.'

Jason gave a low whistle. 'Do you really think she knows nothing about what happened to her?'

'According to Linda, she was physically in a bad way afterwards. She knew something bad had happened and she knew when and where. That's probably enough to put Lord Friockheim in a very awkward position, but no more than that.'

'I suppose if she ever threatened to spill the beans, he could say she was totally up for it. And that she'd blackmailed him into giving her a job.'

'Mutually Assured Destruction,' Karen agreed. 'So the thought of having Sam Nimmo poking about in the events of that night at Fraoch House must have been worrying. Let's not forget this was only a matter of a few months after the event itself. Memories would still have been fresh. Who knows what some of the other party animals might have seen or heard or picked up on? You know how it goes. Things that seemed insignificant in themselves can suddenly loom large when they're put into context.'

'So we're thinking maybe Striven-Douglass was responsible for the murders?' Jason seemed taken aback.

'What makes me consider him is the first death, whether it was an accident or murder,' Karen said. 'You see, I've been reading up about Striven-Douglass online. The picture that comes out from profiles and interviews is of a man who understands strategic thinking. He takes the long view and doesn't rush at things like a bull in a china shop. And in the light of what we now know about Sam Nimmo's murder, someone's response to Rachel Morrison's death was very strategic. Sam was the prime suspect and his disappearing without trace made him look like a heartless killer. Who would believe a negative word he said about anybody else after that?'

'I get that, but ... really?'

'Unless we can stand up your gambling syndicate as being totally ruthless, I can't see anybody else with a motive.'

As she spoke, Daisy walked in. 'She's right, Jason. Where are we up to with the bent referees and their paymasters?'

'OK, I'm not much further forward but I still think it's too soon to dismiss it out of hand.'

'But if you're not making progress—'

'Because I can't do everything all at once and because I've

been focusing on other things,' he said. 'Other things that I *have* been making progress with. Boss, I think Marcus Nicol murdered Bryce Gordon.'

Karen stared at Jason. 'Marcus Nicol? Why were you even looking at Marcus Nicol for Bryce Gordon?'

'I just did what Phil always told me – follow the evidence. And that's where it led me.'

41

Daisy looked incredulous. 'Where's this coming from? Last I heard, we were digging into Sam Nimmo's murder as our number one priority. That's why you were supposed to be sorting out the football bribes allegation.'

Jason flushed an ugly scarlet and his mouth set in a stubborn line. Karen butted in before he could respond. 'That doesn't mean we ignore the other cases on our slate, Daisy. Talk me through it, Jason.'

He opened his notebook and cleared his throat. 'I was following up on the SUV that went up the road after Bryce Gordon's Jag. I managed to make out a partial plate and got my contact at DVLA to get me a list of possibles. I started with the five that were registered in Edinburgh. And one of them was Heidi Nicol. It's an unusual name, and I remembered it was Marcus Nicol's wife.

'I tracked down another cyclist on the road that night who had a better quality camera on his bike. His film covered an area further up the road and there was no sign of the Jag. I guess it could have turned off, though there's only a couple of side roads, not much more than single tracks, really. And Gordon would have had to turn round and go back to the main road because that's where he went off the road. But what I did notice was what looked like signs of an impact on the front wing, and the rear alloy was messed up.'

'Well spotted,' Karen said.

'Meanwhile I'd gone back to DVLA and got the full details on that Mercedes SUV and found out Marcus Nicol – not Heidi but Marcus – sold it two days after the accident that killed Bryce Gordon. Before the wreck of Gordon's car and his body were found. And he went all the way down to Berwick to sell it. All that seemed suspicious to me. So I've arranged for the local boys to send someone round to take a statement from the car dealership.'

'That's bizarre,' Daisy said. 'The suspect in one possible murder turns out to be involved in a completely separate suspicious death only a few months before the one we're already interested in. And the only thing linking them is a mysterious book club. It's like something out of a Sunday-night TV murder mystery.'

'It's a weird coincidence?' Jason didn't attempt to hide his doubt.

Karen was struggling to make sense of what she'd just heard. 'We don't believe in coincidence, we believe in links. So how is the Justified Sinners a link?'

A long pause while they tried to find an answer. Daisy, never shy, came up with the first attempt. 'Maybe Marcus Nicol is the cleaner for the Justified Sinners?'

'Are you using "cleaner" in the organised crime sense? As in, the person who wipes out the problem affiliates?' Karen said, the sarcasm obvious. 'Have you actually read the list of names in the membership list?'

'Of course I have,' Daisy shot back. 'But put together the name of the group, plus the obscure headquarters of the shady Brochan Enterprises that employs Hugh Grieve, and it doesn't exactly sound like a benevolent society, does it? Not to mention that being a Justified Sinner gives you carte blanche to commit any crime without repercussions in the next life.'

'The next life, not this one,' Karen pointed out. 'Even if I thought for a moment there was something in what you're suggesting, it'd be a ridiculous gamble. Me, I'd want a guarantee for this life.'

'But isn't that exactly what this bunch of rich, influential men is? The sort of cabal that could cover your back, come what may?'

'You both sound mad to me,' Jason muttered. 'Like you've been watching too many Netflix box sets.'

'Have you got a better suggestion?' Daisy again, edging towards full stroppiness.

'Not yet, no,' Karen said slowly. 'But like Jason, I'm struggling with the notion of a bunch of Edinburgh high heid yins employing an assassin. I need to think. I'm going for a walk to clear my head. I suggest you two do whatever it is you do for that. And we'll pick this up in the morning.'

The walk clarified nothing, but she'd almost been back home when Rafiq texted her, suggesting a call. Home in 5, she responded. As soon as his call came through, her heart lifted. 'Hi,' she said. 'It's so good to see you.'

His face was unusually solemn. 'Karen, I have news. Something to tell you.' He frowned.

Her stomach cramped and her face tensed. Let it not be someone else in his life. It would hardly be surprising. In the five years since they'd met, they'd spent less than six months in each other's presence. She'd saved up every scrap of leave to travel to Canada, since he didn't yet have the passport

293

that would allow him back into Scotland. She knew she loved him but she felt his past always in the shadows between them. She'd never be as sure of his commitment as she was of her own. Was this the moment she'd dreaded ever since she first walked into his arms in Montreal-Trudeau Airport? 'That sounds serious,' she said.

'It is serious.' His mouth twisted in a complicated movement. 'You know Syria is in turmoil, with Assad gone—'

'Under house arrest in Moscow, I read the other day. And his wife has rediscovered her British passport and she's filing for divorce.' Karen forced a smile. 'Couldn't happen to a nicer couple.'

'I'm sure she will survive. Their kind generally do, except when they don't read the room and try to cling on, like Saddam Hussein or Gaddafi.' His voice was acid. 'My heart is torn, Karen. I did not think I would have to choose between my past and my future, between the two halves of my heart. Between you and Syria. There was no actual choice, you see. I could not leave Canada without losing everything. Again. Becoming a refugee. Again.' He sighed.

'Something's changed.'

A pause. 'This morning, I heard from the Canadian immigration authorities. I have been granted citizenship and I am permitted to apply for a passport.'

When Karen had pictured this moment, she had imagined uncomplicated joy. Delight that at last Rafiq would be able to come to Scotland; that they could decide together where their future lay. She'd shown her commitment by visiting Montreal whenever she could; he'd spoken of his longing to come to Edinburgh to be with her, and to see his extended family members, cousins who had managed to rebuild their lives in Scotland. Now, his words sat like a stone in her gut. 'And you want to go back to Syria,' she said heavily.

'"Want" is not the right word, I think. I feel a duty.' He sighed. 'Karen, I love you. I hope you know this, I hope you feel loved, because you should do. It's what you deserve. But imagine how it would be if we were talking about Scotland, not Syria. Imagine if you had been exiled from the land and the customs and the people, without any hope of return.' He pressed his eyes tight shut, then managed to look at her again. 'It is my country, Karen. And they need people like me, people with the skills to rebuild. So many people whose lives have been blown apart, so many bodies I can help to mend.'

And what was one broken heart to set against that, she thought wearily. She couldn't argue against him. 'Of course you must go,' she said, her voice dull with pain. 'I'd think less of you if you turned your back on your homeland. I always knew that if it came to a choice between me and Syria, I'd be the loser.' *I am not going to cry, I am not going to shed a tear, not here. Not now.*

His pain was obvious now. 'You don't have to lose me. When I met you, I thought I would never dare to love anyone again. That I couldn't take the risk. But you changed that. Your open heart took me in and led me back to contentment. We don't have to give that up. Karen, you could come to Syria. Join me there.'

He doesn't know me at all. 'And what would I do in Syria? How would a thrawn wee Scottish polis fit into a Muslim community? I don't have transferrable skills, and I'd be no use at all as an aid worker.'

'Karen, you're a deeply compassionate woman,' he protested.

'I'm good at one-to-one stuff, Rafiq. I'm not any kind of social worker. I haven't the patience for it. I have a life here. My parents are here and not getting any younger. My friends are here. I can exercise my skills here in ways that matter. I'm not cut out to be a camp follower.' He looked puzzled. 'A woman who follows her soldier husband around from one posting to another. A woman with no identity of her own.' She could hear the anger rising in her voice; it was her default when she was hurt, she knew that. But she didn't want this conversation to veer off in that direction. So she took a deep breath. 'I understand, Rafiq.'

'We can still be together.' She heard the desperation in his voice and it stung. 'You can visit me in Syria and I can visit you in Scotland. We have proved we can sustain our love for each other across an ocean. We have grown closer with every passing year. Why should that come to an end?'

He waited for her to gather her thoughts. 'It worked because we believed it was temporary. Because we talked about the life we would make together once you could come to Scotland. Your work is portable, Rafiq. People have fucked-up joints everywhere. But my work is place-specific. Scottish law is distinct even from English law. I want to spend my life with you, not wee fragments whenever one of us can take time off work. I don't want a permanent holiday romance, I want the dailyness of a committed life together. I thought that was what you wanted too. I thought that's what we were working towards.'

He started to speak but she cut across him. 'I don't blame you. I'm not going to try to talk you out of going back to Syria. Because even if you did agree, there would come a day, sooner or later, when you'd see something on the news, or you'd be having your coffee in Aleppo, eating one of

Amina's pastries, when one of the guys would tell you how things are going back home and you'd want to sit down and cry for what you'd lost. You'd blame me for it. And I can't live my life waiting for that day.'

They stared at each other, each recognising the truth of what she was saying.

When she spoke again, her voice was soft. 'Now away you go and write up your notes on today's surgeries. Make your plans without the encumbrance of having to include me in them.'

'We'll stay in touch,' he said.

No, we won't. Not really. Miran will tell you how I'm doing, Amina will tell me how you're doing. And the hurt will fade a little. We both know this because we have both known loss. And we survived.

42

Daisy was delighted at the prospect of an early cut after a couple of days away from home. Sod the cases, she needed some quality time with the woman she loved. Exchanging a few words in the middle of the night really hadn't counted, not as a proper reunion. It wasn't that they lived in each other's pockets, but Daisy was always eager to be reconnected with Steph. Their worlds were so different, yet each seemed as interested as the other in the minutiae of their days. The incidents and the characters that peppered their anecdotage were a vivid part of the foundation of their relationship.

She stopped off on the way home at the French patisserie for a box of macarons, because she never liked to return from a trip empty-handed and nothing at the airport had excited her apart from the same chocolates she could buy at home. She made it back to their Bruntsfield flat in good enough time to lay out the treats on a plate on the kitchen table and boil the kettle before Steph walked through the door. She exclaimed in surprised delight and pulled Daisy into a tight embrace.

'I thought KP Nuts would have kept you hard at it for ages,' she said.

Daisy pulled away and poured boiling water into the teapot to warm it. 'We were going round in circles and she needed one of her city yomps to clear her head so we were dismissed. Me and Jason didn't need to be told twice.'

Steph took off her coat and spied the macarons. 'Ooh, God bless KP Nuts for lowsing you in time to hit the cake shop!' She embraced Daisy from behind and nuzzled the back of her neck. 'I missed you.'

They sat at the table, drank tea and attacked the macarons. 'God, these are so good,' Steph enthused. 'So, tell me all about your adventures in Rostock.'

Daisy obliged, describing the city and the waterfront before she delved into the details of their meeting with Linda Lawrence. 'She wasn't what I was expecting,' she said. 'I thought she'd be more of a Hemingway sort of figure, you know? A tough cookie in combat pants and a jacket with twenty-seven pockets, a trademark scarf like Lindsey Hilsum always wears. Maybe a cigarette in the corner of her mouth and a clever little camera in her pocket.'

Steph spluttered with laughter. 'But you said she was working undercover.'

'I know, stupid of me, but I had this romantic notion of what I expect a foreign correspondent to look like. Anyway, she looked completely nondescript, which I suppose makes more sense.'

'Was she forthcoming?'

'Kind of. She's clearly still got a bond with William Kidd – they've known each other since they were kids. But equally, I don't think she feels any loyalty to His Lordship. She confirmed that Sam was investigating the allegations of a sexual assault. The big surprise to me was that she told us Kidd had admitted to her one night when he'd been off his face that he'd been goaded into taking part. They'd been doing a lot of drugs and Haig Striven-Douglass had pushed him into it.'

'That's disgusting,' Steph said. 'So they've basically just got away with rape without consequences. Striven-Douglass inherited the title and the big houses and all that goes with it. And Kidd just swans round the world cracking jokes and raking in the cash.'

'Only because Rachel Morrison was probably murdered, Sam Nimmo was framed, discredited and then murdered too, to keep the lid on things. So we're thinking His Lordship was likely the driving force behind the murders. And since Kidd fled the country so soon after Sam Nimmo "disappeared", the boss reckons he's the most likely villain of the piece.' She helped herself to another macaron and bit into it savagely.

'And he's still abroad? Kidd? So you can't touch him?'

Daisy nodded. 'That's about the size of it.'

'What about the victim? Couldn't you persuade her to point the finger so at least they have to face the consequences of the rape?'

Daisy gave a sardonic laugh. 'You know what they say about keeping your friends close and your enemies closer? Guess who's head of marketing for Fraoch House?'

'You're not serious?' Steph clenched her hands into tight fists.

'Oh yes. He brought her into the fold right away and she's still in his employment. If she turns on him now, he could accuse her of everything from consent to complicity, via blackmail. Nobody in her line of work'd take her on after that.' Daisy reached out and covered Steph's hands with hers. 'The good news is that the boss has a kind of plan. Only, I don't see how we're going to make it work.'

'Do you want to share?' Steph drew her hands free and poured them both more tea.

'Her theory is that comedians all have fragile egos. They want to be loved more than anything else. And Billy the Kidd's been away from the home town love for a long time. Selling out theatres in Australia and America and Dubai, having a fuckton of views on YouTube is all very well, but it's not like feeling the love from your own crowd.'

'She's right about that, I'd say. So how is she planning to capitalise on that?'

'She thinks he could be tempted to fly in for a single gig – in and out in twenty-four hours. He's based in San Francisco; KP checked flights. He can arrive one day at lunchtime and fly out again the next afternoon.'

'But surely he'd realise that if the police want to interview him, they could arrest him?'

Daisy looked pleased with herself. 'Only if they knew he was coming. The boss reckons there might be a way. Advertise a big comedy event at a venue like the Hydro with a surprise special guest, keep it a closely held secret, so Kidd will think nobody knows he's coming. He flies in, does the show, disappears to a secret location overnight then boards a flight early in the morning. Maybe even a private jet out of Glasgow into another jurisdiction. He might just take the bait.'

'It's a great idea.'

'With one major flaw. How do we persuade a promoter to organise it for us and keep their mouth shut? I admit my experience is limited, but it seems to me that gossip is the common currency in the entertainment world. The return of the prodigal Billy the Kidd? We'd never keep the lid on it.'

'It's not like you to be defeatist,' Steph said.

'Even optimists have their off-days. This time, I think KP's gone too far.'

'Don't be so sure about that.' Steph's smile was surprisingly mischievous. 'I think you might be able to give her the missing piece of her jigsaw.'

43

Jason was cross with Daisy. Not for the first time, he felt she'd dismissed not just his work but him too. He needed something solid to bring back to Karen to show he deserved his sergeant's stripes as well as his place on the team. That he was worth more than just combing data sources for the next step forward.

It was Wednesday, late in the season with too many fixtures still to be played, so the chances were good that there would be football. Jason scanned the online fixture list and spotted that Jordan Macaleese was listed to officiate at a cup tie that had been postponed from the previous Saturday because a burst water main had flooded part of the pitch. The match was between Alloa and Livingston at Alloa's Indodrill Stadium. Jason didn't really rate Macaleese as a serious suspect, but even a minister of the Church of Scotland might give in to temptation.

He rang Meera. 'I don't suppose you fancy a cold night out in Alloa?'

'Does this involve crap football and a half-time cup of Bovril?'

'A pie too, if you're lucky.'

She groaned. 'This is work, right?'

'Kind of. Probably it'll turn out to be nothing.'

'But if it does turn out to be something, I'm your cover? Mad Asian woman who can't resist a freezing night on an uncomfortable seat watching a bunch of guys making a hash of set pieces?'

He heard the note of merriment in her voice. 'Aye, but it comes with me and I'm irresistible.' Even on the phone, he was blushing.

She snorted with laughter. 'Somebody's got to keep you out of trouble. Karen would kill me if another bad thing happened to you on her watch. Pick me up on your way out of town.'

So he did. They arrived at the ground in good time, but Jason hadn't reckoned with the lack of parking in the immediate vicinity of the stadium. That was confined to directors and officials. Even the visiting team's coach had to decant the players then park a couple of streets away. 'I'm going to have to ID myself,' he groaned. 'Otherwise we've got no chance of following the reverend if he's meeting anybody at the end of the game.'

'You do need to be inside,' Meera said firmly.

The security man on the gate to the parking area was not impressed by Jason's warrant card. Or his concocted excuse for needing to park inside. 'You seriously telling me that you've had threats made against a Livingston director? And they've sent you and a lassie as bodyguards? How come we've not been told about this?'

Meera leaned across Jason and spoke with what he liked to think of as the authority of a librarian. 'Because we're trying to keep it on the down-low. We don't want to freak anybody out. And we don't want to scare off the guy who's making the threats.'

'And you're the deterrent, are you? What, you've got a black belt in sushi?'

'Ukioy-e, actually. Look, there's folk behind us waiting to get in, do you really want your boss tooting his horn at you?'

A sigh with a waft of fried onions came from the security man. 'On youse go. But don't block anybody in, right?'

Jason nodded and drove off, looking for a free spot in the tightly packed area. 'What was that?' he asked. 'Uki- what? I thought I'd heard of most martial arts, but not that one.'

Meera laughed. 'It's a Japanese art movement. You know that famous painting of the big blue and white wave?' He nodded. 'That's an example of it.'

Jason flashed her a quick look then burst out laughing. 'Honest to God, Meera, what do you see in me?' He reversed into a narrow space that offered a view of the officials' entrance. 'I know nothing and you know everything.'

'What do I see in you? I see your big heart, your appetite for life, your eagerness to be the best you can be.' She leaned across and kissed his cheek. 'And your cute arse. Now stop fishing and tell me how we do this.'

A few hundred staunch and stalwart fans huddled into puffa jackets and winter overcoats, scarves wrapped tight around their necks. The wise had heavy-duty gloves, the rest had their hands stuffed into pockets except when play required fists to be pumped or bumped, or faces to be covered in sorrow or disbelief. There was nothing glamorous about a mid-week cup tie, not even for diehard fans who turned out because they always did. Mostly, they'd sooner walk away from their families than their teams. Jason loved the football, had grown up loving his local team, but he'd been relieved of that obligation by Meera's devotion to the game in the shape of Heart of Midlothian Women's FC. Secretly, he'd been grateful for the chance to distance himself from some of his former club's poor decision-making. His brother Ronan did not hide his disgust at Jason's choice, but Jason had learned the hard way not to care what Ronan thought about this or anything else.

The play was dismal by any standard. Neither side appeared to have any shape or tactical plan. But Jason was less interested in the flow of play than in the decisions of the referee. There was little to complain of in the first half, mostly because it was hard to identify any decision that would offer an advantage to either side. At half-time, Jason came back from the refreshment counter with the promised pies and Bovril. 'I'm sorry I've wasted your evening,' he said, handing over Meera's share.

'I've had worse. Wait'll I drag you along to a family wedding.'

'We could leave, if you've had enough?'

'We're here now, let's stick it out. The ref seems to be pretty even-handed to me. If he's supposed to make something happen, he's not showing any signs of it yet. Mind, he's not had many opportunities.'

That changed quickly once the second half was under way. A terrible tackle from an Alloa player in the penalty box led to a yellow card, which provoked Meera into shouting, 'That's a straight red!' She was barely mollified when Macaleese awarded a penalty. 'Quite right too. I've never seen a more stone-cold spot kick.'

Nobody expected what came next. The penalty kick taker paused, took a deep breath, a sideways jig up to the ball and promptly skied it over the bar. A groan ran through the tight cluster of away supporters, while the home crew jeered and laughed derisively. Macaleese was frozen in place for a long moment before he whistled for a goal kick. 'You think that was meant to play out like that?' Meera said.

'There's no way you could plan something like that. Unless the ref was meant to find an excuse for a penalty that the shooter could miss? And he got handed it on a plate. Let's see what happens next.'

What happened next was a second offence in the penalty box. But this time it was a borderline tug on a jersey whose victim made a meal of it. Another penalty to the visitors, and this time the kick was a low shot to the corner but with no real pace. The keeper got a glove to it and turned outside the far post. More jeers and groans.

And that was it for drama. A no-score draw, but two failed penalty kicks. 'You think they deliberately screwed up the penalties?' Meera asked as they hung back waiting for the stands to empty so they could make their way to their vantage point with its view of the door Macaleese would have to depart through. Someone had parked so close to the driver's door of Jason's car that he had to scramble over the passenger seat to get in.

'Friendly bunch here,' he muttered. 'Do I think the penalties were deliberate? It's hard not to think so, even at this level of the game. Let's see what happens now.'

They waited patiently while the away team bus reversed into the gateway and their players and directors filed aboard. Other men emerged in clusters of two or more, then finally, the match officials appeared. The two linesmen got into a car and drove off, leaving Jordan Macaleese standing with phone in hand. It looked as if he was texting. A pause, then more texting. He pulled a beanie out of his pocket and jammed it down over his hair. He wasn't wearing an official jacket, just a plain black anorak. 'Nothing to mark him out as the match referee,' Meera observed.

'Or a minister.'

He walked out of the car park towards the main road, but before he reached the junction, a black taxi swung round the corner, performed a tight U-turn and drew up alongside Macaleese. When he opened the door, Jason could make out the shape of another passenger.

Jason squeezed out of the parking space and left the car park in time to see the taxi turn left. He followed, closing the gap enough to stay in touch. 'Can you take a pic of the taxi licence plate, please? And the number on the white plaque underneath it?'

Meera scoffed. 'On these roads in the dark? I'll go old school, Jason.' She tapped the details into her phone. 'Why exactly are we following them, Jason?'

'I think his handler's probably going to hand over payment and maybe discuss instructions for next time. There'll be no chance to witness that, though.'

'I get that. So what outcome are you aiming for?'

There was, Jason thought, something all the significant women in his life had in common. His mother, Karen, Meera – they all pushed him that wee bit harder to think things through, not just breenge straight into the breach and figure out why afterwards. When it was too late and he was already up to his eyebrows in trouble. 'I want to see where the guy in the taxi goes. I need to know who he is. That's the next step.'

'Sounds good to me.'

They were out of Alloa now, following the signs for the Clackmannanshire Bridge across the Forth. It took them to the sequence of motorways leading to Glasgow and beyond, which made sense since Macaleese was presumably heading back to his parish in Greenock on the Clyde coast. The last of the match traffic soon scattered to the several major roads, and there were few vehicles on the road. Jason hung back as far as he dared while making sure he wouldn't lose the black cab to a sudden swerve into an exit road.

'People think cold case coppering is so glamorous,' Jason said. 'They see it on the telly and they reckon we spend our days in dramatic showdowns and amazing discoveries that the original case officers missed or ignored.'

'If they could see us now, full of Bovril and pie, cruising the scenic motorways of the central belt . . .' Meera chuckled. 'What do you reckon KP's doing right now?'

'Walking,' he said. 'Or drinking gin with Phil's old boss, Jimmy Hutton. Either way, she'll be doing what we're doing. Trying to make a story hang together out of a bundle of loose ends. I hope she's having more luck than us.'

'The night is still young, Detective Sergeant Murray. Anything could happen.'

'That's what worries me.'

44

After the bombshell conversation with Rafiq, Karen knew she needed to walk. Without consciously planning it, she found herself crossing Leith Links and joining the Restalrig Railway path, the former train line where she'd first encountered the Syrians huddled round a brazier on a bitter winter night. It was an encounter that had changed her life, the memory bitter-sweet now. But Karen was determined not to succumb to self-pity; she forced herself to think of the positives. The friendship that had grown between her and Amina and Miran, the satisfaction she'd felt when Café Aleppo first opened and gave the Syrians a place to gather, the delight when they reopened after Covid and the locals flocked back. And yes, the surprise of falling in love with Rafiq.

She realised now how much weight she'd come to place on the idea of a future with him. A Joni Mitchell 'Big Yellow Taxi' moment, if ever there was one. They'd fallen into an easy companionship, in spite of the undertow of griefs they'd both known. When they managed to squeeze time together – in Montreal, on trips to Vancouver and Nova Scotia – their connection had been warm, sexy, funny and surprisingly lacking in cultural incomprehension.

Considering the fact that people from Glasgow sometimes had difficulty understanding Fifers, she'd thought that was no mean achievement. And now it was over. A line had been sliced through their connection. Karen knew there was no way forward or back from this.

She emerged at the other end of the path and walked along the prom at Portobello, listening to the waves curling up the empty beach. The lights on a couple of slow-moving tankers in the Firth were the only signs of life. Not even the dog walkers were out. Karen recalled the fantasy she'd entertained of selling her flat and buying a wee house down here in Porty for her and Rafiq to share. 'Ah, fuck it,' she said and cut up a side street to the main drag. She summoned an Uber and headed home to pick up her car. She needed the company of someone whose compassion she could trust so she drove up to Dundee to see River Wilde because, like her, River thrived on complication and collaboration.

Karen had phoned ahead to order takeaway from their favourite pizzeria and by the time she arrived, River had cleared the papers and laptop from the table in her tiny flat so they could eat 'like civilised people', she said, a note of mockery in her tone.

Karen wasn't ready to break her news so while they munched their way through the Neapolitan pizza with blue cheese, pear, walnut, red onion and chilli honey, she walked River through the journey that the discovery of Sam Nimmo's body had taken them on. 'So it looks like William Kidd committed a double murder. He's certainly got motive. A revelation like this would have wrecked his career. And why else would he abandon his natural audience to chance building a successful career overseas, never coming back to Scotland?' she sighed.

'And of course you never had evidence enough to extradite him.' River shook her head in frustration.

'It was all circumstantial. And without the testimony of the rape victim . . .' Karen shrugged. 'Never going to happen. But we've come up with an idea for how to get him back in the jurisdiction.' She outlined their tentative plan. 'We just need to work out the mechanics.'

'But aren't you still going to have the same problem? A lack of evidence?'

'Now we know who the victim is, though. And the world is a very different place from where it was on Hogmanay 2013. She'd be listened to now. Taken seriously. Men like Haig Striven-Douglass and William Kidd have lost their shiny protective glow since Me Too and Harvey Weinstein, and Emily Maitlis demolishing Prince Andrew. Now, top execs are drowning when the historic accusations come rolling in like the crap that comes in on the tide after a storm. I think I can get her to talk. I really do.'

'You are good at that,' River conceded.

'Not to mention that there will have been other people at the party who will have witnessed stuff without knowing what they were seeing. I know it's a long shot, but we've got to try. For Rachel and Sam's families, we've got to try.'

River frowned. 'You're getting very caught up in this, Karen. I've not seen you this intense about a case for years. What's really going on here?'

'What? I'm not supposed to care?'

'You're not usually this hectic. What's driving you so hard?'

Karen put down a half-eaten slice of pizza. 'Rafiq's Canadian passport has come through.'

River broke into a smile of genuine delight. 'But that's

great news.' Then she registered the darkness in Karen's expression. 'Isn't it?' she added, uncertain.

'It is for him, yes. He's not a stateless refugee any more, he's a Canadian citizen. He can travel freely, cross borders without fear.'

'I hear a lurking "but"? Are you worried about whether you'll manage to handle living together?'

'That's not going to be an issue. He's taking a job in Syria. He's going back home.' Karen sounded as bleak as River had ever heard her.

'But I thought—'

'So did I. But then Assad fell and everything changed. He wants to go home, River. He wants to go back where he belongs and where he believes he can make a difference.'

'You could join him? You've talked about needing a change.'

'I got the change I needed when Ann Markie fucked off down south. River, I love what I do and I'm bloody good at it. I've got my team working well together – well, mostly!' She scoffed. 'What would I do in Syria? I don't speak the language, the culture is alien, I have no friends there. I've seen how being a refugee hollows people out, and I'd be just another refugee, only with privileges. Love can only take you so far and I don't want to live in the back seat of someone else's life.'

'So what are you going to do? Carry on like you're already doing, visiting each other when you can? That'd be OK, wouldn't it? You still have your life, your world, and you still have Rafiq.' River spoke with sincerity but Karen could sense her doubts.

'I don't want that life. I could handle this part-time carry-on when I believed it was temporary, a kind of dress

313

rehearsal for the real thing. But I want more than that, River. I want what you and Ewan have.'

'I spend half the week in Dundee, Karen. While Ewan is back home in the Lakes. And we make it work.'

'I know. But every Thursday night in term time, you get on the train and go home to him. It's not like there are three-month gaps between one kiss and the next.'

'Oh, Karen . . . How did you leave it?'

'I told him I can't do it. And I meant it.' She rubbed her forehead. 'I really thought this was for keeps. Obviously not like Phil, Phil was the love of my life and nobody else could ever occupy that place. And I thought it was the same for Rafiq. I never expected or wanted to replace his wife and son in his heart. But I thought we could make a good life together. A different life, but a life that would matter to both of us.' She looked away, out at the across the harbour. 'Turns out I was wrong.'

'And your heart is breaking and you're throwing yourself into work like a madwoman so you don't have to deal with it.'

Karen's gaze returned to River. 'Not exactly. I'm reminding myself of who I am and what I do best. I don't want to rehash me and Rafiq, River. It's done and now you're up to speed. So can we please move on? I have another case that's split us into different factions and I truly can't see the wood for the mountain of matchsticks. That's really what I wanted to talk about tonight. If it was a movie it'd be called *The Case of the Two Murders that Weren't.*'

River knew when she was being warned off and, in the name of friendship, she was willing to accept it. For now, at least. 'Sounds right up my street. When is a murder not a murder, then?'

'When it's written up as an accident. When it's plausibly an accident if your killer is lucky enough to cross paths with officers that accept things at face value because why would they not be as they appear? Death number one: a successful modern architect's car goes off the road in the Highlands and ends up in a gully where his body isn't found for three days. Terrible tragedy, sloppy coppers who didn't find him or his flashy red Jaguar in spite of his wife reporting him missing. Incidentally, I don't think the delay was programmed in to the murder, I think our killer just benefited from the locus being hard to spot from the road. Anyway, it's recorded as an accident in spite of the wife kicking up a bit of a fuss.'

'Not surprising, really. Highland roads aren't designed for hardcore driving. That's why I've got an ancient Land Rover. Designed for cart tracks and moorland. What happened next?'

'Four months later, the general manager of the Scott Monument Hotel was found dead near the bottom of the Scotsman Steps. Broken neck, broken ankle. The incident happened in one of the CCTV blind spots and the steps are often slippery when wet. Except it wasn't wet that night. An unidentified man wearing a hoodie emerged from the steps at around the same time. But there were no suspicious circumstances, not least because the dead man didn't seem to have a serious enemy in the world. The sheriff ruled it an accident.'

'OK, two deaths that were written up as accidents, misadventure, whatever. So far, so uncontroversial. What changed?'

'The wild colonial boy. The brother of the second man lives in New Zealand. Covid and running a brewery meant it took him a wee while to get here, but he's convinced that his brother was murdered. He tracked down some CCTV from inside the hotel and what looks like the same man in a hoodie follows our victim out of the bar. Presumably going down the steps behind our victim. It's quite persuasive if you're determined.'

'But you're not persuaded?'

'I wasn't even remotely to begin with. Then the Justified Sinners entered the picture.'

River pushed her plate to one side and planted her forearms on the table. 'OK. You've got me. Who are the Justified Sinners?'

Karen told her. River looked increasingly sceptical until Karen reached her account of the stake-out of the meeting. 'Hold up, wait, wait!' River exclaimed. 'The same bloke who was ID'd from the CCTV turns out to be a member of this so-called book club? And so was the guy in the Jag? That's either very spooky or very dodgy.'

'Oh, there's more. Jason's been doing his dog with a bone impression again. You know what he's like when he decides he's going to get to the bottom of something that involves databases and lists. Long story short – we have a cyclist's camera that shows an SUV was following the Jag. The registered keeper of the SUV was the wife of Hoodie Man. Who sold the car two days after the supposed accident. Jason spotted what looked like some damage to the SUV and he followed up with the garage Nicol sold the car to. And there were traces of red paint. Did I mention it was a red Jag?'

'This is sounding very weird.'

'It gets weirder. SUV man is also a Justified Sinner. And by the way, though I can't figure out whether it's connection or coincidence, so is Haig Striven-Douglass, or Lord

Friockheim, as he is now. Like I told you, they're very exclusive. Anyway, Daisy and Jason are convinced that Hoodie Guy is their hit man, who cleans up after someone makes a mess.'

River's eyebrows climbed. 'That sounds more Chicago than Stockbridge, Karen. I mean, the men you described to me – they'd be more likely to politely remove someone's membership credentials to the Royal and Ancient Golf Club than to have them wiped out by a hired gun. It's not very Edinburgh, is it?'

Karen shrugged. 'There are some parts of Edinburgh where I could believe it happens. But not Stockbridge, with its Georgian town houses and men in raspberry corduroys.'

'I can see why you're reluctant to fall in with Daisy and the Mint on this. Have you got any better ideas?'

Karen fiddled with her glass of Diet Irn Bru. 'I'm not sure it's a better idea, but it's a different one. I'm reluctant to try it out, even on you. You'll probably think I've totally lost contact with the mother ship.'

River leaned back in her chair. 'Should I get something stronger than mineral water for this?'

'Just hear me out, then you can laugh all you want.' Karen ran her tongue along lips suddenly gone dry. 'The Justified Sinners are all men with levers of power they can pull for the benefit of their fellow members, agreed?'

'Certainly sounds that way, and we both know the old boys club hasn't ceased trading, it's just sunk below the horizon that most of us have our eyes on. Go on, I'm intrigued.'

'We also know that they sound out prospective members before admitting them.'

'We know this how?'

'The Scott Monument Hotel manager was approached by

one of his regular customers and told about an exclusive book club of limited numbers, by invitation only. He expressed an interest, because he was a keen reader as well as being an ambitious man. What if you'd heard about the Justified Sinners and you were desperate to join? Do you have to wait for a vacancy, or what? How far would you go? Might you run somebody off the road in a remote part of the Highlands? You could just about convince yourself it was almost an accident.'

'Jeez, Karen, that's cold.' River took a deep breath. 'But we both know we wouldn't put it past some of the men we've come across.'

'Exactly. But what if your plan didn't work? What if they didn't elect you to the vacancy? What if they were looking for a man who was ambitious to run an exclusive hotel that would help further their ambitions? If you'd got away with murder the first time, would you roll the dice again? Would you have the balls to give it a second go?'

45

Daisy looked suspiciously at her partner. 'What am I not getting here?' she demanded. 'How might I be able to give KP the missing link?'

'You might not know yet.' Steph got up from the table. 'But right now, I have to do some prep for tomorrow. Give me an hour now and then I'm all yours to cross-examine as you wish.' She headed for the windowless box room she'd turned into a study, pausing to kiss the top of Daisy's head as she passed.

'I'll make a start on the dinner, then,' Daisy grumped. She cleared the table, loaded the dishwasher then examined the contents of the fridge. Clearly Steph had not been near the shops while Daisy had been in Germany, which didn't improve her mood. Half a box of mushrooms, a shallot, the remains of a bulb of fennel and a plastic box with a portion of spicy red pepper and tomato sauce, and that was it. She fried up the veg and added the sauce. When it was time to serve, she'd drain a jar of cooked butter beans and pretend they were gnocchi. And if she remembered correctly, there was an ice cube tray in the freezer filled with wild garlic pesto from their spring foraging. Not bad for a bottom-of-the-fridge dinner.

Daisy stretched out on the sofa, intending to revisit the information they'd garnered in the past few days. The next thing she knew was Steph tickling her neck. Daisy started awake, almost falling on to the floor. She waved her arms around, pretending to fight Steph off. 'You're evil,' Daisy growled.

'That's no way to speak to the woman who's about to make you Cold Case Cop of the year. Budge up!' Steph nudged her upright.

'What are you talking about?'

'I think I know how to solve your problem.'

'Which problem?' Daisy was still groggy from her nap.

'Billy the Kidd.'

That catapulted Daisy right into the moment. 'Please don't wind me up, Steph.'

'It's really not a wind-up. When have I ever pulled a stunt on you about your job?'

'I don't understand, then. How can you fix this?'

Steph leaned into Daisy, head on her shoulder. 'You know I've got more of a past than you, right?'

It was a truth they'd both acknowledged. Steph had a much more chequered sexual history than Daisy and not just because she was five years older and had realised she was gay three years younger. Daisy reckoned what had cemented their relationship had been the first lockdown. While they'd been in the first throes of ravenous hunger for each other, they'd been locked down in separate flats. It had forced them to spend their time getting to know each other properly, learning about each other's backgrounds and interests. That wasn't to say it had been chaste – they'd experimented with different routes to satisfaction. But by the time they were able to be in each other's company physically, they'd come to know each other well and to discover that they wanted to spend time doing more than shagging. But still, Daisy did have occasional twinges of jealousy of Steph's past. Edinburgh was a village; they ran into Steph's former lovers more often than Daisy liked. Her own past had been constrained by the desire to stay closeted as a polis. 'Ah yes,' she said, trying to make it light. 'The slapper years.'

Steph chuckled. 'I prefer to think of it as honing my skills.'

'Am I supposed to be grateful for that?' Daisy poked her in the ribs, not quite gently.

Steph squirmed away. 'Let me speak, woman! Do you remember me telling you I spent a couple of summers working at the Fringe office when I was a student?'

'Of course. It sounded like bedlam. What was it you said? Fifty *thousand* events?'

'And four thousand performers. Bedlam is right. The second year I was there, I hooked up with this gorgeous Irish Nigerian woman, Folasade Cusack. We had a few weeks of fun then she went back to Cork and I went back to uni. She set herself up as an event promoter and moved to Glasgow three, four years ago. She's put on some major comedy tours and one or two big events at the King's Theatre and the Hydro. We've stayed in touch. Just mates, before you freak out. I could ask her if she'd help out?'

'You're amazing, my love! She sounds exactly what we're looking for. But please, don't make any kind of approach to her till I've talked it over with KP. It needs to come from her, not me. But you could smooth the way, right?'

'Of course. Anything I can do to help. These bloody men who think they've got the right to take what they want from women, they disgust me. And just between us, I know Folasade feels the same way. Her sister was raped back in Ireland when she was fifteen. It totally wrecked her. She was planning to go to university to study pharmacology but she dropped out of school and started using. It took Folasade and her sisters years to straighten her out. So yes, I think she's the woman for the job.'

'I'll talk to KP in the morning, see what she says. At least we could maybe set up a meeting to sound her out.' Seeing Steph nodding eagerly, Daisy grabbed her hands. 'But seriously, Steph. Say nothing, do nothing till I've spoken to the boss.'

'OK, OK, I hear you. Can you call her tonight?'

'I'd rather do it face to face. Tomorrow morning is soon enough.' She could see Steph was disappointed at having to wait. 'The mood KP's in right now, I think she'll bite your hand off.'

They followed the black cab through Glasgow, across the Clyde and out the far side to Paisley, where it turned off the motorway and headed towards the town centre. Jason hung back as it slowed down in front of the impressive red sandstone edifice of Gilmour Street railway station. It came to a halt and Jordan Macaleese got out. He stuck his head back inside and Meera muttered, 'That'll be him saying, "Good night and God bless and thanks for the bribe." They're not even giving him a lift home, leaving him to the tender mercies of Scotrail.'

'He's only a wee cog in their machine.' Jason waited while the cab turned round then followed it. To his dismay, their quarry didn't head back to the motorway where there was still just about enough traffic to disguise their pursuit.

Instead, they headed south down a B road that was more or less empty of traffic. 'I've never been down this road before,' Jason said. 'Are we heading for Irvine?'

Meera was already scrolling on her phone. 'We seem to be. There's nothing much between here and there. Is that a good thing?'

'It's a really bad thing from the point of view of tailing him. But it fits with what the boss said Keir Stevens said. Irvine or Erskine, from the rubbish shorthand outline.'

'Should we abandon ship?'

'Not now we've come this far. I'll just have to be careful. Is there a left turn anywhere soon?'

Meera studied the phone screen. 'In about mile and a half.'

Jason nodded. 'Warn me when it's close.' He speeded up till he'd reduced the distance between them to a single car's length.

'Coming up now,' Meera said. Jason flicked the indicator and turned off into a country lane. Almost immediately, he performed a neat three-point turn and rejoined the road he'd just left. 'Wow,' she said, as the taxi's rear lights came into view. 'That was clever.'

'It's a trick I learned from Phil.'

'Ah, the legendary Phil Parhatka. I wish I'd met him. He sounds like one of the good guys.'

'I wish he was still around for you to meet. I bet the boss does too. I'll never forget the look on her face when I broke the news.'

They drove in silence for a few minutes. Then Meera said, 'Promise me you'll never do that to me?'

Startled, Jason flashed her a quick glance. She was staring straight ahead, the profile he loved outlined in the dashboard lights. 'I'll do my best,' he said. 'I'm glad I don't have to worry about you the same way. Being a librarian isn't really a high-risk occupation.'

Her cheeks plumped in a broad smile. 'Especially not an archivist. Nobody's going to batter me for stocking books they don't approve of, or lose their rag because they've got a fine to pay.' She looked back at her phone. 'If you want to try another diversionary tactic, take the next left, then right, then right again and that'll bring you to a roundabout on the road we're on. They'll not be able to go too fast, they'll be in a speed limit.'

'Thanks.' He followed her instructions, hurtling down country lanes at nerve-tingling speed, rough hedgerows flashing past, till they emerged in a cluster of recently completed houses and others still being built. As Meera had predicted, there was a road link to the roundabout. As they approached, Jason saw the cab heading straight on.

'Brilliantly done,' Meera said. Jason held his distance. It was easier to keep track now they were travelling along empty streets lit with lampposts. Conversely, that meant he'd be easier to pick up if the cabbie was paying attention to his rearview mirror. 'We must be on the final strait now. Squeaky bum time.'

'I'm banking on the over-confidence of criminals. They always think they're smarter than us.' He chuckled. 'See when I started? I thought the same. I'm a bit more confident now, though.'

As they approached a T-junction, the cab turned right. There was no one behind them so Jason slowed to a halt before he made the turn. The street was empty. 'Fuck,' he exclaimed. 'Lost them.'

'Just drive, there's no turning. They must have gone

into one of the driveways on the right, the houses on the left don't have anywhere to park. Go slow, I'll check the driveways as we go past.' The houses on the right had high hedges, but Meera had sharp eyes. 'There. The one we've just passed. I caught sight of the glow of the tail lights.'

Jason swerved into a parking spot on the other side of the street and turned off the engine. 'I nearly panicked there,' he said. 'All that effort.'

'Now what?'

'I guess we wait and see if the taxi takes our man anywhere else. I hope not, my heart's pounding as it is.'

She turned in her seat and put a warm hand on his chest. 'You're right, it is. Now kiss me.'

'What?'

'A man just came to the gate of the house where the cab went. Maybe he suspected something, maybe he's just ultra-cautious. But kissing me is the best camouflage.'

So he obliged. It wasn't a hardship, after all. He was just glad it was Meera he was with and not the boss. That would have been weird beyond words. At last she pulled away.

'He's gone?'

'He went ages ago, I was just enjoying myself.' She smirked.

'You'd make a good polis.'

'The hours are terrible. I'll stick to the library. I'd guess we're not going to see much action now, it's gone eleven. Are we heading home?'

'In a minute. I just want to take a wee look. I'll not be long and I'll not take any risks, I promise.' He crossed the road and mooched along the street, hands in pockets, slightly unsteady, an ordinary guy on his way back from the pub. As he drew level with his target, he cut his eyes sideways, clocking the taxi dark and silent next to a Volvo SUV. He muttered the licence plate under his breath. Behind them sat a symmetrical square house built of local stone. It looked like a former manse, so plain was its design. Two upstairs windows were curtained, no visible chink of light. One ground-floor room was dimly lit; Jason barely had time to register details but he thought there was a man leaning on the mantelpiece, a woman in an armchair, and as he passed, he caught a glimpse of a second man entering through an open door from a brightly lit hallway. Its light shone from a plain rectangular fan light above the solid door, casting its glow on three shallow steps that led up from the gravel driveway.

He carried on to the corner, crossed the road and made a note of the address before he walked briskly back to the car. 'Let's head home,' he said. 'I know it probably doesn't seem much like it to you, but we've put in a solid shift tonight. I'll tell the boss she owes you a drink.'

'Or a decent game of football.'

'At least. Preferably one without a bent referee.'

46

By the time Karen arrived in the office next morning, Jason was already hard at work. He gave Karen a full account of his evening with Meera, and when she congratulated him, he said, 'That's not all, boss. According to the council, the house in Irvine is owned by Michael Lee. It's too common a name to be worth chasing on Google, but Lee is a frequent Singapore surname and we've already been told that the betting scam is being organised by a couple of guys from there.'

'Fair enough, but it's hardly definitive.' It was difficult to get excited about so slender a lead. Especially since she'd had a late-night call from Daisy who thought she might be able to set up a meeting with a woman who could help them with William Kidd. Now that *was* exciting.

'There's more,' Jason persisted. 'I spoke to Kayleigh at DVLA. The Volvo SUV is registered to Michael Lee, but the taxi's registration's in the name of Joshua Lee. But here's the thing. I checked the taxi ID plate with Glasgow City Council licensing department, and it doesn't exist. Now, it's not illegal to drive a black taxi as a private car but it is to have one running around under a false taxi ID plate.'

That was marginally more interesting, she thought.

Nobody looked twice at a taxi hanging around at the back door of a football stadium. Or any other sporting venue, come to that. 'What do you want to do about it?' she asked. He'd got this far on his own initiative and although she didn't think a pair of Singaporean scam artists would be behind the murders of Sam Nimmo and Rachel Morrison, it wouldn't hurt the HCU's reputation to expose a betting conspiracy. 'We could just pass on what we've got to Major Crimes? It's more up their street and they've got the bodies to conduct a wider investigation. It's not like we're short of work right now.'

Jason's crestfallen expression told her all she needed to know. 'I wondered whether it might be worth bracing the minister?' he said tentatively. 'I doubt he's got much experience of police interviews and he might just cave? And then we could pass it on for them to finish the job?'

Karen relented. 'It's probably worth a try. I've not got anything on till later – why don't we take a wee run out to Greenock?'

His face lit up and he grabbed his jacket before she could change her mind. 'Great, let's go, I've got the address of his kirk. It's right in the centre, near the station and the cruise ship terminal.'

As they drove cross country to the west coast, Karen brought Jason up to speed with the plans she and Daisy had made to tempt William Kidd back to Scotland for a fleeting visit. 'He must feel homesick, especially when he sees the healthy state of comedy in Scotland. We've got the Fringe in Edinburgh and the Glasgow International Comedy Festival, plus a whole raft of comedy clubs that are rammed every week. It's big business and he's still a big name.'

'He must be gutted at missing out. Did you see that special

he put up on YouTube back at New Year? He goes right near the knuckle, but you can't help laughing. That routine he does about airport security? I nearly fell off the settee, I was laughing so hard. So how are you going to do it?'

'Daisy's Steph is good pals with a woman who promotes big-ticket comedy events. Steph reckons her mate will be so disgusted at how Kidd and Striven-Douglass treated that lassie that she'll be on board to help us out.'

'That's great. What exactly are you going to try and do?'

'Hopefully we can piggyback on an existing event. Something where they've already announced "special guest appearances" or some such thing.'

'It'd be a huge coup to get him on a Scottish stage again. Steph's pal would definitely make people sit up and take notice of her pulling power,' Jason pointed out.

'Well, only if we actually let him perform . . . I'm not sure what I think about that.'

Jason gave her a look. 'How could you not let him do his set? It'd make the arrest headline news round the world.'

'You should know by now, Jason. I don't care about that. All I want is to nail the person who killed Rachel Morrison and Sam Nimmo.'

'I know that, boss. But I also know you're always having to fight the high heid yins for every scrap of support we get. Every time we make a splash, it makes it harder for them to squeeze us tighter.'

He had a point. It wouldn't hurt in her battle to stay out of Gartcosh if she had the leverage of a success like William Kidd under her belt. 'That's true. And you've more than done your bit to raise our profile with the top brass with this football bribery case. That'll hit the headlines too.'

'And don't forget the Justified Sinners. There's going to

be some big names with their heads on the chopping block when that story hits the media. All those powerful men scratching each other's backs to make a bigger buck when half the country are scratching to make ends meet. I tell you, Netflix'll be making a series – *HCU Embra*!'

Karen laughed. 'You're getting carried away!'

'Who'd play you, boss?'

Startled, she thought for a moment then said, 'Ashley Storrie's too young and Michelle Gomez is too old. It's got to be somebody gallus, though. A young Siobhan Redmond, maybe, if we had a time machine. What about you? Rupert Grint? He's not Scottish but he's ginger, at least.'

'I don't know, I was thinking maybe Eddie Redmayne?'

'Too old.' She grinned.

'Jack Lowden?'

'Way too handsome.'

He pretended to be offended. 'I'm gonnae pretend you never said that. We could get Rose Leslie to play Daisy?' He turned his head and caught her eye. They both grinned and said in unison, 'Too posh.'

Now they were relaxed, they discussed how they would approach the interview. By the time the satnav had delivered them to the church of St Brendan the Navigator, they were both confident they could back the minister into a corner. The wooden double doors of the church stood open, leading into a vestibule, tall glass doors protecting the church from the weather. And in Greenock, there would be plenty of weather, Karen thought.

It was a simple interior, typical of Scottish Presbyterian churches, where the nearest they came to decoration was the boards where the numbers of the hymns for the next service were displayed. A pair of women with nylon overalls protecting their clothes were assiduously wiping their dusters along the pews. They looked up as Karen and Jason entered and smiled. 'Can we help you?' the one closest to them said. 'If it's the carpet bowls you've come for, they're in the church hall. Go back out the front and turn left down the side, you can't miss it.'

'Thanks, but we're actually looking for the minister. Is Mr Macaleese about?' Karen returned the smile.

'It's Thursday, is it no', Ina?'

'Aye, Susie, it's Thursday all day. That's how it's the carpet bowls.'

'Right enough.' She made a rueful face. 'I'd forget my head if it wisnae on a string. Thursday morning, he'll be at the manse, writing his sermon.'

'I'm sorry, I don't know where the manse is?' Jason gave them his most obsequious smile.

'You're no' from round here.' It was a statement, not a question.

Susie chipped in. 'We get a lot of strangers, with us being closest to where the cruise ships tie up. Folk want to come in and say a wee prayer.'

'The manse,' Karen said, gentle but firm.

'It's easy enough to find. You go back on to the street, take the first left then second right. It's number seventeen Coral Street. It's got a black door. You cannae miss it.'

She was right. Undistinguished terraced house, two up, two down. Black door, chrome numbers and matching letter box. And a doorbell with a camera. 'Interesting,' Karen said, nodding towards it. 'That's taking the church militant a wee bit far. I wouldn't have thought a minister would need door security.' She pressed the bell and waited. A woman's voice said, 'Hello? Who is it?'

'We're wanting a word with Mr Macaleese,' Karen said.

'Yes, but who are you? I don't recognise you as members of the congregation.'

In response, Karen took out her ID and held it up to the camera. 'Detective Chief Inspector Karen Pirie, Police Scotland.'

'What is it in connection with?'

'That's a matter between us and the minister. Is he at home?'

'It's not convenient. He's working on his sermon.'

'I'm sure he can put it to one side. You never know, it might inspire him to greater things. Mrs Macaleese – it is Mrs Macaleese, yes?'

'Yes.' Long-drawn-out.

'Mrs Macaleese, I'm not sure you're entirely aware of the consequences of obstructing a police officer in the course of their duty, but they're not trivial. I would be obliged if you would either let us in or bring your husband to the door.' Sod the velvet glove, it was time for the iron fist.

A crackle from the doorbell, then silence. 'What was that?' Jason scoffed. 'What a friend I have in Jesus, or what?'

Karen looked at her phone. 'I'm giving him five minutes. Then we'll see how he likes the neighbours enjoying the polis kicking off on his doorstep.'

Macaleese avoided ignominy by thirty-two seconds. The door opened to reveal the minister in a pair of smart indigo jeans and a white shirt, sleeves rolled above the elbows. For a man in his late forties, he was in decent shape, she thought. His wavy black hair was brushed back from his forehead, a few strands of silver beginning to peek through. His face was remarkably unlined; she wasn't sure whether it was Botox or a very diligent moisturising routine. His smile of greeting came nowhere near his eyes.

'My wife says the police are very insistent about speaking to me. I expect you think you deserve my time more than my god.'

So it was going to be like that. *Two can play at that game.* 'God is everywhere, though, isn't she? Me, I've had to come all the way from Edinburgh. We'd like to have a conversation with you, Mr Macaleese. We can do it here on the doorstep, where the world and his dog can hear. Or we can come inside.'

'And if neither of these options appeals?'

Karen gave him a long hard stare. 'Then I'll arrest you. Render unto Caesar the things that are Caesar's, and that.'

'On what charge?'

'This is Scotland. I don't need to have a charge. All I have to have is a reasonable suspicion that a criminal offence has taken place. Which in this case, I do have. Mr Macaleese, I don't understand why you're making this so difficult?'

'Because I watch and read and listen to the news and it seems to me that we're becoming more and more like a police state. Because the likes of you think you can waltz up to my front door and treat me like a criminal.'

Time for Jason. 'The chief inspector has just explained that she has reasonable suspicion that a criminal offence has been committed, so I'd say she was well within her rights. What's it to be, sir?'

He breathed heavily through his nose. 'You'd better come in, then.' There was nothing gracious in his capitulation. He shooed them in and pointed to a door on the right. 'In there.'

It was a comfortless room. A scatter of unmatched armchairs at an inconvenient distance from a low coffee table that featured a panoramic map of the Clyde estuary under clear varnish. There was a reproduction of Salvador Dalí's Christ of St John of the Cross; the original hung in the Kelvingrove Museum in Glasgow, Karen knew. She'd never quite felt it was devotional, somehow. The musculature of Jesus's arms and shoulders was more *Men's Health* than biblical.

He waved them toward the chairs and remained standing, leaning on the plain wooden fireplace that surrounded an elderly gas fire. Wherever the money was going, Karen thought, it wasn't on home comforts. 'Why are you here?' he demanded.

'You're a part-time football referee?' Karen came straight back at him.

'It's not a secret. My congregation knows. And so does the presbytery and nobody has a problem with it. It doesn't interfere with my ministry or my pastoral work.'

Jason's turn. 'Why do you do it? What's the attraction of running about a muddy football field in the rain and sleet and snow?'

'I love the game.' His smile was smug now. Karen felt he was playing them.

'You love the abuse? The names you get called at the matches, the social media badmouthing? Have you got kids? Do they like getting picked on for Daddy's bad decisions?' she said.

'Because you make quite a lot of bad decisions,' Jason said flatly. The minister's cheeks flared red, indignant at the criticism.

He opened his mouth to respond but Karen cut him off. 'What's the nature of your relationship with Michael Lee? And his brother Joshua?'

Macaleese's eyes swivelled from one to the other as Jason continued the barrage. 'Last season, you issued more red cards than any other referee in the championship. Why is that, would you say?'

'And the greatest number of disallowed goals in the top flight before VAR was introduced in 2022. That must have made your side gig a lot more difficult.'

'This is ridic—'

'Does Mr Lee pick you up after every game? Or just the ones that he is – what's the word I'm looking for, Sergeant? Sponsoring?'

'I think the word is "bribing", Chief Inspector. Does Don Rougvie cover your back with the SFA?'

Now the colour had receded from Macaleese's face. 'How dare you come in here making—'

'And then there's the penalties. You hand out a lot of penalties,' Jason observed.

Karen picked up again. 'What do you do with the money?' She waved at their surroundings. 'Obviously not interior decor. And there's a limit to how many pairs of designer jeans you can buy. I bet your congregation would love to know how you've immunised yourself against inflation all these years.'

'Enough,' he shouted, pushing off from the mantelpiece. 'I don't have to listen to this. This conversation is over.'

Karen sighed. 'Mr Macaleese, we've only just begun. You need to start answering our questions. You're looking at jail time here. If you want a lawyer, you're quite within your rights. We can continue this at a police station, or we can do it here.'

He glared at her. 'Or we can just not do it at all. I've got nothing to say to you.'

'We will of course be interviewing the Lee brothers. Don Rougvie too. And your wee pal from the North-East. If I was you, I wouldn't expect any of them to do anything other than throw you under the bus. What do you think, Sergeant?'

'I expect we'll find that Mr Macaleese led them into temptation, offering his services for them to capitalise on.'

Macaleese scowled, his hands curled into fists, his mouth a tight line. It had been worth a try but she reckoned he wasn't going to buckle. Last throw of the dice, she decided. 'A proper wee Prince of Darkness. And we'll be talking to your wife as well,' Karen said. 'I'm sure she noticed a bit more coming into the domestic budget than a Church of Scotland stipend.'

To her surprise, that was the blow that breached the dam. 'Leave her out of it,' he said, the defiance gone from his voice. 'She knows nothing.'

Karen dropped the hectoring tone and assumed an air of sympathy. 'But you know plenty, don't you? If you were to decide to sit down now and tell us all about it, the sheriff would likely take your cooperation into consideration when it came to sentencing you.'

A flicker of hope lit his eyes. 'Would I maybe avoid going to jail? I've got a family, they don't deserve the shame.'

Should have thought about that sooner. 'I can't make any promises, that'd be up to the court. But even a Church of Scotland minister should know, confession's good for the soul.'

His eyes narrowed in anger, but the fight had gone out of him. 'I didn't keep all the money. I gave a lot of it back to the church. We never have enough money to do the work in the community we need to do – that's how it started.'

Karen and Jason exchanged a look that said, 'Aye, right.' She stood up. 'We're going to take you back to Edinburgh where you'll be processed at our base and interviewed by detectives from the Major Crimes Squad.'

'Will I get home tonight?'

He really didn't get it, she thought. Chances were it would be many, many nights before he slept in his own bed again. It was no more than he deserved. His family, though – they'd pay the greater price, in all probability. That was the trouble with corruption. The lives it poisoned went far beyond the obvious victims.

47

Folasade Cusack had chosen a tiny turret room at the top of a winding stone staircase for her office. Her production company spiralled down the turret, sprawling outward as it met the lower storeys of the building in the perpetual dimness of the Cowgate. As they laboured upwards, Steph told Daisy that Comedy Central's HQ had started life as the offices of a company that did the accounting wizardry for one of the many businesses associated with the slave trade. 'Sade thinks it's an act of revenge, her building a comedy empire in it,' she'd explained. Daisy thought her lover was trying to put her at her ease; she'd made it clear she wasn't comfortable having this conversation without Karen. Steph was equally clear that Folasade was only willing to have Daisy present on sufferance because of their history. It was that or nothing, and since this was such a slender chance, Karen had reluctantly agreed to let Daisy take the lead.

'Try not to give too much away,' she'd cautioned her. 'Keep it to the bare bones.' That, Daisy imagined, would be easier said than done.

Folasade's office was surprisingly uncluttered. They walked in through an open door and Daisy took it in at a glance. Two long hangings – one a bright West African waxed cloth, the other a vivid Celtic knot pattern – occupied space on facing walls; the rest was given over to garish posters advertising comedy events. Daisy recognised about a quarter of the names. The rest of the furnishings were basic utilitarian necessities.

The woman behind the desk stood up and rushed round it. She threw her arms round Steph and kissed her on both cheeks. 'It's been too long. You turned into a beautiful stranger,' she said, her Irish accent evident. She wore an oversized multi-coloured jumper over black jeggings, and her hair was braided with beads. At once, Daisy could see the energy and delight that had attracted Steph.

'And you must be Daisy the lion tamer.' Folasade smiled at her but clearly a reserve had sprung up. She offered neither handshake nor hug, instead returning to an office chair that was showing signs of wear.

'I don't think she's entirely tamed yet,' Daisy said. 'Thanks for agreeing to meet with me.'

'Lucky for you, having Steph to vouch for you. Though I always make a point of getting along with the polis. We rely on you guys as a backstop if things get out of hand at a venue. But that doesn't mean we're part of the long arm of the law.'

'I understand that. I don't know how much Steph has told you?'

'Not a lot. Just that you needed some unorthodox assistance and thought I might be talked into helping out.'

'That's about the size of it. Before I explain, I need to ask you to treat this meeting in absolute confidence.' She held up a hand to forestall Folasade's response. 'When I explain the situation, I think you'll understand why.'

'That's a lot. You're tying my hands for I don't know what. Why should I trust you?'

'Because Steph does? Alternatively, because I'm a polis and I'd be out on my ear if I suborned anything illegal?'

Folasade drew a vape from her desk drawer and filled the room with the smell of cinnamon. 'I miss smoking,' she said. 'It bought time in a negotiation in a way a vape just can't.' Another mouthful of vapour. 'Let's hear it then. What happens in Comedy Central stays in Comedy Central.'

Daisy had been rehearsing her approach all morning. She hoped that Folasade's direct brown eyes wouldn't put her off her stride. 'One night a dozen years ago, a young woman arrived at a high-end party. She was hoping to persuade the host to hire her for a role in a major PR campaign. But things didn't go according to her expectations. She was plied with drink and drugs. Then raped, every imaginable way. Then her attackers threw her in the shower to remove any forensic traces. They wrapped her up in a dressing gown and had her driven home by the host's driver. The next morning she had no coherent memory of what had been done to her but she was bruised and battered and her body told her the story her mind had lost. That morning, a massive drift of flowers was delivered to her flat along with a note that offered her the job of her dreams. She took the job and kept silent in what she assumed was her end of the deal.'

'No witnesses, I'm guessing?' There was a sharp bitterness in Folasade's tone.

'Only the men who raped her. And they weren't in any hurry to reveal what they knew. But one man had a conscience. The driver who'd been charged with taking her home. Eventually, a few months later, he talked to a journalist called Sam Nimmo. And Sam started digging. He identified the two rapists. He was close to exposing them when his fiancée was murdered. And murdered in such a way that it looked like he was not only the main suspect, but the single credible one. And then Sam Nimmo apparently did a runner. He disappeared without trace. Everybody – my lot, the media, even Sam Nimmo's pals – followed the evidence and believed he'd murdered his pregnant girlfriend and run. Nobody was very interested in what he was working on because his credibility was shot. And then Sam Nimmo turned up. Did you see the story about the skeleton that emerged when the M73 slid down the hill last week?'

Folasade's hand crept up her neck. 'Oh God, he'd been there all the time?'

Daisy nodded. 'Turns out he wasn't a killer, he was another victim. One other person left Scotland a short time after Sam Nimmo went on the missing list. He didn't disappear, though. He built an international career as a stand-up comedian. Australia, Dubai, the USA. YouTube. Only place he's never played since is the UK.'

Folasade sighed. 'Billy the Kidd?' Daisy nodded. 'Had to be. He's a legend. People post on the socials when they manage to catch one of his shows in Vegas or the Melbourne International Comedy Festival. If I had a grand for every time people like me have tried to persuade him back, I could retire tomorrow. When journalists ask him why he turned his back on his native land, he always says we turned our back on him first. That we didn't love him enough. So fuck us.'

'We think there's another reason for his absence. We think he's afraid of being arrested over the rape. And possibly the double murder of Rachel Morrison and Sam Nimmo. The rape victim's been bought off with a succession of highly paid jobs, but we believe we have leverage to persuade her to talk. And if we can do that, we'll have a chance of putting him on trial. We want you to bring Billy the Kidd back. For one night only. As a secret surprise guest at a big venue. Ideally the Hydro. He'd fly in and we'd be waiting to arrest him.'

Folasade launched. 'Do you think I came up the Liffey on a bike? Why would he put his neck on the block for me?'

This was the hard part. 'Ego and time? Comedians and their fragile egos, it's a cliché because it's true. He might pack them in all over the world, but until he's validated in front of a hometown crowd, in his head he's nobody. Plus, enough time has gone by for him to feel pretty secure, I'd say. There's not been a whisper of a rumour that we can find online or off. Look, here's how you sell it to him. A sell-out event. Nobody but us knows he's the surprise guest. Make the mystery the selling point. Fly him in through Dublin where he's not going to be on any watch list. Soon as the show is over, you promise him a driver waiting to take him across to Europe, where he's free to go wherever he wants. Pretty tempting, no?'

Folasade sighed. 'But you're going to pick him up as soon as he arrives in Scotland, no? That's your plan?'

Daisy nodded. 'We don't want to risk him slipping through our fingers. He's clearly a sharp operator.'

'So what's in it for me?' A challenging stare. 'I've bigged up an event that isn't going to happen. My cred is fucked with the punters and the artists.'

'She's got a point,' Steph said.

'I need the show,' Folasade continued. She leaned forward, elbows on the desk, chin on her fists. 'If I'm going to play along with this, I need the show. Otherwise I'm compromised. I look like I'm in the pocket of the polis. And that's a terrible look for a woman in my position. Daisy, darling, I need the show.' She straightened up, jaw firm.

Daisy hoped the panic she felt wasn't written on her face. 'That's a big risk for us. If he gets a sniff of anything off-kilter, he could run.'

Folasade shrugged. 'That's not my problem. I've got a business to run.'

'It might hurt your reputation more if people realised you'd let a rapist run free.'

'They'd only know he's an accused rapist – innocent till proven guilty – if you leaked that information. Look, I'm willing to play ball with you if you play ball with me. Let me have the show. You can have a team waiting in the wings to bag him the minute he steps off the stage.'

Daisy knew she couldn't make a promise of that order off her own bat. Karen would gut her if she did.

'I'm not asking a lot but I can see we've moved out of your pay grade. Talk to your boss,' Folasade said. 'Then we'll see what I can do for you.'

'Halle-fucking-lujah!' Karen exclaimed. Heads turned in the Major Crimes squad room. She'd been in the middle of briefing the duty inspector when Daisy's call had flashed up on her phone. Daisy had launched straight into the ul-timatum which had provoked Karen's response. 'How did you leave it?'

'I've to talk to you and come back to her.'

Karen had walked away to an empty corner of the room. 'Do you think we can trust her? On keeping it under the radar? And on delivering him to us without a double cross?'

'I don't know her, but Steph says she's someone who can be trusted.'

The gallus side of Karen wanted to seize the moment and go for it. What did they have to lose? Even if they could persuade Claudia Grainger to talk, it'd be hard to make a rape charge stick on William Kidd, never mind Lord Friockheim. All that would happen was that it would become one of those gossipy stories that gets bandied around in bars late at night. And it would stop Claudia Grainger's career in its tracks. Which wouldn't be justice, nor would it persuade women to come forward to report rape in future.

The only chance they had would be to bring William Kidd into custody and use that to leverage testimony from Claudia Grainger, which could give them time to build a murder charge against him. 'We should probably go for it on Folasade's terms. But I want to meet her and make my own assessment. Set up a meeting for me to sit down with her. Just the two of us. This is one time when corroboration is exactly what we don't need.'

48

Somehow, Karen and Folasade Cusack recognised in each other kindred spirits. Karen had walked into Comedy Central's office leading with her chin, but she started to drop her barriers when the impresario greeted her with a grin. 'So you're the woman who nails the bastards who think they've got away with it. Quite a Google presence you've got, DCI Pirie.' She emerged from behind her desk and held out a hand to shake, cupping Karen's elbow with her free hand.

'Good to meet you too.' Karen hadn't quite fallen victim to the charm offensive.

Folasade perched on the edge of her desk, long legs crossed at the ankle. 'My spies tell me they call you KP Nuts. You take that as a compliment?'

Won over, Karen grinned. 'Given the climate I work in, it's a badge of honour. What do they call you?'

'Queen Bitch. Like the David Bowie song. Swishy in my satin and tat.' She waved an ironic hand at her big jumper.

Karen understood the nod. 'I'll take that as a positive. If you say you can do it, you can do it, you don't make false claims. Thanks for listening to our proposal. Daisy explained the situation to you?'

'Broad brushstrokes, I'd say. Not that I need much more.' She held up a hand to stop Karen. 'I'm not pressing for all the details. I understand the problems you guys face trying to make serious sexual allegations stick. The one thing I will say is that in my universe, the one where I'm constantly dealing with men who think possessing a dick makes them entitled, I hear a lot of "she said, he said" stuff that I can't do anything about. It makes a refreshing change to be facing the prospect of maybe being able to help you do the right thing.'

'I appreciate your candour. Just out of curiosity, is William Kidd one of the ones the gossip flies around?'

Folasade shook her head. 'Not on my radar. But I'm not the first port of call when it comes to that kind of chat. So, to business. You want me to craft a mouth-watering offer to Billy the Kidd that will succeed where all others have failed, is that right?'

'In a nutshell, yes.'

'And I'll say to you what I said to Sergeant Daisy, what's in it for me?'

'Knowing you're doing the right thing?'

She let out a loud belt of laughter. 'You should be on one of my stages. Look, if I promise my audience a world-class surprise guest, then I give them somebody whose biggest gig has been *Have I Got News For You*, it'll not be egg on my face, it'll be a whole hen house. If I manage to convince Billy the Kidd that the time is right to come back to a Scottish stage, I need him on my stage. It's not negotiable, KP.'

Karen sighed. 'I understand your position. But I'm going to get one chance to lay a glove on William Kidd and I am not going to take chances with it.'

'What is it you want from this?'

'I want Kidd under arrest in a police station in Scotland. End of.'

'See, I don't think there's a conflict here. We pick him up when he flies in, from Dublin, Daisy darling says. We drive him to the Hydro. No messy business checking into hotels or anything. We give him the best dressing room in the place, supply his every need, bodyguard on the door. He goes on stage, does his schtick. Then straight out the back door, into the waiting limo, and off to the police station of your choice. You can even supply the bodyguard. You must have a couple of heavies you can trust?'

It might just work. There was Jason, for one. And probably Jimmy Hutton for another. He'd enjoy a bit of a change from the Murder Prevention Squad. Karen and Daisy in black with clipboards and headsets, looking like backstage crew. She knew that at one level this was the dictionary definition of reckless. She also knew she wanted hands on William Kidd so badly it hurt her stomach. 'If you could do it, when could you do it?'

She stood up and sat at her desk, attacking her keyboard with the sort of energy employed by people who learned on old-fashioned typewriters. 'Let's see . . . yeah, that's what I thought. Your lucky day, KP. We recently picked up a vacant night at the Hydro, a week on Sunday. Ten days from now. We're billing it as a Comedy Central Showcase with Special Guests. So far, we've shifted about 70 per cent of the tickets so we were due for another push on our mailing list tomorrow anyway. If we pitch it as a once-in-a-lifetime surprise guest – I'll find the words to emphasise what a unique night out this will be – we'll shift the rest of the tickets no bother.'

Karen felt a trickle of sweat on the back of her neck. She'd gone out on a limb before but never this far. 'And can you convince him not to breathe a word? So it can be a true bombshell on the night? To make the socials go mental?'

'I can try. It's in his interests, in a way. He should be thinking, if he can do an amazing night and nothing bad happens, he can start coming back to Scotland again.'

It was more temptation than Karen could resist. Could be career suicide, but if it was, at least she'd be spared a move to Gartcosh. 'Let's give it a go,' she said, her mouth suddenly dry.

Karen's return to the HCU office marked the end of a whirlwind day. So much was going on, it was hard to keep everything straight in her head. Jason was busily writing up the latest developments in the football bribery case, while Daisy was attempting to make sense of his notes on the death of Bryce Gordon. *Wait till they hear what I've got lined up.* Karen allowed herself a weary smile then sank into her chair.

'Report time,' she said, searching her drawer for paracetamol.

'You need chocolate, boss?' It was Daisy's answer to all of life's problems.

'Thanks, but no thanks. My head's nipping, who's got pills?' Without a word, Jason took a blister pack of ibuprofen out of his back pocket and tossed them to her. Karen swallowed two with the last inch of a coffee that definitely predated that morning. 'Good man. Now, let's go with who we've got in custody. Jason, I know we've handed him off to CID, but any word on the minister?'

'Looks like he's been cut adrift from his paymasters. He got his phone call, but there was no lawyer forthcoming. So he's been assigned a duty solicitor who seems to be struggling with the idea of a bent reverend. The CID boys over in Ayrshire have lifted the Lee brothers, confiscated their passports and got them on police bail. They've managed to get warrants for Macaleese's bank accounts and phone records. It'll grind slow, but they reckon they'll get somewhere in the end.'

'Good job, Jason. You ploughed through all those tedious records based on nothing very much and turned it into something solid.'

'Of course, we'll get none of the credit for it, just the usual bitching about staying in our own lane,' Daisy grouched.

'Aye, but we'll know it was us,' Jason said. 'That's what counts.'

'And I'll make sure the Fruit Gum knows that too. Now, what about the Justified Sinners? Jason's been Man of the Match on the databases here too. That and a medal for sooking up to the DVLA to get the skinny on the car nobody else noticed was involved in Bryce Gordon's death. And kudos to the militant cyclists with their handlebar and helmet cams. I've just come out of a meeting with the Fiscal's office and she reckons between the evidence we've got of the paint marks on the car registered to Marcus Nicol's wife, and the photo ID from Drew Jamieson that we've got nearly enough to bring him in. What she wants us to do is bring Hugh Grieve in for questioning.'

'On what basis?' Daisy asked.

'On the basis that there appear to be two suspicious deaths associated with the Justified Sinners. We want to know how long Marcus Nicol has been a member. We want to know the details of their "dead man's shoes" policy. We especially want to know if Nicol was up for membership after Bryce Gordon died, when presumably he was passed over for Tom Jamieson. And we'd really like to know what deals he's achieved with a little help from his Sinner pals since he's been a member. Daisy, that's your job for tomorrow. I'll sit in with you for the interview and our favourite Fiscal Depute will come in and take a watching brief.'

'What if he goes "no comment"?' Daisy asked.

'We'll arrest him on suspicion of conspiracy to murder. If he's just the doorman, or even the consigliere, that should be enough to shoogle loose some serious information. And we'll take it from there.'

'Can we use it as an excuse to bring Handsy Haig in? Just to put him under pressure?' Daisy asked.

In spite of her headache, Karen was brisk and on point, the bit between her teeth. 'I don't want to question him till we have something solid to hit him with. We know he'll be lawyered up with serious players from the get-go. I don't want to give them any wriggle room on the "persecution" angle.' She took a deep breath and arranged her notes.

'Double murder. Rachel Morrison and Sam Nimmo. Bear with me while I run through the verbal version of the PowerPoint. It's no surprise our colleagues fell for the set-up the killer put in place. Although nobody ever came up with a convincing motive, we all fell back on the "nobody really knows what goes on behind the closed doors of a relationship" trope to accept the line that Sam Nimmo had killed his fiancée. There was no evidence of forced entry, no forensic traces of anyone else in the flat and, according to friends and colleagues, no enemies. And not a trace of *cui bono*. He had no effective alibi. Rachel and Sam had wills in each other's favour and the only significant bequest apart from that was a homeless charity. I know there's a homeless crisis going on, but I don't think Shelter Scotland has taken to murdering folk for their legacies.'

Jason stifled a snort of laughter. 'You're probably right there, boss.'

'Next thing we know is that Sam disappeared. He was a successful investigative journalist who had the kind of contacts who could help that happen. From that day to this, there'd been no confirmed sighting of Sam Nimmo. His bank accounts remained untouched, though there was some suggestion he had an offshore account that we'd never been able to trace. Our colleagues believed, not unreasonably, that he'd killed Rachel in a momentary loss of control, thought he could style it out for long enough to build his escape tunnel, then he was gone.'

'And then his remains turned up in the wreckage left by the landslide at the side of the M73. And no question that he was murdered. So a reasonable working assumption is that some unidentified third person murdered Rachel, fitted up Sam then completed the frame by killing him and putting him somewhere they thought he'd never be found.'

'Climate change,' Daisy said.

'What?' Jason looked baffled.

'Heavier and more intense rainfall. Those motorway bankings were designed to withstand a certain level of rain, but that's grown worse. Hence the collapse.'

'Let's not rule out shoddy workmanship, though. Not that it matters. What matters is that it was Sam Nimmo and he was put there when the banking was constructed. When we started the cold case investigation, we thought it would be helpful to take a look at the things Sam was investigating with his three colleagues. Two of them are still alive and from them we got the lead to the football bribes case, which we've now passed on. And we got a whisper about a violent sexual assault at a fundraiser during the Indy Ref campaign.'

'Probably not the only one,' Daisy said bitterly.

'No, but the only one we know Sam Nimmo was following up on. And the fact that it was at a Yes campaign event would have been more interesting to an investigative journalist because pretty much every major news outlet was pro-Unionist, so anything that discredited the Yes campaign was catnip to them. If he'd been able to stand it up, Sam and his colleagues stood to land a big payday. We've got a name for the victim – Chloe Grange, now known as Claudia Grainger. She's currently head of marketing for Fraoch House, and the rest of Lord Friockheim's businesses. Lord Friockheim who was known as Handsy Haig Striven-Douglass. Who, along with his sidekick William Kidd, aka Billy the Kidd, is firmly in the frame for the violent and vicious sexual attack on Chloe. Our source comes via Striven-Douglass's driver, Derek Drummond. Unfortunately, his late driver. Kidd confided in Sam Nimmo's partner in the news agency, Linda Lawrence, that he took Chloe Grange home after the attack. She was completely out of it, wearing nothing but a dressing gown. William Kidd came along to take care of her, we've been told. And that's what we've got so far.'

'What do we think happened, boss?' Jason asked.

'We think His Lordship got wind of the inquiries Sam Nimmo was making. He'd already bought off Chloe with her dream job, working for him in sales and marketing. But Haig Striven-Douglass doesn't do his own dirty work. Billy the Kidd is already in this up to his neck. So my working theory is that Haig blackmails Kidd into stopping the journalistic probe in its tracks. Kidd has a reputation for being very quick on his feet, very smart. The pair of them were also doing a lot of coke around that time. According to an interview I read with Kidd on an Australian website, he had that "master of the universe" sense of himself. But when he left the UK, he cleaned up his act and now he never touches anything more than the occasional pint of lager.

'Between them, they concocted a plan that would destroy Sam Nimmo's reputation as well as his life. There would be no connection to them or what they'd done. I don't know whether the plan was to carry on as if nothing had happened. But whatever the reason, William Kidd took fright. He'd already got an Australian tour booked so he headed out there a bit early and took himself out of the jurisdiction. He's not set foot on UK soil since. Have I missed anything important out?'

Jason shook his head. Daisy said, 'Only the bit where we're going to nail him.'

49

Karen took the tram home to avoid the sudden downpour that arrived as she left the office. She'd barely sat down when her phone beeped with a message. Rafiq wanted to talk to her. Her heart jumped momentarily, then reality kicked in. He'd be feeling guilty, she thought, giving an ostentatiously casual glance to his message, hiding it from the teenager in the seat next to her. I'd like to talk, it said. No emojis; that wasn't his style.

Heartsore and weary, Karen let herself into her flat, threw her coat over a chair and sat down at her laptop. She opened her email program and began typing. 'Dearest Rafiq,' she began, meaning it.

Unless you are contacting me to say you've changed your mind about Syria, I don't think there's any point in us talking. I do not judge you or blame you for giving in to the pull of working to help rebuild the homeland you love. In your shoes, I hope I would have the courage to do what you're doing. But I don't see any point in us pretending we can sustain some kind of relationship with no realistic prospect of being together. I know some people can manage that, but I'm not one of them.

It breaks my heart to say The End, but it would break it even more to struggle on, pretending that was enough for me. I love you, Rafiq. Please don't doubt that. But I can't do this. It's better for both of us to say goodbye. I wish you joy in your new life, and success in all you dream of. I know you will wish the same for me. You will always have a place in my heart.

She didn't know how to sign it. Their usual sign-off was 'XX', meaning a kiss on each cheek. 'Love' felt like she was still clinging to his ankle as he walked away. 'Best wishes' was what you said to someone who wasn't really a friend. 'In sha-Allah' or 'As-aalaam alaikum' felt like inappropriate appropriation. In the end, she wrote nothing, simply pressing *send*.

Karen hoped he would understand she had no intention of hurting him. God knows, she was hurting enough for both of them. But she'd always believed in ripping the plaster from the wound. Nothing would cause quite as much pain afterwards.

Or so she told herself.

She stared out through the rain-streaked glass doors leading to her balcony. Stupidly, she thought the weather was deliberately outdoing her in sadness. Karen stood up and mechanically arranged what she needed for the evening. Harris gin, Glaswegian Raspberry and Rhubarb gin, Arbikie Nàdar gin. Two different tonics. Dried slices of lemon and orange. A bucket of ice. Jimmy Hutton was providing a sounding board. The least she could do was to provide a decent choice of beverages. She was in the middle of filling a couple of bowls of truffle crisps when Jimmy arrived.

By the time she'd fixed their drinks and outlined their

theory of Sam Nimmo's murder, she'd determinedly put Rafiq to the side of her mind and focused on work. She'd almost convinced herself that it wasn't the product of a deranged mind. Jimmy had listened carefully, head cocked to one side, sipping his Harris gin and seaweed tonic. 'So what we've got is kind of a three-way Mutually Assured Destruction,' he said. 'In theory, Claudia can't be named in the media, but we both know that won't hold—'

'And Claudia's already had to rebuild her life once,' Karen interrupted. 'She's a survivor against all the odds, but having to do it once is more than enough. I don't want to be responsible for her life being wrecked again.'

Jimmy nodded. 'Point taken, Karen. None of us wants that. But it's hard to see how you avoid it altogether. If Billy the Kidd talks, OK, he goes to jail, he takes His Lordship into the dock with him but along the way he destroys the life Claudia has built for herself. If Claudia calls them out, she'll be trashed on the socials, she'll lose her livelihood and her reputation, she'll be unemployable though she'll possibly have the satisfaction of condemning Kidd and Friockheim to jail time or, at the very least, a trial that'll make them social lepers. And if Friockheim reveals what happened, even with his money and influence, he won't escape jail. Not as a rapist and accessory to murder. You think you can break this particular triple lock?'

Karen drained her own glass and refilled it, grabbing more ice from the insulated bucket. 'Although he's got most to lose if we're right, William Kidd is the weakest link. He's the one who ran. He's been living high on the hog for eleven years, nobody coming after him. He must think he's untouchable, surely?'

'And that's what you're counting on?'

'We'll soon find out.'

Jimmy frowned, clearly working something out. 'Why are you fixated on Kidd? Why not Friockheim? Surely he's the one with most to lose? His old man was still alive then, if he'd been accused of murder, he could have been cut out of the line of succession, couldn't he?'

'I don't know. More likely to me is that his father – or his pals in the Justified Sinners – would try to pin the blame elsewhere. You know what the upper classes are like under threat. Maybe Kidd knew that, however the chips fell, they'd land on top of him.'

He leaned back in his chair. 'I know you're keen to protect her, and I respect that instinct. But what you're really missing is the lassie. Chloe, Claudia, whatever she's called. Without her, you've barely got an outline. And certainly not a motive for the murders. She's the one who can likely colour it in for you. You need to talk to her, surely?'

'Here's my dilemma, though. Leaving to one side the trauma for her of revisiting it – if she's still in touch with Kidd, and she tells him we've reopened the case, he'll never fall for the bait. Or if she tells Friockheim, the man who pays her wages, he'll do something to bugger it up.'

Jimmy swirled his drink in his glass, musing. 'Since you're keeping it a secret, impress on Kidd himself that you don't want this comeback event to turn into a circus, which it will do if anyone gets wind of it. So you have to impress on Folasade that that's his end of the bargain. If she gets even a hint that he's talking it up, either publicly or privately, the deal's off. Will that work, do you think?'

'Might do. We can hope it holds.'

'Then you can leave interviewing Claudia to the last minute. The day before, or even once he's in the air.'

Not for the first time, Karen had to admit she liked the way Jimmy's mind worked. 'That might just work, if the timings fit. I need Jason to work out the logistics.'

'That lad's come on leaps and bounds.'

'He still goes, "What would Phil do?"' They each took a moment to remember the man whose death had left such a hole in both their lives.

And in an unfortunate concatenation, Jimmy chose that moment to say, 'And how's Rafiq doing?'

'Rafiq's got his Canadian passport. And he's off back to Syria.'

Jimmy recognised the pain in Karen's brusque response. 'Oh, Karen. I'm sorry.'

'Now Assad's fallen, and he's got a passport, he wants to be part of the rebuilding. And honestly, Jimmy, how could anybody blame him, after all he's lost?'

'What about all he's gained with you? Does that count for nothing?'

'This isn't his home. He wanted to keep things as they've been – seeing each other when we can fly in and out. But that's not what I want. I'm tired of a part-time relationship.' She sighed. 'I know I'll never find what I had with Phil again, but I want somebody who wants to share my life, not a permanent holiday romance. That's unreal. It's hollow. I thought the thing with Rafiq was a stepping stone, a station on the way to somewhere more solid.' Karen shrugged. 'Turns out I was wrong.'

'Maybe—'

She cut him off. 'Jimmy, I don't actually need a relationship to define myself. I like me just fine. This is sore just now, but that'll pass. With Phil, I had the best thing. I look around me and realise most folk don't get anything nearly as good as we had. I've got no right to expect that again.' She chuckled. 'Maybe I'll just get a cat, eh?'

Jimmy spluttered gin everywhere. 'Christ, Karen. Don't turn into a cat lady. You could break the bloody internet!'

'Don't tempt me!'

'So what now?'

'We wait for Folasade to work her magic. I have to say, she impressed me. Let's hope she can work some silver-tongued spell. But in the meantime, we've got another high wire to walk out on. A double murder that wasn't even on the radar until a New Zealand brewer walked into the office.'

Jimmy sat up straight. 'Now that sounds right up your street.'

'Showtime tomorrow. Given the people we're dealing with, by this time tomorrow I'll either be charging someone with two murders or I'll be looking for a new job.'

Karen parked behind Jason fifty metres away from the entrance to Surinco's parking area. He'd followed Marcus Nicol from his home to his office that morning; nothing would have been more embarrassing – or potentially disastrous – than turning up to arrest him at his office only to find he was elsewhere. She rang Daisy, who was sitting down the street from 8 Upper Dean Terrace with a constable in his civvies that they'd borrowed from Gayfield Square. Karen wanted to hit Nicol and Hugh Grieve simultaneously to avoid the kind of warnings that might make someone run, and they needed an extra body to cover them under the Scots law of necessary corroboration to keep Fiscal Depute Ruth Wardlaw happy.

'All set?' she asked.

'He's at home. I got the local wine shop to deliver a bottle of wine with an indecipherable signature on the gift message. Grieve came to the door himself and he's not budged since. We're ready when you give the word.'

Karen collected Jason and together they approached Surinco's entrance. 'Prepare to meet the guard dog,' she said, pressing the intercom.

The same receptionist tried the same unwelcoming routine. Karen shook her head wearily. 'It's me again, Detective Chief Inspector Pirie, and I still don't have an appointment. I'm here to see Marcus Nicol and I expect to be buzzed in. If you don't mind?'

She could see the woman harrumphing, but she released the door. By the time they reached her desk, she was already on the phone to Kayesha, who greeted them with the same grin as before. 'Wow, you must really like it here, Chief Inspector. Come away through and I'll tell Marcus you're in the building. He's in a meeting right now but he shouldn't be too long.'

There were still no cups by the coffee machine. Karen pointed it out to Jason. 'Should have brought our keep cups.'

'As well we're not desperate for a drink, eh?' he said.

'I'm not quite sure how to interpret it,' Karen said. 'Are they trying to say, "you're not going to be here long enough for a coffee," or "you're not high enough up the totem pole to deserve one"?'

'Or too slack to stay on top of it?'

'Not the message you'd want to send in a lab, mibbes.'

Kayesha stuck her head round the door. 'Ten minutes,' she said. 'He's just wrapping up now.'

Karen tapped out a message to Daisy. 'Go in ten,' and got the thumbs up in reply. She felt every second of those ten minutes, tension building in her gut. She anticipated a difficult time ahead and wanted to be on her mettle. It wasn't that she was nervous; more that she needed the right level of adrenaline to be at her best.

Marcus Nicol arrived with a flash of scarlet lining as he pulled on his suit jacket. His expression was as welcoming as his receptionist. 'I wasn't expecting to see you here again. I thought I made it clear that your previous visit had been a waste of time for both of us?'

'You did. I didn't agree then and in the light of new evidence, I remain convinced.' She smiled and stood up. 'Marcus Nicol, I am arresting you on suspicion of the murders of Bryce Gordon and Tom Jamieson. You do not have to say anything. But it may harm your defence if you don't mention now something which you later rely on in court. And anything you do say may be given in evidence. We are going to take you to—'

'What the fuck? Are you serious?' Jason put a hand on his arm and he shook it off violently. 'Take your hands off me! Who do you think you are, marching in here and laying down the law?' Jason moved to stand between him and the door.

'We are the law, Mr Nicol. And we are arresting you.' Karen was as calm as if she were discussing the weather. 'You can either come willingly or DS Murray will handcuff you and walk you out.'

Nicol's face was dark with anger. He looked from one to the other. 'I demand to speak to my lawyer.'

'You can certainly do that once we're at the police station. But right now, you're coming with us.'

He glared at Karen. 'You're going to regret this.' His voice was low and vicious.

She smiled. 'You're not the first person to make that

observation,' she said. 'So far, none of them have even been in the ball park. DS Murray, lead the way.'

'We're taking Mr Nicol to Gayfield Square police station, if anybody's looking for him,' she said over her shoulder to the receptionist as they passed. The woman's mouth hung open. Karen knew it was childish but she couldn't resist a smile.

Daisy meanwhile was having a very different experience. Hugh Grieve seemed nonplussed to see her on his doorstep again. 'I'm sorry, I don't recall your name, officer?'

'Detective Sergeant Mortimer,' she said. 'And this is PC Scott. Mr Grieve, we'd like you to accompany us to Gayfield Square police station to answer some questions we have for you.'

He looked offended. 'How extraordinary. Why can you not ask me your questions here in my home?'

'We prefer the more formal setting of an interview room.'

'Am I under suspicion of having committed some crime?' His urbanity had returned, along with an air of mild amusement.

'At this point we would simply like to interview you in relation to an ongoing investigation.'

'And I would like to be interviewed here in my home rather than the more intimidatory environment of a police station.'

Politeness was always harder to fight than aggression, Daisy felt. But fight it she would. 'I'm sorry if this is proving awkward for you, Mr Grieve, but if you refuse to cooperate with my request, I'm afraid I'll have to arrest you.'

'Arrest me?' Now his veneer had cracked a little. 'On what grounds?'

'We don't have to have specific grounds, sir. We can arrest you to facilitate questioning. So you can't simply walk out the door if you don't like the questions we're asking you.'

He gave a wry smile. 'So in effect I have no choice? I take it I may have legal representation?'

'Absolutely, sir.'

'In which case, I will call my lawyer right now.' Before Daisy could stop him, he'd pulled out his phone and tapped a connection. He held up a finger to still her. 'Dougal? It's Hugh. I am in the process of being escorted to a police station to assist the officers in I know not what. Might you meet me there . . . Yes, indeed.' He turned to Daisy. 'Did you say Gayfield Square? Not Fettes?' She nodded confirmation. 'Yes, Gayfield Square . . . Right now, I believe . . . No, not her. A Detective Sergeant Mortimer . . . Thank you, I'll see you there.' He ended the call. 'I doubt our acquaintance will last long, but for now, I will accompany you. Though I can't promise to answer your questions.'

'That is your right, sir. As it is ours to draw inferences from that.'

50

Marcus Nicol wasted no time in getting lawyered up; he made a call as soon as Karen had shown him into the interview room. When she returned a few minutes later, he said, 'My lawyer will be here in an hour. Until he gets here I've got nothing to say so you may as well go and eat doughnuts, or whatever it is you do instead of twiddling your thumbs.'

'The longer I have to prepare, the better for me and the worse for you,' she said conversationally on her way out of the room. She'd no sooner made it to her office than her phone screen lit up with Folasade Cusack's name. Praying for good news, she answered. 'Folasade,' she said. 'What news?'

'I tracked Billy the Kidd down to Atlanta. He's been there for a couple of gigs this week. So we had a long chat all round the houses about why he doesn't want to play the UK. I'm still not sure what's at the bottom of it. He kept going on about respect, not getting the TV gigs, not getting the headline in the big venues even though he's got a massive online following, etc, etc. Which kind of makes sense now, but didn't really back then, before Tubers became mega. Anyway, I sucked up like an industrial hoover. Always been a fan, he's my go-to boy online, I can lip-synch his routines. I tell you, Karen, I made his number one fan look indifferent.' She chuckled. 'All those guys who think I'm a hard-ass would faint to've heard me.'

'I'm sorry if I've hurt your reputation.'

'Nobody heard but Billy. Well, not unless some bastard has my office bugged. Which I wouldn't put past some of the paranoiacs on the circuit.'

'And the upshot of your self-abasement?'

'He's chewing on the bait. He wouldn't say yay or nay, not yet, but I can tell he's aching for it. He wants to hear a Scottish audience shouting his name. I laid it on thick, Karen, told him whenever we have any kind of poll asking who the punters most want to see in a live performance, he's number one. That scarcity value is exactly that – scarcity, not non-existence. I pretended I was worried he might get left behind by some of the new kids on the block who are nowhere near as electrifying live as he is, but they're *there*. You can have a night out with their set as the high point. It's not the same as heading back to your living room and loading up the latest vid.'

'I'd fall for you, Folasade.'

A dirty laugh. 'But are you funny, Karen? Could you fill the Hydro?'

'I couldn't fill a portaloo. What do you think? Is he going to go for it?'

'He's flying back to the West Coast later today, he's promised to give me an answer by the end of the week. I may sacrifice a chicken. Well, a chicken nugget anyway. I'll keep you posted.'

'Anything you need from me?'

'Not right now. I'll keep you in the loop.'

Karen leaned against the wall and let her head fall forward. Jason, returning with takeaway coffee for them, stopped in his tracks. 'You all right, boss?' His anxiety obvious.

She pushed off and smiled. 'Never better, Jason. Never better.'

He followed her into the viewing room where the Fiscal Depute was watching Daisy putting Hugh Grieve through his paces. Ruth Wardlaw looked up when they entered. 'How's it going?' Karen asked, sitting next to Ruth in the narrow space between the two interview rooms.

'So far, so nothing. She's asking about the Justified Sinners and getting an anodyne spiel about a book club of like-minded men who meet once a month to talk books and other matters of interest. He's completely sidestepped the suggestion of any corrupt exchange of information. Though he's admitted that members do occasionally offer a helping hand to each other. "The way friends do. Do you understand how friendship works, Sergeant?" She's working her way round to membership now.'

Karen leaned in, keen to see the body language as well as to hear the Q&A. 'You have a strict limit on membership numbers, I believe?' Daisy asked.

He gave a one-shouldered shrug. 'These things can easily get out of hand. Members want their neighbour, or their bridge partner, or their golf buddy to join and, before you know it, the organisation becomes unmanageable. So the members decided to keep it to a round dozen.'

'You speak about "the members" as if you're not one of them.'

'Very astute of you, Sergeant. No, I am not a member. I merely facilitate the meetings and provide a venue.'

'Is that a paid role, then?'

He gave a quick glance to his well-upholstered lawyer who responded with an almost imperceptible dip of the chin. 'Not as such,' Grieve said. 'I run a company, Brochan, and one of my tasks is to keep the wheels turning of the Justified Sinners.'

'Funny name for a book club,' Daisy said, almost absently.

'Well, it has literary associations that our members appreciate.'

'Because they're members of the Elect? Or should that be "the Elite"?' Grieve had no response.

'She's good,' Ruth observed. 'Could be a wee bit quicker, mind.'

'Here she goes, though.'

'How do you keep the numbers stable, then?' Daisy asked.

'It's very straightforward. When someone leaves, the members elect a new one.'

'So, one out, one in? Death or . . .?'

Grieve gave a deprecatory chuckle. 'Changing jobs. Changing country. Bored with the choices of books. It's not the Hotel California, you can leave any time you like.'

'But you have had a couple of deaths in recent times?'

'Two, three years ago, I think. Not very recent.'

'But two quite close together.' A long pause.

'Was that a question, Sergeant?'

'An observation. Can I ask, how are vacancies filled? Do people apply for a place?'

He shook his head, a patronising smile on his lips. 'Don't be absurd. Members put the names forward of men they think will fit in with the group.'

'Just men?'

'Just men. It's not illegal, it's a private group of

like-minded men. I'm sure you've experienced something similar? A women's book club isn't exactly unusual, as I understand it?'

'When Bryce Gordon died, who was proposed as a new member?'

He gave her a level stare then leaned in to whisper something to his lawyer, who replied in kind. 'I regard that as privileged information,' Grieve said primly.

Her tone changed. The velvet glove was off and the steel was evident. 'Now who's being absurd? You're not a bunch of priests or doctors or even journalists.' Daisy unfolded a sheet of paper that had been sitting in front of her. 'We know these are the twelve current members. So who was proposed as a new member when Bryce Gordon died?'

'I'm not going to answer that.'

'Was Marcus Nicol put forward?'

Grieve couldn't quite command his face. 'No comment,' he said.

'It's a bit late to try that tactic. Was Marcus Nicol proposed as a member after Bryce Gordon's tragic and unexpected death? Or did he have to wait and try again after Tom Jamieson's tragic and unexpected death?'

Daisy's words fell heavily into the silence. Grieve's lawyer cleared his throat and said, 'I must protest.'

'Feel free,' Daisy said. 'It doesn't alter the facts. The reason you're here, Mr Grieve, is that new evidence has emerged about the deaths of both Bryce Gordon and Tom Jamieson. Evidence that contradicts the verdicts of accidental death in both cases. To lose one member to an inexplicable accident may be regarded as unfortunate. To lose two is, in the eyes of the police, regarded not so much as careless as definitely dodgy.'

Ruth snorted with laughter. 'As Oscar Wilde nearly said.'

'She's a shocking show-off,' Karen said, almost missing Daisy's next question.

'So, when was Marcus Nicol put forward for membership?'

Karen got to her feet and hurried out of the viewing room. She knocked on the door of the interview room and entered. 'DCI Pirie has entered the room,' the PC said.

'Sergeant Mortimer, a word?'

Daisy's face froze and she pushed her chair back. As they closed the door behind them, Karen heard the PC say, 'DCI Pirie and DS Mortimer have left the room. Interview suspended.' And he joined them.

'What did I do wrong?' Daisy demanded.

'Not a thing. You did beautifully. Now I want him to sweat while Jason and I get stuck in to Marcus Nicol. If he doesn't crack, we'll take another pop at Grieve and hit him with the new evidence. Him and his New Town cronies, they're not going to want their cosy little backslapping club to be caught up in a murder rap. One way or another, we're going to charge Marcus Nicol with something tonight.'

51

When the word came that Marcus Nicol's solicitor had arrived, Karen readied her file of papers. 'Who's his brief?' she asked Jason.

'Margot Maynard,' Jason said, glum.

'Of course it is.' Who else but the glamorous redhead beloved of every crooked rich bastard who had emptied the wallets of the country before, during and after the ravages of Covid? Maynard was as ruthless as she was lovely, as toxic as she was smart. Karen had never crossed swords with her directly, but she'd seen the after-effects of her savagery on colleagues. It should have made her tremble in her shoes, as she reckoned it was calculated to do. Instead, it switched on her thrawn gene, making her all the more determined to hang Marcus Nicol out to dry.

Jason opened the door and stood back to allow Karen to make an entrance. She'd come prepared not to be impressed by Maynard's beautifully cut charcoal grey jacket and perfectly pressed white linen top, its shallow notch stopping well short of any revelation of cleavage. 'Ms Maynard. I'm DCI Pirie and this is DS Murray.'

She smiled. 'Ah yes, KP Nuts and the Mint. I'm familiar with your reputation. I'm here today to represent Dr Marcus

Nicol whom you have arrested on suspicion of murder without producing a shred of evidence.' Nicol nodded and pursed his lips, apparently confident in his lawyer's capability.

'I'm happy to correct that here and now.' She opened her folder and turned over the top sheet. 'This is a still from a CCTV camera inside the lobby of the Scott Monument Hotel. You'll note the time and date stamp on it. The man whose face is captured here, the man wearing a grey hoodie – that's you, Mr Nicol?'

'No comment,' he said firmly.

'And Mr Nicol will be going "no comment" throughout this interview,' Maynard said. 'So this really shouldn't take long before Mr Nicol can return to his business.' She shot her cuffs, revealing her watch with its trademark emerald bracelet, twelve perfect stones set in yellow gold. It was clearly a seriously expensive piece of kit, meant to demonstrate the value of her advocacy. When she'd first heard about it, Karen had thought it vulgar; the reality was, she had to admit, elegant. Now, she saw Maynard watching her judgement and didn't like it one bit.

'We've got a lot of questions to get through before then, Ms Maynard, so if you have somewhere else to be, better cancel it.' Karen turned over the next sheet of paper, a computer printout. It showed the facial recognition image that had connected them to Nicol. Not in a hoodie but dressed in a suit with a white shirt and a dark red tie. And across the bottom, a banner that read, 'Location match: 1km. Image 99.3% MATCH'.

'It's hard to argue that's not you,' Karen said.

Nicol glanced away and said, 'No comment.'

Next page. 'And here's the same man from the lobby, emerging four minutes later from the bottom of the

Scotsman Steps. Where Tom Jamieson was discovered soon afterwards, dead. Broken neck, broken ankle. The broken ankle was a bit of a puzzle, unless you consider a blow from a metal bar to Tom Jamieson's ankle that caused him to fall catastrophically.'

'Was any metal bar recovered from the scene?' Maynard asked.

'No. It's our contention that your client placed it there in advance, being aware of Mr Jamieson's regular route home, then took it with him after he'd killed him. We have video from another camera that shows him walking down Market Street with his right arm held stiff at his side.'

She scoffed. 'I wouldn't grace this with the epithet of "fishing expedition". You've not even got a bent pin and a bit of string.'

Karen shrugged. 'If you say so.'

'This is a farce. I insist you release my client.'

'We're not done here, Ms Maynard. We're going back in time four months before Tom Jamieson's death,' Karen said. She showed Nicol a photograph of a Mercedes SUV identical to the one that they believed had run Bryce Gordon off the road. 'Have you or your wife ever been the registered keeper of this model of Mercedes SUV?'

Now he reacted. He shot a quick look at Maynard, who shook her head. 'No comment,' he said, his voice tight.

Karen produced the printouts from DVLA and laid them out without comment. Maynard almost frowned. Then Karen turned to Jason. 'DS Murray, can you show us the video footage? These videos were taken on cameras mounted on bikes or helmets, which explains why they're a bit shoogly. Sorry about that. We didn't want to clean them up because we thought you'd accuse us of deepfaking them.

First clip.' They all watched in silence as the date-stamped footage showed the Jaguar F-Type shoot past Alexander Monckton shortly followed by the Mercedes, cutting him up. 'Sorry about the sweary bit, but frankly, I'd have said worse if you'd done that to me, Mr Nicol.'

His brows came down in a frown and he drew in a breath. Before he could speak, Maynard put a warning hand on his arm. 'That licence plate is impossible to read.'

'Not to our forensic technicians,' Karen said. 'But it's even clearer in this second clip. She nodded to Jason, who set Dan Smart's video running. 'A bit further down the road, a bit later. No Jag this time, just the same reckless Mercedes. Pause it there, Jason.' She pointed with her pen. 'And look there, a scrape on the wing and marks on the wheel nuts.'

'I'm afraid I have no idea what the point of this is, DCI Pirie?'

'In that short distance, the Jaguar was run off the road and into a deep gully where it sat for three days before Police Scotland discovered the crash site and retrieved the body of Bryce Gordon.' She picked up the next two sheets of paper. 'Two days after this footage was taken, before poor Bryce Gordon's body was found, Mr Nicol drove the family Mercedes SUV to a garage in Berwick where he sold it. Here's the bill of sale.' She turned it over. 'And here's the condition report on the vehicle. A scrape and dent in the nearside front wing, scuffs and traces of red paint on the nearside rear alloy. Can you explain any of that to me, Mr Nicol?'

'No comment.' His face was pale and there was a sheen of sweat on his forehead.

'Ms Maynard, I'm sure you're wondering what links these two murders?'

'You've yet to convince me there was one murder, never mind two, DCI Pirie.'

'Both of the victims were members of an organisation called Justified Sinners. Named after a novel by—'

'I know about James Hogg's novel and its premise. We in the legal profession do generally have a wider grasp on the culture than police officers. What are you suggesting this organisation is?'

'Well, it's nominally a book group. It consists of a fixed limit of twelve members, all serious players in their own fields. But it's actually more like a high-end masonic lodge rooted in corruption.' Nicol shifted in his seat and threw a pleading look at his lawyer. 'The Sinners help each other out, you might say. Put work their way, make sure they win contracts because they have sight of the other tenders, that kind of thing.' She was out on the high wire now, but she wasn't worried about it. Now the police had their fingers in the pie, someone would talk even if she couldn't get Hugh Grieve on side.

'This is madness,' Nicol said. He turned to Maynard. 'She's talking nonsense.'

Karen leaned back in her seat. 'You desperately wanted into the charmed circle. You'd lined up one of your pals to nominate you for the first vacancy, and you decided to speed the plough by removing Bryce Gordon. But it all went awry. They chose someone else. And you know what they say about murder? Once you've broken the seal, the second one's much easier.'

A knock at the door, and Daisy stuck her head in. 'DCI Pirie, Mr Grieve wants to make a statement.'

Karen affected an air of irritation. 'Fine, I'll be right there.' She stood up. 'I'm sorry, Ms Maynard, but a witness

374

in the case is prepared to make a statement. We'll have to take a break. DS Murray will arrange for coffee, tea, sandwiches, whatever. Interview suspended at 15:27.' And she picked up her paperwork and swept out.

52

Karen clapped Daisy on the shoulder as they made their way back down the corridor. 'Perfect timing.'

'You said, "come and get me when I say 'Speed the plough'," and that's what I did. That Margot Maynard is something else again.'

'She is, but she doesn't have the beating of us yet. What does Ruth think?'

Ruth Wardlaw emerged from the observation room. 'Ruth thinks it's on a knife edge,' she said. 'The Jamieson death is tenuous and circumstantial but the Gordon one might make the charging standard and that'll pull Jamieson along behind it if you can establish connectivity via the Sinners. You're going to need something more from Grieve.'

Karen nodded. 'That's just what I'm about to try now.' She arranged her papers in the right order and entered the room where Hugh Grieve was still sitting with his lawyer. He looked distinctly less calm and collected now, which was what Karen had hoped for. Daisy recited the formalities for the recording and PC Scott left them to it.

Karen made a show of sorting through her papers, then she looked up and sighed. 'Mr Grieve, I'm going to be very direct with you. I don't think you're a murderer. I don't think you're even an accomplice to—'

'Wait a minute, who said anything about murder?' he yelped, all his refinement and finesse fractured.

His lawyer woke up too. 'Where has this line of questioning come from?' he demanded.

'I wasn't aware I'd asked a question,' Karen said mildly. 'We are investigating two murders that are connected to the Justified Sinners book club.' She turned and gave Daisy a stern look. 'Did you not make that clear to Mr Grieve?'

'Sorry, boss, I hadn't got round to it yet.' The picture of contrition.

'Who's supposed to have been murdered?' the lawyer asked.

'Bryce Gordon and Tom Jamieson. Both members of the Justified Sinners,' Karen said.

'I don't understand,' Grieve said. 'Both of these men died in accidents. Case closed.'

Karen pulled a face. 'Yes, it does seem the original investigations were . . . flawed. I can't say at this point why exactly that happened, though I do have my own ideas. Look, Mr Grieve, I'll level with you. Right now, my colleagues are interviewing Marcus Nicol in relation to these deaths. I presume you can confirm he's a Justified Sinner?'

'Yes, but he wasn't a member when . . .' Light dawned and the colour rose in his cheeks.

'My point exactly.' She opened her folder and swiftly went through the photographs from the night Tom Jamieson died and a series of stills from the Bryce Gordon videos. 'You can see why we're pointing the finger at Mr Nicol. It's his car. He's chasing Bryce Gordon down a narrow Highland road. A bit further on, he's tearing along with no sign of the red Jaguar convertible except for the dent in the wing of his car and traces of red paint on the wheel nuts. And the evidence will show that on the stretch of road between those two points, Bryce Gordon's car went over the side. Now, I don't want to drag your cosy wee club and its members through trial by media, never mind trial by jury. But if I have to, I will.'

'I don't understand why you are coming after me. After us. It's not as if any of the rest of us have anything to do with these ... these incidents.'

Karen sighed. 'You say that, but see, you've not been co-operating with the very straightforward questions Sergeant Mortimer's been asking you. The more secretive you are, the more it looks like somebody has something to hide. Now, we suspect a lot of what goes on your wee cabal is technically what we in Police Scotland call corruption. Insider information passed among members. Illegal tendering processes. Whatever. So, do you want me to set the full forces of the fraud team loose on all of your business transactions? Or shall we confine ourselves to the matter in hand? Do you need a minute to think that over?'

Grieve covered his face with his hands and leaned forward, elbows on the table. Finally, he straightened up, his stiff upper lip back in place. 'Let me be clear. We are not members of a criminal conspiracy. We are simply a group of friends who support each other's endeavours in the way that friends do.'

Aye, right. 'When did Marcus Nicol become a member of this coterie of friends?'

His eyelids fluttered. 'He was invited to join after Tom Jamieson died.'

'To make up the numbers to twelve?'

He nodded. 'It's a manageable number.' His mouth

clamped shut as if he was forcing himself not to say too much.

'Was that the first time he had been proposed?'

Grieve pushed up his glasses and rubbed one eye. 'No. His name came up as a suggestion after Bryce died.'

'Who proposed him?'

'Ewan Browning. He's a partner in a venture capital company, But he's not a member any longer, he moved to Grand Cayman about nine months ago. He talked Marcus up, pointed to his impressive response to the pandemic. A few of the members thought it was too soon to make judgements about that, and Tom Jamieson was elected instead.' He closed his eyes momentarily.

'Not a great career move, as it turned out,' Karen said bitterly. 'So Marcus's name came up again? Was it Browning who proposed him a second time?'

Grieve fiddled with a button on his jacket. 'He said we'd be daft not to go for Marcus. That he was a solid businessman. Ewan said his own company had bankrolled an expansion of Nicol's production line and they'd done handsomely out of it.'

'And that swung it the second time?'

Grieve nodded. 'Look, we're all in business in one way or another. It's our job to maximise opportunities. How were we supposed to know that . . .' His voice tailed off before he could say too much.

'Know what?'

He shrugged and said nothing.

'And to your knowledge, has Marcus Nicol benefited directly from his connection to the Justified Sinners?' Not quite the killer question, but one whose answer might give Ruth Wardlaw what she needed to get this over the line.

379

Grieve looked beseechingly at his lawyer, whose mouth turned down at the corners. 'Hugh,' he said kindly, 'your house of cards is going to tumble. The more you help DCI Pirie now, the more chance you have of escaping the worst of the fallout. Is that not the case, DCI Pirie?'

'I make no promises, but it won't hurt.'

'I already told your sergeant, I don't actually attend the meetings, you know? I facilitate them – I organise the drinks and snacks, provide the notepads for them. But I do pick things up from the chat. Ewan Browning has good business contacts in German pharmaceuticals and medical equipment. Before he left JS for the Caymans, he brokered a deal for Marcus Nicol with a German company to licence one of their product lines for the NHS. That's all I know.'

'Not much of a return on murder,' Karen said. 'Mr Grieve, we're going to release you on police bail. Please don't discuss this interview with anyone else, particularly the members of the Justified Sinners. Here in Police Scotland, we're not really into the concept of the elect.'

53

Eight days later

William Kidd stirred his Bloody Mary and squeezed the lemon. He preferred a mezcal-based Bloody Maria, but there wasn't a dedicated Aer Lingus lounge in San Francisco Airport so he'd had to make do with the more puritanical home-grown version. He wasn't normally a nervous flyer, but he thought the strange noises emanating from his gut were less to do with the journey than anxiety about what awaited him on arrival. He'd seized the opportunity to leave Scotland in a hurried flurry eleven years before, even though Haig had told him he was over-reacting, that nobody could make the connection between him and what he'd been part of.

No doubt that would be the outcome for Haig if his name brushed up against any inquiry. People like him – and his father, the old marquess – were Teflon. Nothing stuck to them. The rules were different for men like Billy the Kidd. He reckoned at least half of the lads he'd gone to school with had moved seamlessly along the path from shitty rented flats to shitty youth custody to even shittier prison, their transitions alternately smoothed and scuffed by addiction to street drugs and cheap booze. Not many made it out the other side into what he thought of as a solid working-class life – a job, a marriage, a family. And Billy had had none of those. Come to that, he still didn't, not really. If the police had taken an interest in him, he'd have been an obvious patsy to carry the can.

So he'd run.

And as far as he knew, nobody had come looking for him. But that didn't mean his name wasn't on a list. Cold cases were all the rage these days, you only had to look at the TV schedules to realise that.

Billy the Kidd had built a massive global following in those eleven years. He'd played major concert halls and arenas in four continents, his online subscription channels had bought him an apartment in Sea Cliff with views of the Pacific Ocean and the Presidio Park. He travelled business class when there was no first class available, he stayed in luxury hotels and his personal trainer said he was in great shape for a man in his forties. He'd had a couple of light touches of cosmetic surgery, to keep his jawline taut and delete those bags under his eyes. And the emergence of semaglutide injections had taken care of his weight. He looked at vids and pics of Scottish comedians who were his contemporaries and concluded he looked much better than he would have done if he'd stayed.

And he was careful.

Celebrity was catnip to a certain kind of person; women and men came on to him in more or less equal numbers, and he sidestepped them equally. Not that he lived like a monk; he was a member of an exclusive agency who supplied confidential services, both public and private. There was nothing exotic about Billy the Kidd's sexual tastes so there was a vanishingly small chance of any kiss and tell from the women he saw. Even the *National Enquirer* would struggle to get a headline out of 'Scottish comedian pays for vanilla sex'. He knew why he'd left his homeland and he knew he was never going to be drawn into anything like that again.

He honestly didn't miss his parents. He'd bought them a nice wee retirement apartment on the Ayrshire coast, ironically enough at Maidens. He flew his mum and dad out twice a year for exotic holidays – Thailand, Bali, Hawaii – and they had a good enough time to accept his refusal to come home 'because the weather gives me Seasonal Affective Disorder all year round'. He suspected they didn't really miss him either. Their lives had nothing in common.

But no matter how comfortable his life, no matter how many good pals he was lucky enough to hang out with, he still missed Scotland. Every time he crossed paths with one of his old mates from his former life on the UK comedy circuit, he felt a sharp stab of loss. So many shared cultural references that his US friends would never understand.

He'd been wondering for a while whether it might be possible to return. The prospect of sitting down with old friends to a proper fish supper washed down with Irn Bru, followed by a double nougat wafer almost made him burst into tears. That or a South Indian curry; black dhal and a paper dosa with butter chicken and prawn saagwahla. So when Folasade Cusack had called him out of the blue, he'd been open to suggestion.

Her idea of doing a surprise segment at the Hydro, a straightforward in and out, was overwhelmingly tempting. Testing the water with the home audience but also a way of checking he really wasn't a person of interest to Police

Scotland, as Haig had always assured him. Folasade had promised him absolute secrecy and that he'd be whisked away as soon as he came off stage. Even better, it had a short lead time. No opportunity for apprehension to eat away at his determination.

So here he was, in the departure lounge. Designer jeans and a dark blue dress shirt, understated black sneakers, the glasses with the black oblong frames that changed the shape of his face. Nobody had given him a second glance. And after the show, the waiting car, the drive to the ferry port on the other side of the country and the boat to Holland. Free and clear.

But he did wish there was someone he could share the excitement with. Someone who would understand how far he'd come. Someone from his deep past who would instinctively know how important it was to keep the secret.

The more he thought about it, the same name kept creeping in at the corners of his consciousness. Most people would think the last person you should share this kind of secret with was a journalist. But Linda Lawrence wasn't any old journalist. They'd known each other since childhood. They'd kicked about on the same street corners, understood the griefs and the joys, knew what it had cost to come as far as they had. He'd trusted Linda with a couple of things in the past, tips that had worked out well for her and her crew, and she'd never dropped him in it. They'd met up a couple of times during his exile, private meetings in hotel suites and she'd never let on to her colleagues, Still he swithered. He needed a friend to have his metaphorical back tonight, even if she was half a continent away in some backwater in Germany. Just in case.

When his flight was called for boarding, he made his

mind up. Linda wouldn't let him down. Besides, she'd never get there in time. He took out his phone and typed, Coming out of my shell! Hydro, Sunday, special surprise guest. Sorry you won't see the prodigal return!

Twenty minutes before noon and the flight from San Francisco was on approach to Dublin Airport. Beyond the arrivals gate, Daisy and Folasade were front and centre, flanked by Jimmy Hutton and Jason, who was staring at the app on his phone that tracked the plane coming in to land. 'Nearly on the ground,' he said. He and Jimmy were supposed to be William Kidd's security team so they were dressed in their black uniform trousers, black polo shirts and a couple of black leather jackets that Folasade had temporarily liberated from the wardrobe department of the King's Theatre.

'They owe me a favour,' she'd said. Daisy didn't ask why because she wasn't sure she'd like the answer. 'This is so cool, no cap. I can't believe I'm the woman who's bringing Billy the Kidd back to his neck of the woods. I'm going to be lege.'

'We're really grateful you pulled it off. I can't get over how you managed it.'

'Massage to the ego.' She shrugged. 'To be fair, I think he's got to the point where no matter the reason he had for leaving, he thinks the reasons for staying away are shrinking all the time. The way the Donald is trashing America, Billy told me he has to check everything he says on stage now in case his green card gets shredded. He doesn't want to end up being deported to some Mexican jail.'

'We're not much better here. Politics is totally beyond satire.'

'Yeah, but in Scotland you don't get arrested for saying Kemi Badenoch is a transphobic fascist.'

Daisy winced. 'Not yet, anyway.' Time to change the subject. 'What do you think swung it for you?'

'I wasn't around when he was breaking through in Scotland so we've got no bad history. Working with comedians, you have to be a cross between a shrink and a social worker and you're always walking on eggshells. Even acts I've booked a dozen times or more, I can still put a foot wrong and then they don't take my calls for weeks. But mostly it was the venue – biggest indoor auditorium in Scotland. Fourteen thousand three hundred if you count the standing area. Big audience, big payday and a quick getaway at the end. He was very happy about that. Obviously his past still casts a long shadow over him. I'm guessing you know details you've not shared with me?' Folasade cracked a wicked grin.

'And if I did, I'd have to kill you. Which would be a pity, with you being a lege and all.'

'When all of this is over, you are taking me and Steph for a big night out where you spill the beans. That's the price.'

'I can probably manage that. And you can have enough to drink that you spill the beans about what Steph was like when she was young, free and single.'

'Deal.'

'Bags are being delivered,' Jason said. 'He should be through any minute now.'

None of them spoke. Daisy could feel her heart racing. The first couple of passengers emerged from the customs chicane, then all at once, he was there, a suit carrier slung over his shoulder, a sports bag in his hand, a tweed butcher's boy cap on his head. His eyes were busy, scanning the small crowd waiting for arrivals. Folasade waved to him, catching his attention. He veered towards them, stopped in front of her, tipped the brim of his hat. 'Billy the Kidd reporting for duty,' he said.

54

They emerged blinking into the daylight, Folasade and Daisy flanking Billy, Jimmy bringing up the rear and Jason running on ahead to bring round the MPV they'd hired for the short drive up to Belfast City airport. The route had been at Kidd's insistence, which Karen had been relieved about. Because of the Common Travel Area between the Republic and Northern Ireland, there were no border checks, so Kidd would never actually have to go through a UK Immigration checkpoint. She knew he wasn't on a watch list, but he didn't. His suggestion supported Karen's view of his potential guilt; unless he was afraid of being stopped at the border, why else would he be intent on coming home via the back door?

They climbed aboard; Jimmy driving, Jason riding shotgun, Daisy in the third row, Kidd and Folasade in the second. Kidd stared out of the tinted windows, responding in monosyllables to Folasade's questions about the flight. Was it OK? Did he sleep? Was the food decent? Finally, he said, 'Aye, the food was great but the best thing about business class is you get left in peace.' She took the hint.

They crossed the border seamlessly, Kidd showing interest in the new post-Brexit protocols and signage. In spite of

Daisy's trepidation, they encountered no problems in getting to the airport and catching their Glasgow flight. As they climbed aboard a second MPV, Kidd seemed to wake up. 'So, Folasade, is there any chance of you getting a curry delivered to me before I go on? From Dhakin in Candleriggs?'

'Sure, I'll get one of the team to collect it. Don't suppose you know what you want?'

He smiled broadly, the first time since they'd picked him up that he looked relaxed and happy. 'I came prepared.' He took a crumpled piece of paper from his pocket and read, 'Dosa Masala, meen moli, venchina mamsam and kaikari biryani. Plus a couple of orders of chapalu urundai and keerai bhajji for anybody to help themselves to.' He passed it across.

'You cannae beat a South Indian curry,' Jimmy said. 'Light years away from the chicken vindaloo.'

'I've been dreaming of it all week,' Kidd said. 'I've yet to find a good one in the Bay Area. Though you can't beat the Chinese restaurants in San Francisco.'

The two men were off on a food odyssey; Daisy felt the release of pressure. Kidd wasn't freaking out, he was actually starting to unwind. As they approached the Kingston Bridge carrying the motorway across the river, Kidd started commenting on the changed face of the riverside, which took them down another conversational rabbit hole. Soon they were pulling up at the stage door of the Hydro, a route sequestered from the approaches available to the public. Daisy noticed that the early birds were already gathering at the doors even though there were still a couple of hours before curtain up.

They parked right at the door. Jason jumped out and cleared their entrance, then they all followed. One of the backstage crew led them upstairs to the Artists' Corridor with its Wall of Fame featuring stars as varied as Dolly Parton, Beyoncé and Annie Lennox. In his luxurious dressing room with its artistic upholstery, Folasade got on the phone with the curry order. Jason and Jimmy each grabbed a chair and sat outside, one on each side of the door. And Daisy asked if Kidd had all he needed.

'I'm good, thanks. I'll just sit here and prep my set and tuck into my curry when it comes. You don't have to babysit me. If I need anything, I'll get one of my minders to call Folasade.'

She knew when she was dismissed. As she left the room, she noticed the clock hanging above the stage entrance. 'TIME TO MEET THE BEST FANS IN THE WORLD.' If they had their way, it'd be for the last time. End of Phase One.

Karen had been sitting on Claudia Grainger's home since nine that morning. The job as head of marketing at Fraoch House came with a tied cottage at the far end of the parkland that surrounded the city seat of the Marquess of Friockheim. Not a bad perk, she thought. Claudia's house was one of a cluster of four cottages, each with its own garden and parking space. There was no easy vantage point for her to stake it out. In the end, she found a space on the street outside the park railings, her back to Claudia's front door. Then she put on a pair of sunglasses that lived in her glove box. They were a gift from one of Tamsin Martineau's buddies, a PI from Melbourne. Both lenses had a silvered stripe about a centimetre wide on the outside edge of the inside. It acted as a rearview mirror, effectively giving her eyes in the back of her head. Karen hardly ever used them; she found it almost impossible to concentrate on the double images for any length of time. But today, she needed them.

Daisy had been keeping her up to speed with her team's progress. Karen tried not to feel too relieved once Kidd was safely stowed in the dressing room; she needed to keep her adrenaline on standby till the day was over. There was still immense pressure on her to bring Claudia Grainger on board. Without her, the whole operation was probably a bust, and the killer of Rachel Morrison and Sam Nimmo would go unpunished.

A few minutes after six, the front door opened and Claudia emerged, a liver-and-white springer spaniel living up to its name at her side. She walked briskly down the path to her garden gate; mistress and dog turned into the park and headed away from the road.

She kept a good pace, long legs striding out. It was hard to tell from that distance, but from the movement of her coat, Karen thought she was in good shape. Probably assisted by the dog, who was full of energy, coursing ahead, bounding into the long grass by the rhododendrons then racing back to Claudia's side. But it seemed well trained, responding to her call when she summoned it. They walked for half an hour then returned to the cottage.

Judging by the pattern of light, Claudia had gone into the kitchen at the rear. Then she walked into the living room, turned on the TV and closed the curtains. With relief, Karen took off the ridiculous sunglasses and rubbed her tired eyes. She started the car, drove a few hundred yards and performed a neat three-point turn. Now she could sit facing Claudia's front door without fear of being spotted.

Daisy kept up a running text commentary on the acts on stage at the Hydro. Sometimes, Karen thought, Daisy didn't know what 'enough' meant. Still, better that than sloppy.

Then the important messages started:

About to take to the stage, BTK sending a text(!) to manager then we're on the move.

In the wings. Susie McCabe doing the intro. BTK relaxed. She says his name, audience goes MENTAL.

You would not believe the DIN!

Now he's off. They're loving it and TBH he's very funny. If only they knew . . .

What a performance!!! Defo a night to remember

It was time for Karen to move into action. Kidd was on-stage, he couldn't respond if Claudia sent out an SOS now. Karen took a deep breath and scrambled out of the car and across to Claudia's front door. *Bloody Ring doorbell*, she thought as she pressed it. The disembodied voice said, 'Yes, who is it?'

She held up her ID. 'Detective Chief Inspector Karen Pirie, Police Scotland HCU.' Banking on nobody ever knowing what the HCU was.

'What do you want with me at this time of night?' She sounded puzzled rather than anxious. Karen wondered whether that meant she was untroubled by the discovery of Sam Nimmo's remains, or simply ignorant of it.

'Someone you used to know is on stage right now at the Hydro. He's making Glasgow fall in love with him, which doesn't seem fair.'

Silence. Then, 'I have no idea what you're talking about. Have you got the right house?'

'Billy the Kidd is back in town, Claudia. I need to talk to you about that.'

'Why would I have anything to say about someone I barely knew?'

'Because I'm on your side. The next knock on your door might be a journalist who isn't.'

The door swung open, the dog at her side, her hand on its collar. 'Look, I don't know what business you think you have with me but I can assure you I have nothing to say about William Kidd. Not tonight, not ever.'

'I can't say I'm surprised. Can I come in and talk to you, please? You're not in any trouble. I promise.'

Her mouth tightened. A moment as she made a calculation. Then she sighed and opened the door wide, pulling the dog to one side. 'I'm only doing this to get rid of you.'

Karen followed her down the hall with its framed Highland watercolours and into the kitchen. It was small but well organised. Microwave, air fryer, induction hob and bean-to-cup machine all on display, everything else behind blond wooden doors. A life in order.

She waved Karen to a chair at a table in the window and sat down facing her. Even with the minimal make-up and the simple long bob of her artfully highlighted blonde hair, she was a woman whose looks would still turn heads. The dog padded in behind them and Claudia said, 'Down, Gloria.' Obediently, the dog sat under the table, heavy head on Karen's feet.

'I don't know why you've come to me. I barely knew William Kidd and I haven't spoken to him for more than a decade.'

'My job is to run the Historic Cases Unit of Police Scotland. What drives me is the conviction that nobody should get away with murder. And not just murder. There are other serious crimes that also leave a wide trail of damage in their wake. Nobody should get away with them either. We've recently had fresh information about a double murder in spring 2014. Do the names Rachel Morrison and Sam Nimmo mean anything to you?'

Claudia's lips parted and she drew in a tight breath. 'No more than to anyone else who reads the papers.' There was a slight shake in her voice. She cleared her throat and said, 'Wasn't he the journalist who murdered his pregnant wife then ran away?'

'She was his fiancée. And he didn't run away. He was also murdered. But his remains came to light only recently.'

'OK, I was mistaken, but I'm baffled as to why you think I know anything about this. I'd never knowingly met either of them.'

'Sam was an investigative journalist. So when he turned up clearly murdered, we took an interest in the story he'd been pursuing. Do you have any idea what that might have been?'

'Me? Why would I know anything about it? I didn't have anything to do with the media back then.' She was speaking too quickly, letting her hair fall forward over one eye.

'He was investigating events that took place during a gala fundraiser at the home of your employer, Lord Friockheim.'

'I didn't work for the Striven-Douglass family then. I had nothing to do with the marketing of that event.' Her hands were slowly clenching into fists.

'I know that. But something happened that night that did have everything to do with you.' Claudia said nothing. But her eyes remained firmly locked on Karen's. 'Your life was changed forever that night. Not because of anything you did. But because you were attacked. Violated. By two men.' She spoke gently, a stark contrast with the shock of what she was saying. She hated doing this; it felt as if she was pushing Claudia into fresh victimhood. But she needed her testimony and time was not on her side.

Every word landed like a blow, provoking tiny flinches around Claudia's eyes. 'That's not ... that didn't happen. You've been fed a pack of lies.' Her voice was steady but she was no longer meeting Karen's gaze.

'After they'd finished with you, they made sure to cover their tracks. They scrubbed you clean of all forensic traces, wrapped you in a dressing gown. Because your clothes were ripped and stained. And then they had you driven home.' What was it going to take to persuade her to talk, Karen wondered. Her own discomfort must be as nothing compared to what her words were putting the other woman through.

Claudia pressed her lips together and said nothing.

'What happened to you was a horrifying, disgraceful ordeal. Haig Striven-Douglass and William Kidd' – at the sound of their names her head jerked up and she met Karen's eyes – 'walked away without a stain on their character. Their idea of compensation was to give you a job where you'd have a constant daily reminder of what was done to you.'

She sniffed loudly then said through stiff lips, 'I love my job.'

Karen's phone was vibrating against her leg. She ignored it. This was too fragile to interrupt. 'And then someone else in the know told Sam Nimmo about the terrible things that had been done to you. Monstrous things. And because he was an investigative journalist, he started poking his nose in. I can only imagine what that must have felt like. You were trying to rebuild your life, trying not to let that one night of terror define you. And along comes a journalist, threatening all you'd managed to achieve.'

Claudia shook her head. 'I didn't know Sam Nimmo, I knew nothing about anything Sam Nimmo was investigating. I was just getting on with my life. Why don't you listen?'

Karen couldn't help feeling rage at the position Claudia had been put in. First she'd been the victim of two predatory men. Then as she was struggling to rebuild her life, along came another privileged man willing to exploit her pain. But two people had died, and somehow Karen had to put her personal feelings to one side and conduct her own investigation. Which promised to rip the stitches out of Claudia's wounds again. So she ploughed on. 'And then Sam Nimmo's pregnant fiancée died in such a way that Sam was the obvious murder suspect. Sam, who truly loved Rachel and was so excited at the thought of being a dad. Sam was fitted up, Claudia. Framed for her murder. But while my colleagues were still assembling the case against him, he disappeared without a trace. The word was he'd done a runner. Personally, if I'd been on the team, I would have struggled with that theory because my work in Historic Cases has demonstrated to me how hard it is to actually disappear without a trace,' she added casually.

Karen paused. She thought Claudia's composure was starting to fray and she took no pride in achieving that. And Karen's bloody phone kept vibrating silently, distracting her. 'Now we've found Sam's body, we've launched a major re-investigation of Rachel's death and a full, deep inquiry into Sam's murder. The thing is, Sam was very close to firming up the awful story of what happened to you in Fraoch House. Claudia, I know you don't want to do this, but your evidence could be the difference between the Morrison and Nimmo families finally getting answers about what happened to their loved ones, or not. We'll support you every inch of the way, I promise. But what happened to you was appalling. It should never have happened. It's not right that you've had to carry the weight of it all those years. And I'm sorry that what I've said to you tonight has added to that weight. All I can say in my defence is that I hope it tips the scales in favour of you deciding to tell us what happened, Will you do that, Claudia?'

Their eyes met. Tears blurred the blue of her irises. 'If I do, I'll lose everything. My job, my home, my reputation.' She struggled to keep control.

'But if you don't, they keep on winning.'

'And now you're telling me I'll have Sam Nimmo and Rachel Morrison's deaths on my conscience too.' She bit her lip so hard Karen expected blood. 'How can you do this? You're as relentless as any hack. You're not going to let this go, whether I talk or not. And that means it's bound to leak. You know that. I've struggled so hard not to define myself by what happened that night. I have never managed to have a relationship since. I've never spoken about what they did to me. And it's all been for nothing.' She dashed her hand against her eyes, smearing her mascara. 'I'm screwed either way.' She took a deep breath and released it slowly. 'So, what do I have to do?'

55

In spite of herself, Daisy was enjoying Billy the Kidd's set, grinning at his sharp and savage take-downs of the US President, the UK political scene and the public pronouncements of a gaggle of actors, musicians and celebrities. But that guilty pleasure didn't interfere with her doing her job. Listening to the gags didn't mean she had to have eyes on the comedian, especially since Jimmy and the Mint had that covered. So she kept a roving eye on what was happening in the backstage and technical areas.

About twenty minutes into his routine, Daisy's heart jumped in her chest. As the travelling spot crossed the wings on the opposite side of the stage, she saw a face she recognised. But it couldn't be, could it? 'Fuck,' she said. She tapped Jimmy's arm. 'I need to check something out, stay on Billy every second.' Then she stepped back and round behind the stage. Nobody paid any attention to her. The power of a clipboard, she thought irrelevantly, trying to work out the meaning of who she thought she'd seen.

As she reached the point where she could see into the wings, she slowed down and stayed out of sight. She dodged her head round the stage flat long enough to confirm what she'd thought. The spotlight swung round again and this time there was no room for doubt. Daisy dropped into a crouch and pulled out her phone. She couldn't risk calling Karen and possibly interrupting her crucial interview with Claudia Grainger. But she had to let her know there might be a spanner in the works. All she could do was send a hurried string of texts.

Linda Lawrence is inside the Hydro.

She's on the opposite side of the stage from us.

I've worked my way round to be close to her.

How the fuck does she know BTK is here?

What do you want me to do?

There was no response. Clearly Karen must be in the delicate stage of her conversation with Claudia. 'Fuck,' she breathed. The clock was ticking and although Jimmy Hutton was the ranking officer, it was the HCU's case and her call. She needed to warn the guys, though.

SOS – Linda Lawrence is in the building, Opposite you. I have eyes on her. No idea how she found out to be here. No idea what she's planning.

Daisy still had half an ear on Kidd's routine and now he was clearly working up to a conclusion. 'I hear the Lib Dems are asking the government to set up a refugee programme for US citizens who want to claim political asylum over here. Once you've all finished posting your Instas from tonight, I'll be one of the ones that need it. Only joking, only joking.' The laughter erupted again at his catchphrase. She snatched a look at the stage. She could see the sweat glistening on his face and trickling down his neck. 'But seriously, I'm glad I've had the chance to remind you all how very fucking funny I am. You have lived up to the backstage sign that says you're the best audience in the world. Thanks for tonight.' He spread his arms wide and took an elaborate bow, and waving all the way, he ignored the instructions they'd given for him to leave the stage by the side he'd entered. Instead, he was headed straight to where Linda was waiting.

As he reached the wings, Daisy sprang forward and grabbed his arm. 'What are you doing, Billy, this isn't the way to your dressing room.'

He shook her hand off. 'I want to spend a wee while with my pal. Linda's been my friend for—'

Linda pushed her way between them. 'It's a set-up, Billy. She's a polis. They're coming for you for Sam Nimmo.'

He actually staggered, taking a couple of steps backwards. The real backstage crew were moving towards them now, aiming to defuse what looked like a problem. 'You fucking bastards,' Kidd roared, ramming a hand into Daisy's chest. She stumbled, falling to one knee.

'Come with me,' Linda said, tugging the sleeve of his yellow satin tartan jacket. 'They're going to arrest you the minute you get out of here, I've got a car outside.'

Looking dazed, Kidd allowed himself to be led away, aiming a vicious kick at Daisy as he passed. She somersaulted backwards, crashing into Jimmy Hutton who was rounding the corner towards them. Jason dodged the melee and raced after Linda and Kidd, who were tearing down the stairs leading to the stage door. As they neared the bottom, Jason could see they were going to get away.

He launched himself into the air, yelling at the top of his voice, praying he had enough momentum to land on Kidd's back.

Claudia wanted to change out of her dog-walking clothes, which gave Karen the chance to look at her phone. She couldn't credit what she read there. How in the name of the wee man did Linda Lawrence know William Kidd was going to be at the Hydro that night? More to the point, how did she know far enough in advance to get there from Rostock in time? She'd made it clear to Karen that she had an opinion of William Kidd that didn't chime with the detective's view, but why did she seem to be determined to sabotage their efforts to question him? How far did childhood loyalty go? She texted all three of them. It never hurt to go belt and braces.

Just got Daisy's message. Bring Lawrence in alongside Kidd. Take them both to Stewart Street, I'll meet you there. DO NOT start questioning without me.

Claudia returned quickly, dressed in a stylish bottle green trouser suit over an ecru top. To Karen's surprise she'd regained her composure and repaired her make-up. She looked ready for business and her voice was steady. 'How long is this going to take?'

'It depends on how things develop. We're dealing with a complicated matter.'

'In that case, can we drop Gloria off on the way? I sort of share her with my cousin, she lives near the Squinty Bridge.'

It wasn't far out of the way. Karen nodded. 'Sure.'

The journey to Stewart Street police station was mostly silent. Karen wanted this interview on the record, not a 'She said; no, she said,' version of a chat in the car. When she announced her arrival, the officer at the custody bar raised his eyebrows. 'You lot have had a busy night.'

'Can we put Ms Grainger in a witness interview room, please? She's not under arrest. Is DCI Hutton here yet?'

'Your whole gang's here. William Kidd is in interview room three with DCI Hutton and DS Murray, screaming blue murder about missing a ferry crossing. Linda Lawrence is in interview room four with one of my uniforms. Kidd and Lawrence have both been processed. Oh, and DS Mortimer is being attended to by the duty police doctor in the sick bay.'

'Why? What happened?'

'There was an altercation which resulted in an alleged assault by Kidd on your sergeant. The doc is taping up her ribs and putting a couple of stitches in her eyebrow. The doc had a look at DS Murray as well, but he's just got a black eye.'

'Kids today. You turn your back on them for five minutes . . .'

The custody officer chuckled. 'Who knew Historic Cases could get so rowdy?' He turned to Claudia and smiled. 'All that and the usual Sunday-night nonsense.' He summoned a uniformed officer and said, 'Take this lady upstairs to the canteen and buy her a cup of tea. When DCI Pirie has an officer available, we'll sort you out, Ms Grainger.'

'Before you go, Claudia, can we take your fingerprints and DNA?'

'Why? You just said I'm not suspected of anything.'

'It's for the purposes of elimination. If the case ever

comes to court and either side wants to claim you were somewhere you weren't and we can't produce the evidence that will knock that on the head, we all look pretty stupid.' Surprisingly Claudia didn't grumble or unpick the explanation. Karen knew she would have, in her shoes.

She walked into the room where William Kidd was seated opposite the two detectives. His expression was mutinous, his arms folded across his chest. The image was undercut by the garish satin tartan jacket he was wearing. 'Thank you, DCI Hutton. I'll take it from here.' She leaned over and spoke softly in his ear. 'You can take Linda Lawrence if you like. I want to know how she knew Kidd would be here.' He stood up and nodded, then left.

Karen took his seat. 'Good evening, Mr Kidd. I am DCI Pirie from the Historic Cases Unit. Have you been arrested and cautioned?'

'No fucking comment.'

'Have you been offered the opportunity to consult with a lawyer?'

'No fucking comment.'

'I don't think answering that question puts you in any kind of jeopardy, but please yourself. DS Murray, can you start the recording?'

Jason performed the formalities impeccably in spite of the swollen bruise purpling around his eye.

'William Kidd, you are under arrest on suspicion of the murders of Rachel Morrison and Sam Nimmo at some point in March or April 2014.' She outlined the background; the alleged rape, Sam Nimmo's investigation and the two murders that followed in short order. 'Were you aware that Sam Nimmo had you in his sights?'

He seemed to have forgotten his 'no comment' plan. 'I

didn't have a fucking clue who Sam Nimmo or his girlfriend were.'

'Really?' Karen pulled her laptop out of her satchel and opened it up. 'For the recording, I'm showing Mr Kidd an email he sent to Sam Nimmo in December 2013, inviting Nimmo to a private dinner with Lord Haig Striven-Douglass and "a select group of pro-Indy movers and shakers". Most of us don't invite total strangers to dinner.'

He rolled his eyes. 'Look, we were campaigning for the Indy Ref. I don't know whether you have any political nous but you might remember the Yes campaign didn't have many pals in the media. Haig was trying to build bridges with individual journalists to try to change minds. This was just one of maybe a dozen wee gatherings. I didn't know who half the guests were.'

'Uh huh. So you'd never been to the flat he shared with his fiancée Rachel Morrison?'

'Nope. Not a scooby where it even was till it was all over the papers.' He unfolded his arms dramatically. 'I don't get this. You're dragging stuff up from a dozen years ago. I bet you don't remember who you had dinner with in December 2013.'

'Fair enough. Let's move on to Hogmanay 2013. I'm guessing you've got a better recollection of that night?'

'No comment.'

'There was a fundraising ball that night at Fraoch House, the home of the Marquess of Friockheim. The ball was hosted by his son Lord Haig Striven-Douglass and you. That's right, isn't it?'

He sighed. 'Look, it was Haig's party. My name was on the bill to attract a wider crowd, that's all.'

'But you played the role of host alongside him? Welcoming

guests, talking to them, making sure they mingled with whoever they needed to mingle with?'

'I didn't sulk in the corner and talk to no fucker. I was sociable.'

'You were rather more than sociable with one of the guests. A young marketing executive called Chloe Grange. Now known as Claudia Grainger. I imagine in a bid to distance herself from any gossip about a lassie called Chloe who had a very bad experience with Lord Handsy Haig? And his bosom buddy Billy the Kidd.'

He breathed deeply, his shoulders rising. 'That's bullshit.'

'So you're saying you didn't get her drunk, you didn't give her drugs, you didn't rip her clothes off, you didn't subject her to a series of brutal sexual acts—'

'No I fucking didn't.' He pushed back in his chair and roared. 'You've got a fucking nerve, bitch.'

Karen waited in silence, fixing him with a dead-eyed stare. At length, she said, 'Tantrums cut no ice in this room, Mr Kidd. So, you were complicit in a rape, then you put her in the shower to remove all traces of what had happened, covered her in a dressing gown because her clothes were ripped and stained, then Handsy Haig got his driver to take you home with her, to make sure she didn't drop you both in it while she was still drugged up to the eyeballs. Unfortunately for you, somebody witnessed the state she was in and where she got in that state and they told Sam Nimmo.'

'This is pure fiction. None of this even remotely true. If it was as horrendous as you say, how come Chloe or Claudia or whatever her fucking name is, how come she didn't go to the police?'

Karen lifted her lip in a sneer. 'Because that's always the

first thing women do when they've been raped by rich and powerful men.'

'Sarcasm? Is that the best you've got?' He scoffed. 'You'd better pray you can come up with something better than that when my lawyer comes after you.'

'I don't think you were the ringleader in this. I think you were scooped up in Handsy Haig's slipstream. But when Sam Nimmo came after you both? Swells like Haig Striven-Douglass don't like to get their hands dirty. That's why they keep menials like you on the payroll. So they can cut you loose and leave you to wander from town to town with no direction home. This double murder has cunning written all over it. Frame Sam for Rachel's murder then make him disappear. Not outwith your capabilities, I imagine His Lordship thought. All fun and games till the wheels come off.'

He glared at her. 'You've got nothing on me. If you did, you'd have hit me with it. You need to let me go.'

Karen shook her head. 'Not quite yet, Mr Kidd. I can keep you for twenty-four hours without charge. And if I want to hang on to you a bit longer? I've got not one, but two officers you've assaulted this evening. Police assault's a serious charge and you are definitely a flight risk. Though it might make returning to your lovely life in California a bit more contentious.' She turned to Jason. 'Interview suspended? I've got another interview to conduct and I'm gagging for a coffee.'

56

It was after midnight when the four detectives came together to examine what they had. 'I'm coming at this from the outside,' Jimmy Hutton said, giving Karen a cautious look. 'But it seems to me, as far as the murders are concerned, you've got motive but no evidence. And you've only got motive from Claudia's interview and the tenuous report of the now-dead driver that when he picked her up and took her home, she was in a right state. And that's almost a dozen years ago, which any defence advocate will shred.'

'I can't argue with that.' Karen ran her hands through her hair, frustration written on her face. 'So why did Kidd run if he's innocent?'

'Reputation?' Daisy suggested. 'They heard Sam Nimmo was digging into the rape, Kidd knew he didn't have the protection of being Lord Haig Striven-Douglass and he'd seen how other men in the entertainment business had lost their standing over unsubstantiated rumours?'

'But surely running looks worse?' Jason chipped in. 'The rumours will still spread on the socials, only more so, no?'

'Good point. Except that all running did was take him out of the jurisdiction because we never pursued him at the time. It was like the rumour never really got started, and who's to say that wouldn't have been the case even if he'd stuck around,' Jimmy said. Glum silence all round.

'I've sent Claudia home with a patrol car. We've got nothing approaching proof that she's done anything wrong and she's not going to talk to anybody.' Karen shook her head. 'I hate that this kind of thing still goes on and men like this pair just walk away, living their lives like nothing happened to disturb their smooth progress onwards. It makes me feel complicit – digging all this up again for Claudia. Making her a victim for the third time. And Linda? What the hell was she thinking?'

'How come she turned up?' Jason asked. Karen was sure she'd covered that; either he was slightly concussed or she was losing it.

'Kidd messaged her from San Francisco to tell her about the top secret gig. And because we'd been to see her and she's a journo with a nasty suspicious mind, she worked out that it could be a sting. But she couldn't reach him while he was in the air so she managed to figure out a flight that would get her to Glasgow in time to warn him. And nearly succeeded. Sorry about the casualties, guys.'

'So what do we do now?' Daisy glowered. She was holding herself stiffly, wincing every time she forgot her ribs and moved in her seat. The doctor had done a neat job with the stitches, but having had to shave the eyebrow round the wound gave her a distinctly lop-sided look. She looked exhausted and Karen wasn't surprised. They'd all started the day on a high of expectation and now they were all deflated. Really, she thought, they shouldn't have been so gung-ho to start with.

'We hang on to William Kidd. We can hold him on the police assault. The one slender hope we've got is that the forensics might give us something. Kidd and his buddy were never even looked at in the original murder inquiries. All we need is a single DNA trace or fingermark and we might yet have something tangible to grab on to. I'm going to drop the samples at Gartcosh on the way home. Let's see whether we can get them expedited. Flight risk, and all that.' She stood up and yawned. 'Jason, Daisy – take the day off. Thanks for your work today. It's nobody's fault that the chips didn't fall in our favour.'

'And tomorrow is another day,' Jimmy said.

'It's already tomorrow,' Daisy said, ever the pedant.

'Plus you don't look nearly as lovely as Scarlett O'Hara, Jimmy.' Karen stuffed her paperwork back in her satchel and shooed her team out of the door. She'd felt altogether too much frustration and ambivalence lately. Maybe, coupled with Rafiq's exit to Syria, it was a signal that it was time she thought about doing something different with her life.

Only trouble was, she didn't have the faintest idea what that might be.

It had been past two when Karen finally crawled into bed. She didn't set her alarm and was astonished when she woke to see it was after nine. She'd been expecting a broken night after such a difficult day; every time she had a good night's sleep it felt like a bonus, but this seemed a bonus she didn't deserve.

The weather was depressing too. Gusts of wind tossed rain showers in all directions and just walking to the tram stop soaked her feet and calves. By the time she got to the office, it was after eleven. Nothing appealed less than writing up a report on the previous day's failure, but it had to be done. She kicked off her wet shoes and made a start. She'd been at it for almost an hour when the phone rang. 'DCI Pirie, how can I help you?'

'Girl, you sound as cheerful as a Free Church funeral.' The cheery Australian accent on the end of the line was unmistakable.

'Hi, Tamsin. Sorry, having a run of things not falling the way I'd like. What can I do for you?'

'It's what I can do for you. That stuff you dropped off during the night? DNA samples and fingermark cards? You wanted them expedited?'

'Yeah, can you chivvy someone along?'

'I can do better than that. I can tell you we got a hit on one of the fingermarks. A stone-cold match with a middle finger under the rim of the sink in Rachel Morrison's bathroom. The original report identified the victim's blood in the drain, the surmise was that the killer had washed up there. But the fingermark didn't match anyone the original investigation targeted.'

'But it matches one of the cards I handed in?'

'Our tech says it's as good as he's ever seen: 16 points of congruence, which is as good as it used to get. But we don't rely on the numeric system in Scotland these days. What matters more is the ridge patterns and arrangements. And this is spot on. Text book. It's likely your killer gripped the edge of the sink but thought they'd wiped it clean.'

'Tell me it's William Kidd,' Karen breathed.

'Is that who you'd like it to be?'

'Well, yeah. He's the one the whole sting was set up to catch.'

'I'm sorry to disappoint you, then. The print in the murder victim's flat was left by Claudia Grainger. There's no doubt about it.'

410

Karen was gobsmacked. Claudia? The woman who had looked her in the eye and said, 'I'd never knowingly met either of them.'

There was only one explanation she could think of. And it made absolutely no sense.

57

Back when she'd still had Phil at her side, Karen could rely on him to be a reliable sounding board. He never wanted to grandstand or score points at her expense. On her end, she'd tried not to pull rank and privilege her ideas. But that was history and nowadays, sometimes Karen struggled with the loneliness of leadership.

This was one of those times.

Following Tamsin's startling revelation, Karen had had to go back to the beginning and separate what they actually knew from what they'd only deduced. Or assumed. There was no real doubt about the sexual assault; now she had Claudia's statement, coupled with Linda Lawrence's confirmation of what William Kidd had told her, they had that from two sources. If only the driver who had taken them both back to Claudia's home after the fundraiser and set the whole chain of events running had still been around, it would have been cast iron.

They knew that Sam Nimmo was investigating the events of that night because he'd shared the information with Linda and, less explicitly, with his football mates. They couldn't say for sure that Sam had not murdered Rachel, but the inexplicable presence of Claudia's fingerprint in their flat, coupled with the complete lack of even a whisper of motive, made that seem improbable. And they knew that Sam Nimmo had not gone on the run; he'd disappeared without trace because he was dead and buried under the M73.

But William Kidd *had* run. Only, nobody made the connection between his leaving the country slightly ahead of his scheduled tour and Sam Nimmo's murder because nobody knew there was a connection. Years would pass before his drunken admission to Linda Lawrence that he'd taken part in the assault against Claudia, but when he'd fled nobody knew there was any direct link to Rachel's murder and Sam's disappearance.

With hindsight, putting William Kidd slap bang in the sights of her investigation had made sense. But now? The only way she could twist that into a reasonable conclusion was to assume that Kidd and Claudia were in it together. And that was pretzel logic. Why on earth would she conspire with her rapist to try to kill the story? That was taking Stockholm Syndrome way too far, surely?

But there was no escaping that fingerprint. With a sigh, Karen picked up the phone and set the wheels in motion.

Neither Jason nor Daisy seemed grumpy about the cancellation of the remainder of their day off. Only Ruth Wardlaw was at all unhappy about Karen's plans, and that was only because she was due back in court after lunch. 'I think I can organise a colleague to pick up the baton. Unless you hear otherwise, I'll see you at Stewart Street around two. If I'm not there, don't start without me. I've got a feeling you're going to need all the help I can give you to get this across the line.'

The quartet gathered in the canteen at the Glasgow police

station. Jason's black eye had expanded to cover half his cheek, while the area around Daisy's stitches was puffy and scarlet. She'd travelled over with Karen, wincing at every pothole.

'Talk me through the plan.' Ruth took a sip of her coffee and grimaced. 'I hope it's more palatable than this.'

'I've organised a couple of local uniforms to go to Fraoch House and bring in Claudia Grainger. I've told them to arrest and caution her but to say it's simply an admin thing to get her statement on record.'

'It might have the added bonus of freaking out Lord Friockheim.' Daisy snorted. 'See what I did there?'

Karen rolled her eyes. 'Not here, not now, Sergeant.'

'Sorry,' Daisy said with a look that said, *Not sorry.*

'To get back to the point.' Karen glared at her. 'I'll take the interview with you, Daisy, if you can keep your face-tiousness in check. I'm struggling to see past the image of Claudia as the two-times victim here, but we have to go where the evidence leads us. So I think I need to go straight for the jugular. It makes me uncomfortable, to be honest, but I don't see any way round it. Remind her of what she said, and if she sticks to it, hit her with the fingerprint. And see where that takes us.'

'What if she points the finger at Friockheim as her co-conspirator?' Ruth asked. Karen was reminded of why she admired the lawyer's intelligence, inconvenient as it could be.

'Why would he take a chance on colluding, though? I can see him trying to cover his back by dragging Kidd in. But he couldn't afford to be at the heart of any rumours. At the time, he was the second son, it wouldn't have been beyond possibility for his father to disown him and throw him out.' Daisy had a point, Karen thought.

'And why would Claudia get behind him?' Jason chipped in.

Daisy gave him a 'well, duh' look. 'He'd bought her off with a job she really wanted. She wouldn't want to risk that. It was her chance to rebuild her life after what they did to her. And she could play the sympathy card with another woman in a way that Haig Striven-Douglass never could have.'

'Even so – I'm with Jason here. I don't buy it either,' Ruth said. 'Men like Haig don't get their hands dirty. That's what they have servants for. *He* didn't drive her home that night – he got his driver to take her. He might have pushed Claudia into attempting to get Rachel to appeal to Sam to drop the story, but he'd never have put his own neck on the block.'

'But we still think he might have pushed Kidd into going with her?' Jason again.

Karen sighed. 'Mibbes. I've been juggling "what ifs" ever since Tamsin dropped the bomb. Let's just run it, and see how the chips fall.'

Claudia dressed for work was a different proposition from either version Karen had already encountered. A severely tailored navy suit with a Nehru jacket, terrifying heels, full make-up and hair in an up-do without a single loose strand – it was armour for battle. She launched into her protest as soon as Karen and Daisy entered the interview room. 'What happened to "we'll take care of you every step of the way"? This is really outrageous. What are my team – never mind my employer – to make of a pair of uniformed policemen marching into our office and *arresting* me? I spent hours with you yesterday, I couldn't have been more cooperative, and now this?'

'Your employer? That would be Lord Friockheim, the man you accused of rape yesterday evening?'

Clearly shocked at Karen's tone, she said, 'Have you stopped believing me? Have you been got at? Has Haig been pulling strings already?'

'Nothing like that. We've arrested you because we have further questions and arrest is a mechanism for keeping you here in custody while we ask them. Otherwise you could just walk out the door at your pleasure. Would you like a lawyer?'

'Do I need one? I'm the victim here, not the criminal.'

'It's your choice and you can change your mind at any point.' Claudia crossed her legs and linked her fingers tight together, setting her hands in her lap. *Bad body language.* 'I'd like to return to something you said when we spoke yesterday. When I asked you about Rachel Morrison and Sam Nimmo, you said, and I quote, "I'd never knowingly met either of them."' Karen looked her straight in the eye. 'Do you want to revise that statement?'

Claudia didn't move a muscle. Not even a blink. Finally she said, 'Why would I?'

'And you'd never visited their home?'

If she saw the chasm opening beneath her feet, she gave no sign of it. 'Unlike you, I don't make a habit of walking into strangers' houses.' She allowed herself a tiny smile.

'We asked you to give us a DNA sample and a set of fingerprints yesterday. And you complied.'

'Why wouldn't I? Where are you going with this? I don't get it. If you'd asked me to come in to answer more questions, I'd have obliged. You didn't have to embarrass me in front of everyone. I've done nothing but cooperate with you, why the hostility?'

416

'When our forensic technicians ran your samples, we were surprised to find a match.' Karen paused. Claudia uncrossed her legs and pressed her knees together but said nothing. 'Can you explain how a print from the middle finger of your left hand came to be on the underside of the bathroom sink in the flat where Rachel Morrison was found murdered?'

Claudia's nostrils twitched. Almost a flare but not quite. She gave a forced little laugh. 'Everybody knows fingerprint evidence is dodgy. It's not scientific. It's opinion, not fact.'

'Sometimes that is the case, you're right. Unfortunately for you, this isn't one of those times.' Karen opened the folder she'd brought in with her. She placed two blown-up images side by side. 'Can you spot a single difference?'

'I'm not a fingerprint expert.'

'Neither am I, but to me, and to people who are, these look identical. Claudia, every significant surface in the living room and bathroom was wiped clean of fingermarks on the night Rachel was killed. With the exception of one fingerprint that we couldn't identify until last night. You were there that night. We have no evidence that anyone else was present. On the basis of that single piece of evidence alone, I could charge you with murder right now.'

That hit home. All at once, Claudia's facade cracked. Her demeanour changed completely. Karen had expected shock and fear. What she got instead was anger and defiance. 'All right. I was there. I'd found out Sam Nimmo was poking his nose into what happened. It was common gossip among the girls I knew who'd been at the party. But it was nobody's business but mine. Sam Nimmo didn't give a flying fuck about me or my life. All he cared about was headlines and a payday. And a chance to give the Yes campaign a good kicking, let's not forget that. I wanted to put a stop to it, I'll admit it. I went to their flat to talk to Rachel Morrison woman to woman. To explain what this story would do to my life. In the short time since it happened, I'd gone a long way to rebuilding my self-esteem. OK, you might say I'd been bought off with a job, but it was a job I'd dreamed of and it was going well. I'd gone from shame and despair to hope and I didn't want to end up with my life in ruins again. You have no idea what that's like.'

She closed her eyes momentarily and took a deep breath. When she opened her eyes again, they were damp with unshed tears. 'I thought if I could make her understand how her man would destroy me, she'd agree to persuade him not to go ahead.'

'And she refused?'

A pair of tears leaked from Claudia's eyes and trickled down her cheeks. 'I didn't mean it,' she whispered. 'What I've got to live with – still, I've got to live with – is knowing it's my fault she's dead.'

58

Karen held her breath, unwilling to break the moment. When it was clear Claudia wasn't about to continue, she spoke gently. 'Did you kill Rachel?'

Claudia's head jerked up, horror on her face. 'No, no, that's not what I'm saying. All I meant was that if I'd stayed home that night, she'd still be alive. I didn't mean for it to turn out the way it did.'

'I don't imagine you did, Claudia. Can you tell me what happened?'

Claudia swallowed hard and reached across the table for Karen's bottle of water. She took a long swallow, coughed, then said dully, 'She gave me a lecture about Sam's integrity and how committed he was to justice. And then she accused me of being complicit in violence against women. Every unpunished rapist gave permission to the next one, she said I was the opposite of a feminist. I tried pleading with her, I tried sisterhood but her only answer was to pick up her phone and say she was going to call Sam right now and tell him she had the victim of Haig Striven-Douglass and William Kidd in their living room telling all.'

'I imagine that was horrifying.'

'You could say that.'

'How did you react?'

Claudia squeezed her eyes shut and winced. 'I lunged for the phone. She turned away, I bumped into her and she cracked her head on the mantelpiece. She kind of crumpled to the floor and the blood just flowed. She made this noise like she was choking then nothing. I touched her neck to see if there was a pulse but there was ... nothing, And her head was split open, you could see the white bone. The worst bit was her eyes were wide open, staring. I was frozen. I couldn't believe it.'

'What did you do?'

'I sat down on the floor. I was in a daze. I didn't know what to do. I was in a room with a dead woman, it would look like I'd done a bad thing. Like I'd—' She cleared her throat. 'So I called Billy.'

It wasn't what she'd expected to hear. 'You called William Kidd? You asked a man who'd raped you to come to your rescue?' Karen couldn't help sounding incredulous.

'Because he had his own self-interest at stake?' Daisy knew she was speaking out of turn but she found it impossible to hold her tongue.

Claudia twisted her fingers round each other. 'No. He never raped me. That was Haig. But he still he owed me. I wasn't going to drag one of my pals into my mess. Billy had got me into this, he invited me to that bloody party in the first place. I figured the least he could do was help me out of it.'

'And did he?'

She nodded. Her voice was stronger now. 'I told him what had happened. He freaked out at first. But he was doing a lot of coke around then, and the paranoia kicked in when he grasped what I was saying. He was convinced I'd grass him up to you lot if he didn't help me.'

420

'What did he do?'

'He swore. A lot of swearing. But he came round to the flat. He had a pair of pink Marigolds on. I remember how it looked wrong, like the kind of thing a comedian would do. He made me a cup of tea and told me to sit still while he cleaned everything I'd touched. Then he made me wash my hands in case I'd got any blood on them. That must have been when I touched the sink. Then he took me back to my car and drove me home in it.' She gave Karen a piteous look. 'It was an accident. If it hadn't been for Billy, you'd have arrested me. I'd be in the jail now, and that just felt ... wrong?' She then said, 'There's not a day goes by that I don't think about Rachel Morrison and her baby. What happened that night ... maybe I should just have called the police instead of Billy. Do you think it would still be tearing me up inside if I'd spent the last eleven years in prison instead?'

Karen leaned her forehead against the wall in the observation room. She was still beyond words. 'Talk about blindsided,' Ruth Wardlaw muttered.

'Can you believe that? Calling on Kidd to pick up the pieces?' Jason was bewildered. 'It makes no sense to me. And what a mad idea. Why would Rachel want to talk Sam out of exposing a rapist? I mean, presumably Sam would have left Claudia's name out? You're not supposed to name rape victims, are you?'

'He's right,' Ruth said. 'But given the circumstances, there were probably enough people at that do who would have been able to point the finger at Claudia. She'd be branded in that world. She'd have lost her one chance at the greasy pole and nobody else would have touched her. She was already holding a losing hand; drawing in Billy the Kidd on the deal might have seemed like her only chance.'

'And it was an accident,' Karen said. 'I believe her. I don't think she's gone on her way, tra-la, blithely moving on with her life. Haig and Billy – they've paid no price for what they did. But Claudia – she told me she's never been in a relationship since. She got the job she wanted, but I don't think that's brought her anything like happiness.'

Glum silence for a long moment. Then Karen pushed herself away from the wall, punched one fist into the other palm and said, 'Let's get Billy in front of us. Jason, away to the bar and get the custody sergeant to put him on a plate for us.'

'What are you going to do?' Daisy asked.

'Same as we did with her. Put it to him and see where it takes us. Though the way things are going today, we might end up in the Land of Oz.'

Karen sat down opposite William Kidd and gave him her best hard stare. 'We know what you did, Billy.'

He smirked. 'That doesn't narrow it down. I've done a lot in my time.'

'Not all of it carries a life sentence, I'm guessing.' Karen's voice was hard as glacier ice. 'You must have been bricking it after Rachel's death.'

'Who?'

'Don't, Billy. Just don't. Even before tonight, we knew you and Linda were tight. And if you were Linda's pal, you must have known Sam and Rachel. Or at least, who they were.'

Not even a twitch. 'I didn't know that was a criminal offence.'

'Unlike police assault,' she said conversationally. 'Do you think the immigration authorities in the US will hesitate to tear up your green card once you're convicted of two counts of that? I mean, given that the officers in question aren't black?'

'You don't frighten me, Pirie. I was exiting a venue where there was every possibility I might be mobbed, or even attacked. Your officers both assaulted me without announcing that they were polis.' He puffed out a noisy breath. 'I'm not scared of the outcome of that. The media will murder youse. Fourteen thousand fans were cheering me to the rafters. I doubt Police Scotland could find fourteen hundred to do the same for them.'

'What you did in Rachel Morrison's flat won't go down so well.'

Now he couldn't disguise his reaction. The small muscles round his mouth and eyes clenched then relaxed. 'No comment,' he said.

'Not much point in that now we've spoken to Claudia Grainger.' Karen kept her tone neutral and her expression to match. 'What did Linda say when you told her what you'd done? She must be some pal to have stuck by you after that?'

His eyes widened. Karen thought she'd struck a nerve. 'Leave Linda out of this, it's got nothing to do with her.'

'She's been very loyal. So far. But loyalty has its limits and I've got a feeling we're getting close to hers.' Karen was dancing in the dark now but she felt she had nothing to lose. 'She didn't tell Sam about the rape even though he was her business partner. Out of loyalty to you. But I don't think that loyalty would have stretched to what happened to Rachel. Did she tell him, Billy? Did he come after you?' The limb she'd gone out on was definitely creaking now.

'It was nothing to do with Linda, I'm telling you. Leave her out of it. Look, Nimmo kind of lost the plot after Rachel died. He was convinced she'd been murdered to shut him up and the only story he was chasing that was big enough to provoke that kind of reaction was the one about Haig and Chloe. Because of the referendum and the damage it would do the image of the Yes campaign, it was way bigger than any run-of-the-mill sex story. But he didn't know who the victim was. That's the irony. None of them knew it was Chloe, or Claudia as she'd renamed herself. If she hadn't outed herself to Rachel, she'd have stayed under wraps.'

Karen frowned. 'That makes no sense. If Sam Nimmo didn't know who she was, why did Claudia confront Rachel? I thought Sam's source was the driver who drove her home? Surely he must have been able to find out her identity?'

Kidd shook his head. 'We didn't go to her home. She didn't want to go there because she shared a flat with a pal. I had the keys to a friend's place on the Southside – she was on tour and I was supposed to be watering her plants. So I took the lassie there. I was feeling like shit by then, I wasn't proud of what had happened. I gave her some Valium and let her sleep it off. I sorted her some of my pal's clothes and the next day, I took her back to hers. So Nimmo didn't know who she was. He had my pal's address but he knew it wasn't her because she'd been on a stage in Brighton that night.'

'So why did Claudia go to Rachel?'

'Because everybody knew Nimmo was on the trail of something bad that had happened at the party. Chloe just assumed he knew it was her.'

'But Sam had found out that you and Haig Striven-Douglass

424

were the rapists.' It wasn't framed as a question, even though Karen really wasn't sure of the answer.

'I never raped her, that was all Haig.'

She talked over him, determined to get to an answer. 'So the conclusion Nimmo would draw was that you or Haig Striven-Douglass had gone looking for him and found Rachel instead. Only it had all gone wrong somewhere along the line.'

'It wasn't me,' Kidd insisted.

'So it must have been Haig?' Was he telling the truth or throwing his friend under the bus? Karen swallowed her impatience and stayed calm. 'Is that what you're saying Sam Nimmo thought?'

'He turned up at my flat. He looked fucking terrible. He obviously hadn't slept and he stank of whisky. And he had a gun.'

'A *gun*? You're telling me a journalist was walking about Glasgow with a gun?'

'What's so daft about that? Back when I was living in the city, I could have taken you to at least three pubs where you could get a handgun for a couple of hundred quid. Guns are cheap, it's the bullets that cost. So there's Sam Nimmo in my living room. Waving a gun at me and accusing me of killing his woman and his unborn wean. And I'm denying it, of course I am, because I never did it, not any of it. And all of a sudden, it's like a switch goes in his head and he goes hard and cold and says, just like you, if it wasn't me, it must be Haig because he's the one with most to lose.' He ran his hands through his hair. 'I was fucking scared. Cold, he was even more terrifying than when he was ranting.'

'What happened then?'

For a long moment, she thought Kidd had frozen on her.

425

That he'd disappeared into the dark memory of that moment and she'd lost him. Then, almost robotic now, he said, 'He made me hand over my phone and he sent a text to Haig, telling him to come over to mine double urgent, we needed to talk. Haig texted back, his usual arsey self, saying he was having a drink with some pals and he'd be over after eight. I had two hours of Sam Nimmo going nuts in my living room, drinking my whisky and waving a gun around.'

Daisy dived in again. 'A wee taste of the terror you'd handed out to Claudia, maybe.'

Karen kicked her under the table. *Don't break the flow, how many times do I have to tell you?*

Kidd gave Daisy a dead-eyed stare and said, 'Fuck you. I know I did wrong but I did not rape Claudia. OK, I was there, I did nothing to stop it, but I never—'

'And Haig turned up?' Karen's conversational tone sought to bring Kidd back to where she needed him to be. But he was more than willing to be shepherded back on track.

'Haig turned up. He was fucking outraged. He took one look at Nimmo with the gun and you know what he did? He marched right up to him and smashed him in the face. He had that total confidence that guys like him have got bred into them, he just knew Nimmo wasn't going to pull the trigger. Poor guy went down like a sack of spuds. To be fair, he was pretty much too pissed to stand by that point. He tried to get up, and Haig picked up my Edinburgh Fringe Comedy Award. A big lump of Perspex. And whacked him across the head with it.' He sniffed, hard. 'I still have nightmares. Sort of a wet crack.'

He buried his face in his hands and sobbed. What she was witnessing, Karen thought, was a kind of relief in the release of the burden he'd been carrying alone for so long.

They waited till he recovered himself. It took four tissues to clear his nose after the storm of weeping subsided. They watched him literally pull himself together, squaring his shoulders and clasping his hands on the table.

'I didn't know what to do, I was panicking. Haig was ranting, who the fuck did Nimmo think he was, trying to destroy the independence movement by bringing him down. Like that was what was going on. I felt sick.

'Then Haig turned to me, calm as a fucking millpond, and said I'd better figure out what to do with the body. I'd have a job explaining to the police how I had a dead journalist on my living room floor. He was basically washing his hands of it all. I'd always known he was an entitled arrogant twat, but up till then I'd been on his team, he'd never turned it on me before. I realised I wasn't actually his friend. I was just the help. The entertainment. And I was totally expendable. He wiped the trophy clean on a dishtowel, put it back on the shelf, and walked out.'

Kidd shook his head, the amazement undimmed by time. 'I had a wrap of coke in my pocket and I did a couple of lines to try and get a grip and then I remembered my cousin telling me about a job he was on, building the new bit of motorway out by Gartcosh. It seemed like a good idea to bury him in the motorway verge. My car was in the drive and I reversed close up to the door to get him in the boot. And I drove to where they were finishing off the M73. I buried the gun deep in a skip in Springburn, I thought if it turned up, nobody out that way would be too surprised.'

'How did you get on-site? Surely it was locked up? Security guards or whatever?'

'My cousin had told me how crap the security was. Him and his mate had been pinching all sorts of kit from the site. Wheelbarrows, spades, fence posts. So I drove in along the access road, not a soul in sight, helped myself to a wheelbarrow then manhandled Sam Nimmo back to the embankment.' He shuddered at the memory. 'A dead body, it's fucking heavy.

'I dug a hole. It just about killed me. Solid clay mud, what a nightmare. It took me fucking hours to dig it and fill it back up, to make it look like it the rest of the slope. Then I drove home. Thank Christ there was nobody out walking their dogs to see me looking like the Golem of Gartcosh.' A rare glimpse of the comedian at work.

'I was exhausted but I couldn't sleep. It was the worst night of my life. I'm sorry for everything I did but I did not rape Claudia and I did not kill anyone. I think everything I did was in the name of trying to atone to Claudia for what I was part of.'

Aye, right. Nothing to do with covering your own back. 'So did you also send the fake confession messages to Sam's parents and friends?' she asked.

Now he did look genuinely shame-faced. 'That was Haig's idea. He said the last thing we needed was a Lord Lucan kind of hunt for Sam. He said I had to knock it on the head for good and all.'

Karen shook her head, a wry smile on her face. 'Pity Haig couldn't control the weather as easily as he controlled you.'

59

Karen and Ruth Wardlaw sat opposite each other in the HCU office, each with a premixed can of gin and tonic that Karen kept for emergencies. She'd had them so long they were past their sell-by date; neither cared that they were slightly flat. 'What do you think?' Karen asked.

'The relevant question is not what I think but what a jury would believe,' Ruth said, her voice heavy with cynicism. 'If you follow the evidence, it takes us to Claudia. But she'll make a sympathetic witness and they'll believe her when she tells them it was an accident.'

'And since it *was* an accident, it's hard to see what you can charge Kidd with. There's no legal obligation to report a dead body in Scotland and you can't be an accessory to a crime that didn't happen,' Karen said flatly. 'So we tell the Nimmos and the Morrisons what? "Sorry, it was nobody's fault that your daughter and your unborn grandchild died." Are you happy with that?'

'Of course I'm not. But what's the alternative? We charge Claudia with a crime we don't think she committed and destroy her life all over again?' Ruth drained half of her drink.

'I hate the idea that they get no sort of resolution.' Karen sighed. 'If I don't give the bereaved answers, what am I for?'

'Not knowing might not be worse than confronting this particular horror show. It wouldn't be the first time a case remained unresolved,' Ruth said sadly. 'Maybe we should just focus on what we can work with? Billy did dispose of the body of a murdered man and that's not nothing. Preventing a lawful and decent burial has a maximum life sentence, theoretically. Likewise, perverting the course of justice. You've got a confession to that.'

'But to get there means opening the can of worms that is Sam Nimmo's death. Chances are Friockheim will deny everything and blame it all on Billy. And the best you'll get is Not Proven, plus inevitably destroying Claudia in the process.' Karen felt her conscience was twisting in the wind.

'I know. Even if we can place him in the room, his defence is bound to be that he was protecting his good name against the scurrilous claims of a gun-toting tabloid hack over an alleged rape that was actually consensual sex with a gold digger. All lies, but lies that'll make headlines. Even if William Kidd testifies for the prosecution, we both know what the socials and the tabs will run with.'

'You can't let him walk,' Karen protested. 'Surely not. Two innocent people died. Three, if you count the child Rachel was carrying. We can't just shrug it off and go, "it's too hard".'

'I don't want to do nothing, Karen. But you have to be aware that there's nothing we can do here that will protect Claudia, even if we prosecute the rape separately. We can try, but it won't hold. It never does. All the people in her life will know, plus everybody else with a social media account. This is a decision I have to take upstairs. Let me take it to the boss, and see where we get to.'

Karen sighed. 'We can try, Ruth. We can try.'

*

A week went by before they faced each other again, this time over drinks in the Palmerston, Karen's favourite restaurant for spectacular cocktails, always noisy enough not to be overheard. 'What's the verdict?' she asked as soon as they both had a drink in front of them; a coffee negroni for Karen and a sazarapp for Ruth.

'You want the good news or the bad news first?'

Karen sighed. 'I'm pissed off that there's any bad news, but lay it on me first.'

'The Lord Advocate has decided it's not in the public interest to prosecute Friockheim, William Kidd or Claudia Grainger because there's a lower than fifty per cent likelihood of a conviction. Both in the deaths and the sexual assault.'

Karen groaned. 'Bastard.'

'It's hard to argue against it – it's the criterion we're supposed to use on all cases now. And far be it from me to suggest it might have something to do with Haig Striven-Douglass's connections.'

'The Justified Sinners rear their misbegotten head?'

Ruth's turn to sigh. 'That's a worrying cabal, no doubt about it. But I did also hear today that Marcus Nicol is being charged with one count of murder. They've not got enough to run with the case against Tom Jamieson but they're willing to take a case for Bryce Gordon. I'm sure his brief will plead it down to causing death by dangerous driving, but at least it will put a bloody great spoke in his wheel. And the betting conspiracy's going to trial as well. I think the Lord Advocate was throwing us a bone there.'

'If I didn't know better, I'd have him down as a Justified Sinner. So is that it for the good news? I mean, it's not exactly dancing in the street material, is it?'

'At least you can explain to Rachel and Sam's families that we know what happened, even though we can't prove it. There might be some comfort in that. And the same goes for Drew Jamieson and Jayden.'

'I doubt it, somehow. If it was me, it would just leave me raging at the useless HCU.'

Ruth sipped her drink appreciatively. 'Maybe it's not all bad. Have I ever mentioned my pal Cora?'

'She's the one you were at uni with?'

'That's right. She's making waves writing TV dramas these days.' She pulled a sheet of paper from her bag and passed across a CV printed out from the internet. It featured three award-winning series that had turned recent scandals into riveting drama. 'She says you can tell truth in fiction when the real world clams up. She wants to do a "based on a true story" adaptation of the case. Names changed to protect the innocent but open the guilty up to speculation. She's already pitched it to Netflix. They love a bit of posh. What do you think?'

Karen considered. 'It'll be the talk of the steamie in Scottish high society when it airs. Everybody in the know will know who it is. Billy the Kidd can forget his UK come-back tour. And it'll be long enough in production to give Claudia time to up sticks and start over, maybe changing her name yet again. Which should give her some protection.' A wry chuckle. 'A TV series, that's a different kind of justice. Of course, it depends who they get to play me. As long as it's somebody cool as fuck, I'm fine with it.'

Acknowledgements

Readers are always curious as to where the ideas for books emerge from. It's seldom straightforward, but there are always unpredictable triggers that set the wheels turning. Every year, I spend a few days in the depths of the country-side recording a series of BBC Radio 4's *Round Britain Quiz* in the company of a remarkable bunch of people from an assortment of backgrounds who contain an astonishing range of obscure and arcane gobbets of information. 'I never knew *that*' always crops up multiple times and sometimes it starts a process that ends up in a book. This time my thanks go to Stephen Maddock, the Principal of the Birmingham Conservatoire, whose revelations about his book club set me thinking. I should point out that neither he nor his fellow members engage in anything felonious . . .

I'm always amazed and delighted at the generosity of people who donate significant sums of money to charity for the dubious privilege of having characters with their name feature in books. This time, I'd like to acknowledge Bob Watson for his donation to Playlist for Life; Jacquie Lawrence and Linda Riley for combining as 'Linda Lawrence' in support of DIVA Charitable Trust; and also to Jakki and Sheila

Livesey-Van Dorst for their support of DIVA Charitable Trust and their endless joie de vivre!

And then there are the people whose brains I pick … The staff at the National Library of Scotland, celebrating its centenary this year, always go the extra mile for me. Sarah Springman, Principal of St Hilda's College, Oxford, civil engineer and expert in landslides, kept me on track at the side of the motorway. And Susie McCabe earned her namecheck by introducing me to the backstage world of comedy.

This has been a particularly difficult year for me; I had major spinal surgery, bracketed on both sides by the kind of pain that invades every aspect of life. As well as my gratitude to all the medical professionals who helped me through it, I want to thank the friends, family and colleagues who supported me in very trying times. I'm sorry for the extreme grumpiness, the irritating brain fog and the general 'bad patient' experience you all endured. And I'm sorry for all the cancelled events and visits … I missed the warmth of audiences and the conversations in green rooms and book signings alike.

I'm blessed with a supportive, tolerant and talented team at my back, both at my publishers, Little, Brown, and at my agents, DHA. Particular thanks go to Laura Sherlock, Tilda Key, Lizzy Kremer, Lucy Malagoni and the incomparable Anne O'Brien, whose copyediting skills save my incompetence with timelines on every outing,

But there is one individual whose constant love and support is what digs me out of every hole. Brilliant, funny, inspirational Jo Sharp always finds the light at the end of the tunnel. Lucky me.

Val McDermid

NEVER MISS A THING

SCAN TO SUBSCRIBE TO VAL MCDERMID'S NEWSLETTER
FOR EXCLUSIVE AUTHOR CONTENT, SNEAK PREVIEWS
AND EARLY INFORMATION ABOUT HER BOOKS

SCAN ME

BIT.LY/VAL-MCDERMID-NEWSLETTER

www.valmcdermid.com